Night Voices, Night Journeys

Lairs of the Hidden Gods
volume one

Night Voices, Night Journeys

Lairs of the Hidden Gods
volume one

Edited by Asamatsu Ken
Introduced by Robert M. Price

Kurodahan Press
2005

Originally published as *Hishinkai* by Tokyo Sōgensha, 2002
This edition © 2005 Kurodahan Press
Copyright for the individual stories and translations
remains the property of the author and translator respectively.
All rights reserved.
FG-J0010-L6
ISBN 4-902075-11-3

KURODAHAN PRESS
EDWARD LIPSETT · STEPHEN A. CARTER · CHRIS RYAL
KURODAHAN PRESS IS A DIVISION OF INTERCOM LTD.
#403 TENJIN 3-9-10, CHUO-KU, FUKUOKA 810-0001 JAPAN

Contents

Foreword

Recollections of Tentacles

Asamatsu Ken
Translated by Edward Lipsett

LET ME SPEAK of memories.

Recall the "blackness" you've stored away deep in the drawers of your heart. But what's hidden there is not the sharp knife, the breath of the stalker, or the ring of a telephone at midnight.

Recall instead the sweet darkness.

A darkness to transcend time and space. A darkness which sleeps in the ruins of ancient ages. A darkness where dwell gods, and demons, and sprites. A darkness fusing science and magic into one. A darkness that transforms imagination into reality into an instant. The darkness of, if you will, *mythology*.

Run your consciousness over your oldest memories, your deepest blackness, and reach down into the depths. You'll feel something, down there. Slippery as a swarm of hydra, squirming like a million maggots; perhaps it will sting your finger, like a starving sea anemone.

These are your memories of tentacles.

Recollections of when you were one of the gods, one of the demons... of when dream and reality were still one, of when time and space were still under your control, and when science and magic were overflowing with wonder.

Memories of when you had tentacles.

This is an anthology of newly-written "Cthulhu Mythos" fiction by Japanese authors.

What is the Cthulhu Mythos? The name derives from a work by Howard Phillips Lovecraft, *The Call of Cthulhu*, who had this to say when it was first published: "Now all my tales are based on the fundamental premise that common human laws and interests and emotions have no validity or significance in the vast cosmos-at-large." (*Selected Letters*, vol. 2)

August Derleth, one of Lovecraft's disciples, draws on these words in his later definition of the Cthulhu Mythos.

"All my stories, unconnected as they may be, are based on the fundamental lore or legend that this world was inhabited at one time by another race who, in practicing black magic, lost their foothold and were expelled, yet live on outside ever ready to take possession of this earth again." (*H.P. Lovecraft: Myth-Maker*, by Dirk W. Mosig)

Aramata Hiroshi, one of the first to introduce the Cthulhu Mythos to Japan, explains that "In ages past, the earth was under the control of a race other than Man, and they have come through the mists of forgotten time to invade the present world." (*Kaikigensō no Bungaku* [Weird Literature], *Vol.* 2, commentary to *Ankoku no Saishi* [Hierophant of Darkness].)

The Cthulhu Mythos is the story of the battles of these deposed gods, worshipped by races who ruled the earth before Man, and of their return to our world.

Outstanding stories always leave the reader in silence.

But one very special type of outstanding story, after silencing them, stimulates them into furious action. I'm sure you know what I'm talking about.

A child fascinated by a new picture book will try to create an original picture book. A youth whose imagination has been captured by a hero will mimic him in appearance and gesture. Japanese comic artist Tezuka Osamu was deeply moved by Disney animations, and continued to watch them as he studied their style in his own comic art and animations. His works, in turn, stimulated countless comic-loving children throughout Japan, nurturing them into today's professional comic artists. This is a historical fact, and a universal truth.

But what about the Mythos?

The situation is a bit different when it comes to the grand structure of myth.

Readers who encounter the Cthulhu Mythos also swing into action: they participate in the myth, using Lovecraft's unique terms and tools to write their own stories and novels, as did August Derleth and Donald Wandrei. But there's more. They may illustrate the evil gods, creatures or places mentioned in the stories, as Robert Bloch did. They might collect all the stories dealing with a given god, in the manner of Forest J. Ackerman or Robert E. Weinberg. And they create their own forbidden tomes or magic and evil, as did Lin Carter, for example. Some have even written graduation theses on the subject, collected and annotated Lovecraft's writings, or published mythos and related works, like Dirk W. Mosig, S.T. Joshi, or August Derleth. For readers in non-English lands, it means translation and making lists of translated works. And of course the stories are used as the basis for comic books, games, movies and television dramas.

Some years ago there was a saying in the Japanese SF community: the only American authors with a solid bibliography are Edgar Rice Burroughs, Philip K. Dick and H.P. Lovecraft. Unfortunately, though, I have never heard of a Japanese television drama based on Burroughs, or a commercial publisher founded to publish Dick's works.

We are ensorcelled, possessed by the Cthulhu Mythos. Readers who come into contact with the Mythos feel an affinity, and are lost. This is not the fevered insanity of the maniac, however, but rather than cool possession of the fan.

Why?

In writing this foreword, I reread Lovecraft's works and the Mythos. And as I did, I began to get a glimpse of the broader picture.

Lovecraft writes of an incident, portrays the wider world that makes up the background behind it, and explains the philosophy tying them together. He doesn't write about people at all, and this makes it impossible for the reader to empathize with the characters. What do readers do when faced with such a novel? There are only two choices: Either discard the work entirely, or accept the incident it describes. In short, accept the very *world* it portrays.

In a letter posted in the February 1928 issue of *Weird Tales*, Lovecraft comments "Now all my tales are based on the fundamental premise that common human laws and interests and emotions have no validity or significance in the vast cosmos-at-large. To me there is nothing but puerility in a tale in which the human form – and the local human passions and conditions and standards – are depicted as native to other worlds or other universes. To achieve the essence of real externality, whether of time or space or dimension, one must forget that such things as organic life, good and evil, love and hate, and all such local attributes of a negligible and temporary race called mankind, have any existence at all... I have merely got at the edge of this in 'Cthulhu', where I have been careful to avoid terrestrialism in the few linguistic and nomenclatural specimens from Outside which I present." (*Selected Letters*, vol. 2)

This is acceptance of Lovecraftian hardware, and the language installed into this hardware consists of the Cthulhu Mythos, the outer cosmos, and Lovecraftian names and appearances.

Readers who accept this Lovecraftian hardware try to convert themselves into compatible software, dissolving their own works and characters, thoughts and emotions, dreams and visions, into Lovecraft's world.

Some excellent examples of the products of Japanese authors functioning as software are Kazami Jun's *Cthulhu Opera* series, the *Makai Suikoden* (Demon Chronicles) series from Kurimoto Kaoru, Hanmura Ryō's *Togure Densetsu* (Legend of the Hidden Door), Yamada Masaki's *Gin no Dangan* (The Silver Bullet), and *Yōjin Gourmet* (Weird God Gourmet) from Kikuchi Hideyuki.

To get an idea of what other types of media have had this Mythos, names and appearances "installed," take a look at the lists in this anthology.

The two volumes of the Japanese anthology were completed in about eighteen months.

The theme is "media."

In other words, I have tried to interpret H.P. Lovecraft and the Cthulhu Mythos he created as a type of information media. The stories were grouped into historical and modern themes, each into its own volume. The historical volume pursues the narrative adventure so characteristic of Mythos stories, while the modern volume instead concentrates on the elements of horror, SF and metafiction. I am delighted to read how these authors so well demonstrated their skill.

Detailed lists of written works, comic books and films are also included in the hope that they may serve as a roadmap to readers interested in probing a bit farther.

An overlong foreword only dampens the appetite, but let me add just one more thing.

This anthology is also an attempt to support all the authors who even now are working to expand the horizons of horror fiction in Japan, and to provide an ever-increasing diversity to readers: authors like Inoue Masahiko (*Igyō Collection* [Freak-Show Collection]), Kusaka Sanzō (*Kaiki to Denki* [Eerie Tales and Narratives]) and Higashi Masao (*Gensō Bungaku* [Stories of Delusion]). If you liked this anthology, please, look for an anthology or collection with one of their names on it. I'm sure your nightmares will be darker and more real than ever before.

Well, I'm about done...

Just sit back and listen to your recollections.

Recall the sweet blackness.

They aren't your memories, though.

They are memories of the blackness told by seven authors. Memories of a war-torn Japan, perhaps, or Chicago. Recall images from the trenches, or discover new memories being made even today in Tokyo.

Listen, and you will begin to hear the pitch dark spun through these tales.

...Recollections of Tentacles.

Introduction

Rush Hour of the Old Ones

Robert M. Price

IT IS A privilege to be able to introduce you to a number of highly talented horror writers from Japan, and not just horror writers, but Lovecraftian writers! As any American fan knows by now, the Old Gent has attracted quite a following internationally. A few specimens of the Lovecraftian scholarship of other countries have straggled into print here in the USA, but the fiction spawned in Lovecraft-infected imaginations around the world has been slow in proving the adage: "What goes around comes around"! But now it has come round at last! And we are the beneficiaries. I will comment on each of the stories in turn, as you get to them, but for the present, I want to think with you about the cultural significance of Japanese Lovecraftian fiction.

Alien God and Devil

For one thing, there is a great and happy irony when one asks what Lovecraft would have made of the "foreign" interest in his work on the part of people representing groups he liked to characterize as "Asiatic hordes, winking to alien god and devil."

HPL, a throwback to earlier, nativistic times in colonial America, desperately feared what he saw as the desultory influence of Asian and even South European immigration. He feared that all these cultures, possessing an admirable integrity in their natural homelands, must spawn a bastardized hybrid culture inimical to Western, Enlightenment values if they were allowed to take root in America. He did not attend Klan rallies or any such thing. But he made his opinions known clearly (and to us, repulsively) enough in both letters and fiction, especially "The Shadow over Innsmouth," where the underlying horror is that of race-mixing, in particular breeding between hardly New Englanders and Asian islanders!

What Lovecraft appears not to have anticipated was that Western civilization would latch onto ancient Asian cultures through the twin media of Marxism-Leninism and American democratic Capitalism. Through military conquest and later commercial influence, Japan has in many ways become almost a caricature of what is most Western about the West. And the tales collected here demonstrate that. They occur in a very modern, even post-modern, Westernized Japan.

The Survivor and his Anxiety

Robert J. Lifton has made a great study of the psychological impact of the defeat of Japan in the Second World War, and especially of survivors of the Hiroshima and Nagasaki bombings. One profound and repeating theme in what he calls "survival literature" after the war is that of *survivor anxiety*: when so many died, the survivors feel they have betrayed their dead compatriots by not sharing their terrible fate. They feel and fear they are unworthy to live. I am not the first to speculate that it was such survivor anxiety that produced (perhaps as a cathartic technique for mitigating it) one of the most famous Japanese popular culture products of the post-War period, the Godzilla movies of Toho Studios. Could not one view Godzilla and his successors not only as nightmare allegories of the nuclear menaces that devastated Japan, but also as new and living A-Bombs appearing to finish the job the American warplanes had begun? Here was a fictive second chance to share in the random doom pouncing from fiery skies upon one's countrymen.

An equally fantastic product of the post-War period was the flourishing of innumerable "New Religions" such as Sōka Gakkai (a form of Nichiren Buddhism), the Unification Church (a Korean import) and the Electronic Church of Thomas Edison. These religions presented a kaleidoscope of syncretism, a mixing of demon exorcism, flying saucers, Jesus traveling to Japan, the Lost Continent of Mu, etc. Such a wild mixture of themes had previously been familiar only in B-movies and pulp fiction. Is it possible to understand the embrace by Japanese readers of the Cthulhu Mythos of Lovecraft as something approaching the foundation of a Cthulhu Cult among the new religions? The answer is probably as elusive and as category-spraining as the kindred question as to whether the Elvis cult in America should be considered a genuine faith.

Cult of Death

Such a suggestion may appear to be facetious, even insulting – at least until one reckons with Aum Shinrikyō, a New Religion whose name means "Om" (the Hindu/Buddhist invocation mantra) "Supreme Truth." Founded by ascetic and mystic Asahara Shōkō, the cult was built on the worship of both the Buddha and the god Shiva (the two are connected in Tantra, where the mystical technique is revealed, strikingly, by Shiva appearing in the form of the Buddha, implying that the doctrine was borrowed from Buddhism by Shaiva Hindus). With these elements Asahara mixed biblical themes. He saw himself as something of a Christ analogue and made predictions of the near advent of Armageddon, a breakdown of world society into a chaos from which only he and his followers should emerge unscathed. In the meantime members of Aum Shinrikyō must undertake a rigorous routine of radical asceticism, so radical that one cultist died from the deprivations thus imposed.

The group began a cover-up of the death, fearing negative publicity and trouble with the law. Then they murdered a reporter (with his family) who had uncovered the truth. This was only the beginning of an alarming defensive posture by the cult. They grew quickly and had cells in many nations, but even so they failed to meet their unrealistically ambitious evangelistic goals. This failure signaled that the rest of mankind was just no good, unworthy of survival. A new attempt at spreading their influence in society was an election campaign in which Asahara and other members stood for various offices, only to go down in resounding defeat. This was just too much, and the paranoia of Aum Shinrikyō only increased.

At length Asahara used the cult's considerable resources to build laboratories for the development of biological and chemical weapons of mass destruction, which he told his scientists were only for defense, which seemed to make sense given their paranoia. But in fact, Asahara had a two-pronged strategy. He determined to punish Japanese society for rejecting his God-given mission, and he hoped to simulate the very apocalyptic tribulation he had warned of. His minions never learned the trick to delivering these weapons very effectively, luckily for the sinners, and an attempt to disperse botulin came to naught. But the notorious releasing of vials of Sarin gas on two intersecting subway routes in Tokyo, near the major government complex, was somewhat more successful. A dozen hapless commuters perished, while thousands more were sickened. It did not take the authorities long to pin the blame, and litigation continues at this writing. But the public exposure of the murderous designs of the group has by no means killed it! It has entered a new growth cycle!

What does all this have to do with Lovecraft and Japan? Simply that, at least according to some reports, the doctrine of Aum Shinrikyō led to the attempted mass murder on the subway because the members believed *all human life must be eradicated from the earth to pave the way for the return of the mighty Beings they worshipped, and for a new order in which they, the cultists, would participate, alone of all mankind.* Does that premise sound familiar? Is it so hard to imagine an insidious cult so hostile to their own blood-species, votaries of ancient gods who should return to reclaim the earth and spread mayhem among its inhabitants, rewarding only those who, like Wizard Whateley and Old Castro, had paved the way for their advent?

Indeed, if life mimics art so completely that art is thrust into the shade as anticlimactic, it means that writers in Japan, if they are to make their own contribution to the Lovecraft tradition, must up the ante. There are various ways to do that, and you will find that our authors have found a number of them.

Al Azif and Bardo Thödöl

Some might be skeptical whether the Lovecraft Mythos, at least as popularly interpreted in the wake of August Derleth (*The Lurker at the Threshold, The Trail of Cthulhu, The Mask of Cthulhu,* etc.) could ever even strike a note among those trained in the venerable Japanese culture with its implicit mythic structures. Is the Cthulhu Mythos too similar to the Greek myth of the fall of Kronos to the Olympians, or to the Christian saga of Satan's Fall? Are the Great Old Ones inextricably bound to Western mythologoumena like the fallen angels and the Titans? I think not. Lovecraft sought, he averred, to approximate at least the chilly ring of Tatar or Tibetan folklore with some of the names of his entities, such as Nug and

Yeb. He connected the Bönpa priests of pre-Buddhist Tibet with the cult of the Old Ones in "Clarendon's Last Test." And his famous fictive grimoire, the *Necronomicon*, has a title that boils down to the formula, "Book concerning the dead." And that must remind us of the Tibetan scripture, also sacred to the Shingon sect in Japan, the *Bardo Thödöl*, or "Book of Liberation by Hearing, on the Intermediate Plane," i.e., between this life and whatever comes next. What does come next?

Upon death, one hovers incorporeally about the deathbed for some four days, then beholds the White Light of the Adi-Buddha, which is in fact one's own Inmost Self. One must needs keep in mind the Mahayana Buddhist doctrine that there is no individual *atman*, self, distinct from the one great Self of the Dharmakya, the Buddha-nature. To fail to grasp this is the predicament of the unenlightened. But if one does grasp the significance of the Light, one joins with it and leaves Samsara, individual existence in the world of reincarnation, behind forever. But if one has never meditated, one will not recognize the true nature of the Light and, stunned by it, one will flee into the first intermediate plane.

There one beholds a vista of celestial divine Beings, the Buddhas and Bodhisattvas, penultimate manifestations of the Buddha Nature, and thus of one's own self. As one sees these glorious Entities, one must bear in mind that they are but projections of one's own mind. But if one has lived a sinful life, one's spiritual perceptions are to say the least dulled. And then one sees the Peaceful Deities, as they are called, transform into the bloody-tusked, weapons-wielding forms of the Wrathful Deities. Still oblivious of their true nature as illusions of the Mind, the carnal man retreats into the stage wherein one seeks a new incarnation on earth or in other realms, including existence as a ghost, an animal, or a denizen of one of the numerous picturesque hells.

If August Derleth found it fruitful to interpret Lovecraft's Old Ones as analogues of the Greek Titans and the Christian fallen

angels, the Principalities and Powers, and to oppose to them another group friendly to humanity, the Elder Gods, analogous to the
Olympian gods and the Christian angels, I will venture that it is at
least as productive and enlightening to compare the notion of the
Great Old Ones and the Elder Gods to the notion of the Wrathful
Deities as opposed to the Peaceful Deities. The difference between
them is one created by the unenlightened mind's tendency to split
the Suchness of the Void into sets of opposed half-truths. As in
the *Bardo Thödöl*, where the difference between the Peaceful and
Wrathful Deities is nothing more than the screen of good or bad
karma through which one views them, in the Cthulhu Mythos, the
moral coloring of each or any group of deities is a function of an
anthropomorphic perspective. It is just as Yōzan Dirk Mosig, himself a Zen practitioner, argued long ago: Lovecraft created entities
that are utterly indifferent to the fortunes of man, much like im-
personal cosmic forces. But, Mosig argued, the characters in the
stories cannot help viewing them from a limited anthropocentric
perspective from which it appears that Cthulhu and Yog-Sothoth
are evil, since they are a threat to us, though only in the sense that
a hurricane or tsunami might be. Not intentionally malcious: just
inconvenient for us.

The Origin

How did this particular collection come about? It was the brain-
child of one of the authors, Asamatsu Ken. This notable gent is
a young and indefatigable writer of both historical and horror
novels. He is a dyed-in-the-wool Cthulhu Mythos fan. Asamatsu
first conceived the collection as comprised of twin volumes, one
featuring Mythos tales set in various historical settings, the other
made of tales set in our own day. To this end, he invited a number
of major Japanese horror scribes to join the project. He was successful, and so were they. In fact, the writers found themselves so

carried away that before long the material had far outgrown the original parameters, pretty much like Wilbur Whateley's brother popping the buttons on his farmhouse! So the two volumes grew plump, and the project was taken on by Sōgensha in Japan, a major publisher of mystery and science fiction books translated into Japanese. They were delighted to be able to offer a significant new homegrown product! And so now the shoe is on the other foot: we are offering you the same collection in an English translation! The present collection, *Night Voices, Night Journeys*, is, then, the first volume of a series collectively called *Lairs of the Hidden Gods*. I can only say I am proud and grateful to be associated with the project, and that I can't wait to read the rest of the tales! (One word of warning: you might want to read my comments on each story *after* you've read the story itself, lest certain surprises be spoiled.)

Robert M. Price
Hierophant of the Horde
November 10, 2004

The Plague of
St. James Infirmary

Asamatsu Ken
Translated by R. Keith Roeller

"*Those whom Yog-Sothoth touches are never seen
again… at least, in any recognisable shape.*"
– Letter from H.P. Lovecraft to Willis Conover
(September 1st, 1936)

The Plague of
St. James Infirmary

Asamatsu Ken
Translated by R. Keith Roeller

"THAT WHICH WE have now revealed to you is secret history." So says Allah to the Prophet in the Koran (12:102 and various other passages), as a new version of a familiar story of biblical personalities unfolds. One might say the same thing of Ken Asamatsu's "The Plague of St. James Infirmary," as it supplies a hitherto-unsuspected back story for famous events in early twentieth-century Chicago. At this point, let's just say Asamatsu is able to discern the long shadows cast by historic figures and events, and to see when those shadows are more real and more dangerous than the mortals who seem to cast them but who, in their tenuous flesh, are perhaps the real shadows.

The story is, among many other things, a tribute to the great Henry Kuttner, in particular to his early *Weird Tales* and *Strange Tales* work. These stories, which I collected and introduced in the Chaosium book, *The Book of Iod* (which I later realized uninformed readers probably thought was "the Book of Ten-D"), comprise Kuttner's Cthulhu Mythos legacy, really a preamble to the much more voluminous and more polished science fiction he was once justly famous for. The occult detective, "Michael L," is of course Michael Leigh, the Van Helsing analogue invented by Kuttner for use in his "The Salem Horror" and used again in "The Black Kiss," a tale first penned by Kuttner, rejected by publishers, and rewritten for him by his friend Robert Bloch. Perhaps surprisingly, Asamatsu has Dr. Leigh thumb the pages not of Kuttner's *Book of Iod*, but rather of Robert E. Howard's *Unaussprechlichen Kulten*, for his strategic occult lore. The spectacle of a roomful of flesh containing a legion of human heads reflects Kuttner's story "Azathoth," though Asamatsu's use of the disturbing image is much more imaginative.

Kuttner followed Lovecraft in his use of various items of Theosophical lore in his Mythos stories. The word "theosophy" denotes, in its broadest sense, "divine wisdom," perhaps philosophical speculation, perhaps ostensible revelation. But in its more famous historical sense, the term became the identifying label for Madame Blavatsky's Theosophical Society, a nineteenth-century cult that survives today. Kuttner derives such incunabula as the Vach-Viraj Incantation, the Tikkun Elixir, and the Ch'hayya Ritual from Blavatsky's *Isis Unveiled* and *The Secret Doctrine*. None of that appears here, but the Blavatsky connection is still evident in the characterization of Michael Leigh as an "occultist." Does that designation on one's business card necessarily brand one as a ghost-buster? The term itself is older, of course, as old as the term "occult," hidden, referring to the imagined realm of arcane knowledge open only to the Gnostic adept. But to tag Michael Leigh with it reflects the more recent parochial use of the term (contemporary with Kuttner) as a synonym for "Theosophist," as in Blavatsky's collection *Studies in Occultism* or the Theosophist *Dictionary of Occultism*. Granted, it may seem only a different shade of connotation, but Michael Leigh's epithet implies less that he is a counterpart to Buffy the Vampire Slayer than that he is some sort of Rosicrucian initiate.

The story is also a tip of the turban to Brian Lumley, whose invention the *Cthaat Aquadingen* is. "*Aqua*" means water, and "*din-gen*" is German for "things," but Lumley, to my knowledge, never explained what the heck "Cthaat" meant. Asamatsu has decided, appropriately enough, that it is the name of a marine monster deity. Why not?

Chapter One
Nearer My God to Thee

NOT ONE PERSON in three knew that the large hospital tucked away in a corner of the Jewish neighborhood in the heights had been left abandoned.

Eliot stepped into the reception hall of St. James Infirmary, and as he glanced over his shoulder a bluish, ash gray color reflected in his eyes. It was a heavy, milky white.

"The fog is rolling in. Eliot, switch on the flashlight," said Michael L, leading the way. Whether the fog was a damp wind blowing off Lake Michigan, or a dense smoke from the factory district, it hung extremely heavy, like a wet cape.

The fog carried a foul odor that pierced deep into their nostrils. Moving like some sort of glutinous being, it slipped through the door and into the hospital.

"This fog isn't natural. Can you smell that odor? Just like a strong acid. One of the marks of *them* is *yōki*, contained in the element of water. Tarō, close the door, quickly! Touching them for too long is harmful."

"Yessir, master," his servant Tarō answered in his southern drawl, easily shutting the large glass door with one hand.

Eliot once again marveled at the young Japanese man. Though his left arm hung in a sling, and he wore a patch over his left eye, he was still muscular and powerful. Much of this image had to do with the long, slender object wrapped in a sleeve that he held in his right hand. Eliot stood speechless, recalling the tremendous weight and creak of the glass door.

Eliot's astonished look made Tarō smile.

"What's *yōki*?" Eliot asked, quickly shifting his glance to Michael L, and attempting to regain his composure. Eliot of course knew that Michael L was a renowned occultist long before they had reached St. James, but was still taken aback when Michael L suddenly used such rarefied terms.

Though he was now deeply involved in this affair, Eliot was still very much a resident of the daytime world.

"*Yōki* is a Japanese word, boy," explained Tarō, speaking from behind. "It means 'horrible atmosphere,' or 'gruesome feeling.' The kind of setting in which you might find *them*."

"Them…" The word slipped unconsciously from Eliot's mouth in a whisper. An image of *them* danced through his mind like a revolving lantern.

An explosion of dynamite. A jet-black shadow standing motionless in the center of the light that pierced his eyes, the force of the explosion and the waves of heat. That was what controlled *them*. Hands and feet slashed into gobbets, and entrails spilling out. Fragments of bone and hunks of flesh. A torrent of blood. It was these that as he watched, would pull together, collect together and form a whole, then fall back to their original state. That was one of the marks of *them*. The heads of Italian mobsters, concealing guns in their baggy suits, blown off one after the other. The tentacles that reached out to commit brutal, savage killings were also a part of *them*. And the thing that had contemptibly kidnapped Patty Murphy, confining her in this abandoned hospital as a sacrifice. That was, without question, *them*.

A sharp whistle sounded, driving away the shadows of *them* that had flashed through Eliot's mind.

As he looked up Eliot noticed that the Japanese man had moved in front of Michael L. Eliot shined the light ahead of him. The entrance hall was filled with specks of jet-black darkness. Like a living being, the darkness scattered when touched by the beams of light.

Just like a cloud of gnats, he thought.

Eliot held his breath. He felt that if he drew a breath the grains of darkness would invade his body, and coat his insides with black darkness.

"You ever drink absinthe and water? How about it, boy?"

"No, never. I don't like alcohol, and besides, you're not allowed to drink in this country these days."

"Don't be so straitlaced. Yeah, well, I guess it's no surprise some kid not even twenty don't know nothin' about backdoor drinking."

Tarō suddenly switched to the careless speech of a neighborhood thug.

"Absinthe is one damned strong drink, made from wormwood. But mix it with water and, it's the damnedest thing, it changes into the color of milk."

Eliot said nothing.

"I guess it's some kind of chemical reaction. But the final color isn't pure white. It's a cloudy white with a blue tinge, just like the color of that fog out front."

"Really?" Eliot sniffed. He was a junior in college, and resented being referred to as "boy."

"You're only three years older than I am, but you've had a lot of experience, haven't you? So where was this speakeasy you tried that stuff? Texas? Or maybe New Mexico?"

"Not in this country. Canada. So it doesn't violate prohibition. You ever been to Canada, boy?"

"No."

"Never?"

"Never."

"Well, well," the Japanese man pressed, "you don't just hate liquor, but Canada too, huh?"

Then he grinned. It was a smile that said, "I got you." Eliot at last saw that he was being teased.

"*Waza ari*," he muttered gruffly in Japanese.

The words wiped away Tarō's wry smile. He face turned suddenly serious as he questioned Eliot.

"How do you know that word?"

"I'm learning judo at the university. Didn't I tell you?"

Tarō was silent for a moment. "Really? They have a judo teacher at Chicago U, do they? That sounds like a more interesting job than bartender at a club or bouncer for some underground bar."

Tarō used his teeth to pull back one end of the bag he held in his hand, and showed it to Eliot. A Japanese sword, a *katana* almost a yard long, shown from the bag.

"They're not illegal in this country," he continued, gently waving it around. "Something everybody guard for an occultist should have."

"Silence," interrupted Michael L. "Quiet, both of you." His tone was nervous. Eliot turned his eyes to the tall occultist.

Michael L narrowed his silver-gray eyebrows, concentrating on something.

"There… can't you hear it?" the occultist whispered.

Eliot and Tarō both strained to hear.

The vast entrance lobby was filled with silence.

It was now 11:00 at night. No one was about. All that could be seen were cobwebs, dust and piles of rubbish. The lobby floor, and the chairs and tables strewn about were all covered with a thick layer of dust. Grey particles swirled in the beams of light. It was this great volume of dust that seemed to be the source of the silence.

"Noises in a place like this are probably just cockroaches" Eliot thought, "or a mouse that's…"

They could hear whistling. Like a dark stain slowly spreading from the center of a large white cloth, the sound grew in their ears. A melody was playing. It sounded like a jazz number, but one that Eliot had never heard before.

24

Suddenly, someone very near began singing in a brusque, gravelly voice. The soulful lyrics told of a final glimpse of a girl, cold and beautiful, stretched out on a long, white table.

Eliot's heart leapt into his throat, while at the same time, an image floated in his mind. An image of the worst possible outcome. That of his girlfriend, lying supine on a table in a white-tiled operating room. An image of Patty.

The man who had taken her was the detestable boss of a Jewish gang, an accursed master of black magic, and *that man*, a strange student of the dark arts called Frank "The Pest" Simmel.

As the song went on, describing a final kiss, it chased the ominous image of the man from Eliot's mind. The song was *St. James Infirmary*. Eliot was astonished to realize that it was Michael L who was singing the dark, gloomy lyrics and blues melody.

Eliot stared at the hawklike features of Michael L's face. His eyes ran the length of the dark, high-quality suit covering his tall, slender frame. He was the very picture of an upper class, East Coast upbringing. The embodiment of the scholarly life, buried in old books. What did it mean that he should be singing the kind of blues number more often heard at the Cotton Club, where the philandering gentlemen of leisure gather?

Michael L quietly closed his mouth. With one hand he opened his leather bag. It was similar to that which a doctor might use on a house call, though smaller. From it he pulled out what looked like a rod with a round object attached to it. He held his hand out in front of him.

In his hand, Michael L held a peculiar cross. It wasn't the Celtic cross so often seen in the graveyards of Irish immigrants. And it was different from the cross of the Catholics or Greek Orthodox.

It was a silver cross, crowned with a shining, golden sphere.

"The ankh is responding to the whistling," said Michael L. "The waves of sound contain *yōki*. That… *yōki* in water."

Eliot stared intently at the cross Michael L was holding out. They could now hear the whistling clearly. The sphere atop the cross was glimmering faintly, in rhythm with the rise and fall of the melody.

"So that means," said Eliot, "that what's doing the whistling is…" Even he noticed that his voice was raspy and hoarse, like that of an old man.

"I can promise you it's not your little sweetie."

Eliot was infuriated by Tarō's jest, and he glared at the Japanese man. As his anger subsided, though, he nodded slightly.

Eliot saw that the Japanese man was deadly serious. And as if to prove how serious he was, Tarō was pulling the sword from its bag.

Eliot stuck out his hand.

"I'll hold the bag for you. I'll put it in my pocket."

"Sure. Hold on to it a while. I want to be ready to draw this out at any time."

Tarō passed him the sword's cover. Eliot clutched the cotton bag in his hand. It was cold as ice, as if frost had covered the surface of the cloth.

Putting away the bag without letting go of the light, Eliot shined the flashlight all around the hall. It must have been as large as a billiard hall.

A large painting hung on the south wall. It was a scene from south of the river. The canal as seen from Taylor Street. It wasn't in the picture, but from this angle you should have been able to see the memorial to the Great Chicago Fire of 1871 on the right-hand side.

The pharmacy was to the west. The glass in the little window where medicine was dispensed had turned brown, and a spider had spun a web across it. To the east was the door they had just passed through. Beyond the door was the fog. Michael L's Ford, parked at the curb, was completely obscured by the fog.

To the north were the elevators, and the entrance to the stairwell. They held their breath, and strained their ears to listen even more closely. They could hear a gentle nighttime breathing. And the sound of scampering cockroaches. The soft squeaking of mice.

And also…

The whistling continued.

"The north. That stairwell. It's coming from upstairs," Tarō said confidently to Michael L.

Michael L nodded silently. He shifted the mysterious cross to his other hand, and bent down.

"Shine the light in the bag."

"OK."

Eliot directed the light toward Michael L's bag. As he did so, he caught a glimpse of the contents. It was indeed very much like a doctor's visiting bag. There were items resembling metal instruments. There were other things, of course. Round chips of wood. What looked like gemstones, along with a leather-bound book. Michael L picked up the book, lifting it out with careful, practiced movements.

The items under the book gave Eliot a start.

These were an automatic pistol and a bundle of dynamite. There were also detonators and what looked like a small triggering device.

"Good."

Michael L stood up, preventing Eliot from seeing any more of what was in the bag, and he turned the light upward.

"Stand behind me, and shine the light so that I can read the book."

"OK."

Eliot directed the light as he was told. For a brief moment, Eliot saw the title page of the book Michael L held in his hands. The blackletter printing was probably the title of the book. It was German, in any case. As the son of Norwegian immigrants, Eliot had a fairly good understanding of Norwegian, and could read the similar German, though with some difficulty. The part of the title he was able to make out was *Unaussprechlichen Kulten*.

I should have studied German at college, he thought.

As Eliot was torturing himself so, Michael L began quietly speaking in German, reciting a verse from the leather book. Eliot stammered out a literal translation in his head.

> *Cthugha,*
> *You, ruler of the fiery netherworld,*
> *Guardian of the ancient cosmos,*
> *Protect us from the evil power of the water.*

It's some kind of prayer, thought Eliot. He quietly swallowed the lump in his throat.

Eliot began to feel like one of the characters in the Sherlock Holmes mysteries he used to read as a boy. Maybe *The Hound of the Baskervilles*, for instance.

Who could have predicted it, thought Eliot. Here I was born and raised in Chicago, and I didn't even know about this abandoned hospital. Now here I am, standing in its hall with an occultist and a Japanese man, listening to incantations and an eerie whistling.

It certainly was a situation that would have been unimaginable only five days earlier.

"Cthugha!"

Michael L called out the bizarre name. Eliot wondered what kind of name of a foreign god it could be.

For an instant, the entire hall seemed to warp out of shape. It was just like the time before. Of course, then it wasn't a room that Cthugha had distorted, but *them*.

A strange feeling began to rise from deep inside Eliot's chest. It was like an awareness of a consciousness other than his own, telling him that he shouldn't be here, or perhaps that that this was a place where he ought not to exist. Eliot's throat suddenly went dry. His pulse began to quicken. Sweat formed on his palms.

The room warped again. This time, it's space-time, he thought.

A moment later Eliot's mind flashed back to five days earlier, to that late afternoon on October 26th.

Chapter Two
Here I Am, Oh Lord, Send Me

THE SIGN FOR Wacker Avenue had been defaced with white paint, turned into "Wicked Avenue."

I don't know who did that, but it's not a very funny joke, thought Eliot as he averted his eyes in disgust. Out of the corner of his eye he could see where the wall of the telephone company building had been damaged. A deep hole had been made in the red brick wall, with a series of small holes in the side leading up to it. The nicks and holes stretching along the wall had been circled with chalk as if to provide emphasis. Exclamation marks left by the city police officers.

According to the newspaper, the day before yesterday, a car driven by Judge Clark Van Buren was sprayed with bullets from several men with tommy guns, then crashed into the wall. Judge Van Buren's favorite white suit was soaked with blood as he died. The local police and the federal agents investigating the shooting disagreed about the cause of the judge's death. In the opinion of the city police it was a traffic accident—the judge's neck had been broken. The feds took the position that it was murder, the result of a 45-caliber bullet to the temple—the judge's neck was broken after he was already dead. With the two opinions in opposition, the newspaper said that it would take six months for a final verdict to be reached. By the time the findings were released, however, no one would remember the name Van Buren. That was the way it was every time.

In any event, one thing was clear to the citizens of Chicago. The gangs, getting rich off the illegal production, import and sale of liquor, as well as from drugs, prostitution and gambling, had survived, while the one man who had stood up to and condemned these sleazy lowlifes had died, his body riddled with bullets and his neck broken.

That was how, the day before yesterday, on October 24th, the last mark of justice was erased from the city of Chicago, possibly forever.

Eliot looked at the sign again. Wicked Avenue. He was sickened by the graffiti, and frowned in disgust. To lift his spirits he pulled a magazine from his coat pocket. He had just purchased it from a newsstand at the Deaton Street station on the Loop.

Eliot had bought the magazine to kill time while waiting to meet Patty, and hadn't checked the title carefully. He held the cover up to the streetlight.

"*Weird Tales*. I guess I bought some kind of horror story magazine, not a sports journal." Eliot clicked his tongue, then thought about it some more.

"Oh, well, I guess it's OK. Considering where I am, it's got to be better than *Gangster*, or *True Crime*."

With that he completely forgot about the shooting of the judge. Chiding himself for choosing Wacker Avenue near the telephone company as a meeting place, he flipped through the pages of the magazine. He opened it to a random page, and looked down – it was just for killing time, after all. If it's rubbish, I can just throw it away, he told himself. A young man living in America at this time of unprecedented economic prosperity could certainly afford to throw away a 20- or 30-cent magazine without reading it, and without putting a dent in his wallet.

He began reading the fine writing, printed on pulp paper. Sentences like this one leapt out at him:

I cannot think of the deep sea without shuddering at the

nameless things that may at this very moment be crawling and floundering on its slimy bed, worshipping their ancient stone idols and carving their own detestable likenesses on submarine obelisks of water-soaked granite.

Eliot caught the scent of water. It was a strong, concentrated smell, like standing in front of a large waterfall.

He looked up from his cheap magazine, and sniffed the air.

A cold wind stung his eyes.

It was the wind blowing off the canal that linked Lake Michigan with the Mississippi River. A cold, late autumn wind had picked up the foul odor of the stagnant canal, and had been blowing through Chicago. The smell of that wind, however, was a far cry from the intense watery smell that now filled his nostrils.

"That's strange." Eliot tilted his head to one side in puzzlement, blinked his eyes several times, and continued reading.

I dream of a day when they may rise above the billows to drag down in their reeking talons the remnants of puny, war-exhausted mankind – of a day when the land shall sink, and the dark ocean floor shall ascend amidst universal pandemonium.

"Hey, you, aren't you Hiraoka?"

A man's shout suddenly reached Eliot's ears. It was an overly casual way of speaking, in a rough tone of voice. On top of that the speaker had a Texas accent, or maybe New Mexico.

Some laborer from the Navy Pier, or some kind of cowboy, thought Eliot. He frowned, and looked up. Instinctively he searched for the owner of the voice, casting his eyes back and forth.

"What's the matter? You're Hiraoka, right? You!"

A man was running toward him from the Opera House one block

straight ahead – the very place he had planned to take Patty this evening. Chinese, maybe, or Japanese. His tanned, cork brown skin and refined features were striking. For some reason, the Asian man raised his hand and smiled in his direction. Could this be someone I know? For a moment, the thought passed through Eliot's mind. He was studying judo at Chicago University, and thought that this man might be a friend of his teacher, Mr. Suzuki.

However…

The Asian man suddenly lowered his arm. He took on a puzzled expression. At this point it dawned on Eliot that maybe the Asian man wasn't waving to him.

I guess he's calling to someone behind me, thought Eliot, and looked over his shoulder.

When he did, he saw Patty Murphy. She ran up to him.

There was a small man behind her. It was an Asian man wearing a jeff cap. He called out to the man in front of Eliot.

"Run, Tarō! Get out of here!"

Patty stopped in her tracks.

Eliot also froze where he was.

"What's going on, Hiraoka? What's the hurry?" asked the man up ahead, slackening his pace.

"Get out of…"

As the man called out, a car engine revved. It was about fifty meters behind the man in the jeff cap. It was an eight-passenger, midnight blue sedan. It had a Buick logo, but it was either a special order vehicle, or a model that Eliot had never seen before.

"Get out of the way, lady!"

The man in the jeff cap shoved Patty aside, knocking her down, and ran for his life.

Patty screamed. Eliot reflexively spun around. As he did, the man in the jeff cap ran straight into him.

"Shit."

Eliot threw a punch. The jeff cap man easily dodged it. This guy

32

has had some judo training, thought Eliot. The man kept on running.

But not, however, toward the Asian man who was coming from up ahead. Just before he reached him, the man in the jeff cap suddenly veered off to the left.

"What's going on, Hiraoka? You get yourself in some kind of trouble?"

The Asian man stopped, and was yelling down an alley into which the man had fled. Eliot helped his girlfriend to her feet, staring dumbfounded at the sight of these two men.

"Who was that?" said Patty.

"I don't know. He's certainly no gentleman, though."

"Would you look at this? My dress is filthy. And I borrowed it from my mother, since we were going to the opera."

As she spoke Eliot shifted his gaze to Patty's pearl white dress for the first time.

"That's it, I'm going to say something," he said resolutely, but a voice from the alleyway between the building drowned him out.

"Get down! Tarō, get down!"

It was the man in the jeff cap. His voice echoed, as if he were yelling from deep inside a cave.

"What's the matter, Hiraoka?"

The Asian man called Tarō stood at the narrow entrance to the alley, and kept calling out to the man in the jeff cap.

That was when it happened.

The midnight blue sedan came rolling up slowly. Before it had gone ten meters, it stopped abruptly.

"Get out. It's a time bomb," a deep, gravelly voice said from inside the car. The next moment, all the doors opened. Four muscular men leaped from the car at once.

A flame appeared from near the car's tailpipe. Flames of yellow, orange and purple blended together. The body of the car expanded for one one-hundredth of a second, then shrank. Then it exploded.

Eliot dropped to the ground, shielding Patty. The Asian man on the street instinctively leapt into the alleyway. The evening scene on Wacker Avenue was lit with a flash of light. There was a slight pause before the roar and force of the explosion arrived.

A charred hubcap grazed Eliot and Patty's heads. A hot wind poured blood, lumps of flesh and bone all about them. Eliot saw smoke rising from what looked like a jet-black spider. It took a little less than a second for him to realize that it was the burnt remains of a severed hand. Beside it lay a twisted brake lever.

"Look! Over there!"

Patty leapt up from under Eliot. She stared in the direction of the exploded car. It could have been the no-nonsense nature of an Irish girl, or the fact that her father was chief of detectives, but she just continued to stare. Then she began shrieking.

"That! There... how can it... how can that be!? That body, it's becoming whole again! How can it be that only the body of that man is coming back together!?"

"What are you talking about?"

Eliot turned to look toward the road. Flames and smoke rose from the remains of the luxury car in the road. The shadow of some distorted object floated there among the glowing orange flames that flickered against the veil of darkness. The shadow was barely managing to maintain human form.

It was leaning heavily to the right. Half of its head was missing, like the shadow of a sliced melon. Its right arm hung down to touch the road, attached to the shoulder by several strands of muscle that resembled stretches of half-melted cheese.

"That's horrible. Someone's got to help that man..."

The first thought that came to Eliot's mind was that this was a survivor of the explosion. Even though he had lost half of his head, he was still alive. And he was standing. It's just possible that with a little first aid he might be OK...

"No... that's not it... no... you don't understand!"

34

Patty was shaking violently in his arms. She was practically hysterical. Her expression was one of both crying and laughing.

"What don't I get?"

"Look! That guy, he's... that *thing's...*"

"What the..."

Eliot fixed his eyes on the standing man. He continued to stare. Then he finally began to see it.

His right arm... was it... reattaching itself?

"Oh God, oh God, oh God..."

As he repeated the words its right arm returned to its shoulder, pulled up by the sinews. Its partial head began to grow back, the edges pulling toward the center. A slimy, glistening foam rose from the brain. Beneath the foam the damaged portion of its head was being regenerated. In no time at all the dirty, yellowed pudding of the brain was covered with an intricate network of blood vessels and nerves, hiding its gray, outer membrane. As they continued to watch, the bones of skull were reproduced. The skin of the scalp turned to a blood jelly and poured over the flesh-colored bone; the jelly turned to skin, and hair sprouted from it. But there was more...

The same transformation happened not only to his body, but also to his clothes.

His ruined pants were repaired. The fabric of his suit, soaked in blood and clumps of flesh, became like new. The reddish-brown stains faded, and from underneath appeared a gray cloth with dark blue pinstripes. Fragments of eight shattered buttons leapt up from the ground, settling on the front of the suit like small, legless insects. Flesh began climbing the bare bones of his legs. The burns on his feet disappeared, and were covered by shoes and socks.

Neither Eliot nor Patty was able to utter a sound as they stared at the incredible sight.

Finally, the thing was completely whole again. It was a well-built man, about fifty years old.

The moment his eyes came to rest on the resurrected man's face, Eliot was finally able to let out a scream in his heart–it was Frank "The Pest" Simmel!

The Pest gave his slicked back, jet-black hair a stroke, and looked around. He appeared to be searching for something.

It soon became clear what the man was looking for–a felt hat, a gray borsalino. The hat, too, was slowly but surely being restored. The Asian man was holding it.

"Hira, Hiraoka. What the hell," he stammered.

A hand reached out from thin air and snatched the felt hat from his hands. It was like the hand of an infant, grown large. The skin was pink and soft, and showed not a trace of a scar. It was a hand that had just been regenerated.

"I'll take that back now."

The man's voice similarly seemed to come from nowhere. The pink hand flashed, and the Asian man was flung against the side of the building. The left side of his body smashed against the wall and he bounced off. He fell to the street, blood running from his eye and holding his left arm.

Eliot was taken aback, and glanced over at the man who had suddenly appeared and knocked the Asian man to the ground. He turned back to look at the place where *the thing* had just been standing, but it was no longer there.

It was just a split second… how did he get way over there, Eliot puzzled.

Eliot confirmed for himself that the man who had snatched the borsalino from the Asian man was indeed that same *thing* from a moment ago, a realization that only added to his sense of shock and dismay.

The man calmly put on the borsalino, and smiled at the Asian.

"And now," he said, "where is that *shvuntz* who tried to blow me to bits?"

"Sh… shvuntz?" the Asian man questioned in a quaking voice.

"What respectable people call a fool."

The man curled the edges of his lips. It was an arrogant, boastful grin, the kind of gangster smirk that all residents of Chicago knew well.

"I... I don't know."

Before the Asian man could shake his head, a gunshot rang out from the alleyway. The big man cringed, but not out of fear. He had simply been startled at the sound of the shot.

"Run, Tarō! Get away from that thing! It's not human!"

Hiraoka's voice echoed from between the buildings. Gunshots punctuated his words. Orange sparks flashed from the pitch black of the alley. Hiraoka was hiding deep in the shadow of the buildings, blindly firing his pistol.

The big man mocked Hiraoka's words in a condescending tone. "Run, Tarō, get away." He snorted a laugh, muttering "Piss off!" as he shoved Tarō away with one hand.

It was at least half curiosity that caused Eliot let go of Patty's hand and begin walking toward Tarō. The man who had been blown up by the time bomb in the car was alive. That alone was a heavenly miracle, but even the missing portions of this head and arm were regenerated. That could only be the work of the devil. On top of that, thought Eliot, that "devil" is Frank "The Pest" Simmel. Eliot recalled the words of his brother-in-law Alex.

"We, the citizens of Chicago, are at this moment caught in the grip of two different gangs. One is the Italians, lead by the boss Johnny Trio. This organization has extended its influence from its base in New York, profiting mainly from the illicit production, import and sale of liquor. The other is the Jewish gang that has long had deep roots in Chicago. It is built on understandings with dockworkers and the exploitation of laborers, prostitution, extortion of the general public, and the protection money known as "odds" that it collects from the businesses within its territory. The rise of the Italians nearly drove out the Jewish gang, but some time around 1921 the Jews quickly began to recover lost ground. The man at the forefront of the counterattack was Frank "The Pest" Simmel. He got his nickname because no matter how many times the Italians went after him, he always survived. The more superstitious members of the Italian gang probably believed that Simmel was using some kind of black magic, or that he had made a deal with the devil. Simmel comes from Salem, after all, so that may well be the case."

Eliot's brother-in-law Alexander Jamie knew a lot about the underworld, and as an employee in the Justice Department knew a lot of people on the police force and in the prosecutor's office.

Eliot moved forward as if under a spell, and stood beside Tarō.

Patty walked up slowly behind them. She too had seen the "work of the devil," and wanted to see for herself what else he might do.

The Pest's voice echoed from the alleyway.

"Hey, you there! It's a shame you weren't able to make mincemeat out of me."

The alley was less than five feet wide, and between the evening gloom and shadows of the tall buildings, it was pitch black.

Simmel's body disappeared into the darkness. His dim figure could just barely be seen. Hiraoka, further back in the alleyway, could not be seen at all.

But with a shout of "Shit!" and the sound of gunfire, things began to happen.

Blinding orange flashes lit the alleyway. Hot lead bullets were unleashed in rapid succession. Flames pierced the darkness. They should have gone straight through Simmel's chest, but...

Before the flashes began, Simmel's body became translucent. A translucence tinged by a pale blue light. Small ripples moved over the surface.

Water! Eliot gasped. Has Simmel's body has turned to water!? It definitely appeared to be water in human form.

The bullets passed through Simmel's liquefied body, and flew off randomly.

Peering through Simmel's body they could see a man far back in the alleyway. His face, contorted with fear, was also plain to see in the momentary flashes from the pistol.

"You took me by surprise a moment ago, so I didn't have time to liquefy, but this time it's different. Now, *shvuntz*, you'll taste the power of the water magic," Simmel said in a chanting voice. He stretched out an arm into the darkness of the alley. His arm was glowing with a faint light of pale blue.

For some reason it reminded Eliot of Lake Michigan at midnight.

Simmel's hand reached out from his translucent sleeve. It grew thinner and thinner as it extended through the air. Each of his five fingers grew longer and spread apart, like a blue, liquid casting net or bizarre deep-sea creature. They extended in five directions, close to twenty yards–straight toward Hiraoka hiding in the shadows of the alleyway.

Hiraoka's fear-stricken face reflected the pale blue light.

"It's the face of a ghost," said Patty, as she clung to Eliot's shoulder.

Her voice trembled, and her hands were damp with cold sweat. The face of the man in the jeff cap was being covered by the five-pronged translucent net. It was all happening in a split second, but to Eliot it seemed slower than a turtle's pace.

Hiraoka's head was completely enveloped.

His cap was pulled off, and was floating in the translucent net. It was as if his head had been preserved in a transparent fish tank.

They were able to clearly make out the large bubbles rising from his nose and mouth, opened as he writhed in pain.

"So which is better, drowning or being crushed by the pressure?" laughed Simmel. He remained translucent, bathed in a pale blue light. The arm he had extended outward began to swell monstrously from the elbow, moving along the forearm and finally covering Hiraoka's head.

Hiraoka muttered something. Bubbles of various sizes obscured his face.

"OK, as you wish, we'll make it crushed to death," said Simmel, tightening his grip.

The liquid net wrapped around him tightly. Patty screamed and turned away. She closed her eyes tightly, and buried her face in Eliot's chest. Eliot threw his arms around her, all the while staring at the unbelievable scene before him.

In an instant the net constricted. The pale blue light turned a sticky red.

What was the size of a fish tank contracted to the size of a football, then shrank to the size of a small globe. The crunching of bones could be heard, a sound like someone stepping on stale crackers.

"Fool," said Simmel, tossing him aside. The headless body fell to the street with a thump.

The arm that had survived the damage from the explosion, twisted, bent and stretched out, now returned to normal. As it did, the pale blue light encompassing Simmel's body faded, and he transformed into a perfectly ordinary, fifty-year-old man in a suit.

Simmel drew a white silk handkerchief from his pocket. Then, as if performing for the people watching him, began to wipe the blood from his hands.

"So, I suppose you all are next," he said, flashing his front teeth.

"I," Tarō began to say, and glanced over at Eliot and Patty, standing frozen as they held on to each other. "I mean, we didn't do anything," he said in a hoarse voice.

"You saw what happened just now with my 'water magic,' didn't you?"

Simmel stuffed his handkerchief under the shoulder straps of his coat, and inclined his head in a dramatic gesture.

"It was you that did it in front of us," Tarō snapped. His left eye was hurt and he was holding his left arm, but in speech at least he was still a match for Frank "The Pest" Simmel.

"That's true," said Simmel, nodding deeply. "But then again, that's the same thing that all the ordinary folk say that witness a drug or liquor deal. 'I didn't mean to watch you, you just did it in front of me.'"

With that Simmel turned his palm toward Eliot and Patty, and narrowed his shoulders. Simmel's jet black eyes glowed pale blue in the gathering twilight.

This is the prelude to the water magic, Eliot's gut was telling him.

Chapter Three
All Night Long

MICHAEL L AGAIN caused the name of the god to echo through the building.

The occultist's voice was strong, and projected an absolute belief in the existence that the name symbolized. Michael L himself, however, did not accept that this evil deity was true. He believed only in the element it wielded, in the magical and secret power that the element possessed.

"Yoth-Tlaggon!"

Eliot felt as if the inside of his eyelids flashed with silver sparks. This is different from the other time, he reflected. If nothing else the name is different. The memory of that time came back to his mind – the time that *yōki* was unleashed from the body of Frank "The Pest" Simmel.

"Cthugha!"

The crimson cry rang out.

Simmel pulled back with a start. The confidence and intimidation in his expression instantly drained away, replaced by one of shock and fear that spread across his face. His eyes shifted back and forth anxiously, and he cried out.

"That's not the deal! I still have some time left... yes... I know I do, N!"

The pale blue light faded from his eyes.

"Cthugha! Iä-tslt'algn!"

The strange voice called out again.

Eliot didn't fail to notice how Simmel's body shrank ever so slightly in fright. He opened his mouth as if to speak. Just then, as if hastening him along, they heard the squeal of brakes and a distant siren.

"The police!" yelled Patty. It was a cry of relief, directed to both Simmel and the people gathering in the street.

"Damn," Simmel muttered to himself, and turned toward the main road.

Eliot stared in amazement, unable to believe his eyes. A midnight blue automobile was stopped directly in front of Simmel. Eliot knew in his head that the squealing of brakes a moment ago must have come from this car, but to his eyes the car seemed to have appeared out of thin air.

The side door opened. Simmel slid quickly into the car, but as he was getting in seemed to suddenly remember something, and looked up at Patty. "Hey, you there, girl," he said, pointing at her with the forefinger of his left hand.

"You're Detective Kelly Murphy's daughter, aren't you?"

"No, that's not her," Eliot interrupted, stepping in front of Patty to obstruct Simmel's view.

"You can't hide anything from me. One of the minions of N just told me so. Yes, it'll be two birds with one stone. I'll offer you up to N on the next Day of Blood. I'll cut your heart from your naked body while you're still alive. Then I'll wash your corpse clean with the lifeblood of those two fools over there. Don't forget! On the Day of Blood!"

"Cthugha!"

The strange word echoed for a third time.

Simmel's body – along with the eight-passenger auto – trembled, and Eliot saw him shrink another size smaller.

Simmel pulled the car door shut as if clucking his tongue in disapproval.

The next moment, the car sped off.

"God damn it... that son of a bitch..."

Tarō began stumbling after him, but a white hand reached out and grabbed his shoulder.

"Stop. This is not an enemy we can fight here. Besides, he is more than just the boss of the Jewish gang. He wields the dark power of water, and is a water magician with the protection of N."

The man speaking, with furrowed silvery-gray eyebrows, was in his mid-thirties. He wore a gray coat that covered his tall and lanky frame. He gave off the air of a doctor, or scholar.

"Who are you?"

Eliot abruptly addressed the man.

"This is one of the great teachers in the world of darkness, and my master... for the moment, at least," replied Tarō, turning around.

"Dr. Yamada recommended you as a bodyguard, but you didn't keep our appointment, and when I go looking for you what do I find? You've left the hotel and are in the company of a monster... I may have to rethink your employment."

The tall man spoke softly, and turned toward Eliot.

"Has the lady been injured?"

"No."

"I'm relieved to hear it. However, Simmel seems to have developed a fascination with her."

Eliot said nothing, but squeezed Patty's hand a little tighter.

"The sage I met in New York indicated that the circle of fate would soon revolve toward Chicago. Worse still, he said that N would be involved. It would seem that this is what he meant."

As he finished speaking, the man reached quickly into his breast pocket. Eliot thought that he was reaching for a gun, and instinctively froze. It was a fountain pen, however–a Pelikan–that the man pulled from his pocket.

"Do you have any paper?" he asked, removing the pen's cap.

"Let me see... will this do?" Eliot fished out the magazine that he had stuffed into his coat pocket. Eliot held out the magazine, still folded back to the page he had been reading. "You can write in the margin," he said, adding to himself, though I don't know what you intend to write.

The man took the copy of *Weird Tales*, and jotted down something in the margin.

"This is where I'm staying. Things will probably be all right tonight, but soon you will need my help. Not you – the girl."

"What are you talking about? Her father is a detective for the…"

"It would not matter if her father were President of the United States. The only person in Chicago right now that can defeat Simmel is me," the man asserted, and handed the pulp fiction magazine back to Eliot.

"Master, the cops are here. They were watching the whole thing. Now that they know that Simmel got clean away, they can finally send in a patrol car."

Tarō spoke in the rough speech of Chicago gangsters. The man he referred to as master gave a wry smile, and pulling out his handkerchief held it to the Asian man's left eye.

"Hush now. I thought the Japanese were a more reserved and quiet people. Here, hold this to your eye. I'll put some disinfectant on it when we get back to the hotel."

His tone barely concealed his frustration, and he signaled to a yellow cab that arrived before the police car. The taxi pulled to a stop. The man ushered Tarō into the cab, and gave Eliot a gentle reminder.

"You two *will* need my help. Do you understand? Don't forget to contact me."

"But, your name… you haven't told us yet," Eliot shot back.

"You can call me Michael L," he said, stepping into the taxi.

"L? Your name is L?"

"I can't tell you my name for the remainder of this month. I have sworn a magical oath. Somewhere N might be listening."

"Who or what is N?"

"I can't tell you that either. It's against our occultist code."

With that, the yellow cab containing Michael L and Tarō sped off.

"What was that all about? Who *were* those guys?" Patty muttered anxiously. She pulled away from Eliot as if she had just remembered something. The color drained from her face like melting beeswax, however, and showed no sign that it would soon return to normal.

"I don't know," said Eliot, shaking his head, and looking down at the magazine. There in the margin was scribbled in blue ink a hotel phone and room number, along with a name:

Local 6702
Wacker Hotel, Room 1304
Michael L, Occultist

The sphere atop the ankh Micahel L held in his hand began to radiate light. It was blood red. The light flickered slightly, as if a small flame were burning within. It gently illuminated the surrounding area. The elevator hall, and the entrance to the stairwell to its left appeared from the darkness like ghosts.

"Don't tell me we have to use the elevator, master," Tarō said with a touch of sarcasm in his echoing voice.

"Even if we could use it, as soon as we opened the door the rats would…"

Before he could finish, they heard the sound of five or six small animals scurrying across the floor. Eliot stopped short, moving only enough to look down at his feet. Along with the raucous squeals, several specks of silvery light slipped through the darkness.

"You're something, boy," Tarō chuckled. Eliot shined the light on him, and he turned his face away.

"Knock it off. I'm not poking fun. I really do think you've got guts. Here you see these big old rats, and don't say a thing."

"Hmn," Eliot shot back. "I don't need your compliments. While you're prattling away Patty is…" His voice was growing steadily louder as he spoke. He was frustrated that his beloved had been taken by that monster Simmel, he could do nothing about it, and here he was in this place forced to argue with a Japanese man. The more he thought about it, the less he was able to control his anger.

It was perhaps due to feelings of guilt.

"Come on. We'll climb the stairs," said Michael L, placing his foot on the first step.

The shafts of light danced in the pitch black of the staircase landing.

Black shadows flew through the air, escaping the light. Bats. Their high-pitched shrieks and the beating of unsteady wings. Eliot peered into the darkness. A beam of light, shadows, the fluttering of wings. He felt like something was digging its claws into his heart.

"Let's go, boy."

Tarō signaled to Eliot to shine the light on the stairs.

"Yeah," said Eliot, nodding in response.

"What's the matter? Why are you just standing there?"

"I don't know, it's just that, a moment ago… I got the strangest feeling that I did this exact same thing not long ago."

Eliot looked at the stairs, which rose straight up.

It was a frightening, steep stairway. Each step was unusually high. It also appeared as if each step was a bit warped, leaning to one side. Nor could he tell how far up they went, as they disappeared into the darkness.

"Yeah, that's right," Eliot muttered to himself.

"I did this exact same thing very recently."

There was a loud creak as he placed his full weight on the first step. His heart cringed in response. The sound was loud, enough to make him think that the board had broken in two.

The sound of whistling drifted down from the top of the stairs.

"It's the melody to *St. James Infirmary*."

The melody was drawing in a cold chill, and the smell of water.

"This is the same feeling as before, too."

Eliot spoke softly to himself, half choking on the smell of water, as the air clouded over in a pale white. He placed his foot on the second step. A creak even louder than the first echoed through the building. But this time his heart didn't falter.

Exhaling white breath, Eliot climbed the stairs.

He climbed toward that whistling… toward that monster… that man… *them*… and the events of three days ago.

Chapter Four
Help Me

"ok, this is a secret. When they found Judge Van Buren's body, it didn't have a face," Alex said softly, once his sister Claire had gone into the kitchen. He was speaking as if telling a ghost story.

"What do you mean, no face?" Eliot asked his brother-in-law. He reflexively glanced toward the door separating the kitchen and living room, knowing that Claire didn't like such gruesome talk.

"My friend in the FBI told me. It was like it had been squashed in some kind of giant press – from the neck up you couldn't recognize anything like a head. That's why his trademark white suit was dyed red with blood."

Eliot was speechless, aware only that his mouth had suddenly gone dry. Eliot knew that his brother-in-law Alexander Jamie was a man who deserved respect, but two things about him irritated him. The first was his conceit about his job in the Justice Department. The second was that he always wanted to tell him shocking crime stories, or the bloody gossip he heard from his friends on the police force and the FBI.

It could have been that Eliot's brother-in-law had gotten the wrong idea about him – that he thought he was a fan of magazines like *Terror Tales*, *Horror Stories* and *Weird Tales*.

"But the judge was shot with a machine gun while in his car, wasn't he? Then why the head?" Eliot had finally managed to wring out a reply.

"The machine gun was just to be doubly sure. The judge's head had already been crushed *before* he was riddled with bullets."

"God, that's awful…"

"That's why the feds don't think it was Johnny Trio's gang."

"Why's that?"

"Several members of that gang have been killed in exactly the same way."

Alex leaned forward. As he placed his hands on the table, the newspaper fell to the floor. His brother gave a start. "I'll get it," Eliot said, leaning over and reaching for the paper.

The headline pierced his eyes.

THIRTEEN BODIES DISCOVERED
IN FAR SOUTH WAREHOUSE
Victims' Heads Beat Repeatedly with Blunt Object
Smuggler Feud Suspected

Eliot's face instantly froze.

He remembered the incident he'd witnessed the day before yesterday. Alex saw the expression on his face, mistakenly interpreting it as fear. He whispered in a quiet undertone.

"Those guys were running liquor from Canada for Trio. They were thugs for the Italians. You can't step out of line, I guess. It was just like the judge – their heads were crushed."

At that moment the door opened.

"What was crushed?" asked his sister Claire, as she carried in the tray with the pudding they were having for dessert. Alex jumped, and hurriedly sat up. Eliot handed the newspaper back to his brother-in-law with a wry smile.

"Well, we're not talking about the pudding my dear sister made, in any case."

"That sounds suspicious. You boys aren't discussing something shady, are you?"

His sister had just placed the hand she'd used to serve the pudding on her hip, when the phone behind her rang.

"I'll get it," said Eliot, standing up.

The telephone was brand new, sitting on a side table next to a large box radio. Alex put them on display in the same way he flaunted his position at the Justice Department.

Eliot lifted the receiver, and picked up the body of the phone. He held the mike to his mouth.

"Hello. Jamie residence."

"Uh… Eliot?"

His mother's voice came from the receiver pressed to his ear. She had probably borrowed a phone from the office at the South Side market, as usual. Behind her voice he could hear a din of activity.

"Yeah, it's me."

"Did something happen with you and Patty?"

"Uh… no. Nothing happened."

He had begun to say yes, when an image of Hiraoka's murder flashed through his mind. His mother seemed to know that his flustered denial was a lie.

"Patty's been by to visit three times today. To the store, three times."

Eliot's family ran a bakery at the South Side market.

"I told her that you'd gone to your sister's place in Northwest, but she just sat there, dazed and confused."

"I understand. I'll call her."

"She was really pale, and looked awfully scared. She kept babbling on, saying she couldn't go to Northwest, and such."

"OK, I'll give her a call. Thanks for letting me know. Bye."

Eliot hung up the phone, and turned toward his sister and brother-in-law.

"Can I borrow your phone?"

"Go ahead," his sister replied, looking up from her dessert.

Alex pretended to crush his pudding with a spoon, and gave Eliot a wink. It was just Alex's sense of humor, but to Eliot, at this moment, it only made him purse his lips.

He called the switchboard, and gave them Patty's number. "One moment please," a voice said. Several seconds passed as they waited for the connection. During those few moments Eliot wondered to himself how long it would take to get to Patty's house from here.

"Murphy's"

It was Patty's voice. She sounded nervous.

"Hi, it's me. Did you come by the store several times this afternoon?"

"Yeah," she began, then suddenly began speaking in rapid fire.

"I'm scared. I felt his gaze. Mom and dad won't believe me. On top of that my dad has been put in charge of investigating the judge's murder, so he's been staying at the station. And now my grandmother in New York is sick, and my mom just rushed off take care of her. I've been alone in this house since this morning. I went to the university, but I couldn't find you…"

"I'm at my sister's place. My brother-in-law invited me to go shooting. But that's not important. Look, Patty, are you okay? What exactly happen–"

"It's the water!" Patty yelled, cutting Eliot short. "And the north wind. Yeah, the north wind has this smell of water. I can feel his presence in the wind. Sometimes I can even hear his sinister laugh."

Patty blurted all this out in a single breath, the pitch of her voice rising as she spoke.

"You believe in this, don't you? That *thing* is hiding in that moist wind. That's why I'm not safe anywhere… at school, on the street, in the market. I feel his presence wherever I go. I can hear his laugh. And the water! Wherever there's water, I can feel his gaze. I get the same feeling at the fountain, in cafes, from the corner fire hydrant, even in my own home. From the sink or kitchen, even the fish tank in the living room, I can feel him there. Even from the toilet…"

A silence, then Patty went on.

"So, you believe me, don't you? Even from the toilet, I can feel the presence of that gang boss. But I never see a trace of him. If I tried to tell that to anyone they'd look at me like I'd lost my mind. Has she gone mad? Has this woman been drinking, they'd say."

Patty seemed to be slipping into hysteria. Her shrill voice began trembling violently with convulsions.

"Just stay there. I'll be right over. I'll borrow my brother-in-law's car."

Eliot turned around. Alex had risen to his feet. His cynical expression had disappeared.

"I'm telling you Eliot, it's the water! Listen… can you hear it? The sound of water dripping? I've been hearing it from upstairs all day. I'm scared… I'm hiding in the dining room. There it is again, the sound of water!"

Patty held the receiver out toward the sound so that he could hear.

Eliot held his breath, and listened.

The distinctive static of a telephone. Patty's muffled breathing. Clothes rustling. The sound of an elevated train passing by in the distance. The clattering of the dining room table, chairs and cabinets.

That was all he heard.

"What's going on?" asked Alex, still standing at the table.

"What's the matter? Has something happened to Patty?"

Claire's worried voice chimed in.

Eliot again listened intently.

"There… you can hear it, can't you? It keeps coming closer."

Patty's voice was distorted, like the sound of a radio on a day when the interference was bad. But he could still hear. Eliot pressed the receiver hard to his head, crushing his ear.

"Hey, Eliot…"

Eliot instantly shushed his brother-in-law.

"Quiet. I think I heard something just now."

He did hear something. A soft sound of drip, drip, drip. It was slowly coming closer.

It's the sound of water dripping, his heart whispered, and as he did so a cold chill ran down his spine. It was as if a large block of ice had been pressed against his flesh, on the nape of his neck and slid down his back, and he was held fast by the cold. Goose bumps covered his skin.

"Patty, get out of the house now! Go to the café on the corner. I'll take the car and be down there as soon as I…"

Patty screamed.

A torrential sound suddenly assaulted his ears. Interference, he thought? No, it's the sound of a waterfall. The sound of a tidal wave. The sound of a flood. It was the sound of great mass of water.

Suddenly, the sound stopped.

He listened intently.

Why can't I hear something… *anything*, he thought. The sound of things being tossed about. The sound of a struggle. A voice hissing "You whore!" Patty's screams. But he could hear nothing.

Eliot slammed down the receiver, snatched the car keys from his brother-in-law, and ran outside.

Patty's house had been thoroughly drenched. It looked like it had been through a flood. Pools of water ankle deep remained on both the first and second floors.

Breaking the glass in the back door and entering the house, this was the devastation Eliot encountered. Patty was nowhere to be found. The telephone had fallen from the wall, and was half submerged in the shallow shoal that had formed in the dining room.

Eliot contacted Chief Detective Murphy at the police station.

Three patrol cars rushed to the scene. Patty's father stared in wonder at the wreck of his home, and found himself at a loss for words over the disappearance of his daughter. He did, however, forbid his daughter's boyfriend from entering the house.

"This is the work of the Trio gang. They know that I've been placed in charge of investigating the judge's murder, and they've come to put pressure on me. They'll make their demands tonight, for sure. All we can do is wait. But I won't be silenced, either. I'll tell it to Trio straight. If he touches a single hair on my daughter's head, I'll make him pay for it two, three times over!"

Chief Detective Murphy just kept ranting, refusing to listen to Eliot's explanation. He then began to bark orders at his officers.

It was a comical sight. The detective, stamping his feet in frustration in the flooded dining room, and carrying on in his overblown fashion, while more than a dozen uniformed officers stood shuffling their feet left to right, sloshing in water.

Too comical by far. Grotesquely comical. It was exactly like a scene from a Keystone Cops movie. Eliot was suddenly struck by an extremely perverse thought, and shuddered.

For some reason Patty's father and these men are putting on some kind of amateur drama, he thought. A detective playing the part of a detective... acting the role of a father whose daughter has been kidnapped... a clumsy performance. And the officers, bumbling simpletons in uniforms unable to do anything but push around ordinary people.

His cold chill turned into nausea. Eliot covered his mouth, and ran to the bathroom. He lifted the lid on the toilet, and leaned over. Patty's face was there.

Covering his mouth, Eliot swallowed back the nausea. Even he could tell that his eyes were swollen. The beautiful features of the girl he loved were paler than that of a corpse.

Her face was tinged with the color of a night fog–white, with a slight hint of blue.

Her eyes began to tremble, then opened.

Half transparent eyes looked directly up at him. Her lips quivered as she tried to whisper something.

E– li– Large pockets of air bubbled up from the bottom of the toilet. They rose from around Patty's lips, carrying her voice.

"Help… me… help me… help me…"

These were the only words he could make out.

Ripples surrounded Patty's face. The concentric circles made her beautiful face rise and fall. Her eyes, nose and lips, even her forehead and chin looked distorted.

It's the water, Eliot thought, the water in the toilet. As he realized this, the water began to reveal the face of a completely different person.

A narrow forehead, thick eyebrows, wild eyes, a broad, beak-like nose, and large lips forming a sinister, gloating smile…

It's Frank "The Pest" Simmel!

From the bottom of the toilet Simmel bared his teeth in a smile. Bubbles burst from his lips.

"Just as I promised, I've taken the woman. I'll offer her to N on the Day of Blood. But that day's not here just yet. If you want to know when it is, ask Michael L. But it won't matter. I'll strip the girl naked, and rip the heart from her living chest. By the time the three of you come to rescue her it will be too late. Her corpse will be washed with your blood."

"What do you mean?"

Eliot's distraught voice slipped from beneath the hand he still held over his mouth.

"I'm not going to say it twice, *shvuntz.*"

A large bubble rose to the surface, and burst. A spray of filthy water covered Eliot's fringe and forehead, the back of his hand and his shirt.

"Shit!" he cried in a muffled voice, pulling the chain that hung from the tank.

"Ha, ha, ha! I'll be waiting for you, gallant prince!"

Simmel's laughter vanished in the sound of the flush, his face disappearing in a whirlpool down the drain.

Eliot left the bathroom, and washed his hands and face hard enough to scrub the skin off them. The house was finally beginning to be restored to some semblance of order. Eliot told Patty's father that he was leaving. Chief Detective Murphy simply gave him a slight nod. This gesture seemed like an act, too.

Eliot walked outside, and went back to the car that was parked halfway down the block. He thought quietly for a moment, then put his hand into his coat pocket. In his pocket was a folded page from a pulp fiction magazine. A page from *Weird Tales*. He read the writing in the margin by the light of the streetlamp.

> *Local 6702*
> *Wacker Hotel, Room 1304*
> *Michael L, Occultist*

There was no reason to hesitate.

Grasping the scrap of paper in his hand, Eliot ran to the nearest telephone booth.

"Local 6702, Wacker Hotel."

"One moment, please."

He waited for the connection. As he waited his eyes instinctively ran over the type printed on the slip of paper. Written there were the words he had read the day before yesterday.

> … I dream of a day when they may rise above the billows
> to drag down in their reeking talons the remnants of puny,
> war-exhausted mankind – of a day when the land shall sink,
> and the dark ocean floor shall ascend amidst universal pan-
> demonium.

He clicked his tongue slightly under his breath. His eyes moved from the type to the margin.

The letters made with the Pelikan fountain pen were written in ink the color of azure. Its color seemed to give off a glare, and Eliot blinked several times.

Michael L, Occultist

Tarō's voice came through the receiver.
"Hey. Kinda late, aren't you, boy?"

Chapter Five
Texas Crooner

THE WHISTLING WAS faint, the sound distorted. Unless you listened carefully, it sounded like it was only the wind. Just the sound of the north wind that seeped through the broken glass windows, the crumbling walls and boarded up doors.

But to Eliot, climbing the stairs, it was nothing more than someone whistling the melody to *St. James Infirmary*.

"Let her go," the lyrics rose above the whistling.

"Stop it, Tarō!" snapped Michael L from up ahead. A soft light surrounded his body, like a ghost.

"It's not me, master."

"I'm sorry, that was me singing just now."

Eliot apologized to the occultist, and shifted the flashlight from his left hand to his right. Its cylindrical body was damp. He realized that it was the sweat of his palm, and quietly steadied his breathing.

He felt a tap on his right arm. Turning around, he saw Tarō looking at him through half-closed eyes. It was a friendly, disarming smile. I could learn to like this Japanese guy, he thought.

"You were doing OK with that song just now. Pretty good, there, fella."

"Fella? I've moved up a rank from boy."

Smiling in embarrassment, Eliot wiped his left palm on his jacket to remove the cold sweat that had risen there. He could never have been able to stand being in a place like this alone. He'd even managed a smile. That was certainly thanks to Tarō.

"Well, you know. If you're good enough at singing to be mistaken for me, then I'll have to admit that you're a full-blown fellow." Tarō's voice grew louder and he laughed. The shaking of his body making him grimace. The laughter seemed to pain his eye, and the shaking of his body his left arm.

Tarō had nevertheless been able to recover to the point where no one would have thought that he'd been injured just five days before.

They say there are no more samurai in Japan, thought Eliot, but this man's the genuine article. And not just because he carries a sword. Even without being able to use his left eye or arm, he was able to obtain such a wealth of information.

It was nearly midnight when he took the elevator to the thirteenth floor of the Wacker Hotel, found the occultist's room and knocked on the door.

"Just calm down."

Michael L sipped the coffee he'd ordered from room service, and in a quiet voice chided a desperate Eliot.

"But Patty's been kidnapped!"

"It's OK. Today is only the 28th of October. It's not the Day of Blood. She's safe."

"How can you be so sure?"

Eliot's voice was rising.

"Because that's the only suitable day for making a human sacrifice."

"What kind of unscientific nonsense is that?!" Eliot yelled.

The next moment the door opened, and Tarō entered the room, a wisecrack ready on his lips.

"Keep your voice down, will ya? I can hear that vulgar accent of yours all the way out in the hall."

"You shut up! You don't even know what happened!"

Ignoring Eliot's outburst, Tarō walked over to Michael L.

"I've combed through every seedy bit of Chicago down by the canal. I've asked around in every speakeasy, gambling den, whorehouse, flophouse, and the employment agencies catering to foreigners. Just as you said, all the hangouts for white trash."

"Good. And what did you discover?" asked Michael.

Tarō pulled a pint bottle of bourbon from the pocket of his jacket, took a large swig and went on.

"The boys from the Trio gang are furious about their importers getting whacked. They're planning on doing a little 'pest extermination' in the next day or so."

"You weren't able to discover the exact time and place?"

"Nope. No matter how much I played up the Texas cowboy and gunfighter, that's as much as I got."

"I suppose not. It was wrong of me to expect so much."

"But I did get one of Trio's hoods pretty drunk, a young punk named Alfonso. He told me something interesting."

"What's that?"

"One of the Trio family's lieutenants is putting the word out on the street to every man with guts and who knows how to handle himself to meet at the Canal Stores on the 29th, at one in the morning."

"He's not going? This... Alfonso fellow?"

"He says he's not. He says he's got some kind of guardian angel looking out for him, and whenever something bad is about to go down his old shin wound starts acting up."

"Ha, ha. He's a wise one, this hood. He'll outlive Johnny Trio in Chicago for sure."

As he chuckled Michael L stood up. He walked to the corner of the room, and slowly opened the closet door. He seemed to be choosing among several of the items arranged there.

What in the world, thought Eliot. As Eliot stared blankly, Michael L, his back still turned to him, suddenly asked him a question.

"Do you know how to use a gun, Eliot?"

"Huh?"

"Can you handle a piece? That's what master wants to know," Tarō clarified for the bemused Eliot. He had sat down on the sofa, and begun drinking slowly.

"Oh, yeah. I can use a revolver, and an automatic," Eliot replied to Michael's back.

"You wouldn't being exaggerating there, would you boy?"

Tarō flashed him a broad, ironic smile. *This college boy's all too easy a target* was written all over his handsome face, with its carefully slicked back hair.

"I've had training at the shooting range at the FBI's Illinois office. My brother-in-law works for the Justice Department."

"Wow," Tarō mocked. "A trained G-man. Don't turn your back on this one." He let out a whistle.

"Shut up! I don't need any smart aleck remarks from some Chinese hood!"

"Tough luck, then. I'm Japanese."

"Ah, so you were one of those guys trailing after Madame Butterfly waving a fan, eh? Or maybe a samurai committing hara-kiri in Yoshiwara?"

"Shit. What does it say when a student at that blessed Chicago University doesn't have any more of an international outlook than that? Do you only read pulp fiction or something? Or maybe you believe everything you read in Hearst's papers?"

"What do you mean by that?!"

"There are no samurai in Japan. A decree in 1876 forbade the bearing of samurai swords. It's a good law, don't you think? Helluva lot better than a law banning liquor."

"Shut up, you savage."

"Hmn. It's your so-called 'civilized country' where the words 'daily' and 'crime' have become one and the same. What did the law banning alcohol those fanatical puritans put in place do to this country? In just four years the gap between rich and poor is as wide as that between heaven and earth. The cities are swarming with gangs, festering with syphilis and drowning in bathtub gin. The country's best known product is its crooked politicians, with bureaucrats and cops up to their necks in pay-offs hassling immigrants for fun. You ask anybody in town. They'll tell you that things used to be a lot better."

Eliot sat silent, speechless with anger.

"It's odd. You all think of Asians as just cooks or laundry men, batting their almond eyes and unable to say anything but 'So sorry' to white folk. I'll bet you don't know what the English and French say about you Yanks behind your backs, do you?"

"That's enough, Tarō!"

Michael L, who had been searching through the closet with his back to the pair, finally intervened. As Eliot was about to respond the occultist turned around. In his hand was a type of automatic pistol that Eliot had never seen before. The gun was brand new. Its black luster was menacing.

"Hey, you're not planning to turn your bodyguard into a stiff, are you, master?"

With his jocular remark Tarō held up his right hand as if in a hold up, and rose to his feet.

"If you've nothing further for me," Tarō continued, "I want to get some sleep. We need to be at the warehouse district by one in the morning."

"Yes, do that. It sounds like it's going to be a long night."

Tarō excused himself and began to walk toward the bedroom, then seemed to suddenly remember something.

"That's a German gun. They work a little different, so be sure you get a good lesson in how to use it. I wouldn't want you to shoot yourself in the foot or anything. See ya, boy."

Hurling his insult Tarō disappeared into the bedroom.

"That damn savage," Eliot muttered in disgust.

"Now, don't say that. Tarō's upset too. He saw his close friend brutally murdered before his eyes," Michael chided, giving a wry smile.

"His friend?"

"The Japanese man whose head Simmel crushed. His name was Hiraoka. They came across to America together. When they parted in San Francisco, he had a dream of teaching judo in America."

Eliot was silent.

"Then the day before yesterday, after five years, just as they managed to meet again, on Wacker Avenue in Chicago, he died that horrible death. Of course Tarō's depressed, even angry."

"But Hiraoka didn't look anything like a judo instructor."

"Over the last two days, when I sent Tarō into the Chicago underworld, it was primarily to investigate the movements of the Trio gang. But I was also giving him time to find out about Hiraoka, and what he had been up to these last five years.

"…"

"It seems that Hiraoka became a judo instructor, but then fell into ruin. He became a street fighter, and a bouncer for a secret club. For a time he was known as Panther Joe, and cut quite a figure. But he was just an immigrant, and hadn't even filed his first paper so he could apply for citizenship. When he landed in Chicago he had fallen to the point where, finally, he was reduced to being fodder for the Italian gang."

"I had no idea."

Eliot furrowed his brow.

"There's more. The Japanese people have an exceptionally keen spiritual sensitivity. To the best of my knowledge, this sensitivity is on par with that of the Celts. That is why, as soon as we arrived in Chicago, it was Tarō who led me to Wacker Avenue, to witness that horrific scene."

"So in a sense, he's the ideal bodyguard for an occultist."

"That's right. Tarō's sharp, and he's strong. But even so, I don't

64

think that I can walk through the Chicago underworld unarmed. In a world where men kill each other with pistols, machine guns and dynamite, I too need to provide for adequate protection."

Eliot glanced furtively at the closet. The door had been left open, and inside stood two rifles and a shotgun.

Maybe the "L" in Michael L stands for "legion," thought Eliot, scrunching up one cheek.

"Now then, I'm going to give you this gun. It's a Luger P08, an automatic the Germans used during the last war."

"Does that mean that I... at one o'clock in the morning..."

"Now that things have gone this far, you alone cannot remain a mere bystander. And besides..."

"Besides what?"

"The gods seem to have given you a destiny similar to my own."

Eliot was silent.

"A destiny to do battle with evil."

With that Michael L handed the Luger to Eliot, and began to explain how to use it.

Chapter Six
It Hurts Me Too

THE MOMENT HE stepped onto the landing, his shoes began to sink in the floorboards. It was as if he had stepped onto lumps of fat.

Eliot shut his eyes tightly. An image flashed through his mind. It was an image of stepping on a white belly. Him stepping onto the stomach of a woman, lying supine across the landing, soft and white.

"I smell water."

Tarō's voice swept the vulgar and haunting image from Eliot's mind. He widened his nostrils and sniffed the air. A scent like that in a pool or aquarium hung in the air.

He raised the flashlight from the landing, shining it around the second floor – the floor with its thick layer of dust, the tiled walls showing reddish-brown stains, the high ceiling covered with cob-webs, the long, dark hallway and the doors that lined either side...

He could find nothing likely to be giving off the watery smell.

The circle of light next fell on the signs that hung on the doors. Treatment Room No. 1, Autopsy, Specimens, Nurse's Station, Surgery, Morgue...

The signs were painted green, with bold, block lettering in white. Eliot looked over toward Michael.

The ankh the occultist held rigidly straight gave off a crimson glow. By itself it was bright enough to make one think it was a lamp.

The *yōki* must be more concentrated here, thought Eliot, and as his gaze danced around the room thoughts of gloom began to well up from deep inside his chest. *Something is going to happen. In this next moment, something is going to happen. Something unspeakably awful will befall me.* It was more a conviction than an apprehension.

Eliot suddenly realized that he had put his right hand in his coat pocket. Then to the jacket underneath his coat. Then was sliding it underneath that, fumbling for the gun. For the Luger Po8 Michael L had given him.

In the dead of night on the 29th, he had lost the German pistol, because of that *thing*.

One o'clock in the morning, and the Stores – the warehouse district along the canal – was asleep. It was several degrees below freezing, cold as in the dead of winter. A dense, white haze rose from the glossy black surface of the water.

Canals ran through all areas of Chicago. One stretched to Lake Michigan, forming a link to the four other Great Lakes, to the St. Lawrence River and the Atlantic Ocean. Another cut across to the Mississippi River, and due south to the Gulf of Mexico.

The Stores was the area along the canal where cargo was loaded. A point where the Chicago of the 19th century and Chicago of the 20th century intersected.

Massive warehouses containing corn, cotton and soybeans, beef and dairy products stood in rows. The warehouses were like houses for giants, emblazoned with company names in languages and scripts from around the world. Alongside English there were signs in Spanish, German and French. Dutch, Portuguese, Chinese and Japanese. Many were in roman lettering, but there were also Greek, Hindi and Hebrew alphabets. Arabic, Chinese and Japanese scripts could also be found.

Like the various languages and scripts, the warehouses were a diverse assortment of architectural styles and ages of construction. Among the signs with their peeling paint was the profile of the Mohican Indian representing the G&G Wesley feed company, which had prospered in the 1850s. There was also a girl with a bouquet of flowers, symbol of the O'Hare textile company that collapsed after the Great Chicago Fire of 1871.

The warehouse walls were originally colored green, rusty bronze, Indian red or pale orange, but in the mist and darkness of night they had all become somber shades of bluish green, like shipwrecks at the bottom of a deep sea.

The sound of water flowing through the canal echoed on the hard, concrete streets of the warehouse district, mingling with the slight breaths of air given off by the night, like the breathing of a dying patient.

Suddenly, two beams of light cut through the heavy, drifting fog. The headlights of a large truck.

The truck made a slow, labored circle and stopped in front of one of the groups of warehouses. On the side of the warehouse was written the name Jacobs & Katz, with the catchphrase "Corn Fed Beef" in playful, decorative lettering underneath. At first glance it looked just like any other warehouse full of the beef from the cows raised on the plentiful Illinois corn.

A man got out of the truck and stood beside it.

"You stay in the truck until they get here, ya hear?" the man said over his shoulder toward the truck, and lit a cigarette. He hunched his back against the cold, and peeled the cigarette from his lips. He began to airily whistle *St. Louis Blues*.

Just then, headlights emerged from the north. The beams pierced the fog, dimly illuminating the figure of the man. He took off his Stetson hat, held it in his hand and began waving.

With scarcely a sound, an eight-passenger luxury car appeared, plowing its way through the fog. It was a specially built Buick, painted midnight blue.

The car came to a silent stop in front of the warehouses. The passenger side door opened with a jerk. A large man in a white coat got out.

"You got the merchandise?" the large man asked quickly.

"Have a look in the back if you want. Your agent Niki made the arrangements, so there's no mistake."

The man calling himself Niki proudly placed his hand on the bed of the truck.

"We got everything you asked for. You've got three drums of the red stuff and five of the black."

The rear window in the Buick rolled down. Simmel's voice spilled from the pitch black interior of the car.

"Sam, give Niki the money. Be quick about it, and shut him up."

"Okay."

Sam put his hand in his coat pocket, and casually pulled out a thick stack of bills wrapped with a rubber band. The bills were all crisp, brand-new hundreds.

"As we agreed."

"I don't need to count it. A boss like Frank Simmel with the entire city under his thumb wouldn't try to sell us short."

The wad of bills passed from Sam's hand to Niki's. As if waiting for this precise moment there was a loud metallic clash from the darkness. It was a heavy, dry sound. It began in one spot, then instantly spread, surrounding the entire warehouse.

"Bastards!"

Niki ran toward the truck. Gunfire poured from the darkness, the sound booming. Niki fell as if he'd been struck. He lay prone on the concrete, then stopped moving altogether.

A shadowy figure stirred in the driver's seat of the truck. Dozens of flashes burst en masse from the blackness surrounding the warehouse. The windshield of the truck shattered. The man in the driver's seat reached to pull out a shotgun, but was knocked about like a dancing marionette. Within moments, the body of the truck was peppered with holes.

Young men carrying Winchesters and carbines stepped out of the darkness. There were at least twenty in all. With one exception they all wore grubby hats, cheap coats and jackets, and had wild, crazed eyes. Their hair was black, and their eyes dark. Italian thugs.

Sam threw himself to the ground, and covered his head with his hands. A sign of surrender.

"That's enough! Hold your fire!" came a voice from the midst of the group.

There was a short pause, then the echo of a metallic click. The sound of the trigger guard on a Winchester being released. All surrounding eyes fell on the man who had made the sound.

He had a large scar on his face, and was slightly overweight. As if to cover his feeling of awkwardness, he gave Sam a swift kick in the ribs, who was lying at his feet. Sam groaned with pain.

"Stop it, Scarface!"

The thug was checked by a young man in a well-cut, cream-colored coat and a soft hat pushed far back on his head. Scarface lowered his head, and pulled in his shoulders.

"Isn't that Alfonso? He said he was going to stay out of the fray."

The whispering came from a car parked about thirty yards from the warehouse. The voice was Tarō's.

"Shh." This from Michael L.

"What's that?" asked Eliot from the back seat of the car to the occultist sitting in the passenger's seat.

"That's Simmel's warehouse. One of his Canadian agents has come. Probably delivering liquor or drugs. If Simmel himself is here, it must be something important."

"And Johnny Trio's boys just made the hit," explained Tarō, continuing his master's account. "That's what it's about. I said it at the hotel, didn't I? Every man with guts and can handle himself would meet at the Stores."

Eliot said nothing, but nodded slightly, and placed his hand on his chest. The Luger P08 was there underneath. It gave him a fleeting moment of comfort. Then he turned his attention back to the battle – the fray, as Tarō called it – between the Italian and Jewish gangs.

The twenty Italians surrounded the midnight blue Buick. The thugs stood with their Winchesters and carbines aimed and ready to shoot at the slightest moment.

"Come on out, 'Pest' Simmel. I'm Peter Ferraro, from the Trio family."

The young man wearing the soft hat pushed back on his head spoke brusquely to the man who controlled half of the Chicago underworld. He pulled a pack of cigarettes from the pocket of his cream-colored coat. He took one in his mouth, then struck a vesta against the body of the Buick, and lit it.

Laughter rippled through the gang of thugs. The laughter was metallic, nervous. They were straining to put on a bold front now that they were faced with the real life Simmel.

"I'll come out, but you all had better have a good piss first," Simmel shot back from inside the car.

"What do you mean?"

Ferraro curled his lips.

"You're going to have such a fright, you won't be able to sleep, and you'll wet your beds."

"You don't scare us, you old bastard."

Ferraro signaled his men.

"Destroy the goods in the truck. This old bastard wants to lose his merchandise before he loses his life."

Following Ferraro's order, three of the hoods jumped into the back of the truck.

"Let's do it," they howled, and trained their guns on the drums in the back of the truck. There were eight drums in all. They were each crudely marked with white paint, three with the letter B, and five with the letter M.

"Start with the brandy."

The drums marked with B were hit with rifle bullets from three directions. Sparks flew. Round holes were pierced in the rusted sides of the drums. A thick, sticky liquid gushed out.

"That'll do it. The three of them are flowing freely."

"Just like having a piss."

The second thug smirked, while the third gave a snort.

"Hey, wait a minute! This doesn't smell like liquor."

"What are you talking about? Strike a match, would ya?"

"Is it gasoline?"

"No, it smells too… raw… like the guts of some animal."

The match was lit.

The orange flame was brought down near the drum. The liquid streaming out in long, narrow arcs from the three holes could now be seen clearly.

It was blood. It looked fresh, as if not much time had passed since it had been drawn. Wisps of steam carrying a hint of foul odor rose in thick clouds.

"What… what the hell?!"

"Then, what's in the M drums?"

"Shit!"

Avoiding the streams of blood, the thugs aimed their guns at the drums marked M.

As if by previous arrangement they all pulled the trigger at the same time. Three bullets dug into one of the M drums.

Nothing came flowing out this time.

Instead, a powerful stench wafted from the bullet holes. The reek of rotting meat. The odor of sewage. An overwhelming fetor reminiscent of sludge and feces.

One of the thugs covered his nose and mouth, uttering a strange sound. Another flew into a rage, kicking over the M drum. The floor of the truck shook. The lid of the drum came off, and from inside a black substance poured out.

The third man struck another match. He held it near their feet, so that they could see what had just come from the drum lying across the truck floor.

It was soil. It was mixed with rotting leaves, small stones and tree roots. The dirt gave off a powerful stench. As they looked closer, they could see long, white objects wriggling in it.

"Maggots?!"

"Then that smell... it's from corpses!"

"That's disgusting. The stench could knock you over."

The three men jumped cursing from the back of the truck as if trying to escape.

The door of the Buick opened.

The men surrounding the car reflexively readied their guns. They pointed them at the "gentleman" in his fifties who calmly stepped down from the car. Ignoring the nearly twenty guns trained on him, he gave a toothy grin.

"So what did you think those items in the truck were? That the B stood for brandy, and the M for... mead, perhaps? Or maybe you thought it contained milk."

Simmel narrowed his shoulders.

"Fools. If that's all I wanted do you think I'd have to pay such a handsome sum, and contract with Greek agents? You hear me? Listen, you bunch of *shvuntz*. The B is for blood. And the M the soil from a graveyard. M for the mud of a graveyard, full of the miasma of rotting corpses."

The faces of the three men who had been in the truck froze. Their skewed expressions betrayed a deep shock – worse than seeing the corpses of their parents. Simmel looked in their direction, and raised his eyebrows.

"What's wrong, little boys? You look like you just fucked your mothers. The fun is just about to start."

Simmel placed his left fist on his chest.

"Hey, old man. You should be worrying about your own skin rather than shooting your mouth off."

Ferraro clucked his tongue. In his hand he held a sawed off shotgun. With exaggerated movements he began loading two shells into it.

"Ph'nglui mglw'nafh!" Simmel suddenly called out.

"What?"

Ferraro's hands stopped moving. He looked up at the boss of the Jewish gang, a wry smile on his lips. He narrowed his eyes, and stared into Simmel's face.

"What did you just say, old man?"

Simmel slowly brought his left hand away from his chest. From his fist he extended his forefinger and pinkie. He raised his hand, with his palm turned toward his face.

"Kynu'neyun, naiyalu-latohotta, tser'neguy, utorlyuawinu!"

As he held his beaked nose between his forefinger and pinkie, Simmel continued his chant from underneath his curled fingers.

"Is it some kind of kike prayer? If that's what it is, it won't do you any good. You've really pissed off the boss Johnny Trio. Tonight we'll just be taking care of you and your boys here, but tomorrow all the fucking kikes in Chicago will be swimming with the fishes."

Ferraro pointed the gun at Simmel's face.

Despite the fact that he had a double-barreled shotgun in his face, Simmel just smiled, and narrowed his eyes.

"Little man. I've long since rejected the Hebrew god. But that doesn't mean I've gone and kissed the ass of that Jesus bastard, either. The gods I worship now are…"

In that instant, a shadow fell across Simmel's face, encompassing him in the darkest black. For a moment Ferraro thought that Simmel's face had disappeared. He unconsciously placed a shaking finger on the shotgun's trigger.

"… the water god of darkness Cthaat, the great god of the ocean

Cthulhu, and the fish-god Dagon. And the servant of *them*, the evil gods, the dark god Nyarlathotep!"

As the mysterious names poured from Simmel's mouth, Michael L's left hand moved, almost imperceptibly. In a practically reflexive movement, he extended his forefinger and middle finger, folding the remaining three underneath.

"No, master," Tarō whispered intently. "It's not time for that yet. Right now we've got to figure out what *they* will do – how they'll make use of Simmel."

Michael L was silent. Sitting in the passenger's seat, he nodded his head. From the violent twitching of his shoulders and neck, it was clear that he was trying to suppress a fierce internal conflict. As he watched, Eliot realized for the first time that the occultist sitting before him was not a cold, machinelike student of metaphysics, nor was he one of the hardboiled caricatures that everybody seemed to want to be these days.

Michael L is a human being with feelings, just like me, thought Eliot. As he considered this, Eliot felt himself slipping into Michael L's world.

"Eliot," said Michael L, in a tone that betrayed his attempt to repress all emotion.

"If I try to take a weapon and leap out of the car... please... hit me in the back of the head and knock me out."

"Okay... but... what's between you and Simmel?"

"I have no score to settle with Simmel. Rather, it's the *things* that he worships."

Eliot was silent.

"You heard him invoke their names, didn't you? The water god of darkness Cthaat, the god of the ocean Cthulhu, the fish-god Dagon, the dark god Nyarlathotep – all of them names of horrifying, ancient evil gods. To them... I've... lost my wife... child and friends."

"To those evil gods? Your wife, child and friends…" Eliot repeated in an undertone.

"That's enough," Tarō broke in. "Don't disturb the master's concentration any further. Look! Some kind of strange fog is drifting in."

Tarō spoke quickly, pointing beyond the windshield.

The north wind suddenly grew stronger. It felt like frozen razor blades. It was like the north wind in Chicago that reaches a wind chill of minus forty in the dead of winter.

At the end of October, of course, the wind didn't feel like forty below, but it still seemed as if the skin of their fingers would freeze to the triggers of the guns.

Catching the scent of water on the north wind, Ferraro lowered his brow. It wasn't from the direction of the canal. The canal was flowing behind him, shimmering black.

The smell of water, however, grew stronger with each passing moment. It brought to mind the smell of the bathroom sink. Then the aroma of the bath. The odor of water pipes. The smell of the canal, or the scent that lingered along the Mississippi River valley. It was the smell one sensed near the reservoir, that drifted alongside the Chicago River, or that filled the Chicago harbor on the shores of Lake Michigan.

The watery smell grew stronger, more condensed. It even seemed to be tinged with viciousness. Several of the thugs began to choke violently, becoming a painful cough. Before they were aware of it, the watery scent had become an acidic stench that bleared their eyes, and inflamed their noses and throats.

"Little man," Simmel called to Ferraro, suddenly lowering his left hand. His voice was tinged with laughter.

"What?!"

Ferraro tightened his grip around the shotgun. Simmel smiled at him.

"… sleep in the bosom of Cthaat."

At nearly the same moment "The Pest" had finished speaking, something, like dozens of long, black whips, came racing up from behind him.

The tangle of whips seemed to crack at nearly the moment they began to curl. It was like the movement of the arms of an octopus or squid, though hundreds of times faster.

Ferraro heard a sound to his right. It reminded him of a sound he had enjoyed during the summer, when he had mischievously thrown rocks at watermelons.

It's the sound of breaking watermelons, he said to himself, and in the next instant a hot liquid came pouring down in a shower over the left side of his body. He spun around. The man who had been standing to his left no longer had a head. It was a shower of brains and blood.

In a state of shock, Ferraro let out a hoarse cry. He turned the gun in that direction, but it was already too late for him to fix his aim.

One of the whips, twisting and wriggling, had worked its way through the man at the left. Another, appearing to have drawn back, the next moment whirled into a coil and shattered the skulls of two of the men near Simmel.

The whips were not truly black, only appearing so because they were covered in darkness. In truth they had no color. They were the color of water. And they were not exactly whips, either.

Because they were long and thin like a length of cord, and moved faster than snakes, they looked just like whips. In reality they were jets of water. And there were not a dozen individual *things* to be counted.

From the canal flowing behind Ferraro, water had reached out like the fingers of a demon, cracking like whips to attack the fearless group of young thugs that had surrounded Simmel.

They never hit the hands, feet or torsos. They aimed for the heads, smashing that which identified them as Italians.

Scalps were peeled back. Skulls were shattered. Brain fluid was splattered about. Grayish white brains were squashed like pudding. A spray of blood filled the night with a red mist. Glittering red puddles covered the hard surface of the gray concrete.

It had taken less than three seconds for twelve men to collapse to the ground.

"No… I don't wanna die… not me."

The man's cry suddenly filled the night air, and a gunshot rang out. But it was not fired at Simmel, or at the whip-like strands of water that had come to attack. It was shot into the sky.

One of the thugs ran. It was the man who had kicked Simmel's henchman, Sam. The young one called Scarface. Running like a scared rabbit, Scarface headed straight down between two warehouses. A car appeared to be hidden there in the shadows. The six-passenger Chevrolet immediately sped off.

"Shit. That yellow bastard."

As Ferraro let the words escape his lips, the tentacles reaching out from the canal beheaded their thirteenth victim.

"He's a smart one, that one. He'll go far," a voice laughed from Simmel's car. The window of the eight-passenger Buick was open. From inside, men were watching. They were all Simmel's henchmen. But not a single one of them was holding a gun. The boss's "water magic" was sufficient. They seemed to know perfectly well that they had no role to play.

Ferraro raised the shotgun. As he brought the stock to his shoulder, the fourteenth man was killed. As he had opened his mouth to scream, his lower jaw was left behind as the rest of his head was knocked away.

Ferraro squinted his eyes and took aim. As he did so, the fifteenth and sixteenth men fell to the ground, their heads severed.

"Shit… shit… shit!"

Crying as if tormented by nightmares, he squeezed the trigger. A bloodied head came flying at him.

Reflexively he fired the shot at it. The large-caliber shell turned the head into a red rocket of flesh. There was no body. Those *things* had already plucked off the head.

"No–o!"

The piercing scream resounded.

It was from the last of the thugs. Ferraro turned toward him. It was one of the men who had just gone tearing up into the truck. Now tears were rolling from both eyes, and he was sobbing with fear.

"Mama mia," the man yelled, as he put the barrel of the gun he was holding in his mouth. He closed his eyes. With both hands, he pulled the trigger. The top of the man's head became a party cracker.

The corpse, with its brains splattered around, fell slowly to its knees, and collapsed.

"… Diavlo… fucking devil…" Ferraro kept muttering under his breath.

"No one so small time. I have much more powerful gods behind me."

Simmel put both hands in his pocket, and narrowed his shoulders.

"It was three years ago. Trio put a hit on us up on the northeast side near the Getty Tomb. Dragging my guts, I prayed. The Hebrew God could eat shit. If anyone could help me, I'd sell my soul to the devil. And then, what do you think happened? A miracle. As I lay in agony, slumped against the door of a mausoleum, it opened. I fell far underground. It was the grave of Andreas Lewis Leigh."

Eliot saw Michael L's shoulders grow tenser. He gently placed his hand on Michael's shoulder. Michael spoke to him softly.

"It's OK. I still have control of myself."

Simmel let out a laugh. It sounded just like the clamor of a jackal.

"Punks like you that have just come to America don't know him,

I guess. A.L. Leigh. That's "Leigh" spelt L-E-I-G-H, not some fucking chink. Read some Chicago history. You'll find him there. He was a judge during the colonial period. Made a name for himself during the Salem witch trials of 1692. In his later years he came to Chicago, where he spent the remainder of his life. In the mausoleum of Judge Leigh was a large collection of texts on witchcraft he had confiscated from some sorcerer before he died. There in the mausoleum, a single lamp began to shine. Then my own shadow began to speak to me... 'I am Nyarlathotep, messenger of the great, ancient gods. I exist far and wide amid the darkness in the hearts of men. You, Frank Simmel. If you wish to prolong your existence, open the text there before you. The *Cthaat Aquadingen*!'... I was dying. I couldn't refuse or even argue. I picked up the mystical text near me with bloody hands. Then, as the shadow instructed, I performed the ceremony. I offered up the blood that continued to spill from my stomach, and ten ounces of flesh from my gut. I recited the incantation, then greedily devoured the remains of Judge Leigh, and the soil in the grave. I even ate the maggots that were wriggling in the dirt."

Ferraro felt violently nauseous. A foul-smelling gas rose from the pit of his stomach. He choked back a belch. He thought that if he were to burp, undigested pizza mixed with Cinzano would spew out, filling his mouth.

"And so, from a dying gang, I was reborn as 'The Pest.' As a servant of *Cthaat Aquadingen*, I was endowed with the water magic. Chicago is a city of water. So that means that I was being told to become its king. What a joyous bit of thoughtfulness! A true god provides for you like that. If the Hebrew and Christian gods are like bureaucrats at the immigration office, the Great Old Ones are first-class prostitutes. They are able to perceive everything we desire, and can reach right where it itches. That's why..."

Simmel suddenly turned his back on Ferraro. It was covered with fractures.

Ferraro cast his eyes about. At some point those *things* – the horrible water tentacles – had disappeared.

If I'm going to do it, now's my chance, Ferraro cried out in his heart. It's now or never!

Ferraro squeezed the shotgun trigger. There was still one shell left. Shot burst from the mouth of the gun.

Simmel's body, however, was already radiating a soft blue light, and had turned semi-transparent. He had liquefied.

The buckshot passed straight through the human-shaped water, scattering in every direction. Seeing what had happened, the Simmel-shaped body of water shook its head. It turned back around. Slowly, the semi-transparent body returned to normal.

"That's why even when exterminating fools they give such a first-rate performance. Like this."

A gurgling voice seemed to emanate from under the water. The sound of actual water drowned out the voice. The noise of the water came up behind Ferraro. He glanced back over his shoulder.

A portion of the canal water was coming up toward him. It raised itself up, and forming an arc directly above him, swept down.

"Augh–h!"

Ferraro's scream didn't last for one second. In an instant the water had forced the young Italian to the ground, collapsing his eyeballs. Water gushed into his nose, mouth and ears, pulverizing his head from the inside.

The water that had crawled from the canal was like a giant amoeba. Now all that was left was nineteen bodies and The Pest.

The door of the midnight blue Buick opened. Holding his felt hat, Simmel began to step into the car. Then he stopped, as if he'd suddenly remembered something. He looked up toward Michael and the two young men.

"The show's over for tonight," he said. "The next performance will be the day after tomorrow – October 31st, the Day of Blood. If you want to save the girl, come to the Heights. To the street where the wealthy Jews live. There's an abandoned hospital there called St. James Infirmary. The show will start at 11:00 pm on October 31st, at St. James Infirmary."

Michael L leapt out of the car. His eyes were burning with rage as he glared at Simmel, shouting questions at him.

"What do you mean by telling us all this? What are you planning?"

"The other day on Wacker Avenue, the shadows told me. They told me who your ancestors were. Besides, you're different from all those priests and clergymen. You're different from the feds. You don't have God, the state or any laws to rely on."

"What are you trying to say, Simmel?"

"You're just like me. You've struck a deal with the Great Old Ones in order to extract personal vengeance. Me with the water god Cthaat, and you with the fire god Cthugha."

Michael was silent.

He extended his first and middle fingers from the fist he had formed with his right hand. Simmel immediately formed the same sign as before with his left hand, holding it rigidly in front of his face.

Eliot saw what they were doing, and pulled out the Luger P08. From inside the car, he began firing emptying the gun. But before the 9mm bullets reached Simmel, they flamed pale blue and disappeared. The Pest had thoroughly shielded himself with the water magic.

"Shit!" yelled Eliot, and threw the Luger at him. The German automatic arched through the air at Simmel, but before it reached him was struck by one of the black whips that stretched out from the canal, knocking it to the ground.

"The boy can come to, as I said before. After all, it's for the sake of the girlfriend he's never laid a finger on. I'll fuck her, then rip her heart out and swallow it along with the graveyard soil as a sacrifice to Cthaat. That's a show you don't see too often, eh?"

Eliot was shattered, and Simmel, having rubbed salt in the wound, stepped into the midnight blue Buick.

The car sped off with an explosive roar, but the sound of the Pest's raucous laugh echoed in Eliot's ears for some time after.

Chapter Seven
It's a Mean Old World

REALITY WAS NOT as complicated as Eliot's beloved Sherlock Holmes novels. They found the hospital in the Heights that Simmel had spoke of, almost disappointingly easily, after two days of searching. It was on the north side of the district where the wealthy Jewish families lived – a place that commanded a panoramic view of the majestic expanse of Lake Michigan.

Once they had found it, it seemed strange that it should have taken two days. Stranger still, Eliot never knew that such a large hospital had been left abandoned in the Jewish Heights. It was a three-story stone building, built in the architectural style of the mid-nineteenth century. The imposing design – perhaps due to the gray stonework – gave the impression of the temple of some pagan religion.

Nevertheless, the second floor contained a surgical room and all the facilities of a modern hospital – though everything was decorated with dust and cobwebs, and the mice that scampered about were certainly not doctors and nurses.

"The smell of water is coming from over here."

Tarō pointed with the tip of his sword at the room where the wooden sign reading "autopsy" hung.

Michael L nodded silently. The light from the ankh he was holding in front of him began to shine more intensely. All the while it continued to glimmer with a light that seemed to probe deep into the workings of Eliot's heart, adjusting itself to his pulse.

"Well then, let's start by taking a look in the autopsy room," said Eliot, trying desperately not to reveal to his two companions the fear that was slowly mounting within him. Perhaps the cold was growing more intense. His breath was white. White with a bluish tinge.

Just like the fog outside, thought Eliot.

He unconsciously held his breath. Isn't that the same color as the light emitted by Simmel? Eliot immediately dismissed the thought. It's because of the color of the walls, he decided.

But the next moment, a malicious voice welled up from the bottom of his heart. Never forget that Simmel is a water sorcerer, it said. We are spellbound at this very moment. By him... By *them*... By the gods... The Great Old Ones... The water god Cthaat...

"Don't get spooked there, fella."

Tarō's voice was full, and carried well. His right eye flashed with determination. It was the light of a resolve to bring down Simmel.

I have to get hold of myself too, thought Eliot. I have to save Patty.

Eliot was muttering to himself. For a brief moment, he believed that none of this had anything to do with him. The perspective of the bystander. This was certainly the attitude of university students these days. The role of the carefree student drifting through the roaring twenties.

No, no, thought Eliot. I'll end up just like Chief Detective Murphy or his flatfoots, playing some sort of supporting role in a movie. That's also caused by Simmel's "water magic." What Michael L calls *yōki*.

Struggling to convince himself that he was in control, Eliot focused his mind. He shined the beam of light around in the darkness. At either end of his field of vision a white object seemed to hang in the air, occasionally cutting across to the other side. It looked at once like the naked body of a woman, or a sodden, wrinkled corpse.

... or even like the naked corpse of Patty, hung on the wall.

Eliot held the light on a single spot. He gently bit his lower lip. The sign reading "autopsy" was swaying.

Somewhere the sound of a woman's chuckling could be heard. The whistling they'd heard before seemed to be coming from the autopsy room.

From somewhere behind he heard voices. Men and women, young and old, high voices and low, loud and soft. They seemed to be chattering away, but he could not make out what they were saying. However, he could feel their derision, and their malice toward him.

"I'll get the door," Tarō said brusquely, placing the sword's scabbard between his teeth. He extended his right arm. Grasping the rusted doorknob, he applied pressure and turned it. Slowly he pushed on the door. A creak to set their teeth on edge echoed off the tiled walls from every direction.

Michael L's tension was being transmitted directly to Eliot. Staring at the sphere, which was now pulsing even more rapidly, Eliot realized that even a man like Michael L has never had this kind of experience... this particular type of situation.

Finally beginning to understand, he lightly wet his parched lips.

It seemed to take more than ten minutes for the door to open fully. The air that escaped from the void carried the scent of water, and a chill. And dust. Eliot could not tell whether the cloud of white that came billowing out and filled the surrounding area was cold air or dust.

Tarō crept through the open door into the autopsy room. Next came Michael L, striding boldly with a nimbleness one would not usually associate with an occultist.

So I bring up the rear, thought Eliot. He began to move forward, but instinctively pulled back. Perhaps because of a fearful foreboding. For the first time in his life he was frozen in his tracks by something he could not even see. He recalled Patty's face. The way she moved. The way she talked. He desperately tried to bring the depth of his love for Patty to the forefront of his mind.

My turn to rush in.

"Hurry up. We need the light, fella."

Tarō's voice brought him back to reality. He clenched his teeth. Drawing all his strength he stepped forward, bursting into the autopsy room. At the same time a doubt rose in his mind.

Is this the floor? The belly of a woman? The back of a corpse?

Shut up… shutupshutupshutupshutup!, he repeated to himself. Strengthened by the words, he shined the light forward.

Something white rose up out of the midnight blue gloom. It hung suspended, lying there in the air.

Eliot's breathing stopped for a moment. Straining his eyes, he saw that a sheet was covering the autopsy table.

Is it a body, he thought? Of a woman? Or is it a sheet? Is it just a sheet? Patty isn't under there, is she? She's still alive, isn't she?

Questions rose fast and furious in his mind. It was like a newsreel that continuously flashed horrific scenes. Eliot's hand swung in a long arc. The beam of light danced about in the darkness. It reflected off the underside of the autopsy table, and rose from the floor. It was flickering blue. The smell of formalin wafted past his nose. Straining his eyes further, he saw that there was something like small pool. Nothing of consequence. Just a pool to float or wash corpses. The smell of water must have been coming from there.

Eliot let out a deep sigh. Then he laughed. A laugh of distress and exhaustion.

He moved over to the autopsy table, and grabbed the sheet that covered it. Look at it, he told himself. The sheet is flat. There's nothing underneath. With a wry laugh he pulled back the sheet with all his strength.

He pulled back the sheet in one swift movement – Patty was lying there.

She was completely naked. A large perforation was opened just below her left breast. Her emerald eyes were opened wide.

"Pa… Patty," escaped Eliot's lips.

He stretched out his hand toward the body of his beloved. But she had gone completely pale, and from the dark red wound he caught a glimpse of the bright red fatty layer, the pure white ribs, and the pink and blue-colored organs.

"Patty…"

Is it really her, he thought. Not some doll? A cow, maybe, or a pig?

"Patty…"

Could she really be dead? Is that wound real? Maybe she's really alive.

"Patty," Eliot muttered again, and drew a deep breath. He was about to repeat her name again. But as he formed the first syllable, the word became a trembling sob.

"Pa–atty–y!" Eliot cried, with a forcefulness that nearly brought blood to his throat. He threw his arms around the corpse. To hold her, lift her up, cry for her as he wanted to do…

"You fool, what do you think you're doing?!" he heard Tarō cry.

Shutupshutupshutupshutup!

Eliot held the body in his arms. He held it as tightly as his strength would allow. Then he lifted up the corpse. His head shaking, and tears streaming from his eyes, Eliot called out in his heart again and again the name of the girl he loved. The grief was too intense, and he was unable to form the sounds of her name.

Patty, Patty, Patty…

At that moment, Michael L's spell rang out.

"Cthugha!"

Enormous power was contained with the spell. As if someone were pounding on a drum right next to his ear. The impact came from more than just the sound, but from a vibration that rippled through his entire body.

His head was jolted back and forth. The motion was violent. His neck rose and fell as his spine bent. Both arms began to shake.

Hunks of flesh fell from the carcass he had been holding.

The plopping sounds were brutally graphic, and he had an uneasy feeling of squalor. And the stench. Like that of rotting meat mixed with sewage and feces.

The body is falling apart, he thought. Had the corpse rotted? Is it really Patty?

He saw a sudden movement out of the corner of his eye. Reflexively he cast his eyes in that direction. It was the left arm from the body. It was dressed in a white suit, soaked with blood. It appeared to be a strong, muscular arm.

This isn't Patty!

Eliot took another look at the corpse he held in his arms. He tried to recognize the face.

It had no face. It was gone, as if it had been crushed in a giant pressing machine.

"Augh!" Eliot cried out.

He tried to push the body away. But before he could, the body's left hand grabbed him by the collar. The spongy feel of its rotting flesh attacked the nape of his neck. Struggling, he twisted the hand away, holding it back as it reached out to strangle him. The flesh peeled away. Rotting bits of tissue remained in the hand. It felt like cotton soaked in mucous. Eliot didn't have the time for disgust or nausea, however. The hand, now nothing more than bone, continued to press on his throat. Eliot felt the chafing on his skin, and the tips of the bony fingers as they dug into his neck.

Am I going to die, he thought? Will I be killed here? Am I to be done in by a corpse?

At that moment, Tarō came flying to his aid. The samurai was drawing his sword. There was the sound of the scabbard falling to the floor. The *katana* was over a yard long.

"*Namusan!*"

Tarō yelled something in Japanese, and the bare blade of the sword flashed. The bony hand was severed from the corpse at the wrist.

Tarō brought his right hand, which had brought the sword down, up to his chest, and shifted his weight. He raised his right elbow, then ran it through the corpse in the white suit.

The juice from the rotting flesh was splattered about. Foul stains covered the bandage over Tarō's left eye, and the sling holding his left arm. But the single-eyed, single-armed samurai didn't even wince.

The tip of the sword was pointed at the corpse. His attention was fixed. He pulled the sword back as far as he could, and in the next moment used the full force of his body to ram the sword straight through.

The body flew from the dissection table.

"What are you doing, brother? Your girlfriend is definitely not in here," Tarō asserted.

Eliot responded with gasps, the strength drained from his body. But his blank expression was not because Patty had become a corpse. And it wasn't because his girlfriend's body had changed into a man in a white suit, or that he was shocked by the sudden transformation of that man into a rotting corpse.

It was because a sodden, swollen hand had reached out from the pool used to clean bodies, and had grabbed the leg of his pants.

"*Baka*," Tarō yelled, "kick that thing away!"

Eliot jerked his leg away. The skin of the hand slipped off, like removing a glove. The skin alone kept its grip on his pants leg, like the empty shell left behind by a cicada – a phenomenon common to water-logged bodies.

Eliot shook his leg violently.

The surface of the formalin pool began to rise, and the bloated shapes of men began to emerge. The buttons on their cheaply made shirts looked as if they were about to pop off. The necks of their suit jackets had been swallowed up in flesh, and constricted their arms in an abnormal way.

Eliot leapt backward. The beam of light jumped around the room, illuminating *them* who were rising from the cleansing pool. There were close to twenty of *them*. More than half were swollen to the point where they seemed about to burst, but two or three still seemed to have the same physique they'd had when they were still alive.

Eliot noticed that one of them wore a cream-colored coat draped over him, and covered his mouth. He remembered seeing that coat before. In what was left of its head, Eliot was able to make out the face he'd had in life.

Both of his eyeballs had collapsed into their sockets. His nose had also been sucked into his face. His ears were nothing but holes, and his lips and teeth were curled inward.

But there was something in that face – something unusual about it, that allowed Eliot to tell whose corpse this was.

Ferraro! The young boss of the Italian gang, brutally murdered at the warehouse.

If that's so, thought Eliot, then that body in the white suit was…

A chill ran down his spine. He glanced back in that direction.

The corpse Tarō had brought down was wriggling on the floor like an insect. It appeared to have broken both legs when it fell from the dissecting table. Unable to stand, it twirled around in a circle like a top, propped up on its right hip. It was badly damaged, to the point where hunks of flesh fell from it whenever it moved, but the white suit covering the body plainly told the story of the position he had held in society when he was alive.

The man, the "advocate of law and justice" on which the citizens of Chicago had pinned their hopes.

It's… Once he had finally realized the true identity of this rotting corpse, a chill rose from the bottom of his heart.

Judge Clark Van Buren!

"Shine the light on this book," Michael L suddenly ordered. His voice was loud, but not excited. It was the calm voice of a scholar.

"The light…" Eliot replied. He suddenly realized that he was still holding the flashlight. And that he was standing shoulder-to-shoulder with Michael L, and beside Tarō, holding his sword in one hand.

"Uh, yes, the light."

He tightened his grip on the flashlight, and directed the beam toward Michael L. With an old book in his left hand, and holding aloft the ankh in his right, Michael L opened his mouth to speak.

"Cthugha Fomalhaut n'gha-ghaa nafl thagan! Iä! Cthugha!"

While he chanted this spell, the bodies of the Italian thugs rose one by one from the formalin pool. More than just two or three. All of them.

"Ouon'ghewe natufn! Iä! Cthugha! Fomalhaut natow!"

The corpses moved toward them, dropping hunks of rotting flesh, guts and wriggling maggots as they came. The chemical smell of formalin and a powerful scent of water, the stench of rotting flesh and the odor of graveyard soil, along with the dust combined to form a dense, powerful wave of stench that came square at Eliot's face.

The shock made him want to shield his eyes. But before he did he noticed the bag near his feet. Michael L's bag. In it were a gun and dynamite! The moment this thought flashed through his mind, he crouched down.

"Come, Spawn of Fire,
Children of Cthugha,
Hear my plea,
Descend from the heavens"

Eliot desperately grabbed the bag. He raised his eyes to look forward. The gang of faceless, water-logged corpses inched forward.

Eliot caught sight of one that had only its lower jaw still attached to its neck, and quickly averted his eyes. The gun, the gun. Michael's gun is in the bag. But with just his left hand, he couldn't work the latch on the bag. No, at a time like this, what the hell am I doing? He put the flashlight down on the floor, and used both hands to try and release the latch.

"Iä! Cthugha!"

Michael L caused the name of the God of fire to reverberate. At the same moment, the latch opened.

Eliot stuck his right hand in the bag. He felt the cord. He felt the triggering device. He felt the detonators, and the dynamite. He felt a cold lump of steel.

The Luger P08! His fingers numb with fear, Eliot picked up the German automatic. In the next moment it happened.

The tile wall behind the corpses suddenly disappeared, revealing a bluish-white fog. It was outside the hospital. Beyond the fog rising in thick clouds – far beyond them – orange points of light appeared. In a blink of an eye the lights grew larger. At the same time they began to multiply – from one to two, from two to four, from four to eight. By the time they multiplied from eight to sixteen, the lights had swollen from the size of a fingertip to a basketball.

"Come, Spawn of Fire!"

All the detail could now clearly be seen. Cutting through the fog, the sixteen "things" came flying.

They were rotating spirits of flame. Or rather, blazing fireballs shooting off orange flares. The sixteen fireballs swooped down from the heavens, slipping into the autopsy room through the missing wall. Each of them then burst through the back of one of the corpses that had been advancing on Eliot and the others.

"They've done it!" Tarō yelled. "The flames have thoroughly cleansed those filthy bastards."

Crouching down quickly, he deftly stood the scabbard on end, and with his single hand sheathed the naked blade.

Eliot stared in amazement as the sixteen corpses turned to flaming effigies. Nevertheless, with his right hand he pulled the Luger P08 from its holster, and pointed it at the corpses. In his left hand he held tightly the flashlight and bag.

"Cthugha…"

Michael L offered his heartfelt appreciation to the entity that had sent the fireballs to this place. The corpses were still moving, but each was engulfed in flame. It was plain to see that they would eventually falter and collapse.

Eliot shifted his gaze from the flames in front of him to the place where the wall had been. It was still gone. From the flat, rectangular void that opened up before him, the bluish-white fog swirled as it was sucked inward. The fog carried a strong acidic smell and chill into the autopsy room. Combined with the stench of the burning corpses, it made him nauseous. And still Michael L softly murmured to the god that had provided the flame.

"…we give thanks from the depths of our hearts…"

A bloated arm reached out from the flame. Its fingers flared, and it tried to grab Michael. The hand was impervious to the fire.

"Shit!"

Tarō knocked away the hand of a corpse with his sword, still sheathed in its scabbard. Its arm twisted in an odd direction. In that moment, Tarō kicked in the chest of the corpse, shoving it back into the flame.

"You'd best not forget. There were twenty Italian thugs. Only sixteen were burned up by those *mamzers* of fire."

From behind the trio–from the hallway–Simmel's voice echoed. His voice boomed, as if coming from deep inside a cave.

"There was that one yellowbelly that ran. And one that the Jap just pushed into the flame. So, how many do you think are left?"

"You think we're going to play your game?" Tarō shot back, and looked at Michael.

"Let's get out of here. Patty's got to be in another room."

"Right. Eliot, let's go," said Michael L, closing the old book.

Eliot nodded and returned the gun to its holster, picking up the bag as he stood up.

The three men ran out the door, with Tarō in the lead. Eliot came last, closing the door as he left. From behind the wooden door they could hear a crackling sound. The doorknob was hot. Eliot jerked his hand away. The beginnings of burns had formed on the palm of his hand. This isn't a dream, or an illusion, he thought. It's all real...

The door burst from the inside. A rotting hand was thrust through. With flesh dripping from its bones, the hand snatched the old book away from Michael L. He quickly tried to grab back the book of magic, but the corpse's strength was formidable. The *Unaussprechlichen Kulten* was taken from the occultist, and pulled through the gash in the door.

"Damn," Michael cursed through gritted teeth.

"I'll get it back, master," said Tarō, taking the *katana's* scabbard in his teeth. A chuckle echoed down from the hallway ceiling. It was Simmel.

"*Shvuntz!* Watch this!"

Before the eyes of the startled trio, the door to the autopsy room opened. They could see flames. Burning corpses walking around aimlessly. And toward the exterior the gap in the wall. The fog outside.

The hospital suddenly tilted. It was like being on a ship rocked by a storm.

The hospital leaned further. A great stream of formalin flowed from the pool into the void. The angle became more acute. At last the abandoned hospital began to spill all of the *things* in the autopsy room outside.

The three men in the hall slid along the floor toward the autopsy room door. They scrambled toward the walls. Beyond the wide-open door was a sea of flame. Beyond that was the *outside*–where the outer world of swirling fog was waiting.

Eliot, his body pressed flat against the wall of the autopsy room, held the bag to his chest. He dropped the flashlight. Still shining its beam, it fell through the door. It rolled through the sea of flame, and finally into the void, to the *outside*.

Eliot saw it clearly. The scene momentarily illuminated by the flashlight's beam in the outer world of swirling fog.

He saw the corpses of the Italian gang, slowly churning in the fog. The body of Judge Van Buren. The body of the agent Niki. The corpse of Niki's bodyguard, and that of Hiraoka. That wasn't all. There were the hideous, pitiful bodies of people Eliot didn't know. They'd been shot with guns, stabbed with knives, hacked with axes, beaten with bats, run over by cars, hung with ropes, and blown up with dynamite – the corpses of people murdered in innumerable ways. The bodies seemed to be in water as they rose and sank in bluish-white fog, up and down, right and left, slowly turning in a circle.

"That's the waste dump," explained Simmel. "The halfway point between this world and the next. All those I've slaughtered are put in the waste dump. They drift there, looking as they did at the moment they were killed. Forever. Loathing me. Their hatred becomes the source of my magic."

Simmel roared with laughter. It was a shrill, metallic laugh. It lingered on, reverberating. The laugh slowly grew louder, until at last it became a grating sound that rattled the building. The entire hospital began to shake. More alarming was that the trembling building was tilting even further.

"Look! The autopsy room door…" cried Tarō, still clinging to the wall.

Eliot looked up, his body pressed between the floor and the wall. The rectangular door was beginning to warp. The midsection of the right and left-hand sides of the frame were pulled in toward the center. The corners became rounded. It looked just like a mouth, grimacing in pain.

But there was more to the deformation. The inclined building was becoming cylindrical the more it rumbled, with the autopsy room door at its bottom. The second floor appeared distorted, like an image seen through a fisheye lens. Everything began to twist and bend. The entire second floor was turning into a funnel.

Eliot's body rolled like a ball from the floor to the wall, and then to the ceiling. By shear force of will Tarō drew his sword, and thrust it into the wooden wall. He held it by the hilt to keep from sliding down. But only being able to use his right hand, no matter how tightly he held on it was just a matter of time before he would fall through the doorway. These thoughts ran though Eliot's mind as he rolled.

"Farewell, fools. It's been a fun six days. I won't forget you until the day I die. Of course, I won't die."

Simmel's voice was full of theatrical showmanship. Suddenly, without a moment's hesitation, Michael L called out to him.

"Simmel! Have you forgotten your promise to us? What about that, Simmel?"

The occultist was hanging from the ceiling, holding on to the cord of an electric light.

"Weren't you going to tear the heart from her naked body? Weren't you going to kill us, and wash her corpse with our blood? Was that a lie? An empty threat? Or just the bluster of a petty, third-rate hood? Well!? What about it, Simmel?"

"What?!" Simmel roared. Michael provoked him further.

"I don't think you can do it. I think you're just one of those chicken-hearts that can't even fire a gun during a hit."

"…You… Don't fuck with me!"

The triumphant tone had been swept from Simmel's voice. The second floor, still warping into a funnel, shook violently. Sharp knives appeared around the circumference of the door.

This building is somehow linked to Simmel's mind, Eliot realized. That's why his anger directly manifests itself in this way.

Michael L spoke furiously, in a gangster's tone that shocked even Tarō.

"Where are you now? Crawled up your dead grandmother's asshole? Or peeking out timidly from the bottom of some shit pot? Tell me, Simmel! What have you done with Patty? Don't try to tell me you raped her. I know you've got nothing between your legs. When you were a young punk you went and bought some diseased whore, ended up with crotch rot and it fell off. I read the Feds' report."

"Fuck you, you son of a bitch!"

Simmel's roar cut short Michael L's tirade. The shaking turned into an earthquake. Tiles flew from the walls. The violent shaking made the transformation of the space happen faster, though in reverse. The funnel-shaped space became cylindrical. The corners reappeared. Trembling. Shaking. The glimmering of a pale blue light. The knives around the door were retracted, the flames in the autopsy room extinguished. The wall was restored, and a midnight blue darkness returned to cover the entire scene.

Eliot's back was pinned against the wall. Tarō was slumped on the floor. Michael L was standing motionless in the center of the hallway.

Then, as the silence lingered…

"Come. I'll give you a fight. I said come!"

It was Simmel's voice. The reverberation was gone. The voice echoed from far down the hallway.

"I'm in the room to the right at the end of the hallway. The special operating room for the hospital director. Patty's here with me. No one else… come. It's three against one. Just as I promised, I'll wash the girl with your blood."

"Okay," said Michael L, moving forward. "Though you may be a gangster and practitioner of black magic, you also seem to abhor an empty threat. I'm coming, Simmel."

Me too, thought Eliot, and walked after him, still clutching the bag.

Following the pair Tarō stepped forward, holding aloft the *katana* in his right hand. The patch over his left eye, and the sling and bandage on his left arm were covered in dark stains of soot, blood and the pus of rotting flesh. He walked with his shoulders back and head high, however, as if the stains were a badge of honor.

The hallway was long and dark, but the *yōki* that had lingered until now had disappeared.

Before they had gone fifty steps, a light shot out from in front of them. It was a pale blue light. The light leaked from the partially open door. It stretched from the door along the floor, climbing the walls of the hallway.

The three men stopped in front of the door. It swung open by itself.

"Come on in. I'll show you the ritual. The ritual of the water god of darkness Cthaat."

It was Simmel's voice.

Tarō started to go in. "No. I'll go first," said Michael, hastily pulling him back. The cool-headed expression of an occultist had returned to his face. So different from a moment ago–even Tarō couldn't believe it was the same man who had just raged in defiance.

Michael L stepped cautiously into the room. If the building really is linked to Simmel's mind, he thought, there could be no telling what kind of traps had been set in it. The occultist walked as if traversing the thin ice of a frozen lake.

Simmel saw Michael's caution, and spoke out.

"No need to worry. Nothing is going to happen–yet."

A wry smile rose on Michael L's face, and he quickened his pace. Tarō followed. Then Eliot.

Eliot stepped into the room, still clutching the bag. The moment he was inside, the pale blue light was turned on him. And there was the smell of water. The overpowering smell of water.

The trio silently moved to form a single line, shoulder to shoulder.

Simmel had called it the special operating room for the hospital director, but it didn't look like a place for performing surgery. It was more like the place in a church where mass was held.

The walls on three sides were covered with light blue curtains. Directly ahead a metallic table had been placed. Attached below it were levels and handles, while directly underneath an assortment of gears and wheels were engaged.

Patty lay supine on top of the table. She was covered from the neck down by a white sheet, but the exposed face was unmistakably that of Patty Murphy. Highly polished surgical instruments – knives, clamps, scissors and saws – had been neatly placed beside the table.

Where's Simmel? thought Eliot, his eyes racing around the room.

A bizarre crest had been stitched with gold thread into the curtain hanging in front. Below it was the word CTHAAT, the letters slightly uneven as the curtain gently billowed.

His eyes darted from left to right. Curtains hung to both sides, but only the one ahead of him was adorned with a crest and lettering.

"Simmel!" cried Michael L. "Where are you, Simmel?"

Suddenly Simmel spoke from directly behind the three men, his voice full of derision and mockery.

"Don't yell like that. This is an operating room, as well as a place for ritual. And here you come with your filthy, angry language, and bringing a sword into the hospital. My delicate nerves can hardly bear it."

"What the…"

Michael was about to turn around, an angry expression on his face, when it happened. A human form stood up from behind the operating table.

Eliot froze when he saw it. It was wearing a light blue surgical gown, and a rubber apron. Rubber gloves covered both hands, and it was the very picture of a surgeon prepared for an operation.

But it had no head. There was nothing from the shoulders up.

Is that a corpse? thought Eliot, his heart crying out.

"Simmel!" cried Michael L at that same moment. His voice was hoarse with shock, and trembled with fear.

"What are you looking at? I'm right here. I'm over there. I'm above you, and below you," Simmel chanted.

Eliot looked back over his shoulder. Simmel's face was directly behind them, laughing. His heart stopped. It was only the face of the gangster.

A neck nearly six feet long stretched down from his head. The base of the neck was fused with the floor. It was as if the floor formed a set of extremely broad shoulders.

The floor was completely covered by Simmel's skin. The walls were also wrapped with the flesh-colored membrane – it was the inside of a gigantic bag of skin. The pinkish skin was faintly tinged with a pale blue light, a color that made Eliot think of the flesh of a drowning victim.

Pinkish objects drooped from the ceiling. It was a cloth in the shape of hands. But not simply cloth. The five separate ends moved in different directions.

Fingers, thought Eliot, as he looked up at the ceiling. The entire ceiling was the color of flesh. Objects like thin cloth, pinkish and shaped like human hands – hundreds of them – were descending toward them en masse.

Simmel's hand… the hands of *them*, thought Eliot. For an instant his mind was far away.

"Here I am," came a voice from the direction of the operating table. Eliot turned toward it.

The headless surgical gown was slowly falling backward. The area of the floor under its feet was being forced upward. Veins showed through the floor. It grew fuzzy hair. The floor swelled up, turning into Simmel's head, but not a normal size. It was huge, six feet from the top of his head to his chin.

"I'm *there*. I'm *here*," said the head.

The headless gown hung upside down from the back of Simmel's head. From the ankles down it was sunk into the giant head. And yet its arms continued to move.

That headless *thing* is also a part of Simmel's head, thought Eliot, as his flesh began to crawl.

"Welcome to the director's special operating room. Shall we begin the ritual? The ritual of Cthaat?"

A hand reached out from the floor in front of them. It reminded Eliot of a strange, unknown seaweed, from deep under the ocean. It slithered along quickly, spread out five fingers, and grabbed the front curtain. With all its might it pulled it open to reveal a row of four windows.

Beyond the glass was a night sky of black satin, with stars like a scattering of gemstones. The majesty of Lake Michigan was spread before it. The surface of the lake reflected the brilliant arch of stars. Eliot stared, in awe of its beauty.

Eliot recalled that the Heights offered the best views in Chicago. But he had no time to admire the lake. Directly before him, a hellish metamorphosis was resuming.

The head behind the operating table collapsed. Losing its shape, it flowed into the headless form wearing the surgical gown. The head behind the three men also sank into the floor. After moving like some kind of mucous, the area behind the operating table expanded, and Simmel appeared in the guise of a surgeon. His legs, from the ankles down, were imbedded in the floor.

It's all Simmel, thought Eliot, finally beginning to realize. This entire operating room – it's all a part of Simmel's body.

"Not that I really mind, but I didn't think you'd be able to say anything to me."

Simmel placed one of his hands on the instrument tray.

"So, I'll just go ahead, and while you watch, I'll tear out this girl's heart. Cthaat's been growing steadily more irritable about it for some time now."

"Cthaat..." muttered Michael L, rumpling his cheek. In a sign of contempt he let one of the corners of his mouth droop. Simmel didn't notice, and picked up a surgical knife. He handled it like a real surgeon. Supporting the knife with his forefinger, he brought the blade up to his eye. He appeared to be checking its sharpness.

At that moment Michael spoke.

"Cthaat doesn't exist," he said in a definitive tone. "He's just a wild fantasy."

Simmel's gaze shifted from the blade to Michael. His piercing eyes instantly radiated a smile.

"What's that?" Simmel asked.

He smiled as if he'd misheard. Michael L spoke slowly and caustically.

"I *said*, the water god Cthaat doesn't exist. The fire god Cthugha is referred to not only in the *Unaussprechlichen Kulten*, but also in *De Vermiis Mysteriis* and the *Necronomicon*. But Cthaat isn't in any of those texts. Just the *Cthaat Aquadingen*, and that by an unknown author."

"Silence!" Simmel smiled a snarl. His grin was like that of a wild beast. It was the same look he had when he'd killed the Italians.

"For the sake of argument," Michael continued, "let's say that Cthaat does exist. What can he offer? The best he's able to do is turn his worshippers into monsters."

"What are you saying, you..."

Simmel began moving forward. The floor and ceiling began to ripple. As he did Michael saw his opportunity.

"Cthugha!" He invoked the name of the god of fire. From his fist he raised his forefinger and middle finger. The two fingers cut through the blue space.

Eliot felt as if the room had suddenly shrunk–the mysterious power of Cthugha.

A crimson force shot out from both sides of Michael like a sudden gale. The curtains covering the two side walls fluttered.

Orange flames sprung up from their hems. Pyrokinesis from the fire magic. The tongues of flame crawled up the curtains as they watched. Waves of heat gushed from right and left.

"Go, Eliot!"

Urged on by the occultist, Eliot turned to run. The bottoms of his shoes stuck. It was like he'd stepped in glue.

Looking down at his feet, he saw what looked like pale blue shoots of grass sprouting from the flesh-colored floor. They were small hands, no more than a quarter of an inch high. Moving their bean sprout-like fingers, they tried to keep him from moving. So many covered the floor that it made him stick.

"Damn – *kutabare!*"

Hissing a curse in his throat as he took the scabbard in his teeth, Tarō drew his sword. Gripping the handle with just his right hand, he spun around. He pointed the tip of the upturned blade toward the flesh-colored floor. With all his might he thrust it downward. It pierced the floor, slicing through in an arc.

A splendid incision opened in the floor. A moment of silence, and blood began to flow from it. The room pitched. The floor was thrashing about in pain. Cries of agony rippled off the walls and ceiling.

Mindless of the shaking, Eliot ran. As he did he fumbled in the bag for the explosive switches. But since he couldn't look down, it was impossible for him to set the timing device.

Giving up on the bomb, he pulled out the Luger. A tentacle reached out for him, and as he pushed it away the bag flew from his left hand, almost as if he'd thrown it at the creature.

As long as the detonators aren't activated, he thought, it won't explode.

The bag hit the operating table. Patty lay there, motionless. The bag bounced off the table and fell behind it.

Eliot, gun in one hand, rushed toward the operating table.

"You little bastard…"

Simmel squared off for a fight. A dozen or so hands stretched out from the floor, fluttering like seaweed. Its grotesqueness made him nauseous. Undaunted, Eliot ran straight into Simmel, knocking him to the floor. His chest and stomach responded like rubber. But still Eliot hit him with the stock of the gun, keeping his enemy pinned to the ground.

"Take *this*!"

Eliot squeezed the Luger's trigger, firing three 9mm bullets in rapid succession. Blue droplets spattered from Simmel's head. His hair and scalp stained the floor.

Perhaps because his body was linked together even when he was in this condition, he appeared to feel pain. The walls, floor and ceiling convulsed up and down, and from right to left. Tens, then hundreds of replicas of Simmel's head, the size of fists, rose from the floor. They all opened their mouths and spoke together.

"Nga, eburnga'tnu, ptgepo'gnyo, Cthaat!"

Eliot started to pull back the sheet from Patty, then noticed that she wasn't wearing any clothes. He wrapped the sheet around her, and shoving the gun in his belt, picked her up.

"Good, brother. This way, this way!" called Tarō, waving his sword. He had gone from attacking the floor to the ceiling. Raising the sword, he would thrust in the blade, slice through with a pull, then carve open another spot.

Holding Patty in his arms, Eliot ran from the operating room. The distance was only ten or twelve steps, but to him it felt like a mile.

"Good. Now let's get out of here."

Michael L urged Eliot toward the door. Tarō pulled back his sword, and turned. Making sure that the two of them had dashed toward the door, Michael L reached into his left pocket. He pulled out the ankh. Gripping it tightly, with all his strength he called out the full name of the monster known as "The Pest."

"Frank 'The Pest' Simmel!"

A round object dropped from the ceiling. It was Simmel's head, but the regeneration was crude. He had no hair, and his ears and nose were just vague representations.

Michael L waved his right hand. Simmel's head was engulfed in flame. As he writhed in agony, Michael pulled back the ankh in his left hand as if to throw it.

"The crushing blow of Cthugha…"

"Iä, Cthaat! Water god of darkness!"

Simmel's voice was already distorted, like the static from a radio with poor reception.

And yet, and yet… The curse uttered in the throes of death spawned an evil miracle.

Outside the window flashes of light raced across the star-filled sky. A pale blue light. Light the color of Simmel's "water magic." It wasn't a flash of lightening, or a natural electric discharge. The cloudless night sky was lit with blue flashes. They began to blink.

The lights reflected off the surface of Lake Michigan. When they had blinked four times there was a sudden transformation–in Lake Michigan.

The lake began to rise. Not just one section–the entire lake was bowing upward. From the center, it climbed further. It protruded upward. It looked like an enormous head and shoulders. The lake water rose straight up. A pale blue light framed the entirety. The water ascended even further. Heading toward the sky, it was gigantic, reverse-flowing waterfall. But the higher it rose, the more it took on human form.

Lake Michigan had stood up! It was a giant made of water, nearly fifty yards high.

"Behold, my water god Cthaat!" the crackly voice said with pride.

"Receive the crushing blow of Cthugha, Simmel!" yelled Michael L in a voice to overwhelm his enemy, bringing his left hand down in a flash. "Depart, Cthaat!"

The ankh flew through the air. Michael L turned, and ran toward Eliot and Tarō. The young man held Patty in one arm, pounding on the tentacles and heads amassed in front of the door with the other. Tarō was chopping through the tentacles that hung down from the ceiling. Michael ran toward them.

The ankh flew in a parabolic line to a place behind the operating table. On the floor lay the bag filled with dynamite. Surrounding it Simmel heads popped up like so many mushrooms.

"Gh'neri nryu, hyanste wg'neh, Cthaat!" They chanted the spell of the water god. The ankh fell near the base of the infestation of heads.

The gigantic god formed from the water of Lake Michigan began to spread out its arms. It gathered its strength as it raised one leg. It began to take a step forward, meaning to trample the streets of Chicago under its feet with the power of water. The pale shadow of the water god was draped over Chicago.

The three men ran into the hall. Behind them the floor and walls of the operating room were undulating violently. A flesh-colored *thing* grabbed the door. It was a tentacle mimicking a grotesque human hand. And there were more of them. Hundreds. They held the door, broke through the walls and emerged into the hallway, all the while emitting a pale blue light.

The *thing* was elastic, extending outward like a telescope. It had faces too numerous to count, and snaked its way out through the door. With millions of human hands and feet–large and small–it crawled across the floor.

Like a giant serpent. Like smoke. Like a train. Like an enormous microbe. Like a centipede.

Like a swarm of Frank Simmels.

The sphere atop the ankh that had fallen to the floor was glowing from inside. It was a crimson light. That light was the source of the fire magic.

Eliot aimed the gun at the *thing* coming toward them, and fired. Holes were punched repeatedly in the flesh-colored cluster of faces. But that was all. It only seemed to increase the speed of its pursuit. In desperation he threw the Luger P08 at them.

I've done this before, he thought. Though Eliot was assailed by such notions, they didn't stop him from fleeing. Taking the sheet-wrapped Patty in his arms, he ran with all his might, so that his heart might burst.

The timing device in the bag was switched to ON. The countdown to the explosion was set for one minute. The detonators and dynamite were securely attached to the incendiary timing devices.

Tarō looked back, and threw his *katana*. But the approaching *things* instantly enveloped the samurai weapon, swallowing and absorbing it. Tarō spit out the Japanese word *kusottare*, and resumed running.

The water god Cthaat lifted one of its legs from the lake. Fish deprived of water thrashed about on the muddy bottom. The bones of horses and men, the remains of carts and automobiles–everything that had sunk in the lake–was revealed. Leaving them behind, the giant god prepared to take its first step.

"Down! Go down the stairs!" yelled Michael. Already they were approaching the end of the second floor hallway. The three men entered the elevator hall, then the stairwell. One flight went up to the third floor, while the other descended to the first. They barreled–practically tumbled–down the stairs.

The Simmel hands and feet scampered across the floor after them. What now covered its surface was not just a collection of Simmel faces. There were hundreds of eyes, thousands of lips, tens of thousands of ears and hundreds of thousands of tentacles. They were passing in front of the autopsy room.

A minute is a long time. The minute hand had nevertheless nearly completed a full revolution on the face of the clock. The long and terror-filled day of October 31st was drawing to a close.

The water god was on the verge of taking its first step on land. On October 31st, 1923, the short life of the city of Chicago – city of water – was about to end, destroyed by none other than that water itself, the water of Lake Michigan that was the mother of *her*.

It took less than three seconds for the three men to reach the bottom of the stairs. But the *thing* that was Simmel reached the entrance to the stairwell even quicker than that.

The great length of the creature was almost unbelievable. Though its front had begun to descend the stairs, its torso was still in the middle of the hallway, and its rear stretched back to inside the operating room. Its tail end was wriggling by the window in the operating room, behind the operating table. The floor was also part of the creature. On that was the bag.

The foot of the colossal god was about to trample a small lake monitoring center on the shore. At that moment, the date changed from October 31st, to November 1st.

November 1st – midnight. The timing device moved with precision. The creature swooped down the stairs at once and arrived on the first floor.

The three men ran desperately from the north stairway. Following a straight line, they would head south. A bright light seeped out from the wall. The light of morning. The light was coming from the painting.

The landscape painting. The cityscape with the view of the canal from Taylor street. Downtown Chicago, south of the river. The street lined with buildings, at dawn.

The Chicago business district was still asleep, the building lights extinguished, but the canal flowed ceaselessly. The valley between the buildings was bathed in pink, foretelling the imminent rising of the sun.

The painting was lifelike, as if the scene were clipped out of reality. There was even a refreshing breeze blowing.

"Straight ahead! That's Cthugha's instruction–the guidance of fire."

Michael L's words held an allure that was hard to resist. Tarō, who would normally be making light of the situation by now, was charging straight ahead, head first. A reddish mist began to waft from the surface of the painting. Cutting through it, Tarō dove through to the other side of the painting.

Eliot jumped through next, carrying Patty. Finally Michael L leaped into the painting.

The creature pursued, no less than fifteen feet behind them.

November 1st, one second after midnight.

Electricity flowed to the priming cord, and small sparks flew from the incendiary device. The detonator sent its signal to explode to the bundle of dynamite. The dynamite began to combust at the speed of sound.

At that moment, the purifying fire visited St. James Infirmary. The operating room was demolished. The tail end of the creature was blown to pieces. The fire magic, in an instant, had obliterated the personification of the water magic. A series of explosions rocked the second floor. Doors and floorboards went flying into the walls and ceilings. The stairwell exploded. The first floor lobby exploded.

Them, as Frank "The Pest" Simmel, was destroyed by the flame, blast and shock wave just as its nose drew near the painting on the southern wall. It was completely obliterated, with not a scrap of meat or flake of skin remaining.

The source of the supply for the water magic was suddenly cut off. The entire body wavered unsteadily, the movement of its foot ceased.

Small waves began to run down the surface of the god's fifty-yard high body. Silence, then the giant body began to fall backwards into the drained lake. The angle grew steeper still, as if the lake's depression possessed some sort of powerful magnetic force.

At last the water started to return to the lake bottom. It began with drips and small streams that gradually swelled, finally becoming a cataract, rushing downward in torrents from a height of fifty yards. The roar was tremendous, and fine droplets of water were sprinkled a hundred yards in every direction, but by the time the people of neighborhood came out of their houses, the water had completely returned to Lake Michigan.

Chapter Eight
Love Me or Leave Me

NONE OF THE three men had a clear memory of what had happened after they jumped into the painting.

It seemed that they stood motionless in a reddish fog, alternatively orange or pink in color, and it seemed that they were floating in the sky, surrounded by feathers that reminded them of flames. In any event, what is for certain is that it lasted until morning.

The row of buildings lining the far side of the canal was illuminated by a dizzying light. The light slipped through the valley between the buildings, sparkling golden on the black surface of the canal. The flickering light reflected on the sides of the buildings, quietly proclaiming the coming of dawn.

The first one to notice the morning light was Tarō. He pulled his head right and left in an irritated way, then lifted his right eyelid. His eyes were soon wide open.

"I'm alive," he muttered. He tried to lift his hands, and was reminded of the intense pain in his left arm. His left arm was wrapped in a bandage, and hung in a sling. The bandage and the sling were both stained black, and all he could see were strands of tattered cloth, clinging to his left hand.

"I'm alive. It's morning. I've made it."

As he spoke, Tarō stood up. He had been sitting, leaning against the wall of a building. Looking around, he saw Michael L slumped on the sidewalk. Eliot, his arms around Patty, still wrapped in her sheet, was slumped in front of a nearby building.

Tarō, remembering his duty as a bodyguard, ran first to Michael L.

"Master, are you alright? Wake up."

Lifting the upper portion of his body, Tarō shook him roughly.

Michael slowly opened his eye, finally making out Tarō staring attentively into his face.

"Ah, Kaitarō…" he exclaimed softly. Tarō gave a wry smile in return, his lip trembling.

"Just Tarō. It's easier for you all to pronounce. I told you that the first time we met, remember? Has the shock of that monster made you forget?"

"No, I remember… of course. We've survived. Where are we?" Michael muttered, and sat up straight. Leaving his master's side, Tarō moved over to Eliot. But the young man opened his eyes before Tarō could wake him up.

"We're alive," Eliot said.

"Yeah, so it would seem. We're both fortunate."

Tarō nodded. Then, placing his hand on the bandage covering his left eye, he casually removed it.

"Should you be unraveling yourself like that?" asked Eliot.

"I want to take a better look at the morning sun," said Tarō, lifting his left eyelid, swollen and purple from the bruise. "I can just make it out," he muttered to himself.

"Patty, wake up! You're safe. Patty!"

Eliot called to the girl in his arms. She still had her eyes closed. She appeared to be asleep.

"Don't try to force her. Let's call an ambulance and get her to a hospital. She's suffered more damage than any of us."

"Okay, you're right."

Eliot nodded, and gently laid her down. He reached out to touch her cheek.

"I've got it!" cried Michael L. "I know where we are, and why we've been brought here. Why Cthugha has guided us here."

Eliot turned toward the occultist. Michael pointed excitedly to a spot on a smallish building.

"What is it?" asked Tarō, running over to him.

"Look, look here! The inscription on this building," said Michael L, then turned to explain it to Eliot.

"It says that the first blaze of the Great Chicago Fire began here in 1871. Ha, ha, ha! This is south of the river! Taylor Street. Directly across the canal is Harrison."

"Then... the painting in that hospital... was the view of the canal from around here?"

"That's right. The fire that turned Chicago, city of water, into a sea of flame began on this spot. Now you understand why this area was missing from the scene in the painting, and why Cthugha chose to bring us here."

"I don't understand at all," said Tarō. He shook his head, and continued in an ironic tone.

"But there is one thing I do know. I don't get paid enough to be the bodyguard for an occultist. Let's settle up for my services to now, master. I'm going to go straight to the Wacker Hotel and become a steward or something.

Before long the ambulance Tarō had called arrived, and took them to John Steward Memorial Hospital on Jefferson Avenue.

The admittance nurse at the hospital, following standard procedure, dutifully recorded the names of the four people brought in.

Michael Leigh. Metaphysician. 35 yrs
Kaitarō Hasegawa. Non-citizen. 33 yrs
Patty Murphy. Student, University of Chicago. 19 yrs
Eliot Ness. Student, University of Chicago. 20 yrs

After their examinations, the three men were released from the hospital that same day. Patty Murphy underwent treatment at the hospital for two weeks, after which she was transferred to the psychoneurosis ward in the hospital at New York Medical College. The shock she had received left an incurable scar on her psyche.

Eliot Ness' inability to protect Patty haunted him, while at the same time his hatred toward gangsters like Simmel intensified. He graduated with honors from University of Chicago in 1925, and joined one of the leading insurance companies in America.

In 1927 Ness left his job with the insurance company, and with the help of his brother-in-law Alexander Jamie he was hired on with the Federal Bureau of Investigation. Still only 26, he rose to be the head of a unit investigating organized and violent crime.

As head of a squad of nine agents dubbed the *Untouchables*, Eliot Ness terrified the gangs of Chicago.

Michael Leigh continued to wage his battles against the power of the ancient ones that reigned over the Earth before humanity, in countries around the world. But he never again sought to challenge the power of a god by employing that of another. He had come to know the limitations of trying to resolve events in the third dimension by making use of the power of a different one.

Michael next met the man who had introduced him to Tarō – Dr. Yamada Makoto – in 1937. It was during the affair of the Black Kiss, the battle with the undersea creatures as they tried to manipulate the minds of humans.

Tarō, a.k.a. Hasegawa Kaitarō, returned to Japan in 1924. The day after his arrival in Yokohama, he appeared unexpectedly at the boarding house where his younger brother lived, asking for a place to stay. It was here that he met Mizutani Jun. "So, what do you do for a living?" Tarō asked him. "I write for a magazine called *Shinseinen*." "Really," Tarō replied. "So they buy detective stories even in Japan." After this brief exchange, Tarō ventured on his own to the editorial department of *Shinseinen*, and spoke to the head editor, Morishita Uson. "I've just returned from America," he declared. "I have a lot of fascinating stories, and I'd like you to buy them." The strength of his character won over the heart of the editor straight away. He then began to write about the spirit of a Japanese youth wandering America, under the penname of Tani Jōji. The subtitle to this series was 'Merican Jap. One story involved his experience as a bodyguard in Chicago. He also wrote historical novels for *Tantei Bungei*. The penname he used for these was Fubo Hayashi, aptly implying "not forgotten." In 1929, using the penname Maki Itsuma, he published *True Stories of the Bizarre from around the World* in *Chūō Kōron* magazine. "The bizarre, in a manner of speaking, is absurd," he would say resoundingly, explaining the theme underlying the books. "While at the same time, the facts presented are strictly accurate."

Using these three pennames Kaitarō gained fame as a popular author, but died suddenly of a heart attack on June 29th, 1935. Today Kaitarō Hasegawa is popularly remembered as Hayashi Fubō, the creator of the one-eyed, one-armed samurai warrior Tange Sazen.

Practically no one, however, remembers the book *What is War?*, published under the name Maki Itsuma by Chūō Kōron in 1930. On the inside cover is a pentagon-shaped seal, included at Kaitarō's insistence, taken from the 14th-century text *Maghrib Dementia*. This seal, with three Greek symbols for *tau* in the center of the pentagram, is called the Barque Talisman.

It means, "all evil knowledge should be kept secret."

Chapter Nine
St. James Infirmary

IN A DARK corner of a basement speakeasy, heavy with the smell of rotting cabbage, the gangster was trembling. The hand clutching the bottle of Canadian whiskey was grimy. He had, after all, been on the drink for a month. It had left his jet-black hair stiff with oil, and his sharp Italian features had grown coarse. Already he was nothing more than a bit of rotting garbage called Scarface.

"Hey, what are you muttering to yourself over there?" a curious drunk asked him.

"…a monster… Simmel's a monster… that son of a bitch… the way he controls water… they're all dead… heads smashed every which way…"

"Simmel?"

The drunk spit on the floor as the name of "the Pest" formed in his mouth. He downed what was left in his glass in one gulp. A mouthwash of cheap whiskey. Once he'd rinsed out his throat, he turned to the bartender across the counter.

"Hey. That young punk. Was he a friend of Simmel's or something?" he asked. "He doesn't look Jewish to me."

"Ah, him. He's been on the bottle for a month now. That's why he doesn't know Simmel drowned in the canal."

"Is that so? Then I'm gonna tell him. Hey, you, young fella. First of this month Frank Simmel…"

The drunk suddenly stopped in the middle of his sentence. He stared behind the counter. He had felt a hideous gaze fall on him from the dark shadows beneath the liquor shelf.

"Bless me Lord…"

The drunk crossed himself, placed his glass on the counter, and quietly moved away from Scarface.

With a blank expression Scarface brought the bottle of liquor to his lips and took a swig. That's when he heard it.

The whistling. A sorrowful blues melody. Scarface knew the song. It was *St. James Infirmary*.

Scarface's eyes raced around the room, the bottle still pressed to his lips. The whistling slowly came closer. The man doing the whistling, though, was nowhere to be seen.

"Don't worry. It's not the booze."

A dark shadow slipped out from the recesses of the bar. The shadow was Scarface's own, moving with its own will, and whispering. With a trembling hand Scarface pulled the bottle from his lips.

The whistling of St. James Infirmary began again. This time, it was clear that it was from the shadow.

"Who are you?!" he cried, in a voice husky from drink. "The ghost of Ferraro, or the devil himself?"

"Neither. But if you insist that I reveal myself to you, I might be your guardian angel."

He stared silently at the shadow.

"I was looking after Simmel until recently, but he made a mess of things, so I left him. If you desire it, I'll give my support to you. As much as I did for Simmel. Even more."

Scarface stared for a moment, then shook his head – this is a dream, he thought. Or else an illusion. The drink and the terror have finally given me hallucinations.

"The deal's simple. All you have to do is renounce your so-called god. You a religious man?"

"Catholic."

"Has that god ever helped you?"

"No."

"He ever show you a miracle?"

"None."

"I'll show you one. Look at that liquor bottle."

Doing as he was told, Scarface let go of the bottle. Foam began to rise from its bottom. A bright red foam. The foam covered the alcohol that was left in the bottle in no time at all, turning the cheap whiskey red. The color of blood.

Scarface drew back his chin in astonishment. He swallowed a glob of spit.

"How about that? Now do you believe me? With my power behind you, you can sweep the Jewish gangs from this city. You could be a boss more powerful than Trio."

"I believe you. If it could really be so…"

The shadow nodded.

"Then let's make the deal. Swear to me that together we will spread evil throughout the world. Swear that we will remake the world in violence and murder, prostitution, betrayal and corruption!"

"I… I swear."

"Good. Now say your name. Then, in my name, drink to the last drop the living blood in that bottle."

Scarface bowed his head.

"I… Scarface… I mean, Alfonso…"

"Your full name. And swear in the name of Nyarlathotep!" the shadow cried, shuddering.

Scarface lowered his head once again, and began his vow in a low voice.

"I, Alfonso Capone, swear in the name of Nyarlathotep to spread evil throughout the world."

With that he took the liquor bottle, and brought it to his mouth. He drained the blood from it in a single draft.

As he pulled the bottle from his mouth and wiped his lips, the shadow spoke.

"The Emperor of Darkness is born."

The Import of Tremors

Yamada Masaki
Translated by Kathleen Taji

The Import of Tremors

Yamada Masaki
Translated by Kathleen Taji

WHAT IS ONE of the fungoid crustaceans from Yuggoth doing in far-flung Japan? Don't you remember? Albert Wilmarth, protagonist of Lovecraft's "The Whisperer in Darkness," determined that they lived as far east, at least, as the Himalayas, where they were known as the Mi-Go, or Abominable Snowmen. This was also the area in which the undying Ascended Masters of the Cthulhu cult dwelt.

Masaki's chilling implication that the White Russian had recently, in effect, given birth to the Yuggoth parasite that had grown within him for years, is unsettling in the extreme. But then, come to think of it, so is the implication that even the crustacean Outer One had been but a host to the "wormy parasite" that emerged from its supine form! You will recall that in Lovecraft, the Outer Ones from Yuggoth are by no means supposed to be gods in their own right, not even worshipped as such by ignorant earthmen. No, as in this story, they themselves are worshippers of Shub-Niggurath, and this detail has given rise to August Derleth's perhaps unfortunate notion that the Mi-Go are the minions, a servitor race, for Shub-Niggurath. This business has always seemed to me to empty the whole arrangement, whatever it was, of much of its mystery. Too pat, somehow. The Mi-Go turn out not to be important enough in their own right. I think, though, that Yamada Masaki has gotten the balance right: the peculiar space lobster is alien enough, and yet it stands as a kind of living, concrete pointer to some yet-worse monstrosity.

What monstrosity might *that* be? Specifically, what our author had in mind was the Hanshin Earthquake in Kobe, ten years ago. This would be evident to Japanese readers, not so clear to the rest of us. But one can only muse whether some other hapless fools met tasty-looking Mi-Go somewhere in the interval, because, at the time of my writing, northern Japan has suffered a number of serious earthquakes. Our thoughts are with them.

Finally, there is a bit more to the perhaps puzzling comparison of the narrator and his ravenous companion to "hungry ghosts." You might want to know that, according to the afterlife cosmography of both Hinduism and Buddhism, there are six possible venues of postmortem rebirth. The exceedingly righteous (yet not quite enlightened) may return occupying the positions of traditional gods like Indra and Shiva. Slightly less saintly but still noble souls return as Asuras, the gods of aboriginal India, analogous to the Greek Titans. The third option would be the human race, subdivided into innumerable castes, subcastes, conditions, and fates. The fourth level is symbolically appropriate animal incarnations (the glutton returning as a pig, the thief as a magpie, etc.). The fifth is returning as a *Preta*, or hungry ghost, who drifts about suffering from a huge, empty, extended belly and a pin-hole size mouth fit only for sucking in linguini one strand at a time! This fate is like that of Tantalus, who ate food belonging to the Olympians and for his crime was damned to be suspended in a pool that rose up to his chin but retreated when he nodded to take a drink. He found himself just beneath the laden boughs of a fruit tree, whose branches would lift themselves out of his reach. Obviously, that is where we get the word "tantalize."

The Import of Tremors

1

In OCTOBER OF the year the war ended, I moved to Tokyo seeking the help of relatives, and I have not returned to my home town in the forty-nine years since. Whenever I speak of this to anyone, I candidly explain that I have no home, family, or friends to return to. On June 5, 1945, Kobe City was devastated in an air raid by a three hundred and fifty strong formation of B-29s. My home was completely burned out, and all the other members of my family died in that fire. I am the only survivor – a fact that is painful beyond words. I survived because I had been drafted into the labor force, and was working at a steel mill.

The simple truth is that I haven't wanted to face my grief and pain, which I know would return twofold if I were to go back to Kobe. But there's also another reason why I've never returned – that is, why I couldn't return. I've kept this reason a secret, hidden it in the deep recesses of my mind, and I've never revealed it to anyone. But because of certain changes that have occurred in my circumstances, I've begun to feel the need to leave behind a written record of it. I'll explain the nature of these changes in due course; but, first, I must begin by explaining why I've never returned – why I never could return – to my home town for these forty-nine long years.

In hindsight, my decision to put all this in writing was triggered by a visit to our local video rental shop with my ten-year-old grandchild yesterday afternoon, on my way home from the hospital. There was a certain *anime* she wanted to rent: a story set in Kobe during the war, during a B-29 air raid. It was a most curious setting for an *anime*.

"Grave of *Otaru*"! I froze for a moment when I heard the title. But, as my flash of panic subsided, I realized that she must have said "Grave of the Fireflies" – of "*Hotaru*". Even I knew that to be the successful work of a well-known novelist, Nosaka Akiyuki, although I hadn't read the book myself. Apparently, this *anime* was based on the original story. I had probably been distracted, momentarily lost in thought, and my mind had been elsewhere. I had been listening absentmindedly to her chatter, and I had mistakenly heard her say "Grave of *Otaru*" or perhaps "*Hotare*". In that instant, *something* in me had reacted strongly. Something shivered.

"What's that you say? 'Grave of *Otaru*'?" I sounded like a shrill, foolish old man. And I had probably turned pale.

"It's not 'Grave of *Otaru*', but 'Grave of the Fireflies' – of '*Hotaru*', she said in disgust.

"Oh, I see. 'Grave of the Fireflies', eh?" I nodded, convinced. But my heart continued to race. My mind had set out in a thousand directions on mistakenly hearing that "Grave of *Otaru*". My thoughts were unreasonably confused, and I was unable to stop my mind from wandering off to that strange, faraway place...

I don't remember his surname: I'm sure I heard it at some point in the past; but, then again, perhaps I never did. In any case, all I remember is his first name: Nikolai. He was a large, heavyset man with a distinguished beard; and, from my perspective – I was a fourteen-year old adolescent at the time – he appeared to be very old. It's difficult at the best of times to guess at the age of foreigners; but, in retrospect, he was probably in his middle forties. It was more than just his physical build, and that beard – Nikolai had an indefinable, melancholic air about him that made him seem even older than he was. He was what they called a White Russian émigré – that's a term from the old days that was still in use during the war. I remember that he lived in a mansion somewhere around the base of Mt. Rokko, although I wouldn't be able to pick out the exact location now.

The house was built in the Western style, with prominent gables and a tower; and it was known around the neighborhood as the "White Mansion" – either because of its strikingly white outer walls, or because it was the home of a White Russian émigré. That was what I'd heard from an adult, and this fragment remains stuck in my memory to this day. It seemed that while the basic structure of the White Mansion was done in a Romanesque style, its tower was Gothic – but, of course, at the time these nuances of style were beyond my adolescent understanding. In spite of my ignorance – or, really, because of it – I thought the house was a strange, odd-looking kind of building. The foundations of the house were a mix of bare earth and limestone, which extended through the estate grounds to a solid limestone bluff. This precipitous drop looked out over the distant, isolated town, and the Hanshin shoreline beyond.

But, somehow, my recollections appear to be confused. Even as I write this description of the White Mansion, I have an undeniable sense of its inconsistency. The White Mansion was located at the foot of Mt. Rokko, and looked out over a high bluff... Surely this is improbable topography. These days, I study the map in detail from time to time, but there just doesn't seem to be a place like that around Mt. Rokko. Moreover, such topography doesn't exist anywhere in Japan: a house at the foot of a mountain, yet one which also stands on a bluff. It was physically inconceivable. And, furthermore, does Mt. Rokko have any limestone formations? I must return to Kobe while I still have my wits about me, to confirm if that kind of thing actually exists at Mt. Rokko – although I rather doubt that it does. I've always wanted to make certain of this, but until now I've been unable to do so. One way or another, the entire situation seems unreal: the figure of Nikolai, and the existence of the White Mansion – they were equally surreal. And, recently, I've even begun to doubt that Nikolai himself ever really existed. But, of course, if I'm going to talk about their actual existence... The air raid... Three hundred and fifty B-29s flying in formation, relentless, incendiary bombs strewn in their wake, completely torching the districts of Ikuta, Nada, Suma... The ensuing conflagration, causing an immense number of innocent deaths... Even the event itself has begun to seem unreal.

The unending whine of the firebombs as they rained down on the city made a horrendous noise against the sound of the air raid bell clanging crazily, as the roofs of homes everywhere were bursting into flame. The flames streaked along the eaves, and the townspeople fled through a shower of sparks, pulling large carts, holding on to belongings bundled up in their bedding. A few were even toting their family Buddhist altars, even as flames from the burning wooden shutters rose in the air. They ran for their lives, shrieking in a chorus of screams. I tried to find my way home from the steel mill, but the sky in that direction was stained red. The air-raid warden was shouting through his megaphone "Go back, go back! It's impossible to go beyond this point", and I lost my courage.

The firebombs were like ricocheting jumping jacks, scattering oil in all directions as they hit. Heading for home was clearly dangerous. In fact, people were fleeing in the opposite direction; it was physically impossible to move against the flow of human traffic. I gave up on trying to find out if the other members of my family were all right. It couldn't be helped. I had to think of my own safety. Having made that decision, I fled single-mindedly through the raging fire; and when I finally regained some awareness of my surroundings, I found that I was running shoulder-to-shoulder with a classmate. I don't remember where or when we were thrown together. No matter how hard I try, I can't remember his name. I vaguely recollect an overly mature, seedy looking, acorn-shaped face. No other memories of him come to mind. I don't think we were especially close friends, since I can't even remember his name. In all probability, we were thrown together in a chance encounter as we fled the conflagration. One person became two people in the rush to escape the rain of firebombs. Since being a twosome didn't change the circumstances, it was more reassuring to take flight with a companion than to flee the fire alone. As we beat our retreat, we began to call out to each other.

"Are we going the right way, to get to the ocean?"

"I think so."

"I don't smell the sea."

"Look! Sake warehouses! This must be Nada district."

"All that sake must be nice and hot by now. How about a drink!"

"How stupid can you get! How you gonna outrun B-29s if you're drunk?"

Comforted by the sound of our own voices, we ran on. And yet, as close as we were, no matter how hard I try, I can't remember my companion's name. But it's awkward to continue my narrative if I can't call him by some kind of name, so I'll just refer to him as "S—" from here on.

S— suddenly stopped, and raised his arm. He cried out – startled, astonished – "Look! Over there! What's that?" It was just beyond his pointing finger: the White Mansion.

2

That air raid on Kobe was the most calamitous event in my life. But my recollections have become blurry over the span of forty-nine years, and everything has come to seem dreamlike. I try to jog my memories by watching war movies and documentary films, but that's no longer effective after nearly fifty years – and all the brain cells I've lost along the way. Recently, I've begun to wonder if these events really did occur in this world of ours. However…

For some reason, the White Mansion appeared distant. I will never forget the sight of that queer structure – a view that would never show up in a picture postcard. I had the singular impression that my five senses were subtly off-balance – this impression is deeply etched in my memory and remains with me to this day. There was a vast ocean of fire before us, and the Hanshin Railways embankment in front of us stretched all the way to Mt. Rokko in the distance. The sake warehouse, the military barracks: all were being reduced to charred rubble. Everything was torched and ablaze; purple smoke billowed up and rose in the sky, and then suddenly split apart to reveal the pale outline of the White Mansion in the distance. (Later in life, I was reminded of this moment when I saw the parting of the Red Sea in the movie "The Ten Commandments".) Even the blazing flames that were spewing forth everywhere were cleft in a v-shaped wedge around the White Mansion. A pale pink mist fanned out and it looked strangely *slippery*. The White Mansion shimmered hazily in the heat.

Back then, every Kobe resident knew of the White Mansion. Somehow, it was always in the corner of your eye wherever you looked, and we were constantly aware of it. Of course, this wasn't because it was a notable place of interest to tourists. I don't remember whether I knew Nikolai's name at the time, but I do know that I'd heard a rumor that an enigmatic White Russian émigré lived in the White Mansion. He was considered to be a mysterious figure…

It was rumored that, on the eve of May Day, a passerby had heard a weird buzzing sound – like the buzzing of bees – coming from the far side of the hedge around the White Mansion. Moreover, it had *resonance*, as though it were imitating human speech. No doubt it was a silly fabrication – like that urban legend, whispered among frightened schoolchildren, about a phantom slasher that attacked you in the toilet. But the point of the rumor was that all this supposedly occurred at night on the eve of May Day. According to old European folklore, that was Beltane: the Black Sabbat. (I discovered this fact much later in life.) As a fourteen-year old, I wasn't aware of these details; but, even if I had been, bizarre stories about the White Mansion would have lacked reality and menace before the sweeping expanse of fire around us. The fear of burning to death was much stronger than any scary story.

Looking at the White Mansion, S— cried out, "I'm gonna head up there, to that house. I don't think the fire will reach it." He began running in a panic. I agreed – those firebombs raining from the B-29s were much more terrifying than any childish horror story.

"Wait for me. I'm going too." I ran after S—.

I remember that a question did cross my mind for a moment: why the White Mansion appeared to be so high up, when it was supposed to be at the foot of the mountain.

My memories of what happened next aren't very clear, but we ran for our lives. When we reached the foot of Mt. Rokko and became aware of our surroundings, we found ourselves struggling up a steep bluff on a rugged path with a sheer drop on one side. The path was weakly illuminated by the fire. If we were at the foot of Mt. Rokko, the devastating fire that was consuming eastern Kobe City should have been right before our eyes, but here it spread out below us like a red carpet. Where was there such a towering bluff at Mt. Rokko? If it wasn't there, then where were we?

The rough path was narrow – just wide enough to accommodate two emaciated boys walking side by side. We picked our way carefully, going one step at a time so as not to dislodge the fragile rubble. A thick shower of sparks rose on an updraft beside us, and filled the air around us like a vast swarm of fireflies. The bluff rose sharply on one side, and it fell away frightfully on the other, down to where Kobe City lay spread out. The exposed face of the bluff showed what appeared to be strata of white limestone, reflecting the burning city, like bleached bones.

"I think this air raid unsealed the gates of hell. There's no other way to explain this," said S— breathlessly, his voice tinged with childish fear.

"That's stupid! There's no such thing."

"Have you ever seen a steep bluff like this at Mt. Rokko? There aren't any. This is the gateway to hell."

"Don't talk such rubbish. You'll give me the creeps."

I was in an inexplicably surly mood. Truth be told, I was just as frightened as S—: it was fear that fueled my unreasonable anger. Unlike S—, though, I didn't believe that this was the gateway to hell; but that crag of limestone rising steeply up from Mt. Rokko *was* peculiar, and something strange was happening – something very odd indeed.

The sky enveloped the trail of sparks, and billows of purple smoke rose in the air. I looked up, feeling an unnatural flow in the current of smoke around us. There, a B-29 appeared, massive, out of the purple cloud, like the bow of a ship rending the mist, and bore down heavily just over our heads with a deafening roar. They had come back around. Seconds later, even before we could feel the first rush of fear, the B-29 released a cloudburst of countless firebombs that began to patter to the ground. As we watched from afar, bright flames suddenly erupted all over Kobe City, like the back of a sheet of oilpaper being drawn across a candle. But, as terrifying as all this was, we really broke into a cold sweat when several firebombs dropped down onto the rugged path before us, and for a moment we wondered if it would bring down the bluff. A few seconds passed. Then pillars of fire rose up and drove spikes into the darkness before us. The burning oil scattered in the sky as bright red droplets. The darkness was completely reversed, and an explosion shook through the bright light of the flames, and resounded with a boom in our bellies. The White Mansion was clearly outlined in that flash of light, and a bright flame spewed out from its Gothic tower.

"…"

Without thinking, we looked at each other. There was no mistaking the look of indescribable misery, the expression of ravenous hunger, set into our faces: we were like a pair of starving ghosts, damned to eternal hunger. Clearly, we had both caught the same scent. If so, it was real: it was not an illusion. A seductive smell of something *marvelous* that whet the appetite was emanating from the burning White Mansion. This was the aroma of fish grilled over a charcoal brazier, of salt broiled clams, or shellfish cooked on the beach. The scent-memories welling up left me with a slight feeling of discomfort that you could also liken to a sense of anticipation.

My father was a very stubborn man who obstinately refused to have any truck with the black market. He maintained this very solitary decision at the expense of his family, and it became a source of adversity for me. Thus, I was afflicted with constant hunger during my peak growing years – a time of insatiable appetite – slurping up rice porridge that was little more than a few grains of mushy rice floating in boiling water. Dumpling gruel and dried potatoes were long gone. S— was no better off than I was. In the instant our eyes met, I recognized the selfsame expression on his face as I had on mine. All rational thought burned away to vapor when we realized our sense of smell wasn't playing tricks with us.

It was not uncommon in many homes to hide a supply of food in the air raid shelter. No doubt the White Russian émigré of the White Mansion had done the same thing. And now, a firebomb had come down and deliciously toasted all the food hidden in the mansion's air raid shelter. Since the master of the house was a Russian, it stood to reason that there was more than rice down

there – there was probably canned food, sugar, wheat, dried bis-
cuits. Wow! If a firebomb had fallen on the air raid shelter, there
was probably fresh-baked bread. There was probably butter stash-
ed away in there as well. How many years had it been since I'd had
a piece of freshly baked bread with butter…

We whooped with joy and ran noisily toward the house. We were
overcome by a consuming, ravenous hunger: that unnatural bluff
rising up from the foot of Mt. Rokko, and the dangerously poor
footing of the path – these were no longer of any concern to us.
A buzzing of bees in flight was faintly audible at the bottom of the
bluff. If one listened carefully, the low buzz that crept up the surface of the limestone could be heard to say "*Iä! Shub-Niggurath!
Black Goat of the Woods with a Thousand Young!*" But even this
had become immaterial.

3

I am as ignorant of Western architecture now, in my sixties, as I
was at fourteen. No matter how clever I may seem, bandying about
architectural terms like "Gothic" or "Romanesque", the words are
simply terminology to me – I have neither field-specific knowledge, nor any understanding of the styles the words describe. My
knowledge of Western architecture, and other subjects besides, is
sparse: I am an ignoramus. Despite all this, I *know* that the thick
doors of the White Mansion were Gothic, and that the delicate, detailed open-work design of the columns was Romanesque… I've
always wondered why this knowledge has come to be embedded
in my memory in such detail, even to this day. I am not a scholarly
person, who would set out to research this information later, nor
do I remember ever having been taught about it. Nonetheless,
the memory remains unnaturally vivid. How is this possible? It's
as though another person's memories had been grafted to my

consciousness. At the time, of course, S— and I were completely oblivious to whether we were seeing Gothic or Romanesque styles of architecture.

There was a gap in one section of the hedge around the White Mansion, and a misty smoke issued from that cleft. It was faintly pink in color; and, although common sense told us that it was just a reflection of the fires from the air raid, for some reason that color appeared to be continuously pulsating. An aroma emanating from this strange, vaporous smoke abnormally stimulated our appetites, and our need became more voracious the closer we approached. We salivated uncontrollably. We were like cats in heat. The pinnacle of human lust is undoubtedly the appetite. The queer pulsating and strange color were no deterrent to us, and we didn't hesitate. With cries of desire, we jumped through the opening in the hedge. For a very brief instant, a bizarre thought flashed across my mind – that the gap in the hedge was a crack in the world.

Shoulder-to-shoulder, S— and I landed in the garden of the estate. The bank of smoke had spread throughout the garden, and we were unable to make out its extent or form. Rather our appetites had grown beyond our control, and hunger's fangs were tearing at our innards. It was unbearable. We were giddy and just about raving. We were unable to think straight. Nothing mattered – neither the smoke nor the garden.

In June 1945, in the last stage of the war, all the common people were starving. Dried potatoes had long since disappeared; day-to-day, people were barely able to scrape together a meal of porridge from ground soybeans and wheat husks. All that was on our minds was *food*. It was natural that a delicious aroma of cooked food penetrating the nostrils of two starving boys would made them run all the more eagerly toward its source. We were undoubtedly in an abnormal state of mind. The only thought flooding our minds was of food, and only food. Without a moment's hesitation, the two of us plunged head first into the air raid shelter, undeterred by the smoke streaming out from the entrance. Who in their right mind would dive into an air raid shelter that was belching smoke? They would have to be foolhardy or stupid – or possessed by something beyond their control. If that were true, then what had taken control of us?

As we tumbled into the shelter, there seemed to be a swarm of bees buzzing in unison in a single bizarre voice in the dark recesses of my mind – "Yuggoth, Yog-Sothoth, Magnum Innominandam". It was probably an auditory hallucination. If it was *not* an auditory hallucination, perhaps it was a suggestion, whispered by the innumerable, unknown voices of whatever it was that had taken possession of us. "R'lyeh, Necronomicon, Cthulhu"… But, set upon by starvation, feeling as if our stomachs had been glued to our backs, nothing mattered – neither the "what" nor the "where" of that buzzing. Jostling each other for position, we raced down the few steps leading into the shelter.

The room was about four or five meters on a side. The walls and floors were made of concrete. The private power generator appeared to be working: the interior was dimly lit by a light bulb hanging from the ceiling. The light it gave off was no better than about ten candles of illumination. It was swaying slowly, despite the lack of any breeze or movement in the air, and we felt oddly uncomfortable. Fortunately, there was no sign of a fire, but there was also no evidence of food supplies – none whatsoever. There was only a wisp of that pinkish haze trailing up to the ceiling; but, strangely, it wasn't smoky there. The haze released an aroma that stimulated our appetites, accelerating our starvation, and my stomach felt as if it were being wrung out. Where was the aroma coming from? Where was the source…

As I looked curiously around the shelter, S— suddenly raised his voice.

"It's gourmet food," he exclaimed, and pointed to something in one of the corners.

His voice was unsteady, and he sounded like he was on the verge of drooling. How pathetic: he was a secondary school student! Feeling disgusted, I looked in the direction he was pointing. But in that instant, despite myself, I also cried out. Why hadn't I noticed it before? The swaying light had created a blind corner. There was *something* lying there, about the size of a large dog. Its color was the deep, vivid red of salmon meat. It had a cucumber-shaped body, and there was something like a mouth at one end, with waving tentacles like a sea anemone. Judging from its outer skin, it looked delicious and soft. But the warts on its back were unsight-ly. There were several rows of tubular protuberances around its stomach, which appeared to be legs. It could have been classed as a kind of echinoderm – like a starfish, or a sea urchin – but its bat-like wings made a classification like that somewhat doubtful.

"It's a sea cucumber – a sea cucumber. That's a real delicacy," S— cried out excitedly. As I listened to him, it started to seem like the wings didn't matter any more. "Their dried roe is a delicacy. The skin becomes smoked *bêche-de-mer*. Even its guts are a delicacy when they're salted – it's a mass of delicacies."

"Really? You sure it's not poisonous?"

"What are you – stupid? It's a delicacy. Don't you know anything about sea cucumbers? They're not poisonous."

"But… Look at it…"

I was about to tell him that sea cucumbers didn't have large wings on their backs. But, as I gazed at it, it looked so delicious that I began to salivate uncontrollably. It was unbearable. The creature spread out its wings once, then twice, as if to greet us, which made it seem even more appealing – almost adorable. There was an overwhelming urge… To eat. The urge grew more powerful until it was impossible to think of anything else.

"No need for you lads to stand around waiting. Come on, come on: eat, eat." That was what I thought I heard it saying – I was impressed that it could communicate telepathically. Suddenly, I felt like drooling. Everything else was irrelevant. I couldn't control myself unless I consumed that creature.

S— and I looked at each other for a moment. Our unspoken question – should we eat the thing, or not. We nodded in silent agreement. Turning to face the creature, we took one step forward…

Suddenly, we heard a voice behind us, coming from the entrance of the shelter.

"N–no, don't. Don't be deceived by that thing. Something monstrous will happen if you eat it!"

The owner of the voice was in pain – it was none other than the master of the White Mansion: Nikolai himself. This was the first time I found myself so close to him, this man who had been the talk of the town: I had only caught sight of him from a distance before. And, as fate would have it, this would also be my last time to see him, since he was destined to take his final, dying breath in only ten minutes.

4

I have already described Nikolai as being large and heavyset, but that was before the war hastened the depletion of food rations. In all likelihood, there were no overweight people in wartime Japan. Nikolai was no exception, and his skin tone appeared dull and lifeless. He had that gaunt, unhealthy look typical of obese people who have lost weight quickly. Of course, it was only natural that he appeared dull and lifeless at the time. I was to learn later that he had undergone surgery not long before. Moreover, his postoperative recovery had been unsatisfactory – due to the extreme scarcity of supplies, equipment, and human resources during the war – and he had been given only a few more months to live.

During the air raid, Nikolai had been caught under a burning beam when it fell, and his lower extremities had been completely shattered. Although he had somehow managed to extricate himself and reach the shelter, he would hemorrhage to death within ten minutes. Despite his condition, he could still use the doorframe of the shelter to support his body; his bloody, shattered limbs were splayed out along the stairs. As he lay dying, he said, "Don't eat that thing. Don't be deceived. It cleverly manipulates people into eating itself... It lives in the human body for years, decades, snug and tight, while it nurtures disaster and calamity. When the evil grows big enough, the thing leaves the host's body – and lets loose an enormous disaster in the human world. Look at this terrible devastation, this brutal massacre! It's all due to that thing, the..."

Nikolai then spoke its name – but the sound of the name was very alien, and difficult to voice, due to the structural limitations of the human throat. What has remained in my memory to this day, after a span of forty-nine years, is something that sounded like "Ktulu" or "Kthulhutl." But it could be both, or it could be neither.

There is only an abridged translation of the *Necronomicon* in Japan; and, after the war, I was introduced to a certain Mr. Uchida, a researcher specializing in this tome, through a third party. I asked him what the name of that creature could possibly have been. I was confounded when he asked me if it had been *Magnum Innominandam*, a name that took me completely by surprise. It meant "the great nameless one" and it did sound somewhat familiar. But it was unmistakably something very different from what I had heard Nikolai say. I wrote Mr. Uchida informing him of this; but, for some reason, I never received a reply...

Although I was unable to make out the name of the creature,

Nikolai, drawing painful breaths, continued his story. That's when I heard him mention "the grave at Otaru". Leaving aside the more obscure details of the circumstances, it seemed that Nikolai had made his way to Hokkaido in his escape from the Russian Revolution, and had lived in Otaru for a short period of time. That was when he encountered the creature. The Oshoro Stone Circle, which has inscriptions in an undeciphered ancient language, is in the vicinity of Otaru – thanks to that, Otaru is known as a mysterious place to this day. It seems that Nikolai consumed the creature while he was up in that area. He only mentioned the "grave at Otaru" in passing, and did not give a specific location.

And then Nikolai finished his tale – or, rather, he was forced to end it. The creature's constant, seductive invitations to eat it had become so intense that S— and I were losing our sanity.

"Stop! Don't eat it! If you do, a terrible catastrophe will fester away in you – and the time will come – that someday, the new evil will be let loose on humanity!" He was screaming. But, by this time, his words were lost on S—, who staggered along a wavy line toward the creature. He had an idiotic grin on his face.

I heard the creature's voice in my head – or, at least, that's what I thought it was.

"Oy, it's all right. Right? Everything's fine. Why should humans have to put up with every little thing? It's bad for your health, right? Follow your instincts. Just accept what you need – that's all for the best, right?"

The final words of the creature seemed to echo derisively in my head. At the same time, a tangled mass of white, wormy parasites – or it could have been an intestinal mass – issued noisily from its mouth, undulated on the floor, and wriggled its way towards S—. The brimming mass spread out over several meters along the floor. S— cried out joyfully.

"What do you know! We're gonna die soon in the war anyway. The last battle's going to be fought in the homeland. It won't matter if we eat it. There won't be enough time for any evil to grow in *us*." So saying, he scooped up the white wriggling mass with both hands and started to bite into it.

Nikolai shouted "Stop!" and there was an explosion of sound and a flash of light. The blast of a gunshot resounded in the shelter. S—'s body jerked back, and his feet hung briefly in midair as he landed. There was blood seeping out of his head and spreading out over the floor. Although S— was dead, his mouth continued to twitch, as if he were eating something. It was indescribably pathetic.

"What have done, you murderer!" I shouted furiously as I turned back to Nikolai. But he never heard me.

The gun had fallen from Nikolai's hand. He was dead. The upper part of his body slumped forward, and he slid headlong with a clatter down the steps. I remember feeling very forlorn, seeing the weak illumination from the light bulb reflecting off the back of his bald head.

The creature turned in my direction. As it undulated its mass of intestines – or whatever it was – it said, in a complaining tone, "Well, what's the matter? Eat as much as you like." And it laughed.

I recalled S—'s last words. He was right; it was inevitable. The decisive battle of the war was going to be fought in the homeland. If this creature really was the cause of the air raid, and of the ocean of fire that was consuming Kobe City, it was understandable why Nikolai would be tormented by insane remorse. But all of us were going to die in the war anyway. There wouldn't be enough time for the creature to grow to devastate the city again.

Those wormy parasites, that intestinal mass, began to move in my direction, with a rasping sound. I heard a laughing voice. I remain unsure to this day as to whether it was the creature or me that was laughing…

My story is nearly completed.

An interval of forty-nine years has passed. It's not clear whether the events I describe were real, or if they were all part of a hallucination that came over me while the smoke and fire pursued me. I say that because, shortly after the war, I think I caught sight of S—, once, somewhere – but my memory of this is vague. Likewise, I'm not confident about that reference to "the grave of Otaru." I later came to know that the word *hotare* is a disparaging reference to a sloppy beheading on the battlefield – when an unsightly piece of flesh remains dangling at the point where the head has been severed from the body. So it may have been a "grave of *hotare*" and I do hope I haven't offended anyone from Otaru.

Truth be told, I have cancer. Moreover, it's reached the terminal stage, and I don't have long to live. But that's fine: I've lived long enough, and I leave behind no regrets. Next year will mark the fiftieth anniversary of the end of the war. I'm thinking that I'll make a trip to Kobe early next year, and just forget about the circumstances of my past. After all, I was born and raised in Kobe. Lately, that's what I've been thinking about doing – but there's one thing I've been feeling uneasy about...

Recently, on occasion, in my sleep I've been hearing a faraway, derisive voice saying "*Iä! Shub-Niggurath! Black Goat of the Woods with a Thousand Young!*"

27 May 1945

Kamino Okina
Translated by Steven P. Venti

27 May 1945

Kamino Okina
Translated by Steven P. Venti

WHAT IF THE history we know were merely one half of a telephone conversation? What if, short of hearing a transcript of the whole thing, we could never hope to know what had really happened? Suppose that crucial battles of World War Two witnessed the employment of American and Japanese Imperial forces as mere proxies for the ever-warring factions of Hastur and his half-brother Cthulhu? We have here an excellent case of the ancient biblical belief in Principalities and Powers behind the mundane thrones of what we mortals imagine to be our so-powerful kingdoms. Really just puppets. This portrayal is clear from this story's depiction of Japanese and American forces as equally suffering, equally intrepid, both simply doing the duty someone else has assigned them, and trying to stay alive in the process. They are most certainly not in charge.

The relationship of the Old Ones of Lovecraft to the Shinto deities implied in this story is a good microcosm of that obtaining in the subgenre as a whole. The Shinto gods are a classic instance of a remotely archaic religion synonymous and conterminous with the culture in which it occurs. But, for the story's sake, we are to imagine that the cult of the Old Ones somehow predates it. Since there can be no scientific dating of either faith, even under the terms of the narrative universe of a story like this, what are we to make of competing claims to historical priority? They become symbols of *logical* priority. And the issue of this equation is the revelation of a vision akin to that of Arthur Machen in "The Great God Pan." There Machen presents a model of reality which sees the cosmos of order and sanity as a secondary construct artificially imposed upon the raw and natural state of Chaos. This Chaos is inimical to humanity insofar as "humanity" designates civilized bipeds who strive for a functional society within the confines of reason. As Jacques Lacan puts it, we must accept the minting stamp of "the law of the father" and thus lose a significant amount of freedom and individuality if we are to become dependable and predictable members of a functioning society, such as Japan has always been to an extraordinarily high degree.

If I may venture a probably gratuitous historical allegory, I wonder if the reference in the present story to the invasive Admiral Perry, a powerful "Andromeda Strain" ultimately fatal to traditional Japanese culture, does not call the tune for the whole tale. Was that infection with the West only the beginning of the self-caricaturing Westernization of Japan, drowning in American pop culture, we are witnessing today? Is the invasion of pop Western culture the reality behind the erupting Chaos of Cthulhu that threatens in this story?

27 May 1945

THE STENCH WAS everywhere – sweat, excrement, and decay mingled with something scorched. Repeated bombardment had pulverized the houses and buildings until what little that remained of these devastated communities was not so much rubble as it was gravel. The earth itself had been rent apart, leaving innumerable crevices in which rainwater accumulated and maggots bred.

The dead lay strewn about, neither counted nor mourned, and the bodies of young and old, Japanese and American alike, lay interspersed with the remains of goats, cows, or any other creature that had been foolish enough to move and thereby draw the indiscriminate fire of both friend and foe. Throughout the entire landscape, the only living things enjoying freedom and singing the praises of youth were the flies and maggots that crawled about the corpses.

Of those humans who were still alive, there was hardly a soul on either side of the conflict who cared to do anything other than lie low in the dark, fusty confines of the man-made entrenchments or natural caves that dotted the island. There was, in fact, no better place to hide than one of the gigantic, tortoise-shell-shaped traditional Okinawan mausoleums. There, moaning and shivering in fear, just one wrong step away from lunacy, any sane human could see that madness itself had occupied the island of Okinawa on this day of May 27, 1945.

In the middle of the rainy season, the only thing more oppressive than the muddy boots or the sweat that clung to your skin, hair, and clothes was the stench. It was enough to make a person's nose go numb, except that it didn't, and the only relief to be had was from an occasional sea breeze.

Having gone on for what seemed an eternity, the bombardment from the American battleships died away momentarily.

Crouching at the bottom of a freshly dug trench was a group of men covered from head to foot with dried grass. Each one sported a face streaked with mud, a uniform that had turned a grimy shade of black, and an odor that could only come from the accumulated sweat and filth of a month without a bath. Although free of rainwater, corpses, or maggots, the trench was little more than a crawl space crammed not just with the men but also BARs and other weapons stripped from the enemy dead. The weapons had been propped atop steel helmets and were ready for action at any time. Surrounding the squad leader were the remaining seven men of the unit; some were peering out over the top of the trench while others just waited for orders. The men all carried extra weapons, including Nambu pistols in holsters on their right hips along with Colt automatics that had also been scavenged from the enemy dead.

The squad leader was staring silently across the darkness at the American lines, which were lit up like it was Christmas.

Ordinarily, the last thing anyone on the front lines would do at night would be to shine a light, but the Americans apparently feared the darkness – and the opportunity for a night attack that it presented to the Japanese – even more than sniper fire. They seemed convinced that as long as the area was well lit, the sneaky Japanese would not attack, and they used every light available to keep their own position well illuminated.

Just beyond the glare of those lights was where the enemy lay.

The Americans wielded not only several times the number of

soldiers the Japanese could muster, but also an inexhaustible supply of resources. They were an enemy that came on like a landslide – moving ever forward and never relinquishing an inch in the advance toward the objective: the Japanese headquarters housed in the caves deep beneath Shuri Castle.

Unknown to the Americans, however, was the fact that several days previously, Lieutenant General Ushishima Mitsuru, commander of the 32nd Imperial Japanese Army and the officer responsible for the defense of Okinawa, had given the order to evacuate headquarters. The majority of the army had already headed south, and the only troops remaining were a rear guard, whose objective was to delay the enemy advance for as long as possible.

Actually, the rear guard had two objectives. The first was to provide the retreating 32nd Army with as much time as possible to move south. The second was to kill as many of the enemy as they could before dying in battle themselves.

It was a tactic that smacked of failure, yet there was no defeat in the hearts of the men who had been called on to carry out this duty. After months of forced inactivity due to lack of supplies and day after day of sulking in dark, dank caves with little to eat or drink, all the while enduring a torrential enemy bombardment that afforded almost no chance to bathe or even defecate properly, the opportunity to fight like a soldier at last had, in fact, brought with it a feeling of release to the hearts of Izuma Shirō and his men.

Izuma licked his parched lips and fondled the grip of his pistol. He closed his eyes and tried to rest but was too excited to remain that way for even a minute.

"What's the matter, Lieutenant? Can't sleep?"

The question was followed by a humorless laugh from Sergeant Saitō, the square-headed, narrow-eyed non-com who was sitting next to Izuma.

"Who the hell can get to sleep?"

"That's for sure. Almost every one of these guys has his eyes shut, but there isn't one of them that's asleep."

The two men laughed voicelessly.

There was a very simple reason for these haggard men to feel so invigorated: the prospect of death offered release from this living hell. Each of them had begun to realize that this battle no longer held any meaning beyond buying precious little time for the Japanese mainland. It was a war which they could not win, and the only real word for a war without victory was defeat.

These men knew that their deaths would be meaningless, yet there was a big difference between just sitting around waiting and jumping into the fray feet first.

"You don't suppose they'd be good enough to attack and get it over with, do you?"

"I wish they would," agreed Izuma. "Though I would hate to reach the old soldiers' home in the sky only to find that there's no room left for us."

"There's a lot of good men dead already, even just here on Okinawa."

"Tell me about it," said Izuma, who was clearly affected by the thought even as he continued to peer into the surrounding shadows. Suddenly, he drew his Nambu pistol from its holster and shouted into the void, "Who's there?!"

Sergeant Saitō quickly seized one of the BARs.

"Please. Don't shoot," spoke a voice calmly.

Izuma's finger lay frozen on the trigger as a pale face emerged from the darkness.

For the thousands of American soldiers at the front, the Okinawan nights were the worst time of all.

"Goddamn them!" muttered buck private Roy Whitaker as he huddled in the position he had dug out of the face of Sugarloaf

Hill. This position overlooking Shuri Castle was one that had been taken only after a long, vicious battle.

The intermittent rain of the past few days had soaked the earth to the point where the men had nowhere to dry their feet in the muddy compost they called foxholes.

"Goddamn Japs. Goddamn Japs!"

Whitaker repeated the same phrase over and over again as if he were casting a spell. He finally shut his yap only after realizing that he was keeping others from getting to sleep.

Like almost every other American soldier who had buddied up, Whitaker was sitting back to back with another soldier, a guy named George Conroy, who had fallen into a light sleep. Gaining a sense of relief from the fact that his buddy could sleep, Roy raised his head and looked at the sky.

It was almost eerie how the stars in the skies above this southern island looked so close.

His very first night on the island, he had sat in a nice, dry, freshly dug foxhole, but had been too tense even to think of looking up at the sky. Now, squatting in a messy combination of mud and filth, he had the wherewithal to look around. Anyone who had been able to stay alive on the front line for more than two days knew that the last thing you ever wanted to do was leave your foxhole. Roy's eyes soon returned to ground level as he kept his five senses attuned to any perceptible change in the surrounding area. He had learned in the past few months to be sensitive to any change in sound or appearance, and even to changes in odor.

"This is the pits," he thought. "I'd rather be anywhere than Okinawa."

It made no difference that the US Marines and Army infantry were renowned for their courage under fire. There was no mistaking that this was one battle no one wanted any part of.

Given their overwhelming superiority in manpower and materials, the occupation of Okinawa should have been no more difficult a task for the invaders than crushing a tin can would have been for an elephant. Even so, from L-Day on, the Japanese had resisted with a desperate determination that showed no signs of waning. The Americans had come to be wary of Japanese weapons such as the 50-mm grenade dischargers and the 81-mm light mortars, which were frightening enough to have earned the nickname *Screaming Meemies*. What they had learned to fear more than anything, however, was the nighttime, which brought with it those desperate attacks known as "banzai charges."

Historically speaking, it was standard military strategy to avoid nighttime operations as much as possible due mainly to the danger of casualties from friendly fire. Faced with an insurmountable disadvantage in terms of materials and re-supply, however, the Japanese adopted the strategy of attacking at night in small groups of enlisted men with fixed bayonets led by officers armed with samurai swords. Such groups were less susceptible to friendly fire, and with great care and tenacity could infiltrate the enemy's position. Once all was ready, they would pounce fearlessly upon an unsuspecting enemy, killing as many as possible before slipping away into the darkness.

Countless American soldiers had experienced the horror of waking up to find themselves next to a buddy who had been bayoneted to death, and they feared these night attacks more than anything.

To avoid being mistaken for the enemy, the Americans used a password when moving around at night, but even then there were numerous casualties from friendly fire.

So when Roy heard the sound of boots biting into the dirt somewhere nearby, he instinctively reached for the Colt .45 that was holstered on his cartridge belt. Enlisted men were not ordinarily issued pistols, but several days previously Roy had taken the weapon from the body of the third leader his platoon had had in as many days. Now he held it ready against approaching danger.

"Hey, it's me! Don't shoot!"

At the edge of the foxhole, a big grin on his face, stood the latest addition to the series of officers who had taken over Roy's platoon.

"What the hell is going on, Lieutenant?"

As he put the pistol back in its holster, Roy wondered how any officer could be so stupid, even one who was barely older than Roy himself.

"Where'd you get that?"

"It was willed to me by your predecessor," said Roy brusquely.

When it came to defending a foxhole, a pistol was a lot less unwieldy than an M1 rifle, which was why the more experienced a soldier was, the more he coveted one. Roy had finally gotten his hands on one, and wasn't about to give it up because of some damned Army regulation.

"Is that right."

The lieutenant didn't seem particularly concerned with the issue, and moved on to the next subject.

"Listen, Roy."

It was hard to believe, but in less than a day, this guy had already learned the names of all of the men under his command.

"Doesn't this smell remind you of something?"

"The only things I smell are gunpowder, rotting flesh, and dung."

"Is that right."

The lieutenant sounded somehow disappointed.

"Hey, George. What about you?"

"Yes, sir. I'd know that smell anywhere."

Until just a moment ago, George had been wrapped up in a rancid old blanket, catching some shut-eye, but now he was suddenly wide awake.

"Ah, so you're the one," said the lieutenant, evidently pleased.

"Are there any others, sir?"

"Everyone except the guy behind you."

"Wonderful. This is going to be good."

Roy felt a strange sense of bewilderment run up and down his spine while he listened to these two talk as if they were planning a picnic.

"Lieu… Lieutenant?"

Here he was, about to be made the odd man out, and it didn't take a genius to understand the danger in that.

What the hell is going on? he wondered. *This is the American position. These guys aren't Japs, they're my buddies: the same blond, blue-eyed brothers who have all gone through hell together to get here.*

Roy suddenly realized that his hand was on the handle of the Colt automatic.

"Would it be too much to ask just exactly what you guys are talking about?"

The lieutenant smiled at Roy pleasantly.

"It's all very simple. We're going to take that castle. Platoon! Ten-hupt!"

No sooner had the lieutenant's brisk voice reverberated with that command than the eeriest of scenes unfolded. The entire platoon leapt from their foxholes, which only a moment before had been more precious than life itself, and fell into rank. Although a step behind the others, Roy realized that it might look as if he were refusing to obey a command, and quickly lined up.

"Platoon, prepare to attack!"

Although no one responded with "Yes, sir," it was clear that – with the exception of Roy – the entire platoon was raring to go. Yet the next moment was just long enough for Roy to notice that no one drew their weapon or made any other move to get ready.

"Um, Lieu… Lieutenant?… Sir?"

Roy was bewildered enough by this preposterous scenario to start asking questions when all hell broke loose.

The other soldiers suddenly fell to their knees as the surrounding air began to quiver with the strangest of sounds. Roy saw George's waistline and upper back suddenly expand and his entire uniform bulge from the inside out. With a rip and a snap, buttons, belts, and pieces of shredded uniform flew through the air as more than a dozen pairs of wings burst forth from blood-splattered shoulders. Where a moment before a platoon of American soldiers had stood, a pack of malformed creatures now struggled to rise. The black membranes of bat-like wings spread wide, beating at the air with powerful strokes and shaking away mucus and phlegm. Roy covered his face with his arm as a powerful wind beat the surface of the ground and swirled the dust about.

From the seat of George's pants burst forth a cigar-shaped object. About the size of the torso of a child and sporting a slick sheen of blood, it writhed slowly as if floating in the air. Roy heard something fall to the ground with a thud, and turned to look. The creatures were now hovering in mid-air on bat-like wings, which meant that the cigar-shaped thing, whatever it was, now formed their lower bodies, and those things lying there on the ground below were more than a dozen pairs of human legs.

The creature in front of Roy turned its head to look back over its shoulder at him. Roy saw George's familiar, playful, blue eyes bulging from their sockets until they finally burst, and in their place appeared two bright red disks covered with innumerable hexagonal facets. From the creature's mouth dribbled a number of small white particles. Roy's eyes followed them to the ground where they fell, and saw incisors, canines, and molars lying there between the two discarded legs. Near the teeth also lay a ring-shaped piece of flesh attached to another triangular piece with two holes in it: lips and a nose.

Roy realized what he would see if he looked up, and he knew full well that he shouldn't, but his eyes moved in that direction anyway. There, floating against the background of the night sky was an open nasal cavity that transitioned smoothly into a lipless mouth with gleaming pink gums. All that was left of George was the shape of the head and the hair that adorned it. A spitting sound came out of the back of the creature's throat, and a semi-elliptical piece of flesh fell to the ground. Roy covered his mouth with his hand only to feel vomit seeping out from between his fingers.

With its wings fluttering rapidly, the creature hovered there in the sky, and turned its red, multi-faceted eyes in Roy's direction. Toothless, tongueless, and inarticulate, the creature spoke in George's artless voice: "Khammin'… whiss… huss??"

Roy screamed, and ran blindly into the darkness.

Deserted by the army headquarters staff, the underground facilities beneath Shuri Castle remained occupied only by cold, stale air.

Once inside, Izuma began to search for something that could be used as a torch. Eventually, he found a piece of firewood that would serve that purpose, and darkness at last gave way to light.

What had once been a repository for the official documentation of the Kingdom of Ryūkyū had been expanded and reinforced with a hodge-podge of concrete to create army headquarters. Until just a few days ago it had been filled with a stagnant mixture of dust and exhaled air. The withdrawal of the army, however, had jostled the atmosphere just enough to make it less oppressive.

"Let's head on in, then. Are you ready?"

Izuma spoke over his shoulder in a hushed voice to his companion, who nodded in assent.

For the past several months, Izuma's ability to perceive even the slightest change in the surrounding environment had become almost as keen as that of a wild animal. The same could probably be said of almost every soldier – Japanese or American – who had thus far managed to survive. Now he became aware that this petite woman with finely delineated, pale features and a sweetly feminine fragrance to her perspiration was breathing just as calmly as she had been before they scrambled up the steep foothills surrounding Shuri Castle.

She's no slouch, thought Izuma, half in astonishment and half in admiration, as he slackened the pace just a bit.

His companion was named Ishikina Aya and she was the holder of a hereditary title, called *noro* in the local language, which entitled her to participate in indigenous religious ceremonies. It was a title her family had held since the days when Shuri Castle served as residence to the kings of Ryūkyū. For some reason, she also held a letter from the commandant of the 32nd Army, General Ushishima, that read quite simply:

I would appreciate it if you would perform whatever tasks this woman requests.

Izuma's decision had been all the more difficult because it was not an official communiqué but rather a personal letter, complete with florid signature. In spite of the fact that he had never had any personal contact with Ushishima, the letter seemed to contain some hidden implication.

Aya, on the other hand, had begun issuing directions without even bothering to confirm whether Izuma and his platoon were willing to comply with the request. When asked by Izuma about their objective, she responded ominously: "We are to locate certain critical materials and either transport them a safe location or destroy them."

Izuma had other questions he wanted answered as well. He had no memory of this woman ever appearing at headquarters before, and was curious to know how she had come into possession of a personal letter from General Ushishima, not to mention how she had been able to locate his platoon. He kept these to himself for the time being, however, because he anticipated that all would become clear once this mission had been completed.

So he had led his platoon as far as the entrance to the abandoned headquarters beneath Shuri Castle, where they had remained while he accompanied the woman into the underground.

"Ready to go in?" he had asked.

"Of course," came the reply.

It was a totally guileless answer for a woman about to enter a darkened labyrinth alone with a man, but it seemed entirely natural to Izuma. After prolonged exposure to this interminable battle and its constant shelling, almost all of the men in headquarters had entered a machine-like mental state in which they no longer felt hunger or sexual desire.

The woman appeared quite unfazed and walked briskly forward into the darkness as Izuma hurriedly followed from behind.

"Where is this stuff located? These *critical materials*."

"At the back of this area," said the woman, pointing to a document repository that Izuma himself had been in and out of on several occasions. Izuma followed from behind, shaking his head. After brushing away the dust in a far corner of the room, the woman thrust a crooked forefinger deep into the floor. When she pulled it back out, it held a small metallic ring attached to a chain. She gave a powerful tug, and the sound of stone rubbing against metal could be heard faintly. Dust suddenly puffed out from a section of the wall, which then swung back with a heavy sound. The wall continued to move until a large opening appeared. Izuma had expected it to be pitch black, but from behind the wall came a faint glow.

Not to mention the smell of water.

Where is this light coming from? thought Izuma.

What the…?

Izuma felt his breast well up with a certain human emotion that he had for some time abandoned as having no place on the field of battle: curiosity.

"No need for a torch in here," said Aya quietly. "Leave it in one of the other rooms, please."

"Oh, yeah. I will."

Although he acquiesced to the soft-spoken request, he was left somehow vaguely unconvinced that the torch was unnecessary or that it would be all right just to leave it in one of the other rooms. It seemed to Izuma that such an action could only be a ploy to throw whoever might be following them off the track.

Izuma stomped on the torch until it was out, and then left it a short distance away, in what used to be the communications room.

"Let's be on our way, then," said Aya as she turned and headed through the opening in the wall with such a brisk and nimble step that she seemed to be gliding.

It was then that Izuma noticed for the first time that she never seemed to look at anything higher than her own shoulder level. No sooner had he made his way through the opening than the wall swung itself closed, shutting off all sound from the world outside.

"What do you suppose they're going after, anyway?" said one of the soldiers who had been left behind at the entrance to the underground headquarters. Once Izuma and his companion had gone inside, the rest of the platoon began digging foxholes with their bayonets so as to be ready to defend their position should the enemy attack. Ordinarily, the men would buddy up so that one could get some rest while the other stood watch. Now that they were all awake, however, none of them seemed inclined to go to sleep again, and the conversation naturally gravitated to the question of why they were there and what they were doing.

"I wouldn't mind having to escort her myself," said a second soldier.

Ignoring the second remark, the sergeant addressed the initial query.

"I wouldn't know. But it's something that somebody high up thinks is important. Maybe gold ingots or something."

No one said "Wow!" aloud, but a feeling of excitement spread throughout the platoon, all of whom seemed in rather high spirits for men who might find themselves dead in the wink of an eye. Even though it required an effort to keep their voices low, the conversation just wouldn't go away.

"Come to think of it, Okinawa used to be known as the Kingdom of the Ryūkyūs, didn't it?"

"So what are you saying? That there's royal treasure still in there?"

"Idiot! You've been reading too many pirate stories."

"How would you know what it is or isn't? Treasure or not, what it might be is, you know, one of those new bombs that's the size of a matchbox."

"Oh, you mean the one they took over the whole National Sumo Arena just to build?"

"Yeah, that's the one. I heard it uses a special explosive. Maybe that's what they went for."

"If it is, I hope they bring it out and start using it!"

"If it does have some special explosive, I doubt it would be of any help to us."

The men continued to speculate even while keeping an eye out for the unexpected. Suddenly, with a cry of "It's the Americans!" one of them grabbed a light machine gun and began to spray bullets into the darkness. Hearing the shrill and distinctive voice of automatic rifle fire, the remaining soldiers quickly grabbed their weapons and pointed them in the same direction. In the distance, innumerable red spots of light could be seen approaching rapidly. They swooped in so quickly, it was terrifying.

Having passed through the opening in the wall, they walked for some time down a corridor that ended in a stairway. Taking the stairway down, they came to a long waterway constructed of black marble.

It was clear that the waterway was a man-made construction, although it did not appear to be particularly old. Nor did there appear to be a spot of moss anywhere, despite the volume of water it contained. Some hidden mechanism allowed a soft light to emanate from the bottom of the channel, permitting unimpeded vision.

Where in the world…?

Izuma's first coherent thought was to question why the upper echelon of command had kept the existence of this place a secret.

Why in hell did we have to go so thirsty for so long with all this water here?

General Ushishima was not the kind of man who would allow his officers free use of water when the enlisted men had none, and everyone at headquarters had had their water rationed. But why on earth would he have given this woman that kind of letter if he had not known about this place?

"This place has long been a secret," said Aya, ignoring Izuma's consternation, and plunged into the water with a splash.

The channel was much deeper than it appeared to be, coming up almost to the woman's shoulders.

"Let's be on our way. We haven't much time."

"Wait! Wait just a minute," said Izuma as he hurried to catch up.

The coral reef that formed the wall surrounding Shuri Castle was six meters wide at its base, twelve meters high, and two kilometers in circumference. Even after three days of continuous bombardment by the battleships *Colorado* and *Mississippi*, it was still intact. In the course of that pounding, however, there was one brief lull that had come about as the result of the actions of a single soldier.

This particular soldier was on his way to a hospital ship and a sure trip home when he suddenly began speaking incoherently and jumped from the landing craft that was transporting wounded from the island. He swam as far as the *Mississippi*, a few kilometers away, made his way aboard the ship, and tried to find the powder magazines, where he apparently intended to blow himself up.

Fortunately, this crazed casualty of war was shot full of holes by the guards before he ever had a chance to reach his target, and as he fell overboard back into the ocean, he was blown to smithereens by the hand grenades wrapped around his body.

The captain of the *Mississippi* ordered that the soldier's dog tags be recovered, or at the very least, a description be taken so that his identity could be verified, but the guards who had been involved in the incident looked very pale as they described what had happened: "I have no idea who it was. He looked like the Frog-Footman from *Alice in Wonderland*. I know you're not going to believe me, but the guy had webbed hands and feet."

What the…?

After thirty minutes of walking downstream, they had come to a point where the channel suddenly widened into a chamber or what might even be accurately described as a small pond.

At the center of this circular pond stood a round island made of the same black marble as the channel. Atop this island sat a pedestal that appeared to be made of either stone or metal and to have been hollowed out in an irregular hand. Ensconced in that depression was a mysterious-looking idol made of some dark-colored material. A closer look revealed shiny spots on the surface where it had been handled, clearly indicating that it was made of metal.

Izuma and Aya both came to a natural halt at the same spot.

"There is the deity."

"The deity?"

To an ordinary Japanese like Izuma, the idol bore no resemblance to what a *deity* might be expected to look like. The head was shaped like an octopus with a face made up of innumerable

tentacles. Its sleek body was covered with scales and was otherwise featureless except for a slender pair of bat-like wings folded
on its back and gigantic hooked claws that sprung from the paws
of both its fore and hind legs.

The image had been created according to ideals that were exactly the opposite of the beauty and light inherent in the concept
of a deity, yet with such exacting and realistic detail that Izuma
flinched at its very sight even though he knew it was nothing more
than a sculpture.

It had been carved in relief out of the side of a piece of metal in
such detail that the viewer was given the illusion that the creature
itself was lying right there before his very eyes.

Without realizing it, Izuma raised the barrel of his submachine
gun and pointed it at the carving.

"I don't know what kind of deity this is supposed to be, but
it's…"

He was about to say *grotesque*, but the word stuck in his throat.
Izuma felt some resistance to putting on a display of insolence
while standing before any kind of deity.

"Yes," said Aya in a hushed voice, "It is quite distinct from the
deities of Shinto or Christianity. This is a god of death and misfor-
tune: our Lord of malevolence."

She took the small knapsack she had been carrying, and being
careful not to get it wet, placed it atop the island. Then she began
to undress.

"Whoa!"

Izuma quickly turned his back. To his shame, in the less than
forty minutes that he had been away from the sound of the
battlefield, his mind had already become reacquainted with the
once-forgotten concept of desire.

As it happened, however, there was no need for embarrassment;
Aya was wearing a light silk kimono beneath her soldier's uniform.
The dark red color of the garment, however, seemed to belie its

role as a religious vestment. More than anything else, it evoked the image of blood. Perhaps *evoke* was not even right word because cutting suddenly through the fresh scent of the water was an all-too-familiar odor of the battlefield: the scent of dried blood.

"That kimono... it's been..."

"Yes, it has been dyed with human blood."

And just as if all of this should have been obvious, she took from her pocket a headband also dyed in the same color, which she then wrapped across her forehead.

What the... ?! Why in the world...?

"Our Lord has been enshrined in this place since even before there was a Shuri Castle above." Aya turned slowly to face Izuma as she spoke quietly. "In those days, this small island was inhabited by several factions, who fought among themselves. The leader of one of those factions enshrined the deity in this place as a testament to his covenant with it."

"Covenant?"

Izuma had heard similar stories about the God of the Christians. Now, looking into the eyes of this woman as she told her story made his flesh creep. The pupils of her eyes were dilated just as he had seen on so many of the dead.

"The leader was under the mistaken impression that it was he who would henceforth be the ruler of this island, and as part of the covenant, he had asked that the island continue to prosper as a center of trade. Located as it was almost equidistant from both China and the Japanese mainland, and close to many other islands of the southern seas, it was in fact a most perspicacious request by an insightful leader."

She spoke as if she herself were no longer a mere mortal.

"And the entire archipelago prospered thanks to it."

She was gradually speaking with greater and greater zeal.

"That prosperity continued long after these islands were sub-jugated by an even larger opponent. Did you know that these islands were once so prosperous that even the clerks at government offices spoke four languages?"

There was no doubting the veracity of her story. At the time of Commodore Perry's mission to Japan, this island had already been subjugated by the Satsuma, yet when Perry visited Okinawa just prior to his call on Edo, he found that the officials of the Ryūkyū court were conversant in four languages and in no way inferior to the Qing court officials he had met in Hong Kong and Shanghai.

"The Satsuma came from the north and turned our islands into a puppet of their government, but there was no lessening of the prosperity that was provided to us by the power of our Lord. The covenant remained intact."

"So," said Aya, turning to look at Izuma, "Retribution is now to be visited upon us. Or perhaps I should say, has been visited upon us already."

"What are you talking about?"

"Don't you see? This war is his retribution. The very Earth itself is fraught with madness and crawling with maggots infesting the dead – tens of thousands of voices that moan in pain. The time has come, and the resurrection of our Lord is upon us."

Izuma saw only madness in the woman's smile.

"The only problem to be overcome was access to Shuri Castle and this place."

The woman continued to speak, oblivious to the tormented expression on Izuma's face.

"Weeping, I told General Ushishima that enshrined beneath Shuri Castle was a deity who could achieve a breakthrough in this war, and he quickly gave me his assent."

This woman is crazy.

Izuma was well aware that day after day of lying in the dark, trembling and wondering if you would be next to be blown to bits by the shells that rained down incessantly, was enough to drive any ordinary person insane.

Yet the simple fact that they were here in this place was enough to tell him that the things she referred to were not entirely an illusion.

What's more, it might further be true that she was the descendant of religious leaders and had been appointed a *noro*.

In which case, the knowledge of this underground shrine, passed down from generation to generation, combined with the madness of the battlefield above would certainly be enough to generate the kind of mythological dreams not ordinarily seen by a young woman.

What the hell is this all about?

The irritation running up and down Izuma's spine was almost palpable.

This girl had clearly been contaminated by the madness of the battlefield. Izuma regretted that he hadn't given more thought to why Ushishima might have chosen to write a personal letter rather than an official communiqué.

The general had obviously felt great compassion for the girl. He was by nature a thoughtful and considerate person, and was well loved by his men because of it. Women and children occupied a special place in his personal philosophy of things that a soldier was expected to protect and provide for.

No doubt he had met this young girl while the army was on the move, and she had entreated him to allow her access to the underground caverns. Unable to deny her request, he had written the letter.

Stranger things have happened, thought Izuma.

And now, because of the fantasies of this crazy woman, he had moved his platoon away from their designated station.

Izuma was almost ready to kill the girl then and there.

What is there to live for, anyway?

Leaving the girl on her own in the middle of this living hell of Okinawa certainly would do nothing more than add one more body to the mountain of corpses already piled so high.

In fact, he had already exposed not only his own platoon but the entire rear guard at Shuri Castle to danger.

The few men that had been spared for the rear guard had been carefully positioned so that they would not easily be wiped out by the enemy. Izuma realized that by moving his men, he had potentially upset the delicate balance that might mean the difference between success and failure for the rear guard.

I'll never be able to face my men…

Izuma had not bothered to complete the sentiment by adding *when we meet in the hereafter*.

There was not a single Japanese person in Okinawa who wasn't aware that it was his or her destiny to die in this battle.

Izuma himself was by no means alone in having resigned himself to that fate.

Subconsciously, anger had turned to arrogance, and Izuma's finger began to wrap itself around the trigger of his submachine gun.

For the moment, Izuma seemed to have forgotten that the object of his exasperation was a woman.

This is where I make a stand.

"What is it? Lieutenant Izuma?"

Aya was smiling.

Izuma's finger had just began to close around the trigger when a dull, ponderous sound filled the air. A tremendous crackle, like the bones of a giant being pulverized, was prelude to a sudden invasion by the cacophony of the world outside. Explosions shook the earth as dozens of human beings suddenly dove into and thrashed about in the water. The sound of gunfire was followed by screaming – yammering that might have come from either man or beast. It sounded almost like the gnashing of gears in an old truck, but Izuma recognized it immediately as howling.

Whirling around reflexively, Izuma pulled the trigger and felt the accented recoil of his .45 accompanied by muzzle flash and a heavy, sonorous retort. But still the enemy came on unrelentingly, their eyes burning red as flame as they glared at Izuma. The faint light emanating from the riverbed was enough to reveal the horde appearing out of the darkness. Although dressed in what looked like the remnants of American uniforms, whatever these things were, they weren't human.

Izuma felt a cold sweat running down his back.

The outline of the head and upper body appeared to be human. But their faces had no lips or nose, and from the exposed pink gums grew not teeth but a number of black tubes, large and small. The lower body at first sight resembled a bee, but the wings growing out of their backs were those of a bat. The repulsiveness of these creatures was made all the more enervating by their resemblance to humans. There were twenty in all, no more than a few steps away, in a stand-off with Izuma.

"Beware these creatures. They are servants of the enemies of our Lord."

Aya's voice sounded almost carefree, as though she were convinced that if push came to shove, Izuma could defeat them in a fight.

What the fu– …

Izuma could feel his legs begin to shake even as he suppressed the urge to scream. Squeezing the trigger of his machine gun, he sprayed the area from left to right. The creatures screamed and retreated, but not one of them fell dead. It would take more than bullets to kill them, and now Izuma was sorry that he hadn't brought a grenade launcher with him.

The creatures had fallen back once, but were now inching forward again.

How the hell am I supposed to hold them off on my own?

Izuma would have been relieved to learn that he had gone crazy and was seeing things, but the longer he stood there, the more he realized that whatever was happening, it was no fantasy.

The bombardment outside intensified, shaking the earth above and nerves on either side of the stalemate.

"Iä! Iä!"

A strange sound began to reverberate from between Aya's lips.

"Cthulhu fhtagn! Ph'nglui mglw'nafh Cthulhu R'lyeh wgah'nagl fhtagn!"

Turning around, Izuma saw the figure of Aya. Clad in her blood-red vestment, her eyes shone with a look of joy as she recited the incantation.

A language indecipherable to the human ear continued to resound from her throat.

All the while, the sweet fragrance of fresh water began to bear the pungent odor of the sea.

Izuma felt something touch his legs – something gentle and reassuring.

Huh?

But Izuma wasn't the only one who had noticed something, and just as his eyes glanced down at his feet, the leader of the creatures, who had anticipated the opportunity, came gliding across the surface of the water, straight at Izuma.

Looking up, Izuma began to fire his gun. But in that exact instant, there came from beneath the surface of the water an arm covered in scales, reaching for the approaching creature. Grabbed unexpectedly in mid-flight, the creature lost its balance and tumbled toward the water right before Izuma. The surface of the water rose up as whatever it was that had seized the creature now emerged from below and showed itself to be equally monstrous.

Two dull-looking eyes, set so far apart that they were almost on opposite sides of the head, opened vacantly. A small, round mouth was filled with small, saw-like teeth in several rows, and the ponderous body was covered with scales. Half human, half fish, this new monster let out a howl that sounded like scraping metal as it effortlessly waved the winged invader back and forth.

In an instant, the monster disappeared beneath the surface, after which a moist, gurgling sound was heard from the wall.

Izuma watched as one and then another of the flying invaders had its head smacked against the face of the marble wall and then slithered down into the water.

Now, what appeared to be water eggs rose high into the air, out of which were born the fish-headed, scaly humped bodies of the defenders. Izuma stood there, astounded, as a bloody battle began to unfold before him. Claws tore at bat-like wings and fangs ripped into scaly flesh as eyes were gouged from their sockets and bones snapped apart in a horrific caricature of hand-to-hand combat. Too terrified to move, let alone try to escape, he stood frozen. Yet through all of the horror, he felt with his entire being something that moved him as never before. It was as if he were reliving a moment from his past, when as a young boy he had been surrounded by a gang of schoolyard bullies, only to have his big brother come to his rescue at the last moment. That same feeling of relief and gratitude he had experienced so long ago came to him again now. The scaly monsters were no less terrifying than the winged creatures they were fighting, and yet to Izuma, they seemed not just trustworthy, but absolutely lovable.

Without realizing what he was doing, Izuma began cheering for these scaly defenders. With fists clenched around sweaty palms, he stood there, screaming, "Go get 'em! Tear 'em apart!"

Just at that moment, a tremendous explosion shook the chamber to its very foundation. An ominous vibration sent ripples skimming along the surface of the water as the entire underground began to collapse!

Yet locked in mortal combat, the clawed defenders and the fanged invaders were oblivious to anything but their own conflict.

"Lieutenant Izuma! You must hurry!"

As he turned in the direction of the voice, he saw two arms, holding forth a deity awash in blood that gushed from two slashed wrists.

"You… you're…"

"Never mind me. This is what I came here for," said Aya with a smile of accomplishment. "Take this, and get out of here."

A razor-sharp blade fell toward Izuma's feet, leaving a trail of blood in the water as it sank to the bottom of the stream.

"Hurry!"

Izuma fully intended to knock away those blood-drenched arms and free himself from the grip of this nightmare. But for some reason, he threw down his weapon, took the heavy lump of metal in both hands and held it reverently to his chest.

"I knew we had chosen the right man," said Aya with a smile. Once again, she had in her hand a ring attached to a chain – this time coming from the inside of the flower-bud-like pedestal where the deity had lain.

"Hurry! Make your way to the ocean from here," she said, pulling the chain.

The back of the chamber opened silently.

"At last I have fulfilled my duty to my Lord." Aya closed her eyes as the entrance to the shrine began to collapse. Izuma hurriedly made his way to the exit he had been shown. For some strange reason, the water felt as if it offered no resistance to his movement at all.

Just as he passed through the entrance, the sound of an explosion was followed by the collapse of the entire underground structure. Even as rubble came tumbling down upon Izuma's head, the water swelled into a torrent that swept all before it downstream. Yet caught up as he was in this maelstrom, Izuma felt no fear of drowning and was in fact smiling there in the blackness as he allowed the surging waters to carry him where they would.

"And that is what we speculate happened, based on what we managed to learn from interrogating Izuma Shirō and the sworn testimony of Private Roy Whitaker."

As the officer representing the US government finished speaking, an old man with a remarkable shock of white hair gave a stern look and said, "I see. And where is the deity now?"

"When we captured him on the beach at Wakasa, he had nothing with him."

"In other words, it has disappeared."

"Yes, Professor. That's what we think."

Adjusting his sunglasses, the white-haired old man spoke as if he were groaning.

"Ordinarily, you see, the iconography of the Cthulhu mythos as practiced in the Southern Islands almost always calls for these deities to be carved of stone or of wood. A metal casting would be extremely unusual, and I would have liked to have obtained it."

He folded his hands and long fingers gloved in black leather.

The tropical summer was far from over, even in September, but in contrast with the heavily perspiring American, the old man's forehead was cool and dry.

"I still would like to know just where this 'Aya' person came from, whoever she was."

"She would appear to have been a devotee of this religion," said the old man, as if it should have been obvious. "Part of a cult that had waited hundreds or maybe even thousands of years for its time to come. Generation after generation waiting, each after the other, and even if the day of reckoning failed to materialize in their own time, they handed their beliefs down to their children, who would continue to keep watch – as pious devotees of Cthulhu."

"As are all these islanders, no doubt."

"I wouldn't go rushing to that conclusion," said the old man as if correcting the false assumption of a student, yet smiling at the same time.

"I suspect that those islanders who did know the truth had become frantic in their efforts to do something about the situation.

In fact, we found evidence of a seal to the Shuri Castle underground."

"But how?"

"No doubt the woman was able to *remember* what to do – just as it had been planned a few hundred or even a few thousand years ago."

The old man spoke utterly without affectation.

"As strange as it might seem, both you and I would probably also *remember* when the *time came*, so to speak."

The old man's lips twisted into a cynical grin as both men sank into the stony silence of their own thoughts.

It took a few moments, but the American returned to his senses, and spoke with a sigh.

"No doubt we would."

It was his own lack of emotional response – perhaps even lack of imagination – that had brought the man to this line of work in the first place, but this time even his head was filled with abominable fantasies.

"Would you care to interview this Izuma Shirō? He's in pretty bad shape, but might still be able to talk, I believe."

It had required a bit of effort, but he had returned to his previous, detached tone of voice.

"No, I don't think so," said the old man, dismissing the suggestion with a wave of his hand.

"I expect that he is quite incapable of betraying Cthulhu, or of working for the good of mankind ever again. No?"

"You would appear to be better informed about such things than I," said the American, unable to hide his astonishment.

"It's not terribly difficult to deduce, really," explained the old man. "I requested an authority on Japanese folklore to research the background of the family name Izuma. As it turns out, there is a village of that name up in the snow country of northeastern Japan."

"It seems that long ago, the original name of that region had been Insumasu. After the Meiji Restoration in the nineteenth century, government reforms called for all former peasants to take family names, and it was the custom in those days to fashion a surname from the name of one's birthplace."

"In other words, that's why…"

"Yes, that's probably how the *noro* came to choose him as her… *protector*," said the old man even as he appeared to be thinking of something else. "But how did you ever get anything out of him?"

This time it was the American's turn to smile cynically.

"Truth serum. The Nazis occasionally made some useful things. We had to give him enough for an entire platoon, but it eventually worked."

"I see," said the old man, rising from his chair.

"I'm afraid that I must be getting back in rather a hurry. Since it's too late to do any more here, it looks like we're going to have quite a mess on our hands. I'd better go see if anything can be done to preempt it."

"Let me arrange an airplane for you."

"Don't bother," he said on his way out the door. "I can make it on my own, thank you."

The crisp, sure sound of those steps made it even harder to believe that behind those dark glasses, the old man was quite sightless.

It suddenly occurred to the American that he ought to have seen his visitor out. He followed after the footsteps, but the narrow, grey corridors of the American warship were not so easily navigated.

"Cthulhu fhtagn! Ph'nglui mglw'nafh Cthulhu R'lyeh wgah'nagl fhtagn!"

The bizarre reverberation of this alien incantation stopped the officer in his tracks. There, on the far side of the iron bars to a holding cell, sat the creature once known as Second Lieutenant Izuma Shirō of the Imperial Japanese Army. What little hair there was left on his head – indeed, on his entire body – was sparsely scattered, and four slits ran along his throat, forming flaps of skin that covered freshly grown gills. Dull, clouded eyes were separated by what seemed an almost unnatural distance, and small, round front teeth were followed from behind by several rows of razor-sharp replacements. The creature sat there motionlessly, reciting over and over in a gurgling voice the litany of an accursed deity, which was how he spent the rest of his days until he was sent to a better place.

The officer turned his head slowly, as if it required an effort to pull himself away from the endlessly droning voice, and at last resumed his pursuit of the "professor."

History has recorded that the walls of Shuri Castle were shattered for good by the guns of the battleship *Mississippi* on the evening of May 27, 1945.

Neither that ship's log nor any other official documentation, however, mentions a suicide attack by a wounded soldier on that day, nor are there any records of a visit to Navy facilities by an old man with dark glasses not so long after the battle had ended. The name of Second Lieutenant Izuma Shirō was listed together with so many of his compatriots as killed in action/body not recovered.

Two years later, in September of 1947, a nuclear warhead was detonated on an island somewhere in the South Pacific, but apparently no records were ever made of the purpose of that test or its results.

Work on the restoration of Shuri Castle finally began in 1989. At that time, a group of spiritualists and mediums, known collectively on the island of Okinawa as *yuta*, gathered in a tent on the construction site and spent all day and half the night reciting incantations and prayers in commemoration of the restoration. Rumor had it that sometime thereafter, throughout the islands, groups of *noro* priestesses gathered at local shrines, called *uganjui*, where they performed highly secretive rites. Just as these rumors seemed about to become newsworthy, however, the Japanese government announced plans for the Okinawa G8 Summit, and stories of strange happenings in remote areas were quickly forgotten.

Completed in 1992, the restored Shuri Castle later served as venue for the G8 Okinawa Summit, an occasion that gave rise to yet another rumor: right down to the very day the summit began, it seems the government of the United States pressed repeatedly – albeit entirely off the record – for a change of venue.

Night Voices, Night Journeys

Inoue Masahiko
Translated by Edward Lipsett

Night Voices, Night Journeys

Inoue Masahiko
Translated by Edward Lipsett

THAT IS WHAT we are catching, overhearing, at first not able to understand, as we read this amazing story. But the more we hear of the wispy words of nightmare and desire, the clearer things become. Inoue makes us glimpse old acquaintances we had not seen for a long time and did not think to see again. We see them from new angles and fail to recognize them for a moment, too. But once we do, we realize we have been given precious coordinates with which to begin to locate ourselves on an otherwise chartless desert of dreams.

Not since Ramsey Campbell's "Loveman's Comeback" and Robert Bloch's "Yours Truly, Jack the Ripper" have I been as taken aback by sharing an anonymous narrative focus, only to have the climax be the revelation of just whose perceptions I have been sharing. That fact alone makes this story worth a prize or two, but it has more to offer as well.

"Night Voices, Night Journeys" has a profound grasp of the fact that love is death, orgasm is the little death, and that Plato's Eros holds true even for Doctor Faustus. That is to say, the fleshly desire for carnal knowledge (*eros*, the erotic, the romantic) is ultimately one with (along the same spectrum of continuity with) cognitive eros, the urgency of the mind to fuse with what it seeks to know.

Thus in his tales of intrepid, doomed scholars seeing out irresistible knowledge that will doom them, Lovecraft was writing a kind of implicitly erotic fiction. Inoue Masahiko has made that eroticism explicit. And he provides a sped-up narrative panorama of territory we had thought ourselves already familiar with. The film viewed by the focal character mirrors the way the story itself works, and we see old Lovecraftian moments and insights made new again. What a performance!

AUTHOR'S NOTE

The city where this story takes place is quite unlike the real one, and exists only in the land of the imagination. I made reference to numerous books in touring and writing about these dream excursions, which are becoming a daily infatuation of mine.

Night Voices, Night Journeys

LOVINGLY, THOSE FINGERS toyed with her ear.

Those fingertips, moving so skillfully, soothed along the perfectly-sculpted rim of her ear, cupping; the trace of a fingernail. Sound faded, and then inundated her again. The extravagant seats of the limousine. From the sound system came the crystal clarity of old jazz, the elegant music vanishing, surging back to a head, fading again. Sound – silence – sound – silence... just like the singing crickets in the casino. Or perhaps a different nighttime insect? Fragments of jazz sketched poems through her elegant lines.

Perhaps voices from that night so long ago, or a requiem for a nighthawk of the forest? Or, maybe, cheek-to-cheek in the dance hall. Dancing together, so intimately, are life and death... Sound – silence – sound – silence. The rhythm of his fingers. She lay on the bench seat, facing upward, body stretched out to him. To his fingers. His incessant, gentle, ravenous fingers.

Of course, the fingers would love not only her ear. He would surely walk them elsewhere. From her ear, on down, to other parts. Those unique fingertips, slick with saliva pungent with the scent of myrrh, would glide from that other place to yet another spot, rich in so many secrets, never ceasing their mysterious dance. The hot, brilliant garnet of her self would dull under his distorted fingerprints. The mark of his possession. She was his possession, just like this museum-class limousine, and the audio system that was in itself a work of art; she knew. How well she understood the ways of this man, her master. As an *objet d'art*, he would savor her entirety, her all, until he was fulfilled.

This obsession, almost sad, was not his alone. All of the men who had possessed her had been awed by her very existence, and possessed in turn by the secrets of her flesh. Those that opened her body lost themselves in obscene pursuits. As if falling into cosmic chaos. And yet, it was nothing she desired; nothing she could comprehend. Not even her own existence, nor the terrible fate that awaited them. She could merely drift, on a night voyage, on so many endless night voyages.

She could hear the voices of the night, there on the bench seat. The singing crickets gathering on her skin; the poetry of the night-hawk. The garnet grew feverish, and the song swelled, hot enough for the dead to embrace the living. And then, his fingers froze. He stopped moving his fingertips. Feeling an unmistakable presence, she looked at him. He was holding the fingers of both hands up, staring at his fingers as if they were some strange organs he had seen for the very first time.

The deformation of his hands had progressed considerably.

In the streaming lights of the night his fingers looked like some translucent organism of the ocean depths. Aware of her openness, perhaps, he returned to himself, lowering his twitching hands again, and softly covered her face as if murmuring "Nothing to fear."

His fingers, newly elongated, bizarrely entangled one in the other, made his hands like a soft-bodied organism in shape as well as translucency. She felt the touch of countless tiny suckers on her face, but what she felt was not fear. She had suffered uglier and more fearsome things than this, crawling across her flesh.

The jazz was approaching its end. You could tell that he loved this song so very, very much from the name he gave to this million-dollar tank of a limousine. He flashed a sign to the chauffeur's compartment, separated from the rear seats by an etched glass panel, and "The A–Train" quietly began to slow. She knew that the night's drive was drawing to its conclusion… as had so many other drives of the long night…

"It's been a long time, hasn't it? The smell of the tide…" he said, his hand in its black deerskin glove wrapped around her spine. "Strange that the fog should be so thick here in Wai Tan. Because I brought you, perhaps?"

She shivered, silently.

"It may have drifted here from some distant land…"

The sound of his cane echoed on the paving stones of the Bund wharf road. Her field of vision was obscured dangerously, even at her foot. Even the immobile limousine had sunk its huge body into the milky white sea of cloud, only the gleams from the horns of the René Lalique hood ornament shining through the mist.

"Those who come here from the sea," he said, back to the broad canal. "They always see this scene, first."

Sensing the shadow that drew across his face, she gazed up.

"It's not bad… this view."

In the grayish-white darkness they waited, indigo.

"…As beautiful as the spirits of the dead…"

Spirits, tall and blue. Towering castles, worthy of the name skyscraper. The ghosts of art deco, stretching linear into the sky. Other specters soared in Victorian gothic, pointed towers to the heavens. And yet others, neo-baroque shades in dazzling curves. And Queen Anne revivals, with their glossy brick reliefs; spirits in colonial architecture, with maze-like stone roofs. The stone giants of countless ages of Europe, entombed here, looked as if they had awakened, reborn, to the call of a gong. The indigo spirits of the cityscape, elegant, reaching into the clouds…

"The ghosts of the modern world," he murmured. "The very essence of modern civilization, from every era, has possessed this city, driven by the passion of those on the leading edges of culture. Imprisoned here, they count the passing of eternal hours."

It was true. The original bold modernity of the blue, shadowed city – the Chinese called it Yi Cheng, the "Foreigner's Castle": it was a collection of mansions and buildings erected by cosmopolitans pursuing their colonial dreams of the very latest style – was now covered by ancient growths, revealing the grand visages of the dead, trapped in frozen time.

It was as if a long-dead European metropolis had been wrapped in the ocean fog, and transformed, over time, into a beautiful waxen corpse. Their blue faces were as handsome as death itself.

Still. She knew.

She knew what hid behind the peaceful city streets. Behind the façade.

She knew that behind the handsome chalk death mask raged the rawness of the banquet. The chaos of Asia, ever ready to well up from the alleys running like cracks through the Western-style castles. The formless desire, eating through those graceful, deathly faces. Giant mandibles, antennae, pseudopods and beaks squirming, wriggling, sucking up the blood and meat and mucus, secreting, mating, snaring prey, spawning, reproducing in the gorgeous and sacred banquet of darkness.

And so it was called "City of Demons." This second name of the "Paris of the Orient" derived from its dark, hidden side. He, none other, had explained it to her. The man who was her master. An inhabitant of the *société noire*, the society of darkness; bastard of chaos. When she first met him – when he tore her away from her previous owner – he had already been the master of the port. A Napoleon, ruling over the Paris of the Orient. Though already in his prime, he was richer in welling vitality than any youth she had ever met.

"You are the image of Shanghai," he said, running his fingers over her surface, his face so like the king of spades. "Underneath this chill skin, as cool as a corpse, you hold the unfathomable trea-sure of the cosmos. You are like my woman, but yet refuse to give me your all. You excite the hearts of all who see you, invite them, and lure them to leap into Hell to possess you.

"Just like this city… a beautiful curse," he murmured.

Like a wolf feasting on raw flesh, he continued his loving. And as he did with her form, so he pressed his hot fingerprints into every crevice of the city.

Still, she knew. She knew that this night journey was drawing to an end.

"It's not at all bad, is it? This view."

Looking up at the deep blue of the skyscrapers, with his hand still in its deerskin glove encircling her, he spoke into the smothering fog, but his words were no longer those of a conquering Napoleon. They recalled, rather, the defeated general, exiled to a lonely isle. This man himself understood that the journey was drawing to a close. His pale face under the borsalino still showed the character of the king of spades, even the clear-cut lines of a waxen carving, but his cheeks and lips quivered like ripples on the sea.

"This view – I took it all, all of it, with these hands."

Those hands, black deerskin gloves, twisted into an unnatural shape.

"And yet…"

He shielded his face, like a vampire in the sun, and through his fingers his bitter eyes stared away from the skyscrapers, off into the distant reaches of the Huang Pu River.

On the other side of the canal stood a bizarrely shaped tower, like a space rocket in a science drama: the business district of Pu Dong surrounding the Oriental Pearl Broadcasting Tower filled the nighttime scenery of the twenty-first century.

"There are things I cannot win," he rasped, his voice thin and pinched, as if the words burned his throat. "I can understand it, now; I can understand the feelings of Shi Huang Di, the First Emperor, searching for immortality. Even though this Shanghai is still rich in new culture, new innovations I have not yet devoured…"

He chuckled, rasping, "For me, there is… no more time."

Like a doll with a broken neck, he crumpled, but even collapsing called to her: "Azia… Azia…"

She could not even respond to that, the name that he had given her.

"At the least… you."

She shuddered yet again at her fate.

The same conclusion, the same end for every journey. The fate of the men who had loved her flesh, had been intoxicated by the poison of her cursed skin, and had passed away, calling her name.

"Your all… My Azia."

His silver cane slid down, a dry clatter against the paving stones.

The limousine door opened, the shape of the burly driver bursting out, realizing something had happened.

The man's borsalino skittered away; one of his back gloves slipped off and fell.

She saw them clearly, then – that pair of eyes.

She clearly saw those eyelids of fog blink, rending the white film.

The silent eyes, watching them, piercing them from the depths of the darkness.

Someone had been watching.

No, they were still watching…

She sat in the limousine as it sped home, shaken to the core.

Her master lay on the rear seat, on the other side of the rosewood table. He wasn't on the verge of death, but he lay like a shadow, limp and deep. He looked as if he might begin to rot before her eyes. Half-covered by the borsalino, his face could almost be glowing with phosphorescence.

This journey was drawing to a close. Soon, someone else would take her.

She thought back on her oft-repeated fate.

So… perhaps that was her next master, watching?

"They'll want you, Azia," her possessor had said, his white teeth tearing at a bloody fillet steak. "They all know that your skin, your body, is worth more than the blessings of the axis of the heavens."

He had swept his eyes across the western-style room watchfully. The guests at the French restaurant, popular since the first days of the settlement, had looked elsewhere, as if frozen.

"And that only he who commands you can rule this city – no, the world!"

Every time, washing the territory in blood. At the time, this man had been watching a newly emerging organization that was rising in the south.

"It is always the south that interferes with the unity of the Empire."

He entreated his underlings, too: "The children of Cao Cao and Kublai Khan both fought the flames of uprisings from the south. The Red Cliffs of the Three Kingdoms and the Red Turbans of the Mongols are not a thing of the past. Be vigilant! And especially when their territory, their port, is returned from the British."

Perhaps, then, those eyes belonged to one from the south port.

Those that her master had called "denizens of the other castle that knows no night."

In any case, her fate would play itself out, again.

She looked at the chauffeur, on the other side of the glass partition. The broad-backed driver had shared, to a lesser extent, her strange fate. Hired as a driver–bodyguard by her master for his tough, almost ape-like body, he was yet another spoil of conquest. Like her, he had been taken by force from a former master. His taciturn face was reflected in the rear-view mirror, and under his chauffeur's cap was the face that had earned him his new name from his new master. He was "Qing Wa", "the green frog". The other "Qing Wa" was a three-legged incense stand, one of her master's many curiosities. His melancholy visage, somehow a mixture of toad and prehistoric fish, had not been at all uncommon in one harbor town where she had lived, years ago. Boys in their teens, beginning to masturbate, would already begin showing those features. Some Westerners believed it was just an Asian face, and her former master had been one. He first noticed his mistake when he met the Napoleon of the Orient, come to buy heroin and opium, but by the time his skull had been shattered with a candelabra by his guest, he himself had had a fearsome expression indeed.

Still. She had to admit that her present master's face was undergoing an even more grotesque transformation. Inside those black deerskin gloves, and elsewhere.

The toxins of her skin? The cost of power? The abominable fate that overtook all who partook of her mystery was cursed, indescribable. But she – she suffered an even harsher curse, unable to escape the prison of her eternal form.

The limousine quietly arrived at The Castle.

It was one of the hotels the master owned; another skyscraper, looking out over the Huang Pu River where it merged with the sea. The front entrance was grand, imposing; the private entranceway opened instead, looking somehow like the door to a seamen's clubhouse. The hotel manager, with white hair and moustache, opened the limousine door, smiling like honey. And his smiling face instantly stiffened with tension. From inside the hotel seeped the sounds of old jazz. The master sat up, the king of spades looking out from under his borsalino.

The air filled with the balm of jazz.

The music echoed as they walked along the hotel hallway, decorated in art deco style. Like water seeping up through the hull of a ship, the resplendent sounds of saxophone and trombone boiled up around them. She felt a slight sense of relief as they waded through his Castle, flooded with music. The chandeliers with their parallel cubes and pentagons, and the *objets d'art* like roses painted by a cubist, brilliantly illuminated them. The unique geometry of the art deco designs created the lines and planes that the master loved, as he leaned on his silver cane, protected by the decidedly non-geometrical frog-faced chauffeur, and led by the manager. The enormous Castle, like a bell tower right up to its gargoyles, looked like a crystalline mineral.

"Tonight is a very special night," said the master, looking up at the red, inverted pentagram of the lampshade suspended from the high-vaulted ceiling. "I must change to formal attire, to match you."

His black-gloved hand fingered the silver chain adorning her. The garnet, set into the ebony and silver arabesque, pulsed crimson. His voice came again, as if tormented by a demon: "I'll return shortly, Azia."

She felt a flash of ineffable apprehension, but behind her there were no watching eyes to terrify. This was the heart of her master's domain. Standing near the polyhedral statuary was a black-garbed servant, like a Tang funerary statue, a terracotta warrior guarding its master. There was no gap in the defenses for the southern barbarians to penetrate.

Qing Wa nodded, and the snow-haired manager smiled again, dripping honey.

"I'll return shortly..."

The doors, decorated with a double-happiness symbol drawn in cubist style, closed in front of her, and the elevator with its golden cage carried him upward along the wall, flashing in mother-of-pearl and tortoise shell marquetry.

"I'll return shortly..."

The image frozen in the brandy snifter, endless eons passing.

...Eternity. She smiled her twisted smile. Compared to the night journeys she had come through thus far, a short wait. Only three short requests by the live jazz band in the basement café.

Not even long enough for the ice to melt, in glasses she and Qing Wa shared as they sat in the private lounge.

"Would you like a liqueur, Madame?" The voice was clear, crisp. "Or we have Heineken beer, or J&B or Chivas Regal whiskies."

He was very young for a waiter.

"I already have a cognac, thank you," she said, then looked again. He wasn't wearing a waiter's uniform, but instead white evening formals, with a red rose.

The frog-faced bodyguard, engrossed in the band's performance, didn't seem to notice.

The youth smiled sweetly, with a feminine touch to his eyes. A playboy from the pool bar, perhaps?

"It's on me. And the next request, as well."

She looked at the request card, where the clean, pink finger pointed, and doubted what she saw: "As Time Goes By."

"You can't!… That song!…" she cried, but it had already started. 'As Time Goes By,' the flowing music of the Café Américain in Casablanca. "You mustn't! You can't play that song!"

"But why not?" he laughed. "Just like that old love story."

"It's forbidden!" Her voice roughened. "Only the Master can request that song!"

"Ah… If you prefer cognac, we also have Rémy Martin," he said nonchalantly, winking. "You must be tired of Napoleon by now?"

She felt ice slither down her spine.

She searched that sweet face again.

"Who are you?"

"A specter. A resident ghost of the hotel," he said. "Hah! It seems he cannot perceive me!"

She glanced at the bodyguard. The eyes in his strong, frog-like face were unquestionably open, eyeballs dry and pupils wide. Frozen, immobile. Except for the bubbles – Except for the bubbles of blood frothing out from between his teeth…

She froze.

"Why… Why did you come here?"

"You know full well," he said, chuckling.

The light in the playboy's eyes pierced like a cat stalking its prey.

"Time goes by, and the times change – as does your possessor."

The invader took her hand. "And once again, the modern age sweeps away the old! A man who drowns himself in the forgotten shades of beauty is not fit to be king."

Startled, she looked into his eyes. Deep, black pools stared back into hers.

"As Time Goes By" played on in elegance. The men in black ran closer, as if in time to the music. Some pulled guns from the bulges on their chests, others sported shotguns as if using a stick to dance with. The band played on as time went by.

"You can never escape," she said.

"I wonder," laughed the usurper, unafraid.

But already on four sides, encircling them, a dozen men with guns surrounded them.

"If you would be kind enough to return her?" asked the white-haired manager, carrying a gentle smile and a heavy shotgun of his own. His honey-like expression made him look like a homicidal maniac disguised as Santa Claus.

"We can promise you your life…" he started, and fell silent. Not only his voice, but his movements, and the motions of the surrounding men. They shook as if with the chills, fascinated and trapped by the outstretched pink finger of the young invader. An eerie magic bound them all in place, and from between clenched teeth bubbles began to foam. Just like crabs, she thought to herself. Crabs drowning in the supreme liquor of power.

"What, is the music over already?" he asked, turning to face the band, fallen silent in astonishment. "Play it again, Sam!"

The pink finger, thrust into space, draw back an invisible trigger, and the white-haired man's body stretched, squelching. A little *xiao long bao* dumpling, bitten open. In an instant his body flipped inside-out like a balloon, a waterfall of fresh blood. She could but stand and stare, receiving the crimson baptism with her face, her skin, the depths of her being. As if oblivious to the bloodshed, the band played on. Like beautiful music, the blood spraying onto her skin, toying with her. Still frothing, the men fired their guns, bones shaking violently enough to be heard, shooting each other but unable to fall under the impact. A furious dance. In his seat, the huge, ugly man brought to this Paris of the Orient from a distant and dark abandoned port spurted the thick blood of his ancestry like a geyser to the bullets pumped into his body.

"Well," said the man, taking her bloodstained in hand. "The beginning of a new journey."

Ducking under the gunfire, he ran, drawing her along. Down the hall, the stairs, the art deco hallway.

The mother-of-pearl and tortoiseshell fragmented under the concentrated fire of the gunmen, shards of chandelier and glass artwork raining around them in a polychromatic shower.

And through it all, he ran, holding up his hand as a shield. Under that pink gust the men stopped, fascinated, and turned the sights of their machine guns on each other. She turned to see the black-suited men dancing in a frenzied rhythm, even as they chewed each other's bodies to rags with their bullets. The parallel cubes shattered, the pentagons slivered – the men gradually lost shape, their geometrically patterned organs bursting out as they danced on in a terrible cubism of the living dead…

"My master!" she cried, as they ran. "You've already killed him, haven't you?"

"Someone surely would have," he said, conversationally. "The most likely was the hotel manager."

"What!?"

"Hadn't you noticed?"

The bullets tore away the pentagram lampshade.

"It's just like an action movie!"

They flew like bullets themselves.

"And we are the movie stars!"

Long shadows leaped in the geometric ruin, landed. The safety zone waited near at hand.

"What are you doing?"

"The jazz already told you, didn't it?" he said, pointing at the limousine. "Take the A–Train!"

It was the first time she had ever ridden in the front. The seatbelt was wet with blood.

He put the car in gear and stood on the accelerator, surging the million-dollar tank forward.

And the circus began: pursuing cars full of machine guns. They raced into the city streets, colliding with taxicabs, overturning a trolley bus. And as they scraped off the pursuit and dodged machine-gun bullets, he still joked on.

"This scene really needs some music. I think we've had enough jazz, though. You must be pretty tired of the old man's taste by now. Hard rock! No, even better: heavy metal!"

They drove onto the elevated road, and the opposite lane was full of enemy cars, too. Being shot at from both sides now, she huddled down. He grinned and spun the wheel, soaring off the elevated roadway. Miniskirted girls stood rooted in place, staring at the antique limousine flying overhead as if at a UFO. Behind them, their pursuers crashed into each other, head on, followed by an explosion, bursting flame, then another, more massive blast.

"The Roman Empire in neon," he said, glancing into the rearview mirror at the road, now a raging inferno from the growing pile-up. "Once, a visionary perfectly described this city that way. An Englishman named J.G. Ballard. I dedicate this neon to all those of vision! In celebration of the crowning of a new Emperor!"

Looking at the century-old metropolis alight with explosions and flares, he put his arm across her where she lay, her head angled down.

"What's the matter? You don't seem to be in a very good mood, my bloodstained Empress."

"…"

"Perhaps you are unhappy to leave that old man? You don't want to become the property of the man who killed him?"

"I killed him," she said. "It is my fate to extinguish those who love me, horribly. My curse. A curse on me."

Looking out over the explosion-lit cityscape, she spoke.

"You, too – you, too, will come to understand. The tragic end awaiting all who love me."

She had tried to put a stop to the endless cycle, long, long ago. It had been impossible. She was not even allowed to die.

"The fate of those without the power to possess you," he said. "Dying like those without the qualifications to live in this city. But you… you are the very image of Shanghai."

She looked into his face automatically. Deeply. Into those eyes.

"You speak the Shanghai dialect very well."

"Would you prefer I spoke with a southern accent?" he asked, stealing a kiss. "In Chinese, kiss sounds much like *qi shi*, 'extraordinary man.'"

The sounds of fireworks and screams echoed faintly.

"The night is still long," he said. "There's a very interesting place just across the Hong Kou Bridge."

"An interesting place?"

"A movie theater," he explained. "Hmm, no, perhaps better to call it a cinema, in the old style."

They crossed the steel bridge, entering the old Japanese part of town.

The cinema lurked there, waiting.

Inside, the vast cinema walls were done in red.

The dome and arches were all art noveau, quite unusual for this part of Shanghai. The curving, ivy-like decorations stretched out like blood vessels to the seats, in over a hundred shades of rouge-red.

She stared in amazement that there should be such a huge movie theater – no, a cinema – in the old settlement.

"I've never been here – to the Japanese settlement – before."

"Really?" countered the young playboy, surprised. "That old Napoleon was born around here, you know."

"He was?"

"You never knew anything about him, did you?"

The lights gradually faded out. The hundreds of seats, though, remained vacant…

"We're the only two watchers."

He stole another kiss, another extraordinary man.

"It's a love story, you see," he explained. He spoke as if he were the movie producer, as so many men do when explaining movies to women.

"The title is 'As Time Goes By.'" His white teeth flashed in the darkness. "Or, perhaps, 'Night Voices, Night Journeys.'"

The film began to whirl at his voice.

"And you are the star."

In the next instant – at the image writ so large on the screen – she gasped.

A man's face, gasping in terror.

His expression was driven by his nightmares, eyes bloodshot as if to burst.

She remembered him. No, she could never forget. A night journey from so long ago; he had been her possessor. And this scene – just before they parted.

Why? She turned to face him, but he merely squeezed her gently.

On the screen the man pleaded with someone in the darkness, trembling. She knew it was she herself. Behind him was a collection of oddities: antique mummies, skulls of all shapes in their niches. The voluminous black hangings, the headstones snatched from the oldest churchyards of the world. Yes. It was museum they had owned, her masters. She had had two masters at once, then: collectors of decadence and beauty. She had belonged to them, with all together under a single room, the two of them savoring her flesh in turns. And the end... one of them died horribly on his way home from the railway station. Her flesh crept at the memory. The green jade amulet that no human should touch. Her body had sought it, that statue of a crouching winged hound stolen from the dead body. And then... *it* had come. One of them was horribly eaten, and the survivor disposed of the collection. He discarded even her, and fled. He fled, but he could not forget the touch of her. In the room on the screen he loved her yet again, a revolver gripped in one hand, ready to face the end, his end. He didn't die by the gun, though; instead, *it* came crashing through the window, with a flurry of monstrous wings and a hound's howl. The shriek had been cut off by snapping fangs, fresh blood spurting. On her skin, a crimson spray of the sacrifice. Just like what had happened to the other as he returned from the station, his body torn to gobbets. Her skin drank up the blood, like a desert painted by a bloody rain.

...I hate it!

I never wanted this. I never wanted him to die, but... the sweet blood lured her, stirring her passion. The charnel odor brought her to climax, and over. She hated herself, hated the secret curse buried in her body. And yet...

The film played on. As time, going by...

A close-up of his face.

She could never forget that face, with beard and black-rimmed glasses. It was as he had looked toward the end, after they were together for a relatively long span. She, of course, vastly preferred the bold figure like that painted in a superb impressionist picture, but he had loved costumes, and had demanded them of her as well. She had donned an Islamic robe for him, plucking the Egyptian qanoon. There had been no doubting that the notes and the lure of her body had stimulated his research, but it could not be denied that gradually distortions began to appear. He had been a genius in chemistry. On the screen, surrounded by experimental gear from the era of King George, he entwined with the naked woman, her singed Islamic robe discarded. Bathed together in dark green vapor, he chanted the spells so crucial to his chemistry, blending them with the qanoon melody. Y'ai 'ng'ngah, Yog-Sothot'! The neatly-arranged lekythos urns suddenly shook as countless hideous creatures began to squirm. Monstrous arms gave form to the deformation that had twisted his destiny. Talons searching in the emptiness, overlapping with an image of his arm as he scrabbled against death in those final hours. Yog Sothoth! 'ng'ngah, y'ai zhro! His hand clutching air, his very body, melted away before her eyes. The waves of agony emanating from her lover as he transformed into the bluish-gray wall – more erotic than the blood of the thousand sacrifices he had throttled for her – melted the deepness inside her.

– *Stop the projector!* –

She was tormented by pity and remorse, and even more by the memories of passion that overwhelmed them.

But the film rolled on, and on.

There. That face. There was one who had died a horrible death before he even had the chance to meet her.

The young man, young enough to still seem like a child in ways, had come to find her.

He had heard a rumor of her beautiful portrait, and had come to the strong vault imprisoning her, with fervor to overcome the weakness of naivety. His wild, vital form – even though only seen through a slight crack into the thick steel door – so rich in animal magnetism, had promised a body so ripe it could not be disguised by the mean clothes he wore, and had stimulated her to new heights. Her possessor then, though – that old man had been the only one she never wanted to acknowledge as "master" – had refused to let them meet, or even to allow the youth to see the portrait.

She never did meet him, as it turned out. That night he had climbed over the walls of the university to steal her away, and had been savaged by the fierce guard dog; killed. Listening to his hopeless screams from the other side of the heavy steel door, she had shuddered in grief – even as she flamed with unbearable passion at his final, piercing shriek. She writhed with the onyx cause-and-effect of her existence, and from the depths of her soul she wanted to die.

Her master then – called The Professor – engaged in sterile research, on a table that reminded her of a dissection bench. She felt nothing at all even when he toyed with her body. He was the archetypical scientist, scribbling notes and musings on book margins, and even on their spines, earning the ridicule of his fellows. She knew, though – knew that he absolutely hated his "research material."

She had hoped he would kill her. She had probably asked him to, several times. A man such as he would have known how to kill something like her, no doubt. She had been burned in flames a number of times; by the hand of her master, regretting his ownership; by people tortured by her master; as a witch in a small village; once at the feet of the Pope. But – she could not escape to death. Since Constantinople in the tenth century she had had the chance to reproduce several times, but even though her offspring died in the flames she could not die. Her body, charred black, would flush with blood from deep inside instead of dispersing with the wind, and lush, sensuous skin would be reborn. Her body had never known death. And across the ages, she still had no choice but to continue her night journey. The night she had become the property of the twin sorcerers, who hated each other, and killed each other... the night she had been the catalyst that let a cursed artist realize his rare talent… the night she had revealed the hidden elixir to that young medical genius… The film kept on, and on. Even as she loved the men who mastered her, she was intoxicated by the screams and curses, the blood and flesh; those sobbing nights she reeled at the black abyss of her crimes.

"I never knew you like human beings that much, Nekkie," jibed one of her fellows in this underground room. He was another of her line; she'd met others like him before. That university research room. Later she'd escaped, to be acquired by yet another master, but until then she'd shared confinement with a host of others of her line, and with others from different lines altogether, all sharing a common fate.

"Don't call me that, Misty!"

"Human beings may say everything's black and white, like the Elder Gods, but that's only skin deep. On the inside they're harder to handle than the Great Old Ones themselves," chuckled de Vermis. "They're only here in this world for the blink of an eye, poor things. Compared to the truths of our existence, they're just dust on the wind."

"One thing you can say," broke in a voice as deep as crawling dust, startling them both. The oldster who so rarely spoke, with pieces of his body missing here and there, old Eibon, whom everyone respected. "We are always… together with the humans… that's the very purpose of our creation…"

And as he spoke those words, the film began to roll with a terrible sound.

On the screen suddenly appeared her creator.

The solitary man, standing in the nighttime desert. Listening to the demonic voices of the night as he molded the vermilion sand to form a woman's head. He lowered his head, as if to kiss her on the brow, and the voices of the daemonic insects howled and chattered. And in the next instant, the screen revealed sights beyond imagination: an infinite chaos, wider than the very galaxy… stygian terror from the abyss... eroticism sweeter than death... herself, writhing at her eternal curse.

– *Why?* –

She screamed. Words made blood gushed from her lips.

– *Why did you create me?* –

As if in reply, another image formed. A dream, she thought. A scene from a dream. Though she could not die, she could dream. But this one, this dream she saw on the silver screen, was not the endless, frozen wasteland or the gate that surpassed Time.

It was an image as a youth. – *I am an Arab!* – he cried, sitting at his wretched desk, an illuminated copy of *The Thousand and One Arabian Nights* in his hand. – *I am Abdul Alhazred!* – His hand grasped a pen. In that instant, she was gripped by a deep and inexplicable emotion: she felt that she came into existence in this world the same instant the youth grasped that pen. Her countless night journeys, all the endless centuries, began with that pen stroke in the vermilion desert.

Shaking with an emotion she couldn't express, she suddenly noticed where she was. Not in the cinema seats any more, but propped in front of the screen. From the seats swelled the applause of an audience of hundreds. Surely there had been nobody there, in those wine-red seats? No, wait: if she squinted, she could see them. The red audience, thronging the cinema, packing it with their blood-red presence. Faces as red as if they had been flayed, like silverfish wriggling in the ripples of a rich meat stew, looked at her. They waved at her, cheered, watching her eagerly. Yes. Those eyes. The same eyes as before. The eyes she had felt then, on the banks of the fog-cloaked canal. And for so many of them to be watching her at once...

"I said you were the star, remember?"

Climbing up from the first-row seats onto the stage was the playboy, garbed in his pristine white suit. Handing her a bouquet, he spoke: "They're your fans. They love you."

"But… those horrible faces…" she said, shivering. "They're all my sacrifices."

"No, your recipients. The recipients of your saga," he corrected. "Everyone looks that way, eventually. That's exactly why they are so enraptured by your story; they want to peer inside, and to help you weave the next chapter."

In the front row she could see the bespectacled young man, clutching his *Thousand and One Arabian Nights*. The darkness roiled like red fog, like the night voices.

"They all love you," he said, embracing her. As if to taste her tears he brought his lips closer. "But now, I am your master."

And then, his form slowly faded into darkness, the pink face and white clothes erased. As if melting into black, the packed seats, the cinema, all drained away. The applause and cheers dwindled, gone. All the shadows vanished from the theater.

She stood, numb.

Was this, then, all merely another dream?

Had she merely been fooled by shadows? Perhaps the playboy was indeed merely a phantasm.

Something was moving in the darkness. Dragging its feet like a toad that had been stepped on, the huge clot of blackness approached, halting in front of her to reveal its ruined visage. Qing Wa, his massive frame wrapped in the battered and torn chauffeur's uniform, was still leaking inky blood from gaping gunshot wounds. He caught her as she tipped over and fell.

Carrying her to where the night wind blew, to the waiting battle-scarred "A–Train." She turned toward the cinema once again, and under the light of the gravid moon was a looming ruin, cracked and shattered cement falling off, with only a solitary sign proclaiming this as the future site of a disco, casting a long shadow like a withered reed.

"Indeed, tonight was a very special night, Azia," came the hoarse voice of old Napoleon, lying in his canopied bed. It was the special room, the penthouse suite. At the doorway, Qing Wa stood with his melancholy steward's expression.

Merry flames were dancing in the fireplace, light more than sufficient to show the master's defenseless body, and the advanced state of his condition. The nightmare of his body was more hideous than even the grotesque carvings on the luxurious Chippendale bed. The face of the king of spades had been wrinkled like an old and faded poker card, but the imbalance between the waxwork precision of his features and the decaying body recalled the canvas of that accursed artist.

"It opened with dramatic, cinematic action, and ended as a horror film. Fleeing with your wraith must have been romantic indeed."

His fingers scrawled across her body.

He wasn't wearing gloves, and the transformation had progressed visibly in only hours. His colorless fingers, except for the gnarled knuckles, were the tentacles of some cephalopod of the ocean depths. There were more than a dozen of them – too many to easily count – intertwining with each other, but constantly moving dexterously. In the tiny suckers scattered across them like little pustules grew soft, barbed hooks.

Those skillful fingers caressed her to the sounds of old jazz: "Sentimental Journey," perhaps, or possibly "Stardust." Whichever; it didn't matter. The rhythm was his fingers, scribing poems on her skin.

"He must have been handsome, your young shade," said the King of Spades, seeking her lips, and suddenly – his face slipped, the celluloid mask peeling back onto the bed to reveal his naked, hideously changed face underneath. The visage, a travesty that would freeze a thousand guests at an evening ball in horror, whispered the droplets of its emotions: "He must have been beautiful, Azia."

– *You still are,* – she answered, and pressed herself to his lips, a continuation from the cinema. "Kiss" sounds like *qi shi*, "extraordinary man."

"You knew? All of it?" he croaked. "*You yin yang*: it is not intercourse with ghosts, but liberation of the corpse, living between the worlds of the living and the dead. To be trapped in this frail flesh, and become a specter still living."

The former playboy coughed, like a dog with no jaw.

"It was just possible, before I was destroyed entirely, but even so… there are limits."

He turned his eyes, scintillating as fireworks, toward the window, toward the phosphorescence of Venus, shining clearly.

"Tonight was special," he said. "The stars are right. The Gate of that star, too. And the final method that your body revealed…"

His skilled fingers attacked her. His incessant, gentle, ravenous fingers. No, those strange organs that could no longer be called fingers. Those unique fingertips, slick with saliva pungent with the scent of myrrh, would glide from the folds of her ears to her spine, and on through to that other place. Moving from page to page in her open body. The hot, brilliant garnet of her self would pulse red, and the chaos of the cosmos well up. Inside this ghost-like man, formless arousal quivered and writhed, huge mandibles and beaks. The radiant Sacrament of darkness was about to begin. He chanted the spells, and she panted in the mystery. Outside the window the voices of the nighthawks took up the melody of the old jazz.

"This time I will achieve *shi jie*: the liberation of the corpse."

A gasp of pleasure came simultaneously with his voice.

His form, staring into space, froze for an instant, looking almost like a demonic edifice transforming to yet a new form of modern architecture.

It seemed to all as if the demonic city itself had screamed.

His body collapsed in an instant, like shattered glass, and his indigo spirit howled like a formless sea creature, howled together with the mansions, the castles, the skyscrapers of the city. The rooftiles of the pavilion in Yu Yan Garden flipped, creeping like lizards, and the waters of the Bund bubbled furiously, revealing the unnatural facets and angles of an eerie fortress of dark, mucous green. The rocket-like Broadcasting Tower transformed into a huge sea lily, tentacles seeking. The neon-lit Stonehenge wriggled and writhed as one, and Chaos twisted into a vortex. And those eyes, the hot, red eyes of those countless watchers, sought her out.

Qing Wa's head, burned black, rolled past, clunking along the floor, and fell silent.

The curtains on the window, its lead cames melted, suddenly flurried.

Bathed in furious lights she lay on the Chippendale bed, facing upwards, stretching her body undefended. To the fingers of the wind. The fingers of the wind that could be he.

But this wind was not he; the night journey was not yet at an end.

She believed, never doubting that he would return.

She listened, still. She thought she could hear the cries of the nighthawks, calling together with the beat of heavy metal. Or was it just the howls of the insects on the wind? Straining to catch the footsteps of the wind, she listened, attentive, waiting. Listening. For an eternity… for the night voices of *Al Azif*.

Sacrifice

Murata Motoi
Translated by Nora Stevens Heath

Sacrifice

Murata Motoi
Translated by Nora Stevens Heath

SUSPICIOUS LOCALS IN a rural setting! We know we're in for a treat!
Some people might call it a hackneyed device, but of course they
are wrong! Instead, we may call it a classic theme. The question is
whether the author is able to do something new and interesting,
as well as authentic, true to the tradition, with it. And Murata Motoi can, and has.

The notion of a cult that makes its living off unwholesomely
nourished and yet unusually lush vegetables might be familiar
to readers from three sources. First, we think of H.P. Lovecraft's
favourite among his own longer tales, "The Colour out of Space,"
where a tenuous and insidious gaseous substance from a mete-
orite first enriches, then pollutes the ground into which it had
mysteriously fallen. Initially fabulous growth turns out to be the
superabundant cellular rioting of a cosmic cancer. Second, students of American religious history might have heard of a scandal
connected with the Jehovah's Witnesses sect during the reign of
Judge Rutherford, the successor to founder Charles Taze Russell.
The sect claimed to have the secret to producing larger than normal vegetables – through prayer? Well, the Witnesses might make
a nuisance of themselves from time to time, like when they show
up on your doorstep early Saturday mornings, dressed in immacu-

late but cheap suits, with you answering their knock unshaven and in a hangover and a T-shirt! But they're not very dangerous. For a more risky cult, a cult with some teeth, you might think, thirdly, of the populace of Summerisle in the masterpiece *The Wicker Man*. I think something similar is going on in "Sacrifice."

Ask yourself, did Kanako escape whatever fate had been chosen for her, and which she freely chose? Did her husband intervene in time? What did he save her from, if anything? Note the musings of Katsunori at the end. He seems too little curious as to the ease of their escape. The possibility that things are far from over sounds like a brief note momentarily disturbing his complacency: yes, the cultists of Holly probably *would* dig out the cave, rebuild the shrine, and things would resume. Whatever those things were. Here is no hint that the Soil God was destroyed or could have been. And so one wonders if Kanako had been ritually impregnated, to give new birth to the unimaginable creature within.

And one must wonder if the suspicious Professor Mutō, so obligingly helpful to the cult he was ostensibly suspicious of, was himself a member. And if that is so, then he must have been en-gineering the very confrontation that led to the cave-in. Perhaps Kanako had to be gotten away so she might bear some awful young elsewhere in the country without her husband suspecting the connection.

But then again, maybe the cult planned to *eat* her. Remember how they were wont to combine the Brack mud with human waste ("night-soil") to fertilize it. And remember that the Professor tells Katsunori that the cult would *turn their victims into soil*. My guess is that at some point they would have eaten Kanako in a mystical communion meal and added their own waste to the mud cakes always offered on the altar to the hungry Thing within.

But ultimately we are left wondering, i.e., experiencing a sense of wonder, without a discrete question to which there is a discrete answer. Just think of the possibility that the discovery of some *thing* in the ground, beneath the soil, could affect the possible meaning of life itself.

Sacrifice

1

Izawa Katsunori was moving for the second time in the year since he'd married. His new place was a wood-frame apartment not far from the West Okutama train station on the Ōme line.

West Okutama happened to be the starting point for a hiking trail. On weekends and holidays, backpack-toting hikers in trekking boots descended on the place in droves. Living there meant a two-hour commute to the city, but it was blessed with an abundance of nature and clean air. Maybe this place would be good for his wife Kanako.

Soon after they married, Kanako developed atopic dermatitis. Itchy welts sprang up here and there all over her body. More often than not, scratching them broke the skin and turned it dark red. The hospital gave her steroids, which relieved the symptoms but didn't cure the disease itself. Furthermore, when you go off steroids after using them long enough, they have a rebound effect, making your symptoms flare up even more severely. Kanako found herself treading a path that so many people like her had trod before.

First she focused on their home, getting rid of as many dust mites and airborne allergens as possible. She began eating only natural foods with no additives and chose bottled water over what

211

came through the municipal pipeline. She tried all sorts of cures: Chinese herbs, various lotions and creams, hot-spring therapy, ultraviolet rays, and any kind of folk remedy you could think of. Despite her efforts, her condition only worsened.

Kanako's dermatitis cast a dark shadow on their new life together. She had been proud of her beautiful pale skin; the damage there was psychological as well as physical. There were no welts on her hands or face yet – no one could tell there was anything wrong unless she unbuttoned her collar – but she had grown to hate having her husband see her naked body, and their sex life suffered. Finally, because Kanako worried so much about her illness, any conversation between the two of them had a tendency to grow somber.

Mental stress can cause atopic dermatitis. Knowing that, in Kanako's case, the condition had appeared after they had gotten married, Katsunori often asked her if she was dissatisfied with something. Kanako always answered no.

She had always been introspective and oversensitive, tending not to bother herself over things, even her husband, more than absolutely necessary. Katsunori suspected that living with him might be a source of stress for her. He was cautious about his wife's mental health and tried as much as possible to give her whatever she wanted.

Thinking there might have been something wrong with the newly built apartment they'd moved into after the wedding, the two of them moved into a wooden apartment block that was more than ten years old. That didn't help, either.

After Kanako mentioned the air might be to blame, they decided to move for the second time. They settled on West Okutama because of its clean air and reasonable commute.

2

Katsunori took walks around the house on his days off. It was still cold outside, and there were still occasional traces of snow.

West Okutama was in a valley – a basin, really – and the area surrounding the train station was crammed with shoddy pre-fabs and apartments. Beyond this was farmland, stretching out for miles.

The air was clean here, and the surrounding mountains rich with green. Birds twittered constantly, the river running through the center of the basin flowed with pure water, and it felt good to stroll amidst it all.

When taking his usual walk one day, Katsunori noticed that something was different about the land in the northwest of the basin.

Most farmers seemed to take Saturday and Sunday off, so he rarely caught sight of anyone in the fields, but there was always some sort of farming going on in that particular section of land. He had never seen any machinery there, either; they worked the land with hoe and plow. These men and women often squatted as they worked. On closer inspection, it turned out that they were pulling weeds and plucking insects off the plants by hand.

"Handmade farming" – it might be an awkward phrase, but that's exactly what they were doing out there. It also may have explained why so many of the farmers were bent like old men and women. Their clothes were dirty and ragged, and their faces and hands were caked with earth. They could easily have passed for a group of 18th-century peasants.

Growing interested in these farmers, Katsunori would often shout greetings to them, trying to engage them in conversation. All he got in return were cold stares.

There had never been any contact between the commuting Tokyo businessmen and the farming families living in West Okutama. Still, for all that, these farmers were especially clannish.

Katsunori brought up the subject of this parcel of land at the dinner table.

"Oh, you mean Holly," Kanako replied. "They've been doing organic farming since before the war, and the veggies they grow are supposed to be out of this world."

According to Kanako, Holly used to be known as Hollow. Disliking the negative connotations of the word, however, they changed their name to the more neutral Holly. The land they worked was indeed in a deep hollow.

"Those folks sure seem awfully cliquey," Katsunori commented.

"They do," agreed Kanako. "The government persecuted organic farmers after the war. Apparently that's why they don't mingle much with outsiders, even today."

That might just be the case, thought Katsunori. Organic farming was fashionable and in demand these days, but until very recently chemical fertilizers and pesticides were the absolute latest and greatest, so the government would have wanted to promote their use as much as possible.

"Do they have some sort of special policies, or what?"

"I do know Holly doesn't use any mechanical tools. They say the exhaust is bad for their crops," Kanako explained. "Talk about being thorough."

Ever since they had moved, Kanako's dermatitis had remained unchanged. Because it hadn't gotten any worse, she had begun to hope that it might get better before long. Lately this optimism was buoying her spirits.

"Maybe their vegetables would do you some good. Are you buying any?" Katsunori asked.

Kanako shook her head as if the idea were completely out of the question. "I can't get any. Being totally organic, they're so popular that they have their hands full delivering to people who've had standing orders for ages. You can't buy anything from them directly, either."

"No kidding."

"I heard they were good for my skin condition, though, and I really would like to get some for myself somehow," Kanako continued.

Everything Kanako bought, from her rice to her vegetables, was organic and pesticide-free. There were many different levels of organic farming, though, and it wasn't enough to simply trust a label boasting that something was pesticide-free.

"How about if you gave them a load of cash? They still wouldn't sell anything to you?" Katsunori persisted.

"Nope," Kanako replied, disappointed.

Katsunori decided he would get his hands on some of those Holly vegetables for his wife, and started thinking about how easy it would be to steal a few in the middle of the night. As though reading his mind, Kanako said, "The Holly farmers patrol their fields at night, too. Once they caught someone stealing veggies for their atopic child and beat him black and blue."

"You don't say."

Katsunori remembered the Holly workers and their icy gaze. With all his aimless wandering, they may very well have taken him for a vegetable thief.

In the face of changing times, Holly had clung to organic farming, becoming highly exclusionist in the face of oppression. They intrigued Katsunori deeply.

3

It was spring, and the larks' twittering could be heard everywhere. The trees on the mountains spread their young leaves, and the fields were overflowing with cabbage, cauliflower, and turnip greens, just waiting to be harvested.

Katsunori, exhausted from his daily two-hours-one-way commute, saw his usual weekend stroll as an opportunity to refresh both mind and body.

It was a particularly fragrant time of year, and the aroma of flowers and grass was everywhere. Then again, there was a more unpleasant smell in the air as well – compost. There were compost piles scattered here and there, and just walking past them assailed the nose with the sharp stink of decay.

As Katsunori walked on, he noticed that Holly's compost gave off no odor, apart from a pleasant sweet-sour, almost foodlike scent. This same scent rose faintly from the fields, and whenever Katsunori set foot on Holly's land, he felt as though he had crossed some unseen barricade into a different world.

One day Katsunori paused before a compost pile made up of cabbage leaves and cedar branches producing that same sweet-sour smell.

He took a cigarette from his pocket and was about to light it when a man farming nearby began to shout, waving his hands for him to stop. Katsunori took out a portable ashtray to indicate he had no intention of littering, but the man leaped over furrows and ran toward him.

"Don't you be using fire over there," he admonished Katsunori.

"Why not?"

"Well, the compost'll catch, now, won't it?"

The man looked about sixty years old, but judging from the way he ran over to Katsunori, he may well have been younger. As was to be expected, the clothes he wore on his bent body were ragged and caked with dirt.

"Does compost really burn that easily?" Katsunori asked, putting away his cigarette.

"Sure. Has to do with the gas it makes as it ferments."

In fact, the air above the compost pile was shimmering. The heap generated heat, and probably methane gas, too.

"I see. Sorry about that."

Katsunori decided to take this opportunity to ask something he'd been wondering about for a long time. "The compost around here smells different. Why is that?"

"It's different soil, y'see."

"Different soil?" Katsunori repeated.

"That's right. It's got microbes in it, and we mix some in with the compost. Good microbes make for good smells, and bad microbes make for a real stink. Hasn't your own kitchen garbage ever smelled rancid? That's bad microbes."

"So if all the other farms' compost stinks..." Katsunori mused.

"It's 'cause they've got bad soil," the man finished. "They've been stuffing it with such harsh chemical fertilizers and pesticides for so long, and now suddenly they switch to organic farming – well, the soil hardly has a chance to recover."

"Holly's been organic since before the war, though," Katsunori pointed out.

"Since the 1700s. We've been farming for a long time now, taking good care of our soil the whole time. Of course it's gonna be different from theirs," the man sniffed.

"But why bend over backward for dirt?"

"That's what farmers do," the man replied, cutting their exchange short and starting to leave. Katsunori hastily asked, "Do you think I could have some of your vegetables, by any chance? I'll pay for them."

"No can do" came the man's blunt reply before he headed into a nearby residence. It was quite a splendid home, looking for all the world like a castle behind its high fence. It bore the nameplate "Soeno".

Katsunori walked on. Although the other farmhouses in the area weren't as grand as the Soeno place, they were all handsome. Furthermore, every last one of them was new. They must really be selling their crops for a pretty penny, Katsunori thought.

Choosing a path he hadn't walked before, he came across a tiny

shrine at Holly's northern border. It backed up to a steep moun-
tainside, and beside it sat an explanatory sign placed there by the
local board of education. According to the sign, the shrine was
built in the mid-1700s, when the village was beset by famine and
the farmers had a tradition of eating soil to stave off starvation.
Five or six little mudcakes were set out in front.

Katsunori wondered if Holly's obsession with dirt didn't somehow stem from this soil-eating.

The mudcakes were still fresh. Someone in the area must still be
looking after the shrine.

There was a minuscule clearing behind the shrine, surrounded
by a wire mesh fence whose gate was secured by a huge padlock.
Katsunori found it strange that the clearing would be fenced in
and not the shrine. Venturing a guess, was it because of safety con-
cerns over landslides, given that steep slope?

Katsunori grew curious about how the practice of eating soil
to fend off starvation came about. Maybe they had really been
eating roots or small animals uncovered as they dug around. Or
perhaps Holly farmers had always been this exclusionary, stash-
ing their provisions in the dirt, then pulling them out and eating
them.

On his way home, a thought came to Katsunori, and he picked
up a pinch of soil from the field where he stood. He brought it
close to his face and peered at it intently.

The Holly soil was darker than that found on other farms. It was
tilled and thoroughly aerated, soft and light. Then there was that
old sweet-sour smell again.

Suddenly he was hungry, and the pinch of soil looked perfectly
edible. He wondered what would happen if he did eat it.

He hesitated for some time before deciding it was out of the
question and tossing the soil aside. As he lowered his hand and
looked up, he saw several people working in a nearby field watching him closely. Their stare was as icy-cold as ever, though maybe

it was reasonable enough to expect them to glare like that after what he did.

Katsunori tried to look nonchalant as he walked away.

4

"I found a job nearby. Can I take it?" Kanako was beaming with happiness.

Her dermatitis had had her on a real rollercoaster ride. Often Katsunori would wake up in the middle of the night to find his wife scratching herself all over, almost unconsciously. Kanako knew she wasn't supposed to scratch her welts and tried her best not to, but she was powerless to stop herself when half asleep.

Still, she'd become a little more lively since they'd moved, and had begun looking for a part-time job. There had been no openings in West Okutama, and she had been toying with the idea of traveling as far as Hachiōji for a position.

"What kind of work is it?" Katsunori asked.

"Gathering kitchen scraps from around the neighborhood for composting. Some Holly guy said they had nothing for their compost piles."

"Holly?"

"Yeah," Kanako replied. "The pay's not much, but they did say they'd share some of their veggies."

Katsunori thought about this. Being a housewife out here in the sticks was nothing short of boring. Why not work? Yet the idea of Kanako working with Holly bothered him. He wondered if it was really all right to mingle with the likes of them.

"So have you been hanging out with Holly people, then?" he asked.

"There are some in my cooking class at the community center, and I see them a lot when I go shopping, too."

Perhaps Katsunori had been imagining things when he thought Holly was really full of itself. "How exactly would you go about collecting these kitchen scraps?" he asked Kanako.

"I'd ask everyone in the neighborhood to set them aside for me and not to put them out with the regular trash. Otherwise there'd be too much other stuff mixed in, paper and plastic and God knows what. Then on a certain day I'd come by to collect it," she explained.

"Will all these people cooperate?"

"Oh," Kanako replied casually, "I'm sure it'll work out somehow. I'll just tell them it's recycling and they'll understand."

Katsunori saw no reason to object. After all, it might be nice for Kanako to interact with the locals, too.

"Well, why not?" he smiled.

"Great! I'll give it a shot. They want me to start right away."

Since Katsunori left for work early and came home late, he didn't really know how Kanako was getting along. She told him she'd distributed plastic buckets to each household for them to store their vegetable cuttings and leftovers, which she'd come by to collect twice a week for a Holly representative to pick up. They'd come with a cart and everything, so apparently Holly was going all-out, too.

Eventually Holly vegetables began appearing at the dinner table. There was no disputing their freshness or taste, but they weren't all that different from the organic, pesticide-free foods Kanako had already been bringing home.

"Apparently people with late-stage cancer have been cured thanks to Holly's produce," an animated Kanako proclaimed, her heart set on the possibility that it might work on her own condition.

Katsunori felt a pang of sorrow. Every time his wife tried a new treatment, she was so certain that this time, this time it would work, and every time she found herself betrayed.

"No way. That can't be," Katsunori replied.

"Holly gets lots of letters that say otherwise," Kanako shot back. "People have recovered from incurable diseases, their atopic dermatitis cleared up – things like that."

"Have you actually seen these letters?"

"Yes, I have."

"Something's fishy here. Haven't there been lots of letters like that all along?"

"Yeah, and?"

Among the curative treatments for Kanako's condition were more than a few that verged on the religious. Most boiled down to nothing but sheer money-making schemes.

Holly vegetables – cabbage, spinach, cucumbers, leeks, radishes, and more – continued to grace the Izawa table.

One day, while eating spinach sautéed in butter, Katsunori felt something rough and granular in his mouth. Upon closer inspection, he found black dirt on the reddish area near the spinach's root end.

"This hasn't been washed very well," he remarked.

"No... well, they say it's best not to wash it. The more you wash, the more nutrients are lost."

"You mean you haven't been washing any of these veggies?"

"No. They hardly need a wash anyway – they're organic," Kanako pointed out.

"Can't you at least get off the dirt?" Katsunori asked, irritated.

"But eating the dirt along with the vegetable is the healthiest way."

"Is that what Holly's been telling you?"

"Yes, it is."

Those Holly people really did have a bizarre hang-up about soil. Then again, it wasn't as if eating dirt could actually do any damage. In the interests of placating Kanako, Katsunori decided to keep on eating the veggies, dirt and all.

Kanako's dermatitis hadn't changed at all in nearly a week. When the week was up, however, they saw dramatic results. Her skin no longer itched, and its dry, scaly texture was improving day by day. Then, out of the blue, her symptoms disappeared completely.

It was almost as though all of Kanako's suffering had been a bad dream.

It had to have been Holly's produce; there had been no other change in their lifestyle.

It goes without saying that Kanako was ecstatic. She started smiling again, and Katsunori felt like their life together was beginning anew.

One thing bothered Katsunori, and that was what would happen if Kanako stopped eating Holly food. His two-hour commute was becoming burdensome, and he wanted to move downtown if at all possible. If they did, however, they would no longer be able to procure vegetables from Holly. He didn't think his wife would rebound like she had with the steroids, but it was still worrying.

In the end, Katsunori opted not to mention moving downtown, deciding for the time being to simply wait and see.

5

Kanako's infatuation with Holly's vegetables made her even more gung-ho when it came to collecting kitchen scraps. Her list of contributing households began to grow, and restaurants even started chipping in.

"Coffee grounds and buckwheat hulls make for excellent fertilizer," she would say happily.

Kanako's enterprising efforts had made her a different person, hardly the introspective and meek woman she had been in the past.

The two of them received more vegetables than they could eat, so Kanako went around distributing the surplus to the sick. Some were pleased, but others saw little value in her offerings and declined. Kanako would assail those who refused with an enthusiastic lecture on the health benefits of Holly's produce. It wasn't far from proselytizing.

Katsunori continued his habitual walks on his days off. The Holly people had come to know him as Kanako's husband, and often called out greetings as he strolled through their land. Not so for the other farms. In complete contrast to times past, Katsunori now found Holly to be a warm and friendly bunch.

He had spoken many times with Soeno, the farmer who had chided him earlier for attempting to smoke. Kanako knew Soeno as well; he seemed to be a Holly elder.

Summer came, and Holly's tomatoes, cucumbers, and eggplants grew ever larger as the sun beat down upon them. It was obvious these people had a different way of doing things.

Kanako worked up a sweat as she collected plastic buckets full of kitchen scraps. She had gotten her hands on some Holly soil and worked it into the garbage. Sure enough, this kept the refuse from stinking.

Katsunori tried asking Kanako what made Holly's soil different from the rest. "They got it from the Soil God," she grinned.

"The Soil God?"

"That's what the Holly folks told me," Kanako explained.

"What do they mean?"

"You know that shrine? Well, there's a limestone cave behind it. I guess it's pretty big."

"The part that's fenced in?" Katsunori questioned.

"Uh-huh," Kanako nodded.

There were a handful of these caves in Okutama, popular as tourist attractions. It wasn't unusual for Holly to have one on their land.

"I haven't seen it myself, but there's a sea of mud in there they call the Brack. It smells sweet, and you can eat it."

"You mean like during the famine back in the 18th century? Come on, that's just some random piece of folklore."

"No, it's true," Kanako persisted. "They showed me some of the mud they took out of the cave. I didn't eat it, but it does give off a sweet smell."

"Really? Is it like tar or something?" Katsunori asked.

"I don't think it's tar, since it looks like plain old dirt when it dries out," Kanako replied. "It doesn't look like it'd be tasty, and I can't say if it's nutritious at all, but starving people did eat it once upon a time. Besides, didn't they use night-soil as fertilizer back then? With everyone eating that mud, their crops would have grown like gangbusters."

"You mean because of the mud in the night-soil," Katsunori clarified.

"Right. And it worked even better when they mixed the mud directly into that night-soil before they put it on their fields. That's why Holly's been taking mud out of the cave for their fertilizer ever since. They didn't use any chemical fertilizers because they knew composting made for far better harvests."

"If it's that great, shouldn't they tell everyone about it, maybe help people out?"

"You mean, like, have a scientific study done on it?" Kanako asked.

"Yeah."

"It's not that kind of thing," Kanako insisted. "Mud from the Brack loses potency after a while. Some sort of mystical power must be at work here."

Katsunori was silent, only half believing what he heard.

"You don't believe it?" Kanako asked.

"Do you?"

"I do, because I felt it. How about you? Ever since we started eating Holly's vegetables, how've you been physically?"

"Same as ever," Katsunori remarked.

"Well, sure – you've always been healthy." A faint spark of anger flashed deep within Kanako's eyes.

Katsunori was bewildered. All along he'd tried the best he could to be attentive and caring toward Kanako. Could she still be dissatisfied, after all his efforts?

"A Holly farmer once told me that the microbes in their soil were different because they'd been farming organically for so long. Is that what you mean? Besides, your dermatitis wasn't necessarily cured by some mystical power," he pointed out.

"So what if it wasn't?" Kanako huffed, and the conversation was over.

Katsunori couldn't get the story about the edible mud out of his head. After his walk, he stopped by the little shrine once more. There had been a landslide down the slope behind the shrine, exposing the mountain's rocky face. Katsunori found this odd, given that there had been no significant rains lately.

There were more mudcakes set out in front of the shrine, twenty or thirty where there had been only five or six before.

Katsunori peered beyond the wire fence, but didn't see anything resembling a cave entrance, despite the tracks of people going in and out. What sort of thing was this Brack mud, anyway?

Kanako became more and more enthusiastic about her quest for kitchen scraps, spending nearly the entire day running around collecting while her husband was away at work. Many were the slapdash meals that made their way to the table, and often she hadn't even begun to start preparing dinner when Katsunori came home.

"We're getting ready for the festival," Kanako explained.

"What festival?" Katsunori asked.

"Holly's festival."

"You're not one of them, you know."

"Yeah, but since they don't have any young women in the village, they asked me to help out," Kanako replied.

"Is their shortage of young women really that bad?"

"Uh-huh. All the surrounding villages and farms look down on Holly, so hardly any women marry into that group."

"So what do they do at this festival of theirs?"

"I'm not quite sure myself," Kanako admitted. "They say this one is going to be special."

"Why's that?"

"The Brack's run out of mud, so they have to pray to the Soil God."

"There's no more mud because they keep taking it. How is praying to a god going to fix that?"

"How should I know?"

For the first time, Katsunori was afraid that Kanako might possibly be having an affair. Until that moment, she had been so passive socially that the thought would never have occurred to him.

As far as Katsunori could tell, though, all of Holly's men were awfully seedy, with seemingly no interest in anything but dirt. He couldn't picture any of them with Kanako.

Still, Katsunori had the feeling they'd better move out, and soon.

6

Kanako had left in the morning that day, leaving Katsunori to his beer and television. The fatigue of working all week long meant he had no desire to do much of anything on his weekends. Apart from his weekly walk, he usually just hung around the house.

A man came to the door, about seventy years old and looking like a respectable gentleman – certainly not one of Holly's.

The visitor gave his name as Mutō, and, after making sure that Kanako wasn't home, jumped right in with "There's something I have to tell you about your wife."

Katsunori invited him inside. The business card Mutō proffered identified him as a local historian. By way of introduction, he explained how he had taught in a local middle school for many years and studied local history as a hobby after he retired. He claimed to be especially knowledgeable about the history of Holly.

After the preliminaries were out of the way, Mutō continued with a sense of urgency: "Your wife is in danger. Please leave here as soon as you can."

"What do you mean?" Katsunori asked.

"Have you heard that Holly's about to put on a festival?"

"In passing, yes."

"At that festival – if your wife should – no, I doubt you'd believe me even if I told you," Mutō said finally. "Let's start from the beginning. Do you know about the cave on Holly's land?"

"The one behind the shrine, you mean?"

Mutō went on to tell Katsunori about the edible mud within, eaten by 18th-century farmers and used as fertilizer.

"I've come to understand that when there's almost no mud left in the Brack, the cave appears to be even deeper… and there's something in there."

"Something? Like what?" Katsunori asked.

"The farmers called it 'the Soil God'," Mutō remarked. "It's a gigantic being, not of this world. The edible mud is some sort of secretion or excretion from this – this thing."

"Ridiculous," scoffed Katsunori. "That's just a legend."

"Whenever the mud ran out, the farmers thought they had angered the Soil God, so to placate it, they would offer a young girl from the village as a living sacrifice. Thus its anger would pass, and once again the Brack would be teeming with mud. Afterwards, the farmers began using only a little mud at a time, and not as straight fertilizer, but only by mixing it into compost. By conserving the mud, they wouldn't be caught short," Mutō explained.

"Have you seen this mud?"

"Yes, I have."

"Do you think vegetables grown in it have the power to heal sickness?"

"Holly people hardly ever get sick, and they live a frighteningly long time," Mutō noted. "You probably don't know how old those people are. Ninety- and hundred-year-old Holly farmers are still out there working the fields."

Katsunori remembered the Holly people he had seen. Could they be even older than they looked?

"Holly guarded this secret among them," Mutō continued. "That's why they keep intermarrying, which is probably why hardly any children have been born there lately."

"Surely there's no real basis for these things you're saying, Mr. Mutō," Katsunori said.

"No, there isn't. I've been skeptical myself, until now. Now, however, the Brack is once again running low. What with the popularity of their produce and all the money it brings in, Holly's become profit-hungry. They've taken too much mud, and once again they've seen the gruesome being squirming deep within the cave," Mutō replied.

Katsunori thought of the crumbled cliff face behind the shrine.

"I've been to the inner cave, too," said Mutō. "There was definitely something there. Something that moves, breathes, smells awful, and gives off heat. Something extremely large. In fact, only the merest portion of that huge being, the very tip of its tail, or maybe its nose, is there at the cave's depths."

"What is it?"

"I don't know. It's probably been there since the earth was created. It's not like any creature on this planet, for one, and it's not any god we humans have ever thought up. No, it's something completely different, and Holly is about to offer it a living sacrifice to quell its rage," Mutō said. "They asked me how they used to do it in the old days. I told them any sacrifice would be meaningless – it's impossible for a being like that to have anything akin to a human emotion like anger."

"Then what should they do?" Katsunori asked.

"Leave it alone. It's only responding to being provoked. Leave it alone and it'll be just as quiet as before. The most frightening thing is if this were to get out into society at large, bringing media, police, scientists – all clamoring for a piece of the action. Who knows what that would do?"

"What did you mean when you said Kanako was in danger?"

"Holly is still going to perform the sacrifice. Your wife has been chosen."

"But Kanako's no girl," Katsunori protested.

"She's a beautiful young woman, and that's good enough for them."

"All right, then. Thank you so much for coming all this way to tell me."

"You and your wife have got to get out of here as soon as possible," Mutō persisted.

"You haven't told Kanako any of this directly?"

"I didn't think it would help if I did."

"Why's that?"

"It seems as though she's chosen to become the living sacrifice of her own free will."

"Give me a break!" Katsunori exclaimed.

"That's how it looked to me, anyway. I figured her husband might convince her to leave. Either that, or you can get her away from them by force, if need be."

Mutō stood to leave. As he reached the foyer, Katsunori asked, "Did you teach them how they used to do the sacrifices in the old days?"

"Yes."

"How did they do it?"

"They turn the sacrificial victim into soil," Mutō replied.

"Into soil? What do you mean?"

"Well, you see, it was a long time ago, after all."

With this evasive remark, Mutō turned and was gone.

Kanako returned after dark. Katsunori told her about the historian's visit.

"Oh, you mean that professor. He knows more about Holly than they do. A little weird, though, isn't he?"

"He said Holly was going to make you into a living sacrifice," Katsunori continued.

"Come on! He must be imagining things. It's just this ceremonial thing they do – of course I'm not really going to be sacrificed."

"Maybe those Holly people are just telling you that, trying to throw you off."

"That's impossible," Kanako flatly replied.

"Is it really?" Katsunori pressed.

"Yes, it is, really." A cryptic smile flickered across her lips.

Katsunori dreamed that night, dreams of gigantic monsters running rampant from their underground lairs, of the ruptured earth swallowing him up.

7

When Katsunori came home from work at eight o'clock, just like always, Kanako was gone. Even though she may not always have had dinner prepared by that hour, she'd never actually not been there. His apprehension only grew as he waited for her to return.

About ten days had passed since Mutō had come to deliver his warning. Katsunori didn't much believe the old man's story, especially the part about the huge thing lurking deep within the cave. It only followed, then, that he didn't think Kanako would be its sacrificial victim.

At eleven o'clock, Katsunori made up his mind to go looking for his wife. He had considered going to the police, but he didn't think they'd be able to act as quickly as the situation required.

He headed for Holly's shrine. The surrounding area was dark

and deserted, despite the cart, wheelbarrow, and shovels resting nearby. The entry to the fenced enclosure was open, and Katsunori went inside.

There was something within that seemed like it could be the cave entrance; it was too dark to see much, although Katsunori did hear faint noises from somewhere. He felt his way around, finally managing to slip inside the cave.

The cave interior was black as pitch, with precarious footing that sloped downward at a substantial angle. He moved along step by cautious step until he saw a light in the direction of the cave's depths.

A tangle of flashlight beams crossed a space about the size of a grade-school gymnasium. It must be what they called the Brack, although there was nothing resembling a sea of mud, only a few muddy smudges here and there. The cave's ceiling was dotted with stalactites hanging down in grotesque shapes. About a dozen human figures stood in the space there.

The intersecting beams of light revealed a woman, naked and smeared in mud: Kanako. She was on her knees, scooping mud into her mouth and swallowing it.

She followed a pattern of eating mud, then smearing it over her sensually twisted body, over and over again, looking almost as though she were in a trance. The circle of men crowded around her watched intently; Katsunori took in the scene from behind an outcropping of rock.

Several of the men gripped large sickles in their hands. Katsunori thought back to what Mutō had said, about turning the sacrificial victim into soil. They could slash away at Kanako with their sickles and leave her mincemeat remains where they lay, dripping with mud. Microorganisms would work to decompose the corpse and, eventually, turn her into soil. Is that what was going on? Or was this really just ceremonial after all?

Just then Katsunori was blinded as a flashlight trained on him.

The crowd began to murmur. He stepped out from behind the rock.

"Mr. Izawa! What are you doing here?" It was Soeno's voice.

Katsunori thought fast. Should he come out guns blazing or go the meek and humble route? He didn't have enough of a handle on the situation yet.

Meanwhile, someone had sneaked behind him and cut off his escape path. Katsunori found himself being pushed into the center of the cavern bit by bit.

"You shouldn't have seen this. No, this won't do at all," Soeno said.

"I've come for my wife," Katsunori replied. "We'll be leaving together."

"It's not over yet," said a quiet voice. Bloodlust hung in the air. Maybe they were going to kill him, too.

Kanako continued eating the mud and slathering it over her body as before.

Katsunori, having decided it would be impossible to force his way past the man behind him and make a break for the exit, instead began inching further into the cave's depths. These people were afraid of the Soil God – he had to use that fear.

"Better not go that way," someone said, in a voice that betrayed his alarm.

"Why's that?" asked Katsunori. "Is there something in there?"

It was just as he'd hoped. He started walking boldly into the cave. With all flashlights on him, he had no problem navigating the path.

Katsunori stepped into a layer of mud. It was sticky, like mucus. A sound came from deep within the cave, the sound of something tremendous sliding around. Then a warm breeze began to blow, with a smell that beggared all description.

"Don't let the light hit it!" someone cried, and Katsunori was left in darkness.

There was something huge here, that was certain. Still, he was more afraid of all those men and their sickles.

This monstrous being would react to stimuli. If he did this right, he might be able to drive the men out of the cave. He pressed on, unable to see a thing in the inky blackness.

Katsunori remembered the lighter in his pocket. He pulled it out and lit it, and the space in front of him went blue.

For a while he had no idea what on earth had happened. The men had all collapsed, their flashlights rolling back and forth on the ground between them. Katsunori's ears were ringing, and he caught a whiff of a singed-hair smell.

There had been an explosion; gas deposits had collected along the cave floor.

This was his chance to escape. Katsunori picked up a flashlight and, holding the dazed and muddied Kanako close, turned toward the exit. The Holly men gradually began lifting their heads, trying to make sense of what had happened.

He heard something behind them as rocks came raining down from the cave ceiling. "It's a cave-in!" a voice shouted.

Katsunori ran for his life, Kanako in tow.

8

Katsunori moved back to the city and went into the office every day. Looking back, it was nothing short of a miracle that he and Kanako managed to get out alive. Because Katsunori had been at the explosion's epicenter, he'd felt the least impact and was able to act quickly. That's what saved them. They were also lucky that there was so little gas in the cave, and that their oxygen supply hadn't run out.

Apparently all the Holly men escaped as well, although Katsunori suspected a few of them had been buried alive. It would be a cinch to cover that up as long as the Holly people got their stories straight.

The explosion had made the cave collapse completely.

Katsunori made a single telephone call to Mutō. "Did you see the thing in the cave?" the professor asked.

"I didn't see it, but I could sense it."

"No one would believe you, you know, especially not now, with the cave-in and all. Just let it go," Mutō suggested, and Katsunori agreed. All he could do was let sleeping gods lie, keeping the thing a mystery for all eternity.

One thing still worried him, though. Wouldn't Holly have to dig out that cave again someday to collect their mud?

It didn't matter. By having sensed the existence of that giant being, Katsunori suddenly grew to recognize that everyday reality is itself a mystery.

Kanako was a mystery herself. She claimed not to remember anything at all about what happened in the cave that day, but who knew if that was true? Who could say if the ceremony was meant to be all for show or if they really had intended to sacrifice her?

Kanako's dermatitis never recurred. She went back to being the quiet, introverted person she had always been. She was, however, even more beautiful than before, possibly due to the copious amount of mud she had eaten. When Katsunori told her how she'd grown even more attractive since the "sacrifice", she simply smiled and said, "Really?"

No doubt Katsunori would keep sharing his life with this mystery named Kanako for many, many years to come.

Necrophallus

Makino Osamu
Translated by Chun Jin

"*The most spiritual men feel the stimulus
and the charm of sensuous things in a way that
other men – those with 'fleshly hearts' cannot
possibly imagine and ought not to imagine…*"
– Friedrich Nietzsche

Necrophallus

Makino Osamu
Translated by Chun Jin

WELL, I CAN tell you one thing: Lovecraft would never have written this! But whether he would have been capable of it, or would have approved it, these questions are quite distinct.

And yet it is a Lovecraftian tale; it belongs in this anthology. What Makino Osamu has done, besides, of course, writing an extremely effective and downright extreme horror story, and boy do I mean *horror* story, is to reduce the cosmic horror of H.P. Lovecraft from the *macro*cosmic level to the *micro*cosmic level. As above, so below. The girl from (the planet) next door heralds the end of the world. And in her relentless carving, she *is* ending the world, the only world that we and the narrator know for the duration of the tale. He is an art teacher, and she is Richard Pickman. Only she does not make a flat canvas representation of a monster. She makes a three-dimensional fleshly sculpture into another one with much different dimensions, one fit for life in another dimension.

If our narrator indulges an epistemology of the epidermis, a Nirvana of the nerve endings, he is long past noticing his mistake of mixing two once-distinct colors on his palette: pleasure and pain. Like Sartre who could enter into the acute, hot spotlight of reality only when he stabbed himself in the hand with scissors, our friend Hiroshi can define himself, be sure of the sharp edges separating him from a water-color wash of existence in general (one that anybody might at the moment be experiencing, it being difficult to determine whether it is he or someone else) – when he experiences either pain or fear. But then even here he is, by his own confession, not sure, not safe, because it occurs to him that the thrill of pain and fear may be the same for the sufferer and the sadist. And then, which one is he? He finds ultimate ecstasy in dissolution, which is only fair, since "ec-stasy" means, in Greek, "to stand out from." The visionary ecstatic stands for a moment outside his body, his earthly reality, existing as a ghost and yet so enabled to see the *real* in an objective manner, bypassing the senses. Hiroshi escapes corporeality, not by some imaginary mystical ascension, but by actually escaping the body for good. And then, of course, he has become a being who cannot distinguish life from death, or even tell if there is supposed to be a difference. If not, then no wonder he cannot decide.

Lovecraft, as Fritz Leiber long ago observed, translated the essence of horror into the worldview of science and science fiction. But sometimes he went so far in that direction that a couple of his (best) tales seem to escape the horror genre altogether and become science fiction, period. I am thinking of *At the Mountains of Madness* and "The Shadow out of Time." "Necrophallus" harks back to the former. "Grandpa" must have been one of those explorers or one like them, and he must have discovered such a nameless city. What he found was something on the order of the Shining Trapezohedron, displaying unthinkable worlds of wonder and horror, the difference between them becoming impossible to distinguish. That is the madness out of space, the fun from Yuggoth. "Necrophallus" yanks hard on this concept, this *fabula,* and drags the resultant tale back well within the realm of sheer, unadulterated horror. Finally the relevant question becomes not, why couldn't HPL have thought of a story like this, but rather, why and how Makino Osamu *could.*

Necrophallus

THIS IS NO place. There is nothing here. I am no one.

But of course, I'm just kidding.

In truth, this is some place, there is something here, and I am myself.

Ah, but that is not exactly the truth either.

The moment you say something with conviction, it becomes untrue; so, of course, this is also a fallacy.

Well, be that as it may, in those days, I lived quite separated from reality.

Should you believe me? Should you not? I don't know…

Perhaps I yearned for the 'real' that was out of my reach. Like a nun tormented by desires she does not know, I was hounded by a need to capture the real that seemed always to slip right through my hands.

Like this time –

I'm pushing down this woman's face with my left hand. I am clutching her jaw (that itself would distort a face, but her face is even more twisted with fear) and pushing her against the wall. Her fear is real. Very real.

"Scared?" I ask her, and she tries frantically to nod her head. Her eyes plead.

I raise my right hand and snap my wrist at her face. A slap. It makes an ugly sound.

I leave her left cheek red. The red is real. Even more real are the moment that my hand strikes her face and her face immediately after it is struck. To feel my real, I need to get the details right. Yes, I sharpen the edges of my world, and I find my real. I slap her right cheek. I slap her left. The vague world around me gradually comes into focus.

It requires technique. The human body is amazingly frail. My aim is not to destroy flesh. I chase limits – the limit beyond which damage to flesh would be irreversible. It's a delicate task, knowing just the right amount of force to administer. For instance, when I brought this woman to the hotel, I punched her in the stomach. She bent double and vomited on the cheap carpet like a sick kitten. Can you see how perfect my technique must have been? To make sure I did not hurt my victim's internal organs, yet sap her resistance definitively, and establish without question a relation of dominator and dominated – all with a single punch in the stomach?

There was just once that I made a mistake. I was still learning how to establish my real. And I overdid it. I stared down at the corpse. It nearly made me scream. A corpse is a conclusive thing. It is neither more nor less than just that – a corpse. It slapped home the fact that I had let a precise drop of red spill onto a blurry, vague world. My real, which had so far been clinging on precariously, seemed suddenly to lose its grip and plunge into the depths of nothingness. No, I must not kill. Never!

"Please…," the woman says, "forgive me."

What, I wonder, does she want to be forgiven for? I found her through a dating service. I picked her for her description suggesting prostitution. Is she asking to be forgiven the folly of subscribing to something as idiotic as a dating service? Or is she asking to be forgiven for the illegality of the act of prostitution itself? Maybe she is asking to be forgiven for being stupid enough to come and meet me…?

I ram my knees up between her legs. She lets out a pathetic yowl. Perhaps, if a fish could cry, it might sound like that.

"Don't...," she weeps. She looks amazingly ugly.

I punch her eye with my fist. Even as I watch, the eyelid swells up. In a while, the swelling will go down and leave a black eye. And then the black eye will also go. Her eyesight will not be affected. I'm as dexterous as a surgeon with my hands, you see. As the scars of my violence fade, will the woman's real also fade away?

Most likely, the woman herself will fade away.

I swing her around and push her face into the wall.

"Gimme your hands."

She obeys meekly. I handcuff them behind her. Then, pulling her by her fastened arms, I shove her down on her back and sit astride her stomach. Her arms are crushed under her and she cannot move. I box her head a few times with my fist. I stop for a minute, call out to her, then box again. If I see resignation or despair on her face, I give her a break and start all over again.

Fear always takes birth in these intervals. I savor her fear. I swirl it around on my tongue to taste my real.

Few junior-high school art teachers lack for free time. That's how I can afford so much time chasing after my real. But for that, I would probably be wailing like a lost child in the middle of an uncertain world. Enough to send me straight to the madhouse. However, thanks to my stars, at thirty-seven, I am still around and can face a batch of students as their teacher. It's pretty exhausting, though.

I watch the students as they doodle in the name of art, mark them on their performance, finish my duties for the day, and leave the art room. I walk through the school building, already dusky with evening. It is still early spring and the days are short. The old wooden floorboards in the corridor creak at every step. They're like a bunch of expiring spirits laid in a row.

There is movement somewhere. In the eighth-grade classroom. The door is open a crack; I peek in. There are three boys in there. One crouching with his head in his hands, and the other two kicking him by turns. Like a ceremony of some sort, they kick him again and again, and again and again, by turns.

They stop suddenly, and all three look right at me. All three of them – the one that was being kicked as well as the two that were kicking – look at me with the same eyes. Pitch black eyes, like holes bored through the face. Eyes packed with an endless, evil darkness. I feel a whiff of dry air blow at me from those eyes. I avert my own and leave the scene quickly.

What was it I just saw? Two of them were beating up a third. Without doubt, fear was being produced and consumed there.

But who was the producer and who the consumer? The three boys all had the same expression in their eyes. Is it possible that tormentors and victims have the same eyes? Could it be possible that to find my real, what I need, rather than to terrorize someone else, is to become the terrorized myself? Or are they the same thing? Are they the exact same, completely interchangeable thing? Are they! Are they, really? Perhaps they really are! Still…

"…you know, Sensei."

"Eh?" I turn to find a little girl. She is wearing the school uniform.

"Who are you?" I ask. I am out of the school building and on the road to the station without realizing.

"I was just saying that you must come over to see," she smiles.

She has huge eyes and small lips that pout. A face out of a girls' comic book of not long ago. A face emphasizing the distortion that is beauty…is obviously "beautiful."

"Where?" I ask blankly. "Where should I go to see?"

She contemplates me silently for a moment.

"You haven't been listening to me at all, have you?" She laughs mischievously.

Or rather, she laughs in a way suggesting that she wants it to be interpreted as a mischievous laugh. Like trying to imitate an emotion that is foreign to her nature. Her awkwardness has an inexplicable, perverted charm for me.

"Now lemme see, who might you be..."

"Do I have to explain starting from there?"

"I'm sorry, sweetie. I was thinking of something."

"You're always thinking of something, aren't you? Even in class."

"Like a bad student, eh?"

"Like a bad teacher!" she looks at me accusingly.

"So, where are we going?"

"You'll come with me, won't you, Sensei?"

"Your house?"

"My grandfather's house."

"Is it close by?"

"Oh, just right there."

I end up following the young lady down a never-ending night street.

I have a premonition of something bad about to happen. Or rather, the "something bad" is happening all along. My legs keep pulling me back, refusing to go on. But the girl slips her exceptionally hot hand into my sweaty one and pulls me along. Dusk turns into night in the maze-like suburb, and the street seems to change guise, to become some street in a foreign land. It is a chilling feeling, like accidentally seeing another side to your mother. It suddenly occurs to me that I have been here before.

"We're here!"

Whew! After that endless walk along a tall concrete fence off the road, me pulled along with amazing strength by the small girl, we have come upon a huge iron door. The door, armored with rivets, is lightly rusty and opens reluctantly with a creak as she pushes.

"My grandfather's house," she says, entering.

"Grandpa was American. He was a geologist, who also taught at a Massachusetts university."

A sprawling lawn spreads inside the compound wall. Unbelievable that there should be a house with such huge grounds in this area. We walk across the grounds over the dry grass. It is like a manor house… or perhaps "fortress" describes it better: a huge block of concrete, surrounded by walls. The door to the house is also a sturdy iron one, as though intended to lock something safely up within. The little girl brings out a stout key with old-fashioned openwork. She pushes it through the keyhole. A stout iron key, creaking its way through a rusty keyhole, rammed in by tender fingers – queerly erotic.

I lend her a hand as she tries to push the door in with her shoulder. It is heavy, very heavy. We squeeze in through the gap we manage to open.

"Mind closing it behind you?" she says with a reprimand in her voice.

I obey docilely.

"Grandpa ran away to this far-eastern country." She walks on lightly.

The corridor divides into two inside the doorway. We take the right and come presently to a triple-fork. Not an intersection at right angles – the three lanes have only a small angular difference.

She takes the middle corridor without hesitation.

"Grandpa was hounded, you know. That's why he built a house like this – a maze to throw off pursuers."

She pulls me along, turning now right, now left, going up a staircase and down another, through door after door, until we get to the room. A room like the insides of an ancient ruin. Like a cave scooped out of rock. The door shuts with a nasty grating sound. The only light is from a small bulb hanging from the ceiling, and darkness manages to obscure the far corners of the room.

"This," I stroke the wall… "concrete?"

"Yes, but made to look like rock."

"Your grandfather was a man of very exotic tastes."

"I told you he was being hunted and lived here to elude his pursuers. That's the reason he built a house like this. Behind this wall are thick tiles of lead."

"What exactly was he running away from?"

"Shall I first tell you *why* he was running away?"

She brings out a wooden box from the far end of the room.

"This," she says, "is the reason."

She opens the lid of the old box. Inside is something shaped like a rod, wrapped up carefully like a jewel. The little girl softly peels off layer after layer of wrapping. Each time she peels off a layer, my heart skips a beat.

I can feel cold sweat running down my forehead, neck, armpits and back. I can't stop trembling. The stronger I try to be, the more I tremble. I want to run away. I want to drop everything and flee. My mind fervently wishes for just that, but my legs won't move. My body is petrified. My eyes are frozen as they stare at whatever is trying to emerge from under those wraps.

And then, it shows itself.

"Grandpa called this *Necrophallus*."

It is a dagger. But such a terrifying, ominous dagger! The hilt is leather – leather swollen with gooseflesh, gleaming wet like a sick lizard. The sheath is also leather – but so pale, it looks more like skin. On closer inspection, it does indeed have pores with sparse downy hair growing out of them.

"It is over seventy years since grandpa brought this here. He maintained he had excavated it from an ancient stratum of earth at the south pole. But he was lying. In truth, during a survey of the south pole, grandpa discovered a strange city, and he *stole* this dagger from that city. Stole it and ran. That's how come he had to live in seclusion in a place like this."

The girl removes the dagger from its sheath. The blade of the sword is of a metal I have never seen. A light bluish-gray, a pattern like a network of veins running on the surface. It gleams as though oiled, giving off an ominous, frightening light. A light completely unlike the light of the sky, which rivals and confronts darkness. This light is filthier than darkness itself. A horrific light that will corrode and eat away anything it shines upon, like a powerful acid.

"Well, shall we start?" the little girl says.

She looks at me. Her eyes seem to give off the same light as the blade of the sword.

There is a dull sound like a thud. The impact comes after it. I have been hit.

I put my hand to my brow.

I hear her laugh.

She has struck my brow with the dagger's hilt.

I feel everything go black for a moment.

The collar of my overcoat is in her fists.

I am pushed against the wall.

Even before I have finished being surprised at her strength, which is totally out of proportion with her slender form, she aims her fist straight at my right eye.

I see stars. They're white; now they are red.

She rams her knee up my crotch.

I let out a pathetic howl in spite of myself.

I can feel the strength drain from my legs.

I cannot keep standing.

With my back against the wall, I feel my knees buckling under me.

It hurts… it hurts, oh that hurts…

"What are you doing!?" I look up at the girl, sucking in my runny nose. There are tears in my voice.

"I thought, Sensei, that you were the expert on that," the little girl sounds greatly pleased as she says it, sitting astride me as I slip down to the floor.

Little girl?

How could I be so stupid? Wearing a junior-high school uniform doesn't make someone a little girl. As she brazenly thrusts her glaring face at me, I can see only too clearly that this is – a woman. A full-grown woman. Perhaps not much younger than myself, maybe even older than me.

The woman slaps my face on either side.

"Do you understand now?"

I shake my head.

"But Sensei, you, of all people, must understand me. I mean, after all," she comes close and breathes harshly down my neck, "you're a murderer."

"You were watching…?"

"From beginning to end. But you don't do such things on the roadside anymore, it seems."

"That was the only time I did something like that. Never before and never again."

"Chī-chan…"

"Huh?"

"That's what I call her."

"Oh, she was your friend? A relative? Older sister? …Mother?"

"Just a pet."

"A pet?"

"Yes, Chī-chan is my pet."

She gets up and goes to the far end of the room and pushes at the stone wall. A door opens on the side with a clatter. As though sealed by a jet-black wall, nothing inside is visible. The woman puts her hand into the darkness and pulls out "Chī-chan," somewhat like a conjurer pulls a handkerchief out of a hat.

"Chī-chan" has no legs, and moves by twisting at the waist and bounding up with the stubs that are left where the thighs should be. The arms have also been chopped off at the shoulders. The entrails are falling out of the slit stomach, and keep bouncing up and down like the tentacles of a sea anemone.

"Your work of art, Sensei," the woman says, pointing to Chī-chan.

This thing – Chī-chan – its neck is bent way to the right, as though broken. No, wait, the neck is actually broken. I know. I was the one who broke it. This was ten years ago. I had not been able to grasp my real as efficiently as I do now.

"I…I swear I did not do that! I never use daggers."

"Yes, that's true. You're more a bare-fist guy. I admit you simply strangled her. In an alley quite nearby, no? I dragged the corpse into grandpa's house after you fled. And then I used my own imagination. What do you think, Sensei? Do I get good marks for creativity?"

The "thing" comes up to me taking small bounds. Its lips are still distorted the way they got when I hit them. It opens those distorted lips and makes a small noise like a wild animal.

"*Coo…*" it says.

"B…but I killed her. She should be dead ten years now."

"How right you are, Sensei! She was quite dead. It is the corpse that is now my pet that I call Chī-chan. So, what do you think?"

Chī-chan dangles its entrails over me. They caress my throat, cheeks and crotch very lovingly.

I think I screamed. I must have run from there screaming and lost consciousness…

Coming to, I find myself on a train. The top of my eyelids smart. I feel them with my hands and find them swollen. Could it have been a dream? But it hurts terribly everywhere that she hit me. It could hardly have been a dream.

"Aren't you going to be late?" my wife says, seeing me still in pajamas.

"Oh, I should be fine for class, I think."

"Papa, see you later," my little daughter kisses me on the cheek. She has just started school.

"See you later, sweetheart." I grin foolishly at her vanishing figure. She's just too sweet to be true.

"I'll see you later too," my wife went back to work soon after she had our daughter. She's a clerk at a real estate agent.

"Don't forget to let the dirty dishes soak. Makes it easier to wash them," she says as she leaves.

Left to myself, I silently finish breakfast. Rice with herbs and miso-soup, and something to go. Though busy, my wife always makes it a point to organize a proper breakfast. I told her I had fallen down the stairs at the station. I wonder how much of it she swallowed. Nevertheless, another normal day is looking all set to start. Provided I want it that way.

If I get carted off by the police, the neighbors might want to know why.

"They were such a happy family," they would say.

I wonder about that myself. It feels as though if I continue to sit around vaguely like this, I might just waft up and merge into the surroundings. It is very frightening.

Somehow, I am also very restless. I want to get my edges clear. I want to claw myself out from the rest of the world and make sure of the reality that I am me. Pain and fear – two things that can make me real. Compared with these, everyday life is like a bedtime story, vague and pointless.

So, I must – do what?

I finish breakfast, brush my teeth, and take a shower. By the time I get into my clothes, I have lost any intention I may have had of going to school. I call and make the old excuse about having a cold, and ask for the day off. I wonder what I am doing. There is a me that is the man of action, and there is another me that just stands apart and watches impassively.

Right! If I get it right, things will happen the way I hope. Everything has been gearing up to this from the very beginning. I cannot escape from there. And *where* may that be?

I walk along, dragging my hand against the tall concrete fence. I seem to have left the house without realizing. Ah, there's her voice, so clear.

The door opens from within. I am not sure which way or how I came, but I am in that stone room now.

"Welcome," I hear her laughing voice behind me, but before I can turn, I feel the impact on the back of my head.

Even as I think *uh-oh*, the world sways in front of my eyes. The strength seems to drain easily out of me. I cannot stand. The woman laughs… she laughs… she laughs…

"*Coo…oooru.*" It is Chī-chan making those weird noises again.

Chī-chan is dragging its stumps and marching up and down by my head, where I lie fallen on the ground. The woman sits at my feet.

She holds a naked dagger. Yes, that same horrifying dagger.

"This time I shan't let go," she is holding up my foot, "Of this."

She sticks the tip of the dagger into my ankle.

"No…!"

But my body won't move for all I can scream. She must have drugged me. I raise up my head to see what is being done to me. That is all I can do – to *see*.

The cuff of my trouser-leg has been folded up, and the dagger is being stuck into my naked ankle. I feel a dull, tingling pain. The metal blade of the dagger seems to convulse for an instant.

And then, as though entering slush, it enters my ankle with beautiful ease.

It is scorching! The dagger dives through, leaving the broken flesh as hot as if scalding water had been poured over it. The flesh cools in the same instant. The dagger hits a bone.

It is at this moment – what surges sweetly, heavily down my spine is pleasure. Languid lust that collects in the belly like thick syrup. I break out in an itchy sweat. My penis glows with heat and grows heavy. I let out a slight moan.

"Look," the woman brandishes my right ankle before my eyes.

Chuckling from deep within her throat, she presses a pink cross-section of the stump against my throbbing groin.

"Aaa…ah…" I cannot prevent a pitiful groan from passing through my clenched teeth.

She laughs.

"That's *Necrophallus* for you. The dagger that gives pleasure in exchange for pain, immortality in exchange for death. It is made of a metal called lagh from Yuggoth."

"*Nyo…goos mii goouu*," Chī-chan is prancing around near my head. The dangling entrails sway gently like sea-weeds.

"Yuggoth…"

A faraway look comes into the woman's eyes as she stares into space. She throws away my right ankle and picks up the left, caressing it gently.

I wait, my heart pounding and my flesh creeping. Yes, anticipating the next rush of pleasure.

The dagger digs in. There is heat for a moment, then, before I know, pleasure surges over me once again like a huge wave.

As if pumped with compressed air, my penis swells and lifts my pants upward with adamant rigidity, hard to the point of throbbing painfulness; a very sweetly twinging pain. My leg muscles cramp and a spasm begins.

I feel my toes curl, although of course I no longer have any.

"Have mercy…," I pant.

"Oh, we still have a long way to go," the woman smiles sweetly.

Provoked even by her smile, my semen clamors for release.

The woman sits astride me, pulls out my shirt and bares my stomach. Such a soft, white, defenseless stomach! She runs her slender fingers lightly over it. Her nails scratch the skin.

"Here," she decides, poking with the tip of the dagger.

The dagger smoothly cuts through, widening the slit in its wake. Inside, the blade twists around. It makes a disgustingly sticky swish-swashing sound.

"Don't do this to me…"

Something explodes within. My body writhes and goes into convulsions. Hot, thick sperm spurts out. It keeps flowing never-endingly, as though the stopcock were broken.

"Oh, you came, did you? There's more, of course…"

I can see exactly what she is talking about. The focus of my pleasure is not my penis. As the dagger messes with the organs in my stomach, creating havoc, I continue to ejaculate. Each time it enters the gaping slit, the dagger turns the skin over, and yellow fat oozes in its wake. Blood mixed with lymph dribbles out. I cannot rein in the painful moans that escape with my wild gasps.

"Destroy me! *Finish me off!*" I am screaming before I realize.

My legs have been split vertically from thigh to ankle in many strips. The woman has split them up even more easily than she might split bamboo. I wonder what became of the bones and muscles, but the split legs have now become tentacles of flesh that move according to my wishes. I have turned into something like an octopus. She scooped out my genitals. Words cannot begin to describe the mad frenzy that rocked me when she did that. Now there is nothing there.

Only my intestines, disguised as tentacles, dangling out of the gaping hole. My arms are gone. Quite disinterestedly, the woman cut them off at the shoulders. The skin on my face has been peeled off after the fashion of tiles. The hair, nose, earlobes, eyelids are all gone. She seemed to slice them off in fun. At each stage of this process I mustered and dispatched an additional ejaculation, continuing to climax even after I lost my sexual organs.

The skin and muscles of my stomach and chest form an openwork of vines twined around my trunk. You can see my heart, lungs and other organs through the openwork as they beat with a life of their own. The woman is skillful with her dagger. I rate her skill very highly in my capacity as an art teacher. My body is now an openwork screen, good enough to display as a work of art.

I have lost my body in exchange for the kind of pleasure that is unattainable in this world.

"*Coo...ooooru.*"

That is me, making that noise. My tongue has not been taken away.

"*Roo...curooo,*" Chī-chan responds and comes over. Chī-chan rubs its dangling tentacles against my own. They make a sound like someone slurping their spaghetti. Not to compare with being dismembered by the *Necrophallus*, but such mingling of entrails also holds something like the remnants of pleasure.

"*Ooo ruu,*" I moan. Chī-chan moans in response.

There is no expression on the face above the broken neck lolling at that unnatural angle. Could it be spit dribbling out of those closed lips?

"Hiroshi," the woman calls me by the first name that occurs to her.

Not that I care what I am called. I push Chī-chan aside and glide over to her on my tentacles, eagerly hoping she'll carve me up again. It is possible that this is my true form. I feel no contradictions or strangeness in this form. My edges are very sharp, and I can clearly feel that I am Me. For all people, there exists a form of flesh that is appropriate to their desires. I am now convinced of this truth.

"Come, Hiroshi," the woman holds out her hand.

I press against the hand. The hand steals through the openwork of skin and flesh, sending a tremor right through me. The fingers roughly knead at my internal organs.

"See my grandpa?" the woman asks.

I shake my head breathing raspingly.

"Here, this is grandpa."

She puts her "grandpa" on my chest, and "grandpa" crawls on it like an overgrown caterpillar.

The woman's grandfather was her first creation. Carved over and over again by the *Necrophallus*, he is now little more than a lump of flesh. A small chunk of flesh with tiny hands and legs carved out, that is her grandfather.

"Isn't grandpa cute? He kept running from things all his life, and shut himself up in this dungeon, but the power of the *Necrophallus* caught up with him. When he started hurting himself, my frightened grandmother left him and ran away. It was the right thing to do. Thanks to that, grandma lived and died a human being, unlike grandpa.

"You know, in the end they smoked him out anyway. Grandpa had a daughter – my mama. But scoundrel that he was, he handed mama over to them in exchange for the *Necrophallus*. It was grandpa who carved mama up. They must have liked his creation very much, because they took mama away to their world. That is where I was born."

I begin to see. She is not human. The same way that I am not human. Except, she has no memories of having ever been human.

"Do you know why I came to this world?"

She sticks her fingers into my lung and firmly grasps the swollen spongy tissue, which promptly collapses. A plaintive whistle comes from my throat and I feel the ghost of my penis becoming erect.

"This world will soon end. They – my father and his people – will soon be here. They probably sent me on first to collect information. Or it could be that they sent me on ahead to let me enjoy this world while it still was. Well, come along. You needn't worry about anything any more."

She drops the dagger's sheath. The metal gleams and the light reflected from it trembles. The woman has my jaw in her hands. I suppose my eyes are full of eager anticipation as I look up at her. I must look pathetic, I realize. Indifferent to such things as the end of the world, all I care about is the pleasures of the *Necrophallus*. The sword pierces my forehead.

It goes through… right in…

In the indescribable thrill that follows, my whole world explodes, my consciousness is blown to bits as the dagger dives in… diiivvees iiiiin… diivees iiin. Whaaat could that be… couuuld be…could beee…that sooft twisted tiisssuue iiin the cooorrner of the roooom, that comes and cooomes aaand… coooould it be the eeennnnnnnd of the wooooorld?

Welcome one and all, welcome to the end of the world! Bring your family and friends! Welcome, welcome!

Love for Who Speaks

Shibata Yoshiki
Translated by Stephen A. Carter

Love for Who Speaks

Shibata Yoshiki
Translated by Stephen A. Carter

HERE IS A Lovecraftian allegory of love, perhaps the last thing we expect in the Lovecraft tradition. HPL's women and wives are always monsters and temptresses, as witness Asenath Waite in "The Thing on the Doorstep," Robert Suydam's demon bride in "The Horror at Red Hook," and Marceline in "Medusa's Coil." Asenath turns out not to be human (being an Innsmouth Deep One), and not even a woman! She is the host persona for her sorcerer father old Ephraim Waite (and before *that*, who knows?). Marceline turns out to be a light-skinned "Negress." For Lovecraft, the two revelations were one. At least the identity of Asenath was a symbol for that of Marceline. He loathed race mixing, and that was, of course, the not-so-subtle subtext of "The Shadow over Innsmouth."

But in Shibata Yoshiki's subtle, eerie, and excellent tale, you will find the Innsmouth theme used in a totally different way. Here we cannot but see the airy surface world as an allegory of mundane, humdrum society in the twenty-first century, a place and a time in which romantic sensibility has been exorcised somewhere along the way to facilitate the smooth functioning of human beings as automatons. Even the heroine's marriage, coming after a string of innocent but loveless relationships, is lovelessly pursued and arranged by mediation of a third party: blind date wedlock! And to this arrangement no objection first seems worth making. Until, somehow, as if from an unknown, beckoning world, a call, a mysterious whisper of love intrudes.

The fearful husband, who, as we come to learn, has lost lovers before, need be no more than a fearful husband who loves his wife so much that he literally shackles her to him, alienating the very love he wishes thus to secure. The sea represents that wider world of love and experience his wife has never partaken of. He knows that if she does experience it, he will have lost her. The sea, again, stands for the wide world. Yoshiki tells us this clearly enough when, near the end, he has the husband threaten the wife with the obsessive murder we had earlier been led and tempted to accept as the true answer to the disappearance of his earlier women. Close to the end, we have come to surmise the bizarre, Lovecraftian truth instead; the fact that Yoshiki nonetheless still holds open the seeming possibility that the previous women did after all meet with the wrath of a fanatically possessive husband shows us that it is the all-too-real domestic crisis of the passive wife and obsessive husband that is the real horror of the story. As he remarks more than once, the couple lives for a long time safely in "shells," as if they have not emerged into the broader world of exciting life with its colorful potential.

For fictional purposes the possessiveness of the husband is transmogrified into the selfish disobedience of an official "procurer" for Y'ha-nth'lei beneath the waves. Like the Gnostic Revealer (so ably represented by Morpheus in *The Matrix*), his mission is to contact the members of a breed of strangers in a strange land and summon them back to their dim-remembered home. But, exactly like the Revealer in the Gnostic *Hymn of the Pearl*, he neglects his mission and his senses become dulled, inured to the numbing pleasures of the world into which he had been sent to rescue his kindred exiles. He does not want to leave. And when at length he is forced to become himself, his true form, we realize he could never have been happy with Chisa, or made her happy. Even in the allegorical clothing of fish-people, the two belong to different species. Love would have sealed a bond between them. But then the reason it did not was precisely that, being the sort of creature he was, he lacked the capability for such feelings and such words.

We might sum up the point of this chilling and yet warming tale with Elaine Pagels's version of a saying from the Gospel according to Thomas: "If you bring forth that which is within you, what is within you will save you. If you do not bring forth what is within you, what is within you will destroy you."

Love for Who Speaks

IT WAS A habit she had acquired when she was a child, at the dawn of her awareness of the world, so it never occurred to Chisa to wonder how it looked to others.

That evening, once again, Chisa opened the window wide, raised her arms to the crescent moon, and murmured, "I was a very good girl again today, so please come to me."

Make dark supplications to the new moon,
Big supplications to the full moon,
And supplications small and secret to the crescent moon.

Facing the pale light of the moon barbed like cat's claws, Chisa repeated her supplication over and over again.

Chisa wanted to see him – her father, who had gone away when she was still just an infant. Chisa had memories of her father. Fragmentary memories. His voice, the feel of his arms.

Chisa's mother had remarried, so now Chisa had a new father. Chisa liked her new father. Their life together as a family of three was pleasant, and that's why Chisa could never give voice to her thought – *I wonder where my real father is now?*

But even so, no matter how content her life was, Chisa could not banish the secret yearning that was ever in her heart.

And Chisa believed – if she continued her quiet supplication to the crescent moon, then someday the man with that voice and those arms would come to her again.

1

She had met Izutsu Masaaki, her fiancé, through a relative. And although the circumstances were informal, it was in fact an arranged marriage.

Chisa herself had no solid views on marriage. "Why not just meet him?" her parents had suggested, and so she had – that was all. And even when Masaaki had taken a liking to her and proposed seeing one another with a view toward marriage, she still could not see herself clearly as someone about to wed.

And yet she knew that at twenty-eight she was by no means too young, and figured that if she was going to get married anyway, it might as well be to someone who wanted her. And so she agreed to go out.

It was not as if she'd had no other men in her life up to then. Nonetheless, she had never felt passion so intense that she forgot all else, and though she dated it always felt like it was happening to someone else – she had never given herself over fully to the relationship, and so time and again the other party had broken it off. And when the break-up occurred, the man she was dating always said the same thing: "I feel like you don't really love me. I'm tired of being the only one who's trying, and getting nowhere."

Do I really like him? What does it feel like to truly love someone? Chisa wasn't sure.

Yet whenever a suitor told her he wanted to end it she felt neither heart-rending sorrow nor a fervent wish to stay together, which made her wonder vaguely whether a part of her heart was missing. Even so, she never knew what to do, or even felt the need to do anything at all.

And after all, there must surely be women in the world who live their whole lives without ever experiencing passionate love. People's feelings change, and you cannot chain the heart. And if that's so, then never falling in love must be happier than the alternative – because never falling in love means never knowing pain when feelings change.

Besides, marriage and love are two different things.

Wanting to be with and gaze upon a person forever, and wanting to make a life together and start a family, were two totally separate matters. On this point Chisa had no illusions.

Even so, she hoped Masaaki would be pleasant to be around. Since they would be spending the rest of their lives together under the same roof, this was only natural. That is why Chisa spent six months going out with Masaaki, like any ordinary couple, before getting formally engaged.

Weekend dates – meeting up, seeing a movie, walking in the park, dinner, cocktails in some hotel bar, then going their separate ways. What could be learned from doing this over and over? What was the sense in it? Chisa had no compelling answer to these questions, but it would be enough to find out whether she could enjoy being with him, that they could converse without strain, that their views weren't hopelessly divergent, that there were no habits or quirks that she just couldn't live with.

And it turned out that nothing about Masaaki sparked any unease along such lines.

Except for one thing.

It was a truly small thing, no cause for concern.

One Sunday, Masaaki came for Chisa in his car. The weather was good, and Masaaki asked Chisa to go for a long drive. Chisa was glad, because she had become a bit bored with dates in the city.

"Is there anywhere special you want to go?"

Masaaki's question brought an immediate response from Chisa.

"I'd like to go to the ocean… if that isn't a problem. Some place not too far would be fine."

Chisa noticed that Masaaki's reply was a little longer in coming, but eventually he said in his usual manner, "The ocean sounds great, but the traffic on the roads to places like Shōnan or Chiba is probably pretty bad, so it might be better to take the expressway – that would make it easier coming back, too. It's not the ocean, but how about Lake Kawaguchi? It should be beautiful there this time of the year."

Chisa wanted to see the ocean, not a lake, but she didn't want to be unreasonable. She knew the Sunday traffic to Shōnan and Chiba was awful, and that if they wanted to go someplace else to see the ocean, they would either have to go very far out of the way, or make do with someplace like Odaiba down at the port, which wasn't quite the real thing. What Masaaki said made sense.

Lake Kawaguchi turned out to be pretty enough, the views of snow-capped Mt. Fuji and the mountains of Yamanashi were also lovely, and Chisa was quite content with how their date turned out that day.

They headed for the mountains again the second time they went for a drive, and the third time as well, but Chisa still thought there was nothing strange about it, for fall had given way to winter and the color of the skies was too desolate for going to the ocean.

Eventually Masaaki told Chisa he wanted them to get formally engaged. Chisa found no reason to refuse – Masaaki was fun to be with, and he had no odd habits that she simply couldn't stand. The company Masaaki worked for was a solidly established firm, so financially their lives seemed secure. They could also converse easily enough, and nothing in their ways of thinking or values seemed so disparate as to make compromise difficult.

If she married Masaaki, they would be able to make a reasonably happy, reasonably settled, cozy home together.

In a few years there would be children, and the family would gather around candle-strewn cakes on birthdays and Christmases.

Imagining such scenes gave Chisa a sense of pleasantly warm comfort, and for the first time the idea of marriage began to arouse in her a sense of longing.

So she assented to the engagement, and they even exchanged traditional engagement gifts.

They had a little more than five months to prepare for the wedding. There was much to do. First they needed to reserve the venues for the ceremony and the reception, plan the honeymoon, choose what to wear, and decide who to invite, and at the same time look for a new place to live. Five months was definitely not a long time.

Chisa herself worked for a midsize manufacturer of medical equipment, but because her job consisted of clerical work in General Affairs she had no regrets about quitting after her marriage. Even so, before she left she had to bring her replacement completely up to speed to ensure a smooth transition.

The days passed in a frenzy of activity. Their weekend dates were devoted entirely to wedding preparations: discussions at the hotel where they would hold the reception, trips to department stores to buy furniture, meetings to coordinate what they would wear. Chisa was renting the kimono for the wedding, but she wanted to buy her wedding gown, so her time was also taken up with fabric selection and fittings at the dressmaker's.

Spring came and went. Because the weather might be a problem for their guests once the summer rainy season started, Chisa gave up the idea of being a June bride and they decided to hold the ceremony in May. One morning a little less than a month from the event, Chisa awoke early to the sunlight of early summer. Opening the window and breathing in the fragrance of the breeze, a thought struck her.

She wanted to see the ocean.

Judging by their schedule, this would likely be their last date before the wedding. From the next week on, every weekend was booked solid. Chisa telephoned Masaaki and prefaced her entreaty by saying it was her last request as an single woman.

"I want you to take me to see the ocean. I've decided that the last date of our engagement will be at the sea. I know it's a long way away, and I'm sorry, but please."

The discomfiture of Masaaki, at the other end of the phone line, was palpable. He was clearly not eager to go for a long drive now, in the busy period right before the wedding. They had to be at the hotel that evening for another discussion about the reception, but if the traffic was bad they might not get back in time.

Yet Chisa was unyielding.

"A quick look is all I want. Let's just have a quick look at the ocean and come right back, so we won't get held up in the evening."

"All right," Masaaki said in the end. Then, in an especially jovial voice, "In that case, let's leave right now. If we get caught in traffic we'll be late getting back, and then we'd really be in a bind. So let's be sure to get started back home well before evening."

"Of course. I'm really grateful for this, Masaaki." Chisa was elated. *I want to see the ocean. I don't know why I want this so badly, but I want to see the ocean.*

The salt breeze felt pleasant on her cheeks.

Masaaki had cheerfully brought her to the sea at Izu. Chisa's earlier impression that Masaaki was tremendously reluctant to visit the sea must have been groundless.

The caress of the fragrant salt spray calmed Chisa's heart.

It was not as if Chisa had loved the sea from childhood. Far from it – the waves had frightened her, and she had never once set foot in the water. The instant the waves had tugged at the sand at her feet, she was struck by the terror that they would drag her down, to a place deep down at the bottom of the sea, never to be seen again. There on the beach Chisa had burst into screams and tears. Since that time no one in her family had ever taken her to the beach.

This was probably the first time she had ever wanted herself to see the ocean.

Chisa stayed silent, gazing at the waves. Emptying her mind of all thoughts, forgetting even Masaaki beside her, she just stared out at the sea.

Chisa could see it.

There, swimming between the waves, a silver man, supple and powerful as a dolphin.

Chisa understood. She had been summoned here by this man.

His long hair, like a woman's, twisted away delicately to disappear in the foam as his lithe limbs stroked through the waves. Powerfully, powerfully, he continued to swim.

"Who are you?" Chisa asked without speaking.

"It really doesn't matter," the silver man laughed as he swam. "I like you. Come here. Swim to me."

"I can't swim."

"Of course you can. Just come into the water. I like you. I love you. So come to me. Come here."

"We'd better head back soon, or we'll get stuck in traffic," said Masaaki with impatience. He looked terribly pale.

"Masaaki, are you feeling all right? Your face…"

"Yeah, I know," said Masaaki, forcing a smile. "It's just that I don't do well at the sea. I've never liked it. I can't stand the smell, and

I don't like watching the waves. I'm sorry – if you like the ocean, then I'll try to learn to like it, too."

"Don't worry about it. I've seen enough," Chisa said with a laugh. "I've seen enough."

2

Make dark supplications to the new moon,
Big supplications to the full moon,
And secret supplications to the crescent moon.

Married life was good.

Masaaki was everything a good husband should be, and nothing was missing from their lives. They had the happiness they deserved in the degree they deserved, and Chisa was content just to scoop it up with both hands and drink her fill.

They never went to the ocean again.

It was not that they did not want to go, or were afraid to go. It was just that they were happy enough without going.

In the ocean was a man who said he loved her. Just knowing that was enough for Chisa.

Masaaki had never told Chisa he loved her. Their engagement and marriage had come about through arrangement by a third party, so there had never been any need to say "I love you," for the understanding had been that their courtship would naturally progress to marriage, provided neither backed out. And it had been the same even before she had met Masaaki. Even though she had been asked out by others, none had ever told her he liked her. And yet, when the break-up came, the man always said, "I feel like you don't really love me. I'm tired of being the only one who's trying, and getting nowhere."

Chisa knew that the cause lay with her. She was always peeking out from her shell at the other person. She understood that the other person never tried to open his heart to her because she never attempted to come out of her shell. Masaaki had married Chisa shell and all. For Masaaki, that was preferable – for he was the same kind of person as Chisa, a man living inside a shell.

In the ocean is a man who loves me and waits for me. For Chisa, that was sufficient.

Sleep would not come on nights of the crescent moon.

After they were married, Chisa gave up her habit of opening the window and making supplication on nights of the crescent moon – sleeping in the same bedroom as Masaaki made it impossible.

The nights when the moon was a crescent, Chisa lay still in the bed, completely motionless, until the sky whitened and grew light. Only one thing was in her thoughts: the silver man.

Chisa realized she had fallen in love with the silver man. And yet, she had no thoughts of acting on this. *I can't swim. I can't go in the water, so I can't go to him.*

But that's just fine, she thought.

Calm, quiet, and modest, this lifestyle suited her. She was suited to a life in which she and Masaaki took care of one another, both remaining snug in their rigid shells.

One morning, into this calm and quiet daily life came a visitor.

When Chisa opened the door in response to the chime, a young woman stood on the doorstep.

"Where's my sister?" she demanded without preamble. "Ask that Izutsu man where my sister is!"

Chisa had no idea what the woman was talking about.

"Izutsu knows where my sister is!"

"You're looking for… your sister?" said Chisa. "Excuse me, but what's her name?"

"It's Takagi Sawako!" said the woman. "You mean to tell me you don't even know my sister's name? She used to be engaged to Izutsu, and you didn't even know!"

Masaaki had never once even hinted that he had been engaged before.

"When Sawako broke off her engagement with Izutsu, she said she was going to travel, and we never heard from her again," said the woman, breaking down in tears. "Everyone thought she disappeared out of disappointment because she couldn't get married. They said she must have killed herself. But that's impossible – I know! Because *she's* the one who broke off the engagement! And that Izutsu man wanted to marry her. But as soon as Sawako disappeared, he started looking for a wife again and got engaged to you! I know what's going on. Izutsu knows where Sawako is!"

Chisa led the woman inside.

The woman's name was Takagi Emi. According to Emi, her older sister Sawako had been Masaaki's fiancée until a year and a half ago. Then one day the two had suddenly announced that their engagement was over.

"Sawako and that Izutsu hadn't been seeing each other all that long – maybe only around two years," said Emi. "They got engaged about half a year after they met, and got along really well. But one day when Sawako came back from a date she told me, 'Emi, it looks like I made a mistake. I'm not going to get married to Masaaki.' Then the next day she broke off the engagement. But she never said anything more about why. And then all of a sudden she was gone. She just left a note saying she'd decided to do some traveling."

"What reasons did Masaaki give for breaking off the engagement?" asked Chisa.

"He just kept saying he didn't know – that he didn't understand it," said Emi. "He said it was all Sawako's fault, that she was just being selfish. But Sawako wasn't the kind of person who would do something so... so senseless! So I began to suspect that Izutsu had done something terrible to her."

Chisa shivered. Masaaki had never shown the slightest inkling that he could be such a person, at least not to her.

"That day – the day Sawako told me she'd made a mistake – the two of them had gone down to the sea at Izu," said Emi. She shook her head slightly, as if trying to remember some small detail. "Now that I think about it, there was something strange."

"What was it?" asked Chisa.

"Sawako told me once that Izutsu seemed to... dislike the ocean," said Emi. "Sawako didn't like it much, either. She had delicate skin and burned easily, and she also tended to get feverish. So she could never lie on the beach in the summer, and she hardly ever suggested going to the sea. She said it worked out perfectly that Izutsu didn't seem to enjoy the ocean either. Yet one morning she said she wanted to borrow a hat and some sunglasses. I asked her where she was going and she said she had an urge to see the ocean. I did think it was unlike her, but I just figured the upcoming wedding had put her in a strange mood. But then when she came back... all of a sudden she said that she'd made a mistake and wouldn't marry Izutsu. If something happened between the two, it must have been at the ocean."

Shuddering, Emi covered her face and continued, "I don't want to think about it – I don't want to imagine it, but what if my sister... Sawako... was murdered by Izutsu? I mean, even though he was so attached to her and blamed her for ending the engagement, as soon as she disappeared he started up with you as if nothing had happened, and he never said one word to you about my sister. That's not natural. It's not natural!"

"I'm sure that he just didn't want me to worry, because our marriage was arranged," said Chisa.

"Do you really believe your own words?" Clutching Chisa's arm, Emi spoke in a low voice. "You... you could end up like Sawako. Sawako must have found out Izutsu's secret. So Izutsu –"

"Masaaki's secret?" asked Chisa.

"Sawako wasn't the first woman he saw to have disappeared," said Emi.

Chisa felt her spine turn to ice. Noting the change in Chisa's expression, Emi nodded triumphantly.

"I checked it out," she said. "Before Izutsu started up with Sawako, there was another woman he almost married. And she's disappeared, too. Surely even you can understand – it can't be a coincidence. But the police refuse to look into it. They say that even if Sawako and the woman before her are dead, Izutsu wouldn't have anything to gain! But they just don't get it. Money isn't the only reason people kill!"

"But to accuse Masaaki of murder based on nothing more than that..." said Chisa.

"Then how else would you explain it?" said Emi. "Sawako found out Izutsu had killed his earlier fiancée and broke off the engagement. Izutsu figured out the real reason for Sawako's change of heart, killed her, and married you. That has to be it. I don't want to believe my sister is dead. That's why I've been doing everything I can to find her for more than year. But not only hasn't she turned up, there aren't any signs of her at all. What other explanation could there be? Sawako wasn't the kind of person who would just up and leave me and my parents. If she really were traveling she would definitely have gotten in touch, and even if she had gone into hiding for some reason, she would have found some way to let us know. I've decided not to cling to baseless hopes. I'm going to face the facts, and find out the truth as quick as I can, and... and... I'm going to get revenge!"

Emi stared out into space with wide, bloodshot eyes.

"I'm certain Izutsu knows where my sister is. He has to know where her body is."

Standing, she let out a choked laugh.

"You don't believe what I'm telling you, do you. Fine. I don't care whether you believe me or not. But let me give you some advice. If Izutsu suspects you know the truth, he'll probably kill you, too. So leave Izutsu and get away before you live to regret it!"

So saying, Emi fled from the room.

In the room vacated by Emi, Chisa was thinking hard. But no matter how hard she concentrated, only one single thought swirled in her mind.

Could Masaaki really have killed Sawako?

Before Sawako there had been another woman who had disappeared. Could that really be true?

Chisa dug out the guestbook for their wedding reception from the closet where it had been stored. It contained the names and addresses of all their guests, in their own handwriting. Only five people had been invited to the reception as Masaaki's friends. One of them was a friend of Masaaki's from college who had also visited the newlyweds at their new home, and seemed like someone Chisa could trust.

She picked up the telephone receiver.

3

"That story isn't exactly a lie."

Ueshima Masahiko shook his head slightly, a look of consternation on his face.

"It's true that a long time ago Izutsu was seeing someone I think he intended to marry. Her name was Shioda Keiko. They were in the same study group in college. They went out together all through college. Everybody thought they made a great couple, and figured they'd get married when they finished school. But maybe three years after they graduated, Izutsu told me that Keiko had gone missing. He told me that she'd left saying she was going to travel alone for a while and never came back, and that her family was frantic. I suppose that in the end she never did turn up."

"There's someone who thinks that Masaaki was involved in her… disappearance," said Chisa.

"Would that be a woman named Takagi? Takagi Emi?" asked Ueshima.

Chisa looked up. Ueshima gave a sardonic smile.

"Ms. Takagi came to see me, too. It seems she's Takagi Sawako's younger sister."

"Did you know about Takagi Sawako, too?" asked Chisa.

"I hadn't heard many of the details," said Ueshima. "Because Izutsu is the kind of guy who doesn't talk much about himself. But… with Takagi Sawako, I really think *Izutsu* was the victim. They got engaged and exchanged engagement gifts, and even reserved a hall for the ceremony, but then she broke off the engagement without giving him a reason. Her sister said that Izutsu blamed Sawako completely and kept calling up and bothering her, but under the circumstances that would only be natural. They'd gone so far as to exchange engagement gifts, and Izutsu must have told everyone he was engaged, so it must have been embarrassing for Izutsu's parents. At the very least she should have given her reasons – if she had some problem with Izutsu she should have pointed it out, and then they could have agreed to dissolve the engagement. Isn't that the way such matters are supposed to be handled?"

"But… what if she broke off the engagement for a reason that she could tell anyone about?"

"That's just another of Takagi Emi's claims, right? That Izutsu killed Keiko, and Sawako found out, and so he killed Sawako. Listen, Chisa, Takagi Emi is deluded. Keiko definitely disappeared while she was traveling. Even her family says so – it seems the last time they had any contact from Keiko, it came from Izu. What I heard was that she sent them a postcard saying she was in Izu because she wanted to see the ocean. Of course it's not impossible that Izutsu chased her down in Izu and killed her, but as a couple they got along great. Izutsu had no motive for killing Keiko. I don't know whether she met with an accident, or killed herself, or decided on her own to vanish, but I'm certain that Izutsu had nothing to do with her disappearance. And that makes it hard to believe that Izutsu had anything to do with Takagi Sawako's disappearance, either."

"So… she went to the sea, too," Chisa said, thinking about the silver man who called to her from the waves.

Could it be possible?

Could it be that Shioda Keiko and Takagi Sawako each saw that silver man? She wanted to find out for sure.

"I wonder where it was in Izu that Keiko went last," said Chisa.

"Well, I don't know the specific details," said Ueshima. "But the postcard had a picture of Yumegahama."

"Yumegahama?"

"It's a beach just beyond Shimoda, close to the tip of Izu Peninsula. It gets crowded in the summer, but the postcard from Keiko came in February, in the dead of winter. Even though Izu is warmer than other places at that time of year, taking a trip to Yumegahama alone in the middle of winter is a strange thing to do."

Yumegahama was where Chisa had gone with Masaaki before they were married. As a day-trip destination it was a bit far to travel, she had thought, but Masaaki had said that as long as they

277

were making the trip they might as well go where the ocean view was the prettiest, and she had happily taken him at his word.

It couldn't be a coincidence. Could it?

After leaving Ueshima, Chisa called Takagi Emi from a pay phone.

"If you know where in Izu it was that your sister and Masaaki went on their last date, I'd like to know."

Emi answered without hesitation, "It was Yumegahama. Sawako told me that when she said she wanted to see the ocean, Izutsu said he'd take her."

Chisa couldn't drive, so she took a bus from Shimoda. The mid-December seaside was deserted.

Even so, the sea at Izu was calm and bright, seeming so gaily brilliant that one had the illusion it would be warm to the touch. How wondrous that this sea was one with the ocean in far-off Micronesia.

What had Shioda Keiko and Takagi Sawako glimpsed in this sea?

It could only have been one thing.

Chisa continued to stare out at the waves.

Five minutes… ten… fifteen.

"So you finally came to me!"

A silver hand appeared between the swells.

"I've been waiting all this time. I knew you'd come."

"No!" said Chisa. "I'm looking for some people. A woman called Shioda Keiko, and another called Takagi Sawako. I know they came to you, both of them!"

"I don't know their names," laughed the silver man as he swam. "What meaning would names have? Forget about that, and come to me now! I like you. I love you!"

"I can't!"

"Why not?"

"I can't swim. I've always hated the ocean!"

"Come in the water – you'll be able to swim, you'll see. It's a very simple thing. You were born here, and this is where you should return."

"I can't! If I go in the water I won't be able to get back. Isn't that so? Just like the others – I'll never be able to get back again!"

"Whether you go back or not is up to you. We won't force you to stay. The people you're looking for are here too only because they like it. So stop worrying and come to me! Just put your feet in the water. That's all you have to do!"

Almost automatically, Chisa took off her shoes. Still wearing her tights, she took one step from the beach, then another. The surf lapped at her toes.

It was cold.

Chisa came to her senses.

"No!" she screamed. "I won't go! I'm not going back to the sea!"

Covering her ears to shut out the voice of the silver man, Chisa ran from the beach.

That night, coming to her bed, Masaaki sniffed her hair and shouted, "You went to the ocean!"

"Yes," said Chisa. She wanted to know what was in Masaaki's heart. "I did go. To Yumegahama. The place by the sea where you and I went just that once."

"Don't go to the sea!" shouted Masaaki, his features terrible.

"But why not?" asked Chisa. "Why is it that I shouldn't go to the sea?"

Masaaki suddenly hid his face and sobbed. "I… I don't want to lose you. I don't want the sea to take you from me."

"So you did know, didn't you," said Chisa. "Your girlfriend, Shioda Keiko, and your fiancée, Takagi Sawako – you knew that they both disappeared in the sea at Yumegahama!"

Masaaki continued to weep with heaving sobs, like a child.

"I don't want to lose you. You especially. Please promise me you'll never go to the sea again. Please, Chisa…"

"So you didn't kill either of the others?" asked Chisa is a soft voice, stroking his hair. "That, at least, is true, isn't it?"

Weeping, Masaaki nodded.

"Then all right," Chisa murmured. "I'm happy the way things are now. I won't go to the sea again."

I love you. Come to me now.

The voice of the silver man went around and around in her head. Chisa tried her hardest to ignore it.

Her calm, quiet, shell-enclosed life. She didn't want to jeopardize it. She wanted her life to go along quietly, just as it was.

She had no desire to go back to the sea.

4

When she awoke, Chisa was startled by an odd sensation. One of her legs was hard to move. Her left leg felt very heavy. Something was touching it. Something cold.

Chisa sat up and whipped off the covers. Then screamed.

Around her left ankle was a shackle, the other end of which was fastened to a leg of the bed.

"Masaaki!" she screamed. "Why did you do this!"

"It was just a precaution, to keep you from leaving while I was asleep," said Masaaki, his face studiedly nonchalant.

Chisa felt light-headed with shock.

"Don't worry," said Masaaki. "I'll take it off when I leave for work. You can move around as you like in here."

"What do mean, 'in here'?"

"I put a lock on the front door that can't be opened from inside. You'll have to let me lock it till I get home from work. It's okay, I'll take care of all the shopping. And after this I'm going to the post office to arrange for them to hold all our mail for pickup at the window. Parcels, too – I'll have the delivery services hold everything for pickup. You might get a bit bored, but it's only until I come home from work. After I get back we'll go for a walk together. Today I'll rent a bunch of videos you'll like, and I'll buy some paperbacks, too. Okay? All you have to do is relax and enjoy yourself. Everything will be fine just as long as you never, ever think about going to the sea."

It was a nightmare.

Chisa, unable to resist, submitted to Masaaki's wishes. She feared the darkness in Masaaki's heart that had let him force such an empty, abnormal life upon her.

All she had wanted was an uneventful life of quiet contentment.

From that day on, Chisa could never go outside before sundown. She was able to move freely only within their blocky, two-bedroom condominium. Masaaki took her out for a walk when he came home in the evening, but he put a metal shackle on her left wrist, holding the chain attached to it clenched in his fist in his pocket, so after the first time Chisa took to refusing to go out. Even if no one saw them, the thought of being walked like a dog on a leash so filled her with shame she became almost feverish. Even more humiliating were the nights, when they went to bed. To keep Chisa from escaping while he slept, Masaaki shackled her left ankle every night. Even though he told her she could wake him if she had to go to the bathroom, the feelings of humiliation inhibited her; the only thing for her to do was to stop drinking anything at all from nightfall on.

Despite all that, she seemed much too afraid to resist Masaaki. Chisa was intimidated by Masaaki, able to put her in chains while continuing to smile and speak in a gentle voice, and whenever his hands touched her body her heart quailed and shriveled, and her radiance faltered.

Her desire to go on living gradually waned.

Day after day, to escape its reality, Chisa's mind plunged into a fantasy world.

Chisa dreamed of the silver man. When she dreamed she did not have to confront her painful reality.

The daytime hours she passed in the cramped rooms of their condo, Chisa spent dreaming even though she remained awake. Past the glass door that Masaaki had made unopenable, far past the streets of the city spread out beyond, Chisa fixed her eyes on the blue sea.

Come to me now.

The silver man began to call.

I've been waiting for you all this time. Why don't you come to me?

Shedding tears, Chisa gazed at the silver man waving to her, and asked herself with regret why she hadn't stepped out into the waves when she had the chance.

If she had only stepped into the water, she would not have had to live trapped, like a bird in a cage.

She had no idea how many days the nightmare had gone on. It seemed that Masaaki had lied to Chisa's family, telling them that she had disappeared. The telephone was disconnected. The windows were hung with cloth to block the view. Chisa had lost even the will to try to take it down.

"Don't think about trying to escape," said Masaaki in a tender voice, as he combed up her hair with gentle movements. "Please. If you try to run away, you might be destroyed. If you go to the sea, you might be destroyed. By me."

Sleep would not come on nights of the crescent moon.

Chisa raised the palm of her hand to a forlorn moonbeam slant-ing in through a gap in the cloth covering the bedroom window. Careful of her bound leg, she sat up in bed and pressed her face to the gap. The dull orange glow of a crescent moon reached her eyes.

Secret supplications to the crescent moon. She realized that she had not sent a supplication to the crescent moon since her life of confinement by Masaaki had begun. Because she felt as if all hope to live life had been stripped from her, it had not even occurred to her to ask anyone for anything.

Masaaki's sleeping breath droned in her ears.
If she was going to do it, now was time.

"Father."

Chisa spoke in a whisper.

"My true father. Please, I want to see you. Come to me. Take me away from this place. Set me free. I want to go to the sea. To the silver man."

Chisa whispered the words over and over again. Just as she had always done ever since she was a child.

The orange light of the moon shining in through the gap in the cloth trembled and wavered.

Chisa stared at the light with amazement and expectation.

Thunder. Lightning. Flash. A scream! … A shadow slips in.

A black shadow. A colorless space. Empty. And yet, *he* is there.

"My daughter."

The shadow spoke.

"Why do you lie there shackled?"

"My husband has shackled me," said Chisa. "He says he does it because he doesn't want to lose me… lose me, also. So he has shackled me so I won't go to the sea."

The shadow laughed.

"How foolish. You are bound to return to the sea. At the bottom of the sea, in the city of the Great Old Ones, it is your destiny to become the wife of the Great Old Ones and gain new life. Is the one who lies there sleeping not a minion reared to gather the daughters of the sea?"

Chisa turned. Masaaki had opened his eyes and was glaring at the shadow, his face twisted by terror and hatred.

"Do not touch my wife!" shouted Masaaki. Enraged, he clutched Chisa's arm. "Chisa, come here!"

"Minion!" sneered the shadow. "Is it not your task to gather my daughters and return them to the sea? And yet by becoming attached to a daughter of the Great Old Ones you risk your own existence."

"Chisa is my wife!" Masaaki shouted angrily, in tears. "She belongs to me!"

The shadow shimmered. Chisa rose into the air. The shackle on her ankle melted into black liquid that dripped down under the bed.

"Let us return to the sea," the shadow spoke. "To your home."

"Yes," Chisa nodded. "...Father."

Those arms. Their touch was the same as the arms and hands she remembered. He who had held Chisa so very, very long ago was the shadow.

The cloth came apart and fell away, and the glass in the window turned insubstantial, evaporated, and was gone.

The moon, orange and thin. The shadow, cradling Chisa, glided swiftly up into the sky.

At the windowsill, Masaaki bellowed.

Chisa covered her ears.

They crossed the sky.

Cutting through the jet-black darkness, they arrived within moments at the sea, where the orange light rained down upon the waves.

Silver people poked out among the waves and waved to her.

A throng. A multitude.

Countless numbers of heads bobbed in the waves, stretching upward to welcome Chisa.

The shadow gently let her fall into the waves.

The water was warm. Her breathing stopped once, and after an agony, she breathed again with ease. When she moved her body her limbs stroked back and forth through the water smoothly and with grace, like the fins of a fish, and Chisa was able to swim down to the seabed with no effort at all.

Around her were gathered untold numbers of silver people.

Their eyes had no lids, their mouths no lips. Their ears were small holes in their skulls, and at their necks she saw gill slits, gaping like mouths.

The silver sheen came from their scales.

With no fear or doubts, Chisa accepted the fact that in time her body too would be so transformed.

A new world awaited Chisa in the eternal city at the bottom of the sea.

The glory of forgotten days long ago.

The joy for the revival that would someday come again.

In the glittering old city at the bottom of the sea, Chisa encountered Sawako and Keiko. Each had a graceful form of silver scales, but Chisa somehow knew instantly that each had once been loved by Masaaki.

"So you finally came."

At the sound of his pleasant voice, Chisa linked hands and floated with the silver man.

"I like you a lot."

A new life began. For Chisa it was the glorious future she had been promised. Eternal happiness in an everlasting world.

"More and more of the daughters are being gathered," said the silver man who had become her companion, pride in his voice. "The daughters whose destiny is to return to the sea. We are finding the daughters who carry the bloodline of the Great Old Ones and bringing them back to the sea. Soon the seabed will be overflowing with those of our kind, and our time will come again."

Chisa saw Masaaki only once after that.

It happened when she was swimming in the courtyard of the kingdom under the sea, a silver newborn baby in her arms.

Masaaki had the form of a giant moray eel, black and yellow blotches on brown. He twisted away out of Chisa's sight, as if ashamed of his hideous form.

Yet Chisa knew at once that it was Masaaki.

She knew because the glittering black eyes in the fearsome face, those painfully beseeching eyes, spoke out to her.

I loved you, they said. *I didn't want to return you to the sea.*

"If only you had said you loved me – just once, just a whisper," said Chisa to the grotesque eel, as it sped out of sight in a cloud of sand. "If only you had whispered it to me before you put on the chains."

Lovecraftian Landscapes

Four Decades of H.P. Lovecraft and Manga

Yonezawa Yoshihiro
Translated by Ryan Morris

Lovecraftian Landscapes

Four Decades of H.P. Lovecraft and Manga

Yonezawa Yoshihiro
Translated by Ryan Morris

FOR MANY YEARS, comic book artists and writers have tried their hands at adapting H.P. Lovecraft's fiction to their medium, sometimes with greater, other times with lesser, or no, success. Some have created comic book renditions of particular Lovecraft tales, and it is fun to compare various comic book versions of the same original story. Others have created their own stories using locales, names, and monsters from Lovecraft, resulting in the comics equivalent to a prose author writing Cthulhu Mythos pastiches. Still others have borrowed Lovecraftian trappings for tangential use (which was, after all, the way Lovecraft himself often made use of them!) in stories essentially about something else, heroic adventures, for example. Fritz Leiber's first adventure of Fafhrd and the Grey Mouser, "Adept's Gambit," used the Lovecraftian deities as background supernaturalism. Lovecraft himself felt it was extraneous in that case and advised his protégé to drop them, which he did. Others, like Richard L. Tierney, have succeeded fabulously well in knitting the Mythos into Sword-&-Sorcery tales.

But one might suspect that comic book adaptations of Lovecraftian elements in any of these three senses would face a special challenge. Since so much of Lovecraft's horror is a matter of chilling *implication* and of the Unseen – how can these features of his vision ever be adequately translated into a largely visual medium? Lovecraft movies face the same hurdle, and most have failed to surmount it. But it is interesting to note that Lovecraft does once or twice intimate that sheer visual representation might after all convey the chill he was after.

I am thinking, first, of "Pickman's Model," the story in which the blood-freezing horror of the ghouls is depicted with the clearest and sharpest techniques of artistic realism. Artist Pickman used no evident tricks, unless they were so exceedingly subtle that the viewer is not even aware of them, only of their effect. But by the climax of the tale we learn we had been giving Pickman too much credit! He was just recording on canvas the sober reality posing before him, the actual ghouls inhabiting the underground labyrinths of South Boston.

Second, recall the explorers of the South Polar city in *At the Mountains of Madness*. They reconstruct the entire history (even the sociology!) of the Elder Ones from examining their wall-cut bas reliefs covering hall after hall of their morgue-like city. There are no intelligible captions or legends to help the reader. But Lovecraft's intrepid delvers manage to dope the whole thing out. It must have been like reading a Mythos comic book in a language one does not speak! So perhaps Lovecraft was able to admit that explicit visual depiction could convey what he himself sought to convey through words alone.

Except that it was a cheat. When you think about it, he does not show us Pickman's live model. He simply uses *words* to suggest the narrator's shock at the sight of it! Nor does he show us any of the wall murals of the Elder Ones. He merely *tells* us that the pictures paralleled the *verbal* description he is even then providing. And that about sums up the situation of our author, Yonezawa Yoshihiro, who is trying to *write* an ostensible introduction to an artistic medium! Good luck to him!

Lovecraftian Landscapes
Four Decades of H.P. Lovecraft and Manga

MY FIRST ENCOUNTER with H.P. Lovecraft was with the book *Great Stories of Horror and the Supernatural* (published by Tokyo Sōgen-sha) that I borrowed from a rental library, which I had initially noticed because of the name Edogawa Rampo. A few days later, I returned to borrow the *Anthology of Great Horror Stories*, found in one of the deeper reaches of the establishment and covered with dust. After reading this work, Lovecraft's name had been committed to my memory. Indeed, how could one forget the palpable depictions of what were normally obscured monsters, the almost comic-book sensibility, so different from other works where the reader was left not knowing exactly what had transpired. Granted, this impression of mine was surely influenced by the editorial commentary by Rampo, but for certain, *The Dunwich Horror* and *The Shadow Over Innsmouth* were just the kind of horror novels that children could get excited about: science-fiction-like works that gave us a glance into a world where the abnormal bled into the everyday.

Around 1965, *The Shadow Over Innsmouth* appeared twice in monthly manga magazines targeted at teenage boys: once in the form of an illustrated story, and again as a horror short. In both cases, it appears that Ōtomo Masashi was one of the people behind the project. The two magazines were *Bokura* (Us [September 1964]) and *Mainichi Chūgakusei Shimbun* (Mainichi Jr. High News

[August 4–11, 1968]). Presumably, this horror story's clear imagery made it appropriate fare for a young boy's magazine.

This was not, however, the first time the story had appeared: that would have been 1959, when it also appeared as an illustrated story. It was entitled *The Fishmen of Innsmouth* (illustrated by Shōgo Matsumiya) and appeared as a part of the featured article, *The Greatest Horror Stories from Around the World, Illustrated* in issue three of *Ugoku Kao* (Moving Face), the "tabloid strictly for men," originally published as an offshoot of the very popular 1950s erotic entertainment magazine *Hyaku-man nin no Yoru* (One Million Nights of One Million People). The subtitle read "Horrors! My face – it's become… a frog!" The story featured pictures of half-naked women with such outrageous captions as "The Khanakai tribe made sacrifices of young virgins. The bosoms of these fast-maturing tropically-raised maidens, with their black skin, breasts like ripe peaches, dark eyes that could seduce any man, lips with scents like durian, and gently curving waists hidden only by grass skirts, were but decorations on the altar: offerings to the Demon God." The illustrations were fine black-and-white ink pieces that had all the mood of a Western horror novel, and although the Fishmen looked more like frogs, they were certainly grotesque. These drawings were perhaps made more accessible thanks to their being in a similar vein as the "lost world" monster stories of Oguri Mushitaro and Kayama Shigeru. It was only a four-page illustrated story, but it is most likely the first ever domestic H.P. Lovecraft visual work.

Incidentally, the other stories included were *The Monkey's Paw* (W.W. Jacobs, illustrated by Yoshizaki Masami), *The Werewolves* (F. Marryat, illustrated by Akiyoshi Ran), *The Upper Berth* (F. M. Crawford, illustrated by Kameyama Hiroshi), and *Strange Adventure of a Private Secretary* (A.H. Blackwood, illustrated by Yanazawa Gen). Personally, I long to see Akiyoshi Ran's interpretation of Lovecraft. The same magazine included an erotic monster story called *An*

Astonishing Illustrated Story: Human Monster Mitchi Attacks the Contest (Kitayama Ken, illustrated by Kimura Shūji). We should not forget that sado-masochist oriented magazines such as *Kitan Club* (Strange Story Club), *Ura Mado* (Black Window), and *Tanki Shōsetsu* (Strange Stories of Decadence) ran horror stories based on their merits as deviant and grotesque. Once, *Tanki Shōsetsu* even ran a vampire special.

Around this time (1957 to 1959), horror manga was emerging as a genre in girl's comics and in rental libraries. Thriller and horror detective stories were appearing in boy's manga, but most works were adventure-detective stories in the vein of Rampo. In them, the young male hero was forbidden to scream or be frightened by the unknown, and was instead charged with the task of defeating "fear" with an arsenal of intelligence, strength, and bravery. Furthermore, these heroes had to unmask terror and solve mysteries with modern logic. Many horror comics appearing in girl's manga, on the other hand, were being premised on the three core concepts of "sad, scary, and sweet," and the comic rental industry experienced a boom in short-story anthologies, resulting in major hits with *Kaidan* (Horror Stories, published by Tsubame Shobō) and *All Kaidan* (100% Horror, published by Hibari Shobō), which contributed to the creation of the horror and ghost-story manga genres. More than half the readership of works of horror from rental libraries was female.

This success was, of course, partly due to the fact that horror stories were well-suited to the short-story format, but also because of a new trend that was occurring in the rental library industry toward more atmospheric and realistic depictions. It surely owed something to the traditions of "karma stories" about characters getting what they deserved, for good, or more typically, for bad, and Japanese ghost stories that lived on in *kami-shibai* (traditional picture-storytelling plays) and popular novels. At the time, most of the works set in modern times and outwardly labeled "horror stories" were in fact thrillers. However, there were certainly exceptions: during this horror short boom Umezu Kazuo illustrated the *Ichirō Misaki Series* and Mizuki Shigeru edited the short-story anthology *Yōki Den* (Strange Tales), to which he contributed his own work, including the first appearance of his character, Kitaro of *Gegege no Kitaro* fame. Mizuki, who illustrated works of science fiction, humor, war, and other genres depending on the requests of clients, began to shift his work toward horror stories during this period. In contrast to most other rental comic artists, who wrote stories inspired by (in other words, rip-offs of) movies and bestselling popular novels, Mizuki began building an original universe based on elements borrowed from translations of [Western] science fiction, horror novels, and a host of other resources, including surrealist paintings, the photography of Domon Ken and others, Japanese folklore studies by Yanagida Kunio, and American comics (including pre-restriction day horror comics).

Then in 1963, Mizuki published *Thriller Theater: Footsteps of the Underworld* (published by Bunka Shobo), a creation based on *The Dunwich Horror*. The cover features a typical Mizuki rendering of "man fleeing from terror," likely inspired by a foreign horror illustration or comic. The locations in the book were transplanted, quite seamlessly, to Japan: Arkham became Tottori prefecture (the location of Mizuki's home town), Miskatonic University became the Tottori University Folklore Department, Dunwich became Hachime village, and Whateley became Adachi. "Necronomicon" became "Spirit Revival" (described as a book written eight hundred years ago by a Persian madman named either Atobalana or Galapagolos; which was intended is unclear), Yog-Sothoth appears as Yogurt (an odd choice!), and the story itself remains nearly the same.

I was left with an indelible impression of the demented scholarship, strange events, and engulfing atmosphere of the comic, which I happened upon as it was being released. Never before had such a strange world been depicted in manga: the unrelenting series of eerie scenes, the strange character named Snakey (the younger of the twins), and the various notes on spirits and explanations of the other-world. Within a year of my encounter with the comic, I got my hands on the original source. But even after finding out that Mizuki's *Footsteps of the Underworld* was an adaptation of a foreign work, it lost none of its appeal. Even today I am grateful to Mizuki and Rampo for introducing me to the world of Lovecraft.

Incidentally, I must point out that this was a pioneering work in the Japanese genre of "science fiction manga fables." Mizuki's storytelling was unique even when compared to novelists: he subtly links a mysterious monk named Enku to a legend, introduces folklore and ancient scripts into the story, and otherwise develops the story of a strange land that hovers betwixt the realms of fact and fiction. Many comics published after the *Footsteps of the Underworld* used a similar approach, including *The Martian Chronicles* (unrelated to the work of Ray Bradbury), *Cursed Village* (not Wyndham's, but J. Finney's *The Body Snatchers*) and *The Great Mystery of the Tumulus* (F. Brown's *The Mind Thing*). Osamu Tezuka made forays into science fiction fables with such works as *Dr. Thrill* and *Hero Dan* in the 1950s, but it was Mizuki's technique of infusing realism by introducing ancient texts into the story that became a standard formula for later science fiction fable writers.

For the frontispiece of *Bessatsu Highspeed Kaiki Nyūmon* (Highspeed Special Edition: Horror Primer) (Sanyōsha), Mizuki illustrated a *Kyōfu Hakubutsukan* (Museum of Terror) which borrows the Lovecraft phrase "The oldest and strongest emotion of mankind is fear, and the oldest and strongest kind of fear is fear of the unknown" as the motto of the anthology. This book includes a powerful Mizuki illustration called Nekomata, inspired by *Lucundoo* (H.L. White). Another heavyweight, Umezu Kazuo, presents a piece called *Hone* (Bones) which examines the very Lovecraftian theme of decay. Yet in the end, Umezu did not gravitate toward Lovecraftian themes. Mizuki, on the other hand, has probably read either *Great Stories of Horror and the Supernatural* or *Great Tales of the Supernatural and Uncanny* (Hayakawa Shobō) and found similarities between his own proclivities and Lovecraft's. In the late period of the rental library era, the technique employed in much of Mizuki's work was to adapt Western science fiction to a Japanese period-piece context, but *Footsteps of the Underworld*, a pioneering work of grandiose modern horror, is an atypical work for Mizuki. And perhaps readers did not respond favorably to it, because from that time on he rarely illustrated stories in modern settings.

In the work he began in 1965, *Green Leaf Flute*, Mizuki introduces an invisible monster summoned from another dimension that grows with each passing day. This work exhibits strong shades of folklore, seen in the way the deformed Tsushima natives revive an ancient god to revolt against their oppressors. A similar theme is found in *Akuma-kun* (Devil Boy), but *Green Leaf Flute* should be considered an original extension of *The Dunwich Horror*. The Lovecraftian monster (deity) is revealed when charcoal dust is thrown upon it, and disappears into a volcano. This spectacle is unmistakably a recreation of *Footsteps of the Underworld*. The author shows the green leaf flute, the key to the other-world, and encounters with a mermaid in the introduction and at the ending of the story, creating an unresolved tale of tragedy while still remaining accessible to a general audience: all traits that are testimony to this work's Lovecraftian roots. Why Mizuki never put his hand to *The Shadow over Innsmouth* continues to baffle me.

One other thing that I found strange was that when Mizuki began working for magazines in 1966, he did remakes in one form or another of nearly every one of his works from the rental library era, but did not remake either *Footsteps of the Underworld* or *Green Leaf Flute*. I am not sure if this was due to a change in

Mizuki's feelings toward supernatural beings and other-worlds from his experience during the monster boom, or if there was a copyright issue. In any case, this made these two works unavailable for more than twenty years. Once Mizuki's honeymoon with Lovecraft ended, the traces of Lovecraft vanished from the pages of manga. Lovecraft's influence was not seen in the manga boom of the late 1960s, when the genre transformed into a type of science-fiction horror.

Unlike the anarchic world of rental comics where copyrights were all but ignored, magazines could not afford to ignore literary property rights. In the early 1970s, many horror novels were adapted as manga, as seen in the competitive rush to adapt short stories by Saki, but Lovecraft was now a forgotten author. Oguri Mushitarō's *Mirror to the Other World* series, an "illusory demon-world" story from that period, certainly seems to have some core features in common with Lovecraft. And from the same period, one can detect a trace of Lovecraft in Gō Nagai's *Demon Lord Dante*, and in the vengeful character in *Devil Man*, but the chain of influence is not direct. Stories such as *Devil Man* that depict apocalyptic battles between humans and resurrected evil gods started roughly with Hirai Kazumasa and Ishinomori Shōtarō's *Battle of Genma*, and perhaps should be classified along with the stories of large-scale wars that would eventually culminate in the epic science fiction tales of Kurimoto Kaoru. By the end of the 1970s, starting with Maeda Toshio's *Urotsukidoji* (serialized in *Erotopia*), an evolution of the genre appeared that might be called sex-violence horror tales, a format which enjoyed a moderate explosion. Maeda Toshio illustrated many more manga in this vein, including works of other authors like *Jashin Densetsu* (Legend of Evil Gods), *Chōshin Densetsu* (Legend of the Overfiend), and *Juma Densetsu* (Legend of the Demon Elf), and in these titles one certainly senses the Cthulhu Mythos.

Morohoshi Daijirō made his debut in 1974. In his series *Yōkai*

Hunter (Monster Hunter [the movie adaptation was released in English under the name *Hiruko the Goblin*]), which started that same year, Morohoshi illustrates a world of horrors that we encounter through the field work of heretical folklorist Hieda Rejirō. Two of the early works are extremely Lovecraftian: in *Kuroi Kenkyūsha* (The Dark Truth Seeker) the other-dimensional Hiruko beings writhe far beneath the earth; *Shijin-gaeri* (Return of the Dead) features a being that is reminiscent of Azathoth, or even Ubbo-Sathla. In these stories, we find banished evil gods, summonings of beings from other dimensions, folklore studies, and demented scholarship. These are all things that Mizuki had experimented with, and most certainly owe some debt to Lovecraft.

However, in 1972, Hanmura Ryō's Densetsu (Legend) series began. Science fiction tales became an accepted form of entertainment during this period. There was a boom in apocalyptic stories, and soon Deniken's super-ancient studies and space archeology would make waves. The occult spirit boom began in 1975 and centered around works like Tsunoda Jirō's *Ushiro no Hyakutarō* (Hyakutarō Lurks Behind) and the movie *The Exorcist*. In 1972, Saigetsusha published *Gensō to Kaiki* (Fantasy and Horror [and subtitled *Roman Fantastique* on the cover]). The fourth issue ran a Lovecraft feature article, and represents the first in-depth look into the concept of the Cthulhu Mythos. Fantasy literature and translations of American and British horror novels flourished: Sōdosha published Lovecraft's *The Dark Magic* and C.A. Smith's *The Empire of Necromancers*. The magazine *Chikyū Roman* (Earth Fantasy [subtitled Believe it or Not]), published by Gen'eisha, advanced themes of strange esoteric scholarship of ancient legends and scripts of gods with works like *Takeuchi Monjo* (Takeuchi Document). The 1970s was a turning point for the common man's fear of apocalypse, since he viewed the world through not a scientific but a pseudo-scientific and occult lens, and could not help but be affected by the state of events brought about by the oil crisis. The interest in the mythical universe built up by Lovecraft must be considered in this context. In the mid 1970s, Lovecraft became by far the most popular author in the field.

In the manga industry of the 1970s, rip-offs and adaptations of English horror works were off limits. Not even insider playfulness in the form of tributes was possible. One can catch glimpses of Lovecraft, but as for clear renditions, there are none. Morohoshi, while making no attempt to hide his Lovecraft orientation, also made no direct references. It was only in the early 1990s that he referenced Lovecraft in the fantasy-horror parody series, *Shiori to Shimiko* (Shiori and Shimiko), which centers on the strange events that seem to daily surround the strange inhabitants of Ino-kashira Village (the name is based on a pun involving the Japanese homonyms "stomach" and "water well"). The wife of the eccentric horror writer Dan'icchi (a pun on Dunwich) is a being from another dimension with a gigantic face and countless legs, and the daughter, little Cthulhu, chirps "Tekeli-li." Her small pet is named Yog (as in Yog-Sothoth). In the story, the wife's parents are called upon in an altar ritual, and the wife appears to be one of the Old Ones. These elements are all just so much insider fun, but they are an essential part of the myriad mysteries and surprises that populate the original Morohoshi universe.

In the world of girl's comics of the 1970s, vampire stories gained popularity with Hagio Moto's entrance on the scene, setting off a rush to create gothic romances. And yet, girl's comics never really crossed paths with Lovecraft. The only girl's manga writer of the time who makes any mention of Lovecraft was perhaps Yamada Mineko, who refers to black magic and the *Necronomicon* in her debut rental comic, *Manatsu no Hōmonsha* (Summer Visitor). Even the rediscovery of Lovecraft in the mid 1960s hardly made a ripple in the manga world. Yet, starting around 1980, one begins to witness a great many scattered insider references being made (the type with no relation to the main storyline), which can be partly attributed to the increased use of parody as a standard format for humor. I remember seeing several references to Lovecraft, starting with horror-fan Maya Mineo's *Astaroth Gaiden* (Astaroth Side Story). As for niche magazines, Kagemizo Yōji (that is, Tani Kōji) had been a consistent creator of illustrated works for magazines like *Garo* that conjured up the imagery of foreign fantasy novels, and in the late 1970s illustrated such works as *Kaijin: Haeotoko/Yōmu no Aieki* (Fly Man / Exotic Dreams of Love Juice) with a touch that reminds one of Virgil Finlay. All of his following works, until he switched over to fantasy action-adventure, had hints of Lovecraft. *Matenrō no Kage* (Shadows of Skyscrapers) appears in the 1987 issue of *Bessatsu Gensō Bungaku 2: Kurabu Cthulhu* (Special Edition Fantasy Literature 2: Club Cthulhu) and describes the meeting of H.P. Lovecraft and Whateley in New York. The depiction of Lovecraft is simply brilliant.

In 1985, another horror boom occurred. This time splatter movies were all the rage: violent horror movies by the likes of Yumemakura Baku and Kikuchi Hideyuki. Many stories began to focus on clashes of light and dark in battles reminiscent of Armageddon. We begin to see quite a few works about "supernatural heroes" that revolve around a ghost hunter, exorcist, or shaman. Horror-dedicated manga magazines, like *Halloween* and *Susperia*, began cropping up. *Horror House* (from Tairiku Shobō publishing) was running a serial called *Postwar Horror Manga History*, and I often spoke with the editors about ideas for new projects, and I recall that one of the suggestions I made was to adapt Lovecraft to manga. An anthology of the Lovecraft serials that were later created was released in 1990 as *Lovecraft no Gensō Kaiki Kan* (Lovecraft's Fantasy and Horror Museum). The works included are Matsumoto Chiaki's *The Horror in Red Hook*, *The Music of Erich Zann*, and *The Outsider*, as well as Okamoto Ranko's *The Hound*, *In the Vault*, and *The Colour Out of Space*. These were the first domestic manga adaptations of Lovecraft, but it seems that the style of girl's manga and the world of these stories did not mesh well. The titles were not met with any particular enthusiasm, and can justly be considered failures, if for no other reason than the fact that no follow-up projects grew out of them.

Itō Junji made his debut when he was awarded the Kazuo Umezu Award established by *Halloween*. Many of his early works certainly suggest Lovecraft, but only in atmosphere. When *Re-Animator* was released (based on *Herbert West: Reanimator*), he illustrated a tie-in special called *Sword of Re-Animator*. While space does not permit me to delve into the details of the fantastic and visually spectacular original universe created by Itō, at least let the record show that he professed a great personal love for Lovecraft. Incidentally, the film *Re-Animator* was adapted into a manga title on the pages of *Halloween* by Abe Yutaka in 1987.

Takahashi Yōsuke, who had been writing horror shorts since around 1980, wrote *Gakkō Kaidan* (School Horror Stories) for *Shōnen Champion*, his first serial to run in a major weekly. *Gakkō Kaidan* was a series of short stories based on various themes and motifs. The book release was a collection of the entire series, and in the comments the author states that he was conscious of the Cthulhu Mythos when he created the monster in *Konnichiwa Akachan* (Hello, Child) that appears in book ten. Many of the stories in this series deal with the sea, and every last one of them seems to suggest the fishmen of Innsmouth. The impressive thing about this series, with its parade of adorably grotesque monsters, is that all of the stories go over quite well. The use of of Lovecraft employed by Takahashi is the referential type that targets those in-the-know. In one installment of *Mugen Shinshi* (Dream Gentleman), there are also references to names of documents and evil gods.

For a time, there was a sharp increase in novelists expanding upon the Cthulhu Mythos, such as Kurimoto Kaoru and Kazami Jun, and in the world of manga, Yano Kentarō's *Jashin Densetsu*

Series (The Legend of Evil Gods Series), serialized in Comic NORA in 1987, represented a full-fledged contribution to the Lovecraft universe. The five-part series made up of *Lamia*, *Dark Mermaid*, *Last Creator*, *Confusion*, and *Re Verse* portrayed a war surrounding the resurrection of the evil gods. This series used the framework of the Cthulhu Mythos as the basis of an action-horror story that featured the familiar pantheon. In contrast to previous Lovecraft tie-ins, which were adaptations, parodies, or just Lovecraft-inspired, this series showed a clear and earnest intent to add to the Cthulhu Mythos. Yano Kentarō, who made his debut with a love comedy, was a fan of science fiction and belonged to the animation generation. He adapted a different side of Lovecraft than Mizuki or Maboroshi: Yano's Lovecraft focused on animation-like visuals and action rather than shadowy grotesqueness. He did the illustrations for the *Cthulhu Basic Story Guide* and *Cthulhu Evil-God Picture Book* that appeared in the *MU special Edition: Everything About the Cthulhu Mythos*.

In 1986, the name Lovecraft became widely known with the release of *Cthulhu no Yobigoe* (Call of Cthulhu), a role-playing game localized by Hobby Japan. With Gakken, a well-known firm, as the publisher, what had essentially been a sub-culture was on the verge of becoming fair game for new manga proposals. In the late 1980s, Lovecraft adaptations were appearing in various forms including games, novels, and manga, but soon the trend reached its limits. And thus it was that straightforward marketing of Lovecraft dried up.

Death (written by MEIMU and published by Kadokawa Shoten), presently being reissued in book form, is probably the most recent long-running Lovecraft-related manga. *Death* was serialized in Comic Comp from 1993 to 1994. The jacket blurb reads, "The forbidden 'Record of the Dead' has resurrected the ancient evil gods in the present. The young heroine, with the Mask in hand, sets out to face the writhing creatures of the dark in battles that transcend time-space." Simply put, it is a super-heroine story set in a foreign country that is a cross between *JoJo's Bizarre Adventure* (Araki Hirohiko) and the Cthulhu Mythos. Not only is the story based on the resurrection of Old Ones from a deep sleep, but this pseudo-Cthulhu Mythos comic is replete with words that ring with an unmistakable familiarity to those in the know: there is Mislarik Girls School of Autumn State (Miskatonic University of Arkham), the "Record of the Dead," which describes a world crafted by a mysterious author, and chapters called "The Fishmen Legend" (*Innsmouth*), "The Light Ones" (*The Colour out of Space*), and "The Groo Dark Order." It is difficult to determine whether or not the author intended for the average reader to pick up on these Lovecraft references, but in any case this action tale is enjoyable even to the non-Lovecraft reader. Once can also find Lovecraft references in the works of fanzine authors like Amiya Mia, Gotō Juan, Shirow Masamune, and Senno Knife. Incidentally, although I was unable to confirm the names of the fanzine titles, there was a series about "Dagon-chan the Costume Girl," and I recall that the horror illustrator Pelican Project did a manga adaptation of Love-craft. At the height of the role-playing game's popularity, there were several Lovecraft-related clubs at the Japan Comic Market, but none remain today.

Yōshin Kōrin Shin Cthulhu Shinwa Comic (Descending of the Gods: The Authentic Cthulhus Mythos Comic) (ASCII Corpora-tion), edited by Tanaka Fumio and published in 1995, was an anthology that included manga adaptations of the Mythos by vari-ous authors including Lovecraft. In it we find *Fair Below* (Robert Barbour Johnson, illustrated by Itahashi Shūhō), *De Vermis Mys-teriis* (Robert Albert Bloch, illustrated by Itsuki Takashi), *The Black Kiss* (Robert Albert Bloch and Henry Kuttner, illustrated by Raiga Tamaki), *The Temple* (H.P. Lovecraft, illustrated by Goblin Matsu-moto), *Medusa's Coil* (Zealia Bishop, illustrated by Sakura Mizuki), and *Hydra* (Henry Kuttner, illustrated by Fujikawa Mamoru). The failure of every cinematic depiction of the Lovecraft universe seems to suggest that the Mythos, despite its visual nature, defies pixellization. This suggests that the "fleshed-out" images achieved by moving pictures are in fact inferior to the magic of language and its ability to conjure up images from the depths of the reader's psyche. Perhaps the strange and indescribable forms of the nause-atingly sinister only exist in the reader's mind.

This chronological examination of Lovecraft and manga reveals that there is no large number of Lovecraft-related works, and that only a few manga artists openly express their faith in Lovecraft. In the present manga industry, which so favors innovative hits, the prospect for a significant resurfacing of Lovecraft is gloomy indeed, but there will always be artists who paint worlds using shades borrowed from Lovecraft's palette. The universe of Love-craft, replete with forbidden pleasures, has a way of creeping under your skin, a timelessness that explains its periodic resur-gences. As the antithesis to the Doraemon universe, when readers traverse the wonderland that is Lovecraft, they gain access to an exclusive world. They may soon sense that they belong to a chosen few. Indeed, they may even begin to doubt reality itself. Despite, or perhaps because of this, the world of Lovecraft will continue to lure those who dare become entangled in its web.

(*Written to the music of the H.P. Lovecraft band and the other ga-rage bands on Dunwich Records, of course!*)

Bibliographies

Cthulhu Mythos Manga List

The Cthulhu Mythos in Japan

Cthulhu Mythos Manga List

Compiled and Edited by Hoshino Satoshi
Translated by Ryan Morris

Abe Yutaka

Deddorī Naito [Deadly Night]. In *Triangle High School,* Vol. 2, from
Halloween Comics (Asahi Sonorama Ltd., 1988), and Halloween
Shōjo Comics [Halloween Girls Comics] (1989).

Deadly Night is a comic version of the movie Re-Animator. It ran
in two installments as *Shiryō no Shitatari* ["Droplets of Death," the
subtitle for the Japanese release of Re-Animator] in the March and
April issues of *Halloween* in 1987, and later appeared in book form
under a new title.

Amiya Mia

Ishiki no Yoru [Night of Ishiki]. In *C-LIVE 3* (Mugensha, 1986).

Yuki goes to Yoshino, Nara and marries into the Shūjitsu family,
who are rumored to possess a precious text that is highly sought
after by ancient historians. Yuki's mother-in-law never shows herself, and every night Yuki hears a slithering sound coming from
her room. Yuki entrusts the Shūjitsu Family Text to her friend, a
teacher's assistant at a university, whose supervising professor
analyzes the text with a computer. What is the significance of the
"name of the god" that he discovers? And what is the thing that the

madams of the Shūjitsu family have passed down for generations? The mixing of Cthulhu Mythos with Japanese myth and the use of standard items of pseudo-history, like the script of ancient gods and the theory of common ancestry of the Japanese and Jewish peoples, are just the kinds of elements that you would expect to find in a Mythos manga, yet Amiya's ideas are the first of their kind, and the realistic style of the illustrations matches the theme well.

Chō Gōkin

Return. World Comics Special (Kubo Shoten, 1991).

The human race, in danger of extinction, futilely resists the legions of monsters that have seeped out from the depths of the earth in this *Dawn of the Dead*-like tale replete with apocalyptic despair. The leader of the monsters is called Ghatanothoa.

Eno Akira

Horla (Fujimi Publishing Co., Ltd., 1997).

After Horla is reincarnated as a vampire, he is taken to a whorehouse of young girls called Arkam House. In the afterword, the spelling is corrected to "Arkham," and it is described as an "American horror publisher."

Fujisawa Naoto

Death Rocker II: Kongō Yasha-hen [Death Rocker II: Vajrayaksa].

   Rapport Comics (1998).

In this manga we find a world called Kadath ("Olympus"), created by the Elder Things in another dimension for the purpose of controlling and maintaining the human world; the banished old gods Yog-Sothoth, Nyarlathotep, Hastur, and Byakhee ("demons/lesser creatures"); and the magical tome the Al Azif that has recorded all events of the earth since the beginning of time (the Necronomicon, Pnakotic Manuscripts, and the Eltdown Shards are all considered alternative names for the same book).

Fujiwara Yoshihide

Jesus (13 volumes). Shōnen Sunday Comics (Shōgakukan Inc., 1993–
1995). Also released in "wide" format (7 volumes, Shōgakukan
Inc., 1993–1995).

Story written by Nanatsuki Kyōichi. A special corps of a crime syn-
dicate is called the Night Gaunt, and an armed limousine is called
the Hound of Tindalos.

Gotō Juan

Alicia Y. Ninjin Comics (Akane Shinsha Co., 1994).

The descendants of the Whateleys, seeking revenge, use black
magic to cause Alicia, the heir to the powers of Yog-Sothoth, to be
born into the Armitage family. John Dee, a great scholar of renais-
sance England, black magician, and experienced reanimator, uses
Alicia to awaken Cthulhu, the first step toward accomplishing his
dream of becoming one with Yog-Sothoth, the bearer of ultimate
wisdom.

However, Alicia, with her love for the human world, and Nyaar
(Nyarlathotep), who has a certain attachment to the chaotic
and conflict-ridden world of mortal men, band together with a
werewolf who was left on the earth as a guardian of the seal on
the Elder Gods, and together they face the threat presented by
John Dee's plot. This work cleverly depicts the Elder Gods not as
mere monstrous beings, but as "gods" who reign over time-space
itself. An epilogue to the story, following Alicia and Nyaar after the
events occurring in this manga, is told in *Shirly Holmes* (Fujimi
Publishing Co., Ltd.).

Hiroe Rei

Hisuikyō Kitan [Mysterious Tale of Jade Valley] (2 volumes). From
Comp Comics (Kadokawa Shoten Publishing Co., Ltd., 1994–
1995).

This excellent series depicting the conflict between the Nazis, a

Japanese archaeology youth group, and a secret military organization which surrounds the awakening of the God of Inca from the bosom of the oracle's daughter, was unfortunately cut short. At the beginning of the story, one of the objects found by the Nazi Ahnenerbe (Homeland Artifact Association), a group which seeks out the mystically imbued O-Parts ("Out of Place Artifacts") and magical tomes for the purpose of global domination, is the "Revelations of Glaaki" of Turkey.

Phantom Bullet. In Comic Gum: March, April, May, and June 2000 issues.

The story takes place in a lonely village in Poland occupied by Nazi Germany. When a girl's mother is murdered by the German Schutzstaffel (ss), the Tome of Chaos is bequeathed to her, which she uses to summons a dragon to mete out vengeance on the German soldiers. However, it turns out that the Tome of Chaos is a trap set by Nyarlathotep (the Crawling Chaos), who revels in stirring up conflict in the world of humans.

The Gunslinger, a gun that takes the form of a human girl, is the only one who can prevent Nyarlathotep's plot, and thus begins the fierce battle between the Gunslinger and the girl's summoned dragon.

Hotaka Ayumu

Jaen no Yōshin [Dark Flame God]. Asuka Comics (Kadokawa Shoten Publishing Co., Ltd., 1994).

This comic is an adaptation of the *The Haunted Palace Providence* movie directed by Roger Corman, which is in turn based on *The Case of Charles Dexter Ward* (the movie takes place in Providence, not Arkham). In the movie Curwen Ward is played by Vincent Price, but in this manga Curwen has long hair and is beautifully handsome, suggesting a touch of homo-eroticism.

Ida Tatsuhiko

Gedō no Sho [The Book of Outsider]. In Young Magazine KC Special (Kodansha Ltd., 1991), and from Kowloon Comics (Kawade Shobo Shinsha, 2001).

Throughout history, The Book of Outsider has been banned and burned. Despite this, it has been passed down through the ages amongst those who seek the dark knowledge that it offers. According to legend, the book reveals a method of changing humans into books, and he who collects twelve such volumes gains ultimate knowledge and power. A girl whose older brother was turned into a book joins forces with a man who was halfway transformed into one, and together they pursue a grade schooler who is collecting the evil tomes. There is no mention of Cthulhu Mythos or any Mythos proper nouns in this manga, but the afterword says "Special thanks to Abdol Elhazzared [sic]," and the English title is given as "The Book of Outsider." It is worth special mention for its extensive exploration of the theme of unholy texts.

Ishigaki Yūki

MMR Shinta naru Chōsen, Yomigaeru 1999 Nostradamus Ankoku Shin Yogen!! [Magazine Mystery Reportage's Latest Report: Terrifying New Predictions of Nostradamus for 1999 Revived!!] (2 volumes). In Weekly Shonen Magazine, combined March/April 1995 issue and May 1995 issue.

This documentary-style manga claims to be coverage by a special team of Weekly Shonen Magazine editors of a plot that threatens the future of the human race. We learn that the Necronomicon actually exists, that the elder gods are aliens that landed on Earth in ancient times and later created a subversive international organization called the "Counsel of Three Hundred." The Necronomicon is sacred scripture for the group, which is plotting to domesticate the human race.

Ishii Hisaichi

>   *Omocha Shūriya* [The Toy Repair Shop]. In *Comical Mystery Tour 3:*
>   *Psycho no Aisatsu* [Comical Mystery Tour 3: Psycho Says Hello]
>   (Sōgen Suiri Bunko, 1998).

Omocha Shūriya is a comic strip parody of Kobayashi Yasumi's *Omocha Shūrisha* (*Reanimator;* the Japanese title means "toy repairman"). The sheer idiocy of the toys that are entrusted to Yog-Sothoth for repair are alone enough to readers quake with laughter. This may well be the shortest Cthulhu Mythos story in existence.

Itahashi Syufo

>   *DAVID* (2 volumes) (Tokyo Sanseisha, 1986–1987).

DAVID is set in a future when the surface of the Earth is desolated and the elite live in space colonies. A brain with a will of its own is contained in a book called "Odd Brain Tome of Alhazred."

Itō Takehiko

>   *Uchū Eiyū Monogatari* [Tale of the Space Hero] (2 volumes). From
>   Comp Comics (Kadokawa Shoten Publishing Co., Ltd., 1989)
>   and from Home Comics (Shueisha Inc., 1996).

In this science-fiction comedy manga, the main character visits a hot spring where an evil cult that believes in Asuta chants "Iä! Iä! Hastur!" and "Hastur cf'ayak 'vulgtmm"

Kanzaki Masaomi

>   *KAZE* (11 volumes). Shōnen Captain Comics (Tokuma Shoten,
>   1992–1997).

Oda Nobunaga returns to the world of the living with monstrous retainers in tow. As it turns out, the "evil tome" that drove him mad was the Necrominocon.

Karasawa Naoki

Hospital (2 books). From JETS Comics (Hakusensha, 1990–1991).

In this manga, we meet Herbert Nishi (Herbert West), a surgeon who toys with reanimation of corpses and bodily alteration. In the final scenes, he builds a dubious machine and attempts to summon The Crawling Chaos. Herbert West also appears in Act 12: Rakuda (Camel) of *Zoro Zoro* (Crawling Droves, published by Seirindo and later revived in Aspect Comix) as the royal doctor who prescribes an analeptic to revive the lord who has died from eating poisonous blowfish.

Tales of the World's Terrors: The Dankichi Horror. In *Kinmirai Baka*
(Futuristic Idiot), (Seirindō, 1990). Revised edition published by
Seirindō Kōgeisha, 1999.

Story written by Karasawa Shun'ichi. Dankichi finds a mysterious ancient text in the altar worshipped by the Relatively Poisonous Snake gang. He finds out that the ancient text was discovered in the "Dog Ruins" ("Cthulhu" written with ideograms) and deciphered by Professor Aikura (Lovecraft, also in ideograms), who hid the dangerous discovery away. When Dankichi chants the ancient spell, he mutates into a disfigured beast and wreaks general havoc, all in a manner befitting of this humor piece.

Komai Yū

Sonna Yatsu-a Inee! [These People are Unreal!] In Kōdansha Wide
KC Afternoon, (1995–2001).

Sonna Yatsu-a Inee! is, for the most part, a four-panel humor strip manga. In book 3, Aida Yukari was voted #1 in the reader poll for favorite character. Next to her name reads "When this young girl saw Yog-Sothoth lurking in the school, she screamed "Te Keli Te Keli!" And in the "Be Like Aida Yukari" test designed for readers, one of the requirements states "I have read the entire works of Lovecraft. Duh!" In the "Traumatic Loneliness" episode, the class goes quiet when a high-schooler retells the story of when he failed to get a reaction when he turned a grade-schooler red-and-white cap vertical and said "I'm a fishman," and hearing this, one of his classmates thinks to himself "That's nothing...when I mentioned 'Innsmouth,' it caused a panic!" The mysterious foreign exchange student using the name "Tanaka" wears armbands that read Nyarlathotep, Yog, and Dagon, and in one scene mutters "The land I come from cannot be pronounced in Japanese."

MEIMU

Laplace no Ma [Laplace's Demons]. Comp Comics (Kadokawa Shoten Publishing Co., Ltd., 1989).

This comic version of the PC game is written by Yasuda Hitoshi. The heroin, Mina, and her allies must defeat the professor of dark arts Weathertop who is attempting to summon the elder gods so that he may control destiny (Laplace).

Deathmask (4 volumes). Comp Comics (Kadokawa Shoten Publishing Co., Ltd., 1993–1995).

High school girl Celia Segal's big brother Lloyd is engrossed in study of the Record of the Dead, an evil tome that can unlock the power of the Old Ones, a task which he nearly succeeds at. Celia, using the Deathmask, a special mask bequeathed to her by her older sister Cremieux and which gives her special powers, fights Lloyd ("Grand Mask"), who, according to prophecy, is destined to surpass the power of both the Old Ones and the Light Ones and to annihilate the earth.

Death Shadow: Kuro no Mokujiroku [Death Shadow: The Black Records] (2 volumes). Young Teiō Series (Bunkasha Publishing Co., Ltd., 1996).

Members of the Makabe bloodline have the power to both summon and nullify evil gods. Beautiful young Nana (from the nullifying side of the family), with the power of the seven "shadows" that watch over her, and together with her twin sister Luna, the "dancing prophet," challenge the Groo Dark Order in order to thwart their attempts to uncover and revive the evil god that sleeps in the Japan Trench. Luna has the title of Master Rouvier, and two leaders of the Dark Order are called d'Erlette and Azathoth.

Death (4 volumes) (Kadokawa Shoten Publishing Co., Ltd., 2001-
    2002).

This is a reissue of *Deathmask* and *Death Shadow: Kuro no Moku-jiroku* [Death Shadow: The Black Records] under a new name.

Omocha Shūrisha [Reanimator; title means Toy Repairman in Japa-
    nese]. In *Omocha Shūrisha*, from Comics Ace Extra (Kadokawa
    Shoten Publishing Co., Ltd., 1998).

This manga is based on a story by Kobayashi Yasumi, but with changes made to several aspects, including the final scenes.

Maeda Toshio

Jaseiken Necromancer [Necromancer, the Unholy Sword]. Takara-
    jima Comics (JICC Publishing, 1989).

The lord of the dark dimension defeated by brave Cain is named Azathoth.

Maya Mineo

Astaroth Gaiden [Astaroth Side Story]. Princess Comics (Akita Pub-
    lishing Co., Ltd., 1996).

The episodes entitled "The resurrection of the ancient beast Nyarlathotep," "The Necronomicon," "Manuscript of Ashurbanipal," "Descent of the Gods," and "The Dark Demon" all suggest the Old Ones and other elements of the Mythos.

Bencolin vs. Beelzebub, Part 1. In *Patalliro*, book 69, Hana to Yume
    Comics (Hakusensha, 1999).

Patalliro VI, descendant of the King of Marinera, recorded the secrets of the creation of the world which he heard while serving the
Grandee of the Demon World in his diary. According to his writing,
the utterly corrupted evil beings referred to as the "Ancient Demons, otherwise known as the Cthulhu Fiends," were born from
a dimensional wrinkle in the ancient universe, and later banished
by the benevolent Old Gods from the planet Aldebaran region. It
would appear that this is the same universe as that of *Astaroth
Gaiden* (Astaroth Side Story). The conflict between the Old Gods
and the Old Ones (Ancient Demons) on the intergalactic level and
the hostilities between the Lord (God) and the devil on earth over-
lap. Also, in other episodes of *Patalliro* there are references to the
Cthulhu Mythos and to Lovecraft: in "Prince Maraich" (book 6),
and "Return to East Kalimantan" (book 62).

Mike Mignola

Batman/Hellboy/Starman (English version: Dark Horse Comics, Inc.,
    1999. Japanese version: Shōgakukan Production Co., Ltd., 1999).

Hellboy and his allies face the Knights of October, remnants of
the Nazis, and the evil god that they have summoned, Suggor Yogeroth, a squid-like beast. According to the story, tens of millions
of years ago, Suggor Yogeroth, along with the Lemuria civilization,
were both neutralized as a result of a conflict between them. One
of the conversations in the comic goes, "Elder god? As in Lovecraft
elder god?" "Yeah, it's not as weird as it sounds. Lovecraft knew
some stuff." The fact that Hellboy himself is a by-product of Nazi
experiments in summoning demons gives the other titles in the
series a Cthulhu Mythos feel.

Minagawa Ryōji

Striker (3 English volumes, 11 volumes in Japanese under the

Spriggan title). English version: Viz Communications Inc., 1998. Japanese version: from Shōnen Sunday Comics Special (Shōgakukan Inc., 1991–1996; new edition printed in 8 volumes, 2001–2002).

Story by Takashige Hiroshi. Corporations and several nations seek the relics of an ancient civilization that promise fearsome military applications, and it's up to the Arcam Foundation to stand up to the perpetrators and make sure the relics never see the light of day. In another manga, *ARMS* (available from Shogakukan Inc.), the same artist makes bows to Lovecraft with the names of people and places, such as Lavinia Whateley, the supernatural woman from Dunwich, the middle eastern country of Kadath, and the genius professor from Miskatonic University, Tillinghast. However, these may be the ideas of Nanatsuki Kyōichi, one of the contributors to the original concept.

Mizuki Shigeru

Chitei no Ashioto [Footsteps of the Underworld] (Akebono Shuppan, Bunka Shobo, 1963), and in *Mizuki Shigeru Kashihon Manga Kessaku Sen Hachi Haka no Machi / Chitei no Ashi oto* [The Best of Mizuki Shigeru Rental Books 8: Graveyard Town / Footsteps of the Underworld] (Asahi Sonorama Ltd., 1986), *Mizuki Shigeru Kaiki Kessaku Kashihon Sakuhinshū II* [Collection of Horror Rental Books by Mizuki Shigeru, Volume II] (Kodansha Publishing Co., Ltd., 1998), *Mizuki Shigeru Kashihon Kessaku Daizen 1* [Great Collection of Mizuki Shigeru Rental Books 1] (Jinruibunkasha, Ōto Shobō, 1999).

Chitei no Ashioto is an adaptation of *The Dunwich Horror*. It is also one of the earliest works introducing Cthulhu Mythos to Japan. Mizuki seamlessly transplants the story from the backward, murky New England town of the original story to the deep countryside of Tottori prefecture.

Akuma-kun: Seikimatsu Taisen [Devil Boy: Apocalypse Battle]
   (Kōbunsha Co., Ltd., 1989).

A fish-man who inhabits the sea, the Evil God of Cthulhu, and the she-beast Hydra appear in this manga. Asamatsu Ken and Takeuchi Hiroshi both assisted with the scenario writing, but apparently Cthulhu was Takeuchi's idea.

Mizushima Sei

Seima Densetsu [Legend of the Ero-Beast] (3 volumes). Gekiga King
   Series (Studio Ship/Koike Shoin Corporation, 1990).

Millions of years ago, a God of Evil was defeated by the God of Good, and its essence banished to a mirror dimension. But the God of Evil, with his eyes on the domination of the present world, targets the female teachers at an earth high school in his search for an appropriate Queen of Evil. His plans may be thwarted, however, by a male teacher with latent mystical powers (despite being a lazy, overeating lech) who wants a female teacher of his own in order to give birth to the savior of humankind. One of the evil gods comes to teach at the school in the form of a Western teacher and is named Yog-Sothoth.

Morohoshi Daijirô

Yōkai Hunter [Monster Hunter]. Jump Super Comics (Shūeisha
   Inc., 1978).

Kuroi Kenkyūsha [The Dark Truth Seeker] and *Shinin Gaeri* [Return of the Dead] are about a pseudo-lifeform called the Hiruko, creatures that followed an alternate path of evolution from humankind and are planning an invasion of the present world. No proper nouns from the Cthulhu Mythos appear in the story, but it exhibits strong hints of the Mythos. The author, in a conversation with Hoshino Yukinobu, mentions that "I was writing that manga right around the time that I was deep into horror novels" including Lovecraft and Arthur Machen (from *Munakata Kyōju Denki Kō*,

Tokubetsu-ban [Reflections on the Reports of Professor Munakata Tadakusu, Special Edition] (Ushio Shuppansha Co., Ltd.).

> *Shiori to Shimiko no Namakubi Jiken* [Shiori and Shimiko and the Detached Head Incident].
>
> *Shiori to Shimiko to Aoi Uma* [Shiori and Shimiko and the Blue Horse].
>
> *Shiori to Shimiko no Satsuriku Shishu* [Shiori and Shimiko: The Massacre Verses].
>
> *Shiori to Shimiko: Yoru no Uo* [Shiori and Shimiko: the Night Fish].

In *Nemurenu Yoru no Kimyōna Hanashi Comics* [Strange Stories for Sleepless Nights Comics] (Asahi Sonorama Ltd., 1996-2001).

In this manga we meet the writer Dan'ichi's monstrous wife, on par with *The Dunwich Horror*, who can hardly be contained by the family home, young Cthulhu, who chirps Tekeli-li, and the family pet, Yog. Overall, an excellent blend of horror and humor.

Nishikawa Rosuke

> *Shōten Command* [Skyward Command]. From Wanimagazine Comics (1999).

Shōten Command is an adult humor comic about a survival game that features Dagon and other Cthulhu-related creatures. Many of the titles are puns on Mythos books, such as "Cthuttle Little Mermaid," "That Who Coughs over a Cold," and "The Shadow over Christmas."

Okada Megumu

> *Nirai-kanai: Harukanaru Ne no Kuni* [Divine Utopia: Land of Great Roots] (5 volumes). In Afternoon KCDX (Kōdansha Ltd., 1999–2002).

The survival of the human race is threatened by evil gods who can create disasters at will and who possess awesome regenerative capabilities. Humanity's only hope lies with the wizards of sound, masters of an ancient Japanese art that makes it possible to topple even gods. The depictions of the evil gods are reminiscent of the Ancient Ones, in particular Nyarlat-Hotep. Readers are invariably awestruck by the dense artwork, the action-horror intensity, the suggestions of ancient legend presented by the myths and traditions of mainland Japan and the Ryūkyū kingdom, and the implication of connections between the Japan archipelago and ancient South American civilization. The naming of the chapters of the Necronomicon in Uchinaguchi (the Ryukyu tongue) is an artful fusion of Japanese legend and Cthulhu Mythos.

O-BO-RO (2 volumes). Dragon Comics (Kadokawa Shoten Publishing Co., Ltd., 2001).

This horror-action comic is the inspiration for *Nirai-kanai* which ran in the latter half of 1997 in Monthly Comic Dragon and was cancelled before its completion. In the future, most of the world is submerged in the sea, a fate from which "mystical civilizations" like the Empire of Japan were just able to escape. The story takes place in future Kantō, Japan, which sets the stage for an assortment of tricky East-West occult occurrences. The story begins in an excavation site uncovering the remains of a squid-like being (if it is a being at all), where we are introduced to the "Great Book of Evil," which has been translated into Latin and Greek but can never be fully comprehended. Names of evil gods and spells can be seen inscribed in objects throughout the manga. Furthermore, in the latter half, we encounter Nyarlathotep, the Crawling Chaos. Unsettlingly, there are premonitions of defeat for the heretofore unrivaled hero before his battle with Nyarlathotep. And at this point there is a clear mention of the Necrominocon, and a reference to the "Quest of Unknown Kadath."

Okuda Ippei

Barong. In Monthly Afternoon (April 2001).

Minamoto Yorimitsu, charged with the investigation of the bizarre massacres that occurred at the hands of a mysterious being at the Kyōgoku mansion and in Matsubara, enlists the help of Princess Kumara, leader of the Kurama Tengu sect and master of magicians and giant Izuna beasts in northern Heiankyō (ancient Kyoto). When Princess Kumara arrives in Kyoto, she discovers that the evil cult the Paradise Society that worship Devas and originates from the mainland (China) are involved in the incidents. Eventually she faces off with their leader Olivia in the cult temple. The Society brands the backs of captured orphans with a pentagram-and-eye pattern (the "Ancient Sign"), conjures up the Great Old Ones and the Outer Gods, and infuses the orphans with the essence of Shub-Niggurath, transforming them into Black Goats of the Woods. Members of the Society, in addition to Christian and middle eastern devils, worship the fire god Cthugha and the wind god Zarr, and in one scene Olivia calls out "Iä!! Cf'ayak 'vulgtmm Ai!" to summon Shugoran to fight Princess Kurama. This manga, with its excellent art and exceptionally well-told story, is an achievement based on its merits as an ancient monster tale alone. But perhaps more importantly, the use of terminology borrowed from Indian mythology and Christianity creates a convincing depiction of conflict between the evil cult of Cthulhu and Japanese mysticism set in the Heian era, a technique which suggests an approach for Japanese mythological tales to come.

Onishiba Takushi

Call of Cthulhu '97.

This manga received honorable mention in the fifty-fourth Tezuka Award. To the editor's knowledge, the piece has not been published in a magazine or book. In the articles announcing the award (in the January 1998 edition of Monthly Shōnen Jump and issues 1 and 2 of Weekly Shōnen Jump from the same year), the plot outline is described: "His father, the archeologist, killed?! The writer Kyōji seeks to resolve a terrible mystery surrounding the Cthulhu sea god of times past."

Ōtsuka Eiji (Concept) Mori Mika (Art)

The Tale of Hokushin (Book 1). From Newtype 100% Comics (Kadokawa Shoten Publishing Co., Ltd., 1997).

This series of strange tales depicts horror incidents occurring in the early Showa era. Yanagita Kunio and Hyōdō Hokushin are both minor characters essential to the development of the plot. Hyōdō Hokushin is the successor to the study of "dark arts," a hidden branch of Yanagita Kunio's folklore studies that even Yanagita himself did not reveal to the academic world. The afterword introduces a "real" person named Hyōdō Hokushin, who supposedly "is setting up an antique bookstore near Hongō, Tokyo" and who also translates and independently publishes novels and occult documents related to "Lovecraft Cthulhu mythos." However, such "facts" are no facts at all: they are clever extensions of the story. Book 2 was published in 1999.

Saitō Kazusa

Aka no Crusade [The Red Crusade] (Enix GFC, 1994).

Secret construction is underway on a holy site to revive the evil gods that were banished there in times long past. A local occult sect, the "Order of Cthulhu," is used to create a distraction from the plot.

Saitō Kuniko

Rifujin na Umi [Strange Seas], *Ningen Miman* [Not Human] and
Hydra. From *Rifujin no Umi* [Strange Seas], from Bunkasha M
Comics (1994).

Near a certain sea, drowning victims seem to be returning from the dead, but with one important difference: they are now unharmed even by mortal wounds. Their newfound invincibility makes them the targets of witch-hunts in human society.

As it turns out, a monstrous Hydra lives within the sea that resuscitates the dead by sharing its own cells with them, at times giving them immortality, and other times making them a part of itself. The Hydra is not an other-dimensional being, and in the story only Greek myths are mentioned. Yet the manner in which the writhing Hydra makes the drowned corpses part of itself is reminiscent of the Hydra in the Cthulhu Mythos that hunts intelligent lifeforms from planets across the cosmos and claims their heads.

Saitō Misaki

Masatsu Note: Taimashin [Notes of a Monster Killer: Hunter of
Evil]. Volumes 1–7 (Scholar, 1995–1999); volumes 1–11 (Sony Magazines, 1999–2001); and the entire series in 7 volumes (Gentōsha, 2001–2002).

Taimashin: Mashin Taidō-hen [Hunter of Evil: The Quickening of
the Beasts] (2 volumes). Gentōsha (2001–2002).

Original story by Kikuchi Hideyuki. The descendants of the band of evil-ridding shamans, the Night Hunter Society, fight to the death against the evil gods summoned by a rich lord. The connections to established Cthulhu Mythos are clearly described early on in the story, but the evil god that is thought to have destroyed the continent of Mu in antiquity, and which the heroes must battle with, is an original creation. In "The Quickening of the Beasts," there is a road that leads to the residence of the Toka family, owners of a large estate in Kyushu. Ever since a fire occurred on the land surrounding the road eighty-five years ago, it has remained desolate. Not so much as a single tree has since grown upon it, and it becomes the site of a series of strange and mysterious incidents. The Toka family road is clearly modeled on "the blasted heath" in *The Colour Out of Space.*

Sakura Mizuki

Magical Blue (2 volumes). From Kyōfu no Yakata Comics [Haunted
  Mansion Comics] (Reed Publishing Co., Ltd., 1994–1995).

Original story by Asamatsu Ken. The leader of the league of dark
sorcerors (ODT) plotting to destroy Japan chants "Iä! Yoth Trag-
gon!" and in one scene a sorcerer underling controls "the hellish
Hishisen aphids which come from the depths of the dark world of
K'n-yan."

Shibusawa Kōbō

Angel Foyson (2 volumes). Dengeki Comics EX (Media Works,
  2000–2001).

The ever-feeble Kudō Susumu is viewed as an "opportunity" by the
Outer Gods since he exchanges his "yang energy" (vitality) with
the "yin energy" (exhaustion) of others. This manga is a love-com-
edy detailing the surreptitious activities of the dubious characters that converge upon Kudō: the Red Phoenix, Nyarlatotep (also
called "the chattering chaos"), Atlach-Nacha, Nefertiti, Azathoth
(also referred to affectionately as Azalin), and finally, a group of
vampires.

Shiozaki Noboru

Hissatsu! Shōryuken! [Deadly Move! Shōryuken!]. Combat Comic,
  November 1996.

This humor/essay manga focuses on military and science fiction
themes, as well as video games. Under "things that could very well
come out of the ice of Antarctica" we see, along with The Thing,
the Apostles, and demons, a depiction of "Cthulhu" (old one) as a
withered tree with bat-like wings.

Shirow Masamune

Orion. Japanese version (*Senjutsu Chō Kōkaku Orion*): Seishinsha,
  1991. English version: Dark Horse Comics, 1992

In this manga we find such dubious names such as "Varuna Ru-riie (R'lyeh)" and "Yamatanoorochi the Nine-tailed Kyutoryu (Cthulhu)."

Signora Satoshi

Fukaki Monodomo [Deep Ones]. Comic Master 5, 1991.

This manga short associates a social phenomenon, which was popular for a short time in the 1980s, with the Cthulhu Mythos. The fad involved writing letters to the editor of a certain magazine with blurbs like "Seeking: other people who were warriors in a past life."

Sōma

Es Hoteishiki [The Es Equation]. Appears in Comic Fantajennu (issue unknown).

A manga version of a game from Abogado Powers by the same name which features items from the Cthulhu mythos. Original story by Sawano Kakeru.

Takahashi Yōsuke

Kakashi-tei [Scarecrow Inn]. In *Mugen Shinshi* [Dream Gentleman] (Asahi Sonorama Ltd., 1983); in *Mugen Shinshi: Boys Manga Edition* [Dream Gentleman: Boys Manga Edition] (Asahi Sonorama Ltd., 1985 and Sonorama Bunko, 1998), and in *Takashi Yōsuke Sakuhinshū 7: Mugen Shinshi* [Collection of Works by Takahashi Yōsuke 7: Dream Gentleman] (Asahi Sonorama Ltd., 1987).

In this story, Mugen Shinshi (the Dream Gentleman) stays the night at an inn that stands all alone on a heath. A row of scarecrows would suggest a farm, yet there is none. The quarters of the inn master are cluttered with strange books titled "Cultes des Ghoules," "De Vermis Mysteriis," "Liber-Damnatus," and "Necronomicon," and the guest book has entries for arrivals but none for departures. Mugen Shinshi is attacked by a monster in his room, but is able to drive it back. When he witnesses the inn master casting spells on scarecrows named Azathoth, Byatis, and Cthugha, he devises a certain plan...

Shokkaku [Antenna]. In *Yōsuke no Kimyō na Sekai Part 2: Kamen Shōnen* [Yōsuke's Strange World Part 2: The Masked Boy], from Sun Comics (Asahi Sonorama Ltd., 1979); *Takashi Yōsuke Sakuhinshū 2* [Collection of Works by Takahashi Yōsuke 2] (Asahi Sonorama Ltd., 1987); and from Sonorama Bunko 1999.

When Haida confides in a fellow fanzine reader that the grotesque monster illustrations that he submits to fanzines are based on real creatures, his friend pokes fun at him, saying "That sounds like something straight out of Pickman's Model!" Haida lost his left eye in an accident, and the antenna that grew in the eye socket allows him to see "the true forms" of man and beast alike.

Haunted House. In *Umi kara Kita Doll* [The Doll that Came from the Sea] (Hakusensha, 1985); in *Takashi Yōsuke Sakuhinshū 6: Neko Fujin* [Collection of Works by Takahashi Yōsuke 6: The Cat Wife] (Asahi Sonorama Ltd., 1987); and from Sonorama Bunko (1999).

A house in the town of Red Hook lures visitors to the "other" world. One scene in the story looks precisely like the cover of the June, 1936 issue of Astounding Stories, which featured Lovecraft's *The Shadow Out of Time*.

Kumo [Spider]. In *Medium 12*, (1987); *Mugen Shinshi: Kaiki-hen 2* [Dream Gentleman: Strange Stories 2] (Tokuma Shoten, 1987); from Asahi Sonorama Ltd., (1992); and from Sonorama Bunko (1998).

An entomologist shows his daughter a picture of the ancient spider, the Atlach Nacha. According to legend, the spider transforms into a young girl...

Konton no Shima [Chaos Island]. In Comics Master 1, (1990); in *Kai-*
dan KWAIDAN [Stories of Horror] (Asahi Sonorama Ltd., 1991);
and from Sonorama Bunko (1999).

When a man tires of life with his sterile wife, he visits an isolated
island, where he saves a young girl who is washed up on the beach
and who resembles his wife in her younger years. Later, in the caverns of the island that lead to the sea, he shows her the "pool of
life," a pool which continually creates new lifeforms only to de-
vour them, and tells her "you were born from this." The pool of life
is likely based on Abhoth.

Kage Otoko: Dokusaisha o Ute [Shadow Man: Shoot the Dictator].
In *Takashi Yōsuke Sakuhinshū 20: Teito Monogatari* [Collection
of Works by Takahashi Yōsuke 20: Tale of an Empire] (Asahi Sonorama Ltd., 1993).

A cruel dictator named Yog-Sothoth IV appears in this story whose
Ring of Tindalos symbolizes the crown.

Konnichiwa, Akachan [Hello, Child]. *Gakkō Kaidan* [Strange School
Tales], book 10, from Shonen Champion Comics (Akita Publishing Company Ltd., 1998).

The eldest daughter of teacher Hinode goes to the maternity clinic
to pick up her new baby brother, but a different baby is accidentally handed to her. The baby's real mother, who comes to claim
him, turns out to be an Old One. Also, in the conclusion in book
15, teacher Kudan's fiancé, Professor Munakata mentions that "I've
been asked to serve on the supernatural research committee at
Miskatonic University."

Kuroko (4 volumes). From Shonen Champion Comics (Akita Publishing Co., Ltd., 1998).

Tōge Shinkurō, to save his sister, Ōka, who was turned into a medium to tell prophecies against her will and eventually fused with

a being from another world, fights along with Kurogami Shinano as the Kuroko (Men in Black), clandestine masters of magic-nullification. In the course of their fight against evil, the Kuroko face the "Descendants of Fishmen," and a beast which appears to be a tangle of antennae who melded with Ōka and has an insatiable appetite for modern-world information, (according to the afterword in book 2, the former is the artist's "attempt at Innsmouth," and the latter is based on *The Dunwich Horror*).

Tanaka Masato

The Camp. In *Killer Ghost* (Shinshokan Co., Ltd., 1987).

A meteor falls on a camp site where a group of students are staying, and a being hidden inside it slaughters the students in succession. The occult-crazed teacher in charge of the camp worships the deformed being, alternatively calling it the "Evil God Eschu" and the "Great Cthulhu."

Tani Kōji

Mukuronomikon: Kōrei Mahō –Tantei Kagemizo Yōji– [Corpse Spirit: Summoning Magic –Detective Kagemizo Yōji–]. In *Mugen-jō Satsujin Jiken* [Mugen Castle Murder] (Atelier Peyotl, 1995).

An occult-crazed old man, after going through much trouble to acquire the Tome of Evil by the master of magic Abdul Alhazred of medieval Arabia, claims that he followed its scripture to dig up the grave of a beautiful young boy that he was infatuated with in order to reanimate his corpse. But could this be the whole story? Written under the Kagemizo Yōji name.

Kaijin: Haeotoko/Yōmu no Aieki [Fly Man / Exotic Dreams of Love Juice] (Seirindō Co., Ltd. 1993).

In this manga, we find the "Dark Planet Hyades" and the "Snake God Cthulhu."

Matenrō no Kage [Shadows of Skyscrapers]. In *Bessatsu Gensō Bungaku 2: Cthulhu Club* [Special Edition Fantasy Literature 2: Cthulhu Club] (1987) and *Bara to Kenjū* [Guns and Roses] (Seirindō Co., Ltd., 1993).

Illustrates the visions that Whateley shows Lovecraft in New York.

Nÿogtha. Four separate titles. *Sore wa Rokugatsu no Yūbe* [An evening in June]. *Chiisana Fūkeiga* [Little Landscape Painting]. *Ippu-kun no Omoide* [Ippu's Memories]. In *Kaiketsu Shinkirō* [Gallant Mirage] (Seirindō Kōgeisha, 2002).

In *Nÿogtha*, in the quarantined city Necropolis (the Graveyard), a paranoid young boy is chosen to be a gateway for beings from the other world and is transformed into a mess of feelers, yet his pitiful weakness makes him the target of a witch hunt, and eventually even Nÿogtha abandons him. In the other three stories, Celephaïs appears in the dream sequences.

Tanuma Yūichirō

Princess of Darkness. Hot Milk Comics (1990), and in a new enlarged and revised edition from the same publisher (1994), and from Core Magazine Co., Ltd., in a new enlarged and revised edition (1996).

When the young girl Kurohara Maki's parents die in an accident, the only book that remains from the collection of her bibliomaniac father is Alhazred. When she faces danger, she opens the pages of the forbidden Alhazred, and with the powers of darkness and a special costume, sets out to punish those who betray and affront her.

Tsukishiro Yūko

Shōkan no Banmei [Fiendish Names of Summonings]. Roleplaying Game Magazine (printed in certain issues starting with the March 1997 issue and ending with the July 1999 issue).

Young Tochikusa Hifumi, after being transferred to a Theosophy High School that trains sorcerers from the fundamentals up, struggles with a variety of subjects that are utterly foreign to her, including magical arts, Hermes studies, Latin, and Greek. The class leader, Amano, is assigned as her tutor / protector, and they both become caught up in the magical wars surrounding the mystical tomes such as the Necronomicon, Unausprechlichen Kulten, Celaeno Fragments, and involving the summoning of the Old Ones themselves. *Shōkan no Banmei* seamlessly weaves ideas and objects from the Cthulhu universe and elements of Western magic into the story. The concept that any true magical tome must have a powerful master, and the delightfully grotesque student's pet that was summoned from outer space, hungers insatiably for human knowledge, and feeds on humans are just some of the elements that make us all hopeful for a publication of this title in book form. The November 1997 issue features a documentary-style manga with appearances by Crowley and Derleth entitled "Fact? Or Fiction? The truth behind the Necronomicon witnessed by Tochikusa Hifumi."

Ushijima Keiko

Necromancer. From Asuka Comics (Kadokawa Shoten Publishing
Co., Ltd., 1989).

This comic contains a scene in which the necromancer, who possesses corpses to turn them into assassins, thrusts a wicked sword up and calls out "In the name of the power of Azaroth!"

Watanabe Shin

Shito [City of the Dead]. In *Deathtopia Seiten: SF / Horror Eiga no
Mokujiroku* [Deathtopia Bible: Forbidden Record of Sci-Fi and
Horror Movies] (Filmart-Sha Co., Ltd., 2000).

This short story decorates the beginning and end of this book that reviews movies about the decimation of the human race. In a crumbling Tokyo, danced upon by Hydras, zombies, mushroom people, and radioactive ants, nuclear missiles from countries around the globe descend upon the head of a man who has transmutated into Cthulhu after being possessed with a thirst for destruction.

Berni Wrightson

> *Cool Air.* English version: *Creepy* #113 (Warren Publishing, November 1979). Japanese version: *Starlog Bessatsu: Vampirella 2* [Starlog Supplement: Vampirella 2] (Tsurumoto Room Co., Ltd., 1980).

Cool Air is a comic adaptation of the Lovecraft story of the same name. One of the few Japanese translations of an American Lovecraft / Mythos comic. Translated by Kuromaru Hisashi.

Yamada Akihiro

> *Kaiki Kottō Ongakubako* [Strange Old Music Box]. In *CRASH Kūsō Kagaku Dai Bōken Katsugeki Kyōsaku Daizenshū 8* [CRASH Fantasy Science Adventure Stories, Various Authors Grand Collection 8] (Tokyo Sanseisha, Inc., 1988), in *Beniiro Majutsu Tanteidan* [Crimson Detective Society of Magic], Nora Comics Deluxe (Gakken Co., Ltd., 1989), and from Paper Comics (Nihon Editors, 1999).

Doctor Who swipes a record from the shop-front of an antique shop, which, when played, emits an other-worldly tune so eerie that it would make even demons see nightmares, and in fact causes several neighbors to go mad. When the record is set on fire, it dances wildly within the flames and screeches. Finally, the label peels off, revealing the previously indecipherable words, Erich Zann – yet nobody knows whether it is the song title or performer.

Yano Kentarō

> *Jashin Densetsu Series* [The Legend of Evil Gods Series] (5 volumes). Nora Comics (Gakushū Co., Ltd., 1988-1993).
> *Lamia* (contains *Lamia* and *Chaos Seekers*).

Dark Mermaid (contains *Dark Mermaid*, *Nagisa Crisis*, *Simple Case*, and *Point of Curse*).

Last Creator (contains *Last Creator* (newly titled as *Furuki Kami no Kikan* [Return of the Old God] and *Jashin Meikan* [Evil God Encyclopedia].

Confusion (contains *Confusion*, *Nefertiti*, *Summer Wind*, and *Call of Cthulhu*.

Re Verse.

This series follows the activities of the Chaos Seekers (CS), a human organization formed to face the evil gods, as well as the conflicts amongst the evil gods themselves. In *Lamia*, the great sorceress Lamia of ancient Zothique, after a failed return from spirit-travel to Azathoth, borrows the body of the modern-day young boy, Tachikawa Jun, who was born into this world from a mirror-dimension earth. However, Lamia, on her next inter-dimensional trip, accidentally comes in contact with Yog-Sothoth, and summons his servant the Fire God Cthugha to earth. In *Chaos Seekers*, Cain, an agent of the Chaos Seekers, prevents the servants of Hastur, the survivors of the Land of the Wind, from using the body of Hoshima Nagisa to perform a summoning, saving Lamia. After that point, the story revolves around Lamia, who inherits the Spirit of the Wind God and gains supernatural powers, and her efforts as a member of the Chaos Seekers. One of the more memorable stories is *Confusion*, which depicts a horrifying nested relationship between the past and present worlds when CS agent Mia experiences the confusion of reality and illusion surrounding the mystery of Stregoicavar, the location of The Black Stone, and Chernobyl. According to the artist, the inspiration came from Hirose Takashi's *Kiken na Hanashi* [Dangerous Ideas], and from Bangō Moto's *Ato kara Kuru Mono he* [Message to the Next One] (Serialized in *Bessatsu Gensō Bungaku 2: Cthulhu Club* [Special Edition Fantasy Literature 2: Cthulhu Club]), which claims that the works of Lovecraft prophesied the nuclear age.

Yasuda Tatsuo and Dynamic Pro

> *Yōsen Chitai* [Monster War Zone]. In *Shōsetu Gendai Extra edition:*
>> *Kikuchi Hideyuki Special* (1986).

The story by Kikuchi Hideyuki is a well-known homage to *The Dunwich Horror*.

Yatsufusa Tatsunosuke

> *Senboku no Kajitsu* [Fruit of the Ancient Tree]. Media Works/
>> Dengeki Comics EX (Kadokawa Shoten Publishing Co., Ltd.,
>> 1998).

In this horror series, we meet Jack, a sorcerer who resides in England, and his assistant / bodyguard Genevieve, a woman who is as fierce with magic as she is with her bare hands. In *Tobiuo* [Flying Fish], the duo visits a forest where creatures that once inhabited the seas lived on ground due to tectonic plate movements, and they encounter the "water race" (Dagon). Jack explains, "Make one false move, and you'll get impregnated" and "Well, I guess I'm thinking of a Deep One."

> *Yoiyami Gendō Zōshi* [Evening Tales Under a Dim Lamp] (4 vol-
>> umes). Dengeki Comics EX (Media Works, 1999–2002).

In this horror-action series, appearing to take place in 1930s Japan, a female antique shop owner with strange powers, a Western gentleman sorcerer, a boy possessing the powers of a Tengu goblin, and a doctor with no supernatural abilities whatsoever are drawn into various incidents involving all manner of creepy crawlies. The story that runs from the middle of the 3rd book through the 4th book is a wonderful homage to *The Shadow Over Innsmouth*. It takes place in the run-down village of Yog in Southern Chiba where the faces of the villagers are transforming into what appears at once fish and frog. The immortal fishmen, without food, shrink into frog-like critters, and with it, exhibit limitless giant growth. In the climax, fishmen who have grown to monstrous proportions rage across the village. This manga offers more than just compelling action; the underlying theme of fishmen reproduction, which runs from the initial outbreak of the incident to the ending where the conflict is barely resolved thanks to an offering to a sea god, adds depth to the horror elements of the story. And, in *Fukujō nite Kau* [Kept on the Saddle], the antique shop owner forcefully sells a dubious ancient book to a customer with the line "It's sure to take well to a beautiful woman like yourself." But when the store lackey fetches the book for the duped customer, the owner yells at him, saying "No, not the Greek version! That's part of my personal collection...There's extras of the Latin version! Over there!" When the customer returns home and opens the book, it begins with "That is not dead which can eternal lie." There is also mention of the Pnakotic Manuscripts in book 3.

Anthologies

Lovecraft no Gensō Kaiki Kan [Horror Vault of Lovecraft]. Horror House Comics (Tairiku Shobō, 1990).

Includes Matsumoto Chiaki's *The Horror at Red Hook*, *The Music of Erich Zann*, and *The Outsider*, and Okamoto Ranko's *The Hound*, *In the Vault*, and *The Colour Out of Space*.

These comic adaptations are very close to the original stories. Commentary by Ōtaki Keisuke.

Yōshin Kōrin Shin Cthulhu Shinwa Comic [Descending of the Gods: The Authentic Cthulhu Mythos Comic] (ASCII Comics, 1995).

Includes Itahashi Shūhō's *Fair Below* (written by Robert Barbour Johnson), Itsuki Takashi's De Vermiis Mysteriis (written by Robert Albert Bloch), Raiga Tamaki's *The Black Kiss* (written by Robert Bloch and Henry Kuttner), Goblin Matsumoto's *The Temple* (written by H.P. Lovecraft), Sakura Mizuki's *Medusa's Coil* (written by Zealia Bishop), and Fujikawa Mamoru's *Hydra* (written by Henry Kuttner).

This anthology, edited by Tanaka Fumio and with commentary by Asamatsu Ken, is based on *Shin Cthulhu Shinwa Daikei* [The Authentic Cthulhu Mythos Taxonomy]. One particularly astonishing scene is in *De Vermiis Mysteriis* when the messenger lands from outer space and attacks the protagonist's companion. Certain illustrators, some more than others, have adapted the original story.

The Cthulhu Mythos in Japan

Works Related to H.P. Lovecraft and the
Cthulhu Mythos by Japanese Authors

Compiled and edited by Hisadome Kenji
Translated by Edward Lipsett

Information as of June 30, 2004.

Adachi Yō

Sekai Saishū Bishōjo Sensō [The World's Final Bishōjo Battle]. KK Bestsellers Prelude Bunko, 1998.

Aikawa Shō

Tatakae! Ikusā 1 [Fight! Ikusā 1], 2 vols. Kadokawa Sneaker Bunko, 1989.
(Novelization of animation of same name by Hirano Toshihiro,
based on idea by Aran Rei.)

Asamatsu Ken

Gyaku Uchū Hunters [Hunters of Inverse Space], 5 vols. Sonorama
Bunko, 1986 & 1987.
Yami ni Kagayaku Mono [Shining in the Darkness]. *Bessatsu Gensō
Bungaku* 2, May 1987. Published in *Cthulhu Kaiiroku* [Weird Re-
cords of Cthulhu], Gakken Bunko, 1994.
Bakuyaku to Reijo [Explosives and the Chairman's Daughter]. In *Shitō
Gakuen* [Private Battle School], Sonorama Bunko, 1988.
Shishoku Kairo [Ghoul Corridor]. Chuo Kōronsha, 1989. Republished
by Haruki Bunko, 2000.

Majutsu Senshi [Magical Warrior], 7 vols. Tairiku Novels (vols. 1 to 6), 1989 to 1992. Republished by Shōgakkan Super Quest Bunko (vols. 1 to 3), 1997 to 1999, and Haruki Bunko (vols. 1 to 6, 7), 1999 to 2000.

Hirasaka File – Maboroshi no Onna [The Hirasaka Files – Femme Fatale]. Sonorama Novels, 1992. Republished by Haruki Bunko, 1999.

Otte Kuru [Pursued]. *Shōsetsu Cotton* (August 1991). Republished in *Mashō* [Gremlin] by Haruki Horror Bunko, 2000.

Kuroi Ruby [Black Ruby]. In Haitoku no Shōkanka [Song of an Immoral Summoning], Futami Shōbō, 1993.

Kunyan no Joō [Queen of K'n-yan]. Kadokawa Horror, 1993.

Zosu no Ashioto [Footsteps of Zoth]. *SF Magazine* (February 1994).

Necronomicon: The Novel. Gakken Horror Novels, 1994.

Mouth of Madness. Gakken Horror Novels, 1995. (Novelization of film of same name.)

Magical City Knight (2). Shōgakkan Super Quest Bunko, 1995.

Sassengai [Ten Deaths]. *Gekkan New Type* (December 1995 & January 1996). Published as *Jū no Kyōfu* [Ten Terrors] by Kadokawa Shoten, 1993. Republished by Kadokawa Horror Bunko, 2002.

Kimotorimura Kitan [A Village to Steal Your Heart Away]. Kadokawa Horror, 1996.

Suikoron [Water Spirits]. In *Igyō Collection V* [Freak Show Collection V], Inoue Masahiko, ed., Kōsaidō Bunko, 1998. Republished in *Hyakkaisai* [Festival of the 100 Strange], Kōbunsha Bunko, 2000.

Hishin Mokuji Nekuronōmu [Necronome: Apocalypse the Hidden Gods], 3 vols. Mediaworks Dengeki Bunko, 1998 to 2001.

Kaichigo [Monster Basket]. In *Igyō Collection VII* [Freak Show Collection VII], Inoue Masahiko, ed., Kōsaidō Bunko, 2000. Republished in *Hyakkaisai* [Festival of the 100 Strange], Kōbunsha Bunko, 2000.

Yatouraryō Ibun [Temple of the Gates]. In *Hishin – Yami no Saishitachi* [Hidden Gods – Hierophants of Darkness], Asamatsu Ken, ed., ASCII Aspect Novels, 1999. Republished in *Yami Kenran Hyakkaisai 2* [Festival of the 100 Strange Vol. 2], Kōbunsha Bunko, 2003.

Jashin Teikoku [Empire of the Evil Gods]. Hayakawa Bunko JA, 1999.

Migō Hichō [Secrets of the Migo]. *SF Magazine* (February 2001).
Yōden Sunomatajō [Weird Tales – Sunomata Castle]. *SF Magazine* (August 2001).

Ashibe Taku (as Kobata Toshiyuki)

Taihei Tengoku Satsujin Jiken [The Taiping Heavenly Kingdom Murder]. *Bessatsu Gensō Bungaku 2* (May 1987).

Fushimi Kenji

Celephaïs. *Dengeki hp* 1, (January 1999). Published in expanded form by MediaWorks, 1999.

Road to Celeph is. Mediaworks, 1999.

Shōjo, Sarishi [Girl, Gone]. *Shōsetsu non* (1999). Reprinted in *Yukidomari* [Dead End], Shōdensha Bunko, 2000.

Hastur. Mediaworks, 2001.

Rainbow Layer. Haruki Bunko, 2001.

Hanazono Ran

Kuro no Danshō [Black Fragments]. Paradigm Novels, 1997. (Based on *Abogado Powers*, a novelization of a game of the same name.)

Es no Hōteishiki [The Id Equation]. Paradigm Novels, 1997. (Based on *Abogado Powers*, a novelization of a game of the same name.)

Harada Minoru

Miskatonic Daigaku no Sanji [Tragedy at Miskatonic University]. *Tsuki no Hikari* 23 (August 1988).

Hayashi Jōji

Shōnetsu no Hatō 8 – *Mōshū! Brisbane Daikūshū Sakusen!!* [The Fiery Waves 8 – Air Assault on Brisbane!!]. Gakushū Kenkyūsha Rekishi Gunzō Shinsho, 2000.

Atogaki [Afterword]. In *Ankoku Taiyō no Mezame* [The Black Star Awakens], Vol. 2, Haruki Bunko, 2001.

Higuchi Akio

Yūrei Yashiki no Evil Fire [Evil Fire in the Haunted House]. Sonorama Bunko, 1997.

Ino Fumihiko

Shūmei [The Tell-Tale Crab]. In *Hishin – Yami no Saishitachi* [Hidden Gods – Hierophants of Darkness], Asamatsu Ken, ed., ASCII Aspect Novels, 1999.

Wa ga Tsuma – Ravi ni Tsuite [My Wife – About Ravi]. *Shōsetsu non* (October 2000).

Inoue Masahiko

Yōgetsu no Kōkai [Sailing Under an Eerie Moon]. Keibunsha Novels V Series, 1992. Republished by Sonorama Bunko NEXT, 1999.

Nakoto Shishashitsu [The Pnakotic Screening Theater]. *Fangoria Japan* (November 1995). Republished in *The 1001 Seconds of Horror Movies* by Bunkasha, 1997.

Hydra no Chōkyō [Funeral Bells for Hydra]. KK Bestsellers Wani Novels, 1996.

Kurara – Kaibutsu Sendan [Kurara – Monster Flotilla]. Kadokawa Horror Bunko, 1998.

Ao no Shirushi [The Blue Sign]. In *Hishin – Yami no Saishitachi* [Hidden Gods – Hierophants of Darkness], Asamatsu Ken, ed., ASCII Aspect Novels, 1999.

Izumi Makoto

Jashin Hunter [Hunter of the Evil Gods], 2 vols. Seishinsha Bunko, 1998.

Hofuri no Yakata [Hofuri Hall]. *Dengeki hp* (August 2001). Republished by Mediaworks Dengeki Bunko, 2001.

Kai Tōru

Shikumareta Miraizu [Buried Plans]. In *Persona: Another Vision – Ashita Deau Jibun e* [To the You You'll Meet Tomorrow], DNA

Novels, 2001. (Novel related to games Megami Ibunroku, Persona 2 – Tsumi and Persona 2 – Batsu.)

Kamata Sanpei

Alone in the Dark, (vol. 1). Shōgakkan Super Quest Bunko, 1995. (Novelization of game of same name.)

Kazami Jun

Cthulhu Opera, 4 vols. Sonorama Bunko, 1980 to 1982

Hakugin ni Nemuru Yōma [The Demon Sleeping in the Snow], (Zombie Watcher Series No. 5). Kōdansha X Bunko, 1997.

Kikuchi Hideyuki

Yōshin Gourmet [Weird God Gourmet]. Sonorama Bunko, 1984. Republished by Sonorama Bunko NEXT, 2000.

Izurumono [They Who Come]. *Genshi no Bungaku 1985*, Gensō Bungaku Shuppankyoku (1985). Republished in *Yōmu Tokkyū*, Kadokawa Shoten (1989). Published by Kadokawa Shoten, 1992. Republished in *Cthulhu Kaiiroku* [Weird Records of Cthulhu], Gakken Bunko, 1994. Republished in Gakken M Bunko, 2000.

Yōsen Chitai [Weird Battlefield], 3 vols. Kōdansha Novels, 1985 to 1988. Republished by Kōdansha Bunko, 1988 to 1991.

Makai Sōseiki [Demon World Genesis], 3 serialized vols. *Shōsetsu Suiri* (July 1991 to February 1992, February to October 1993 and March to December 1993). Published by Futaba Novels, 1992. Republished by Futaba Bunko, 1995.

Marionette Ballad. *Griffon*. (Fall 1992, Fall 1993 and Fall 1994). Published by Sonorama Bunko, 1994.

Yōma Hime, [Demon Princess], 3 vols. Kōbunsha Kappa Novels, 1994 to 1995. Republished by Kōbunsha Bunko, 1998 to 1999.

YIG – Bikyōshin [Yig – Beautiful and Evil Goddess], 2 vols. Kōbunsha Kappa Novels, 1996. Republished by Kōbunsha Bunko, 2000–2001.

Taimashin [Demonspike], 2 vols. Scola Novels, 1997 to 1998. Republished as a single volume by Shōdensha, 2000.

Sarakin Kara Mairimashita [I Came from the Loan Shark]. In *Igyō
Collection XII* [Freak Show Collection XII], Inoue Masahiko, ed.,
Kōsaidō Bunko, 1999. Republished as *Yūgengai* [City of Spirits and
Illusion] by Shinchōsha, 2002.

Mashi Ingi [The Masseur and the Succubus]. *Shūkan Shōsetsu.* (January 8 to August 6 1999). Republished by Jitsugyō no Nipponsha Joy
Novels, 1999.

D-Jashintoride [D-Fortress of Evil], Vampire Hunter Series 13. Sonorama Bunko, 2001.

Kobayashi Yasumi

Gangu Shūrisha, [Reanimator], in novel of same name, Kadokawa
Shoten, 1996. Republished by Kadokawa Horror Bunko, 1994.

Kyūketsugari [Vampire Hunt], in *Ninjūzaiku* [Man-Beast Mosaic], Kadokawa Shoten, 1997. Republished by Kadokawa Horror Bunko, 1999.

Misshitsu – Satsujin [Sealed Room – Murder]. Kadokawa Shoten, 1998.
Republished by Kadokawa Horror Bunko, 2001.

Myakuutsu Kabe [The Pulsing Walls], *SF Magazine* (1998). Published in
Nikushoku Yashiki [The Carnivorous House] by Kadokawa Shoten,
1998. Republished by Kadkawa Horror Bunko, 2000.

Kioku [Strange Memories]. Shōdensha Bunko, 2000.

Kokuin [The Carven Seal], in *Ka Collection* [Mosquito Collection],
Mediaworks Dengeki Bunko, 2002. Republished in *Me wo Kosuru
Onna* [The Woman Who Rubbed Her Eyes]. Hayakawa Bunko JA,
2003.

Konaka Chiaki

Insumasu wo Ō Kage [Shadow Over Insumasu]. In *Cthulhu Kaiiroku*
[Weird Records of Cthulhu], Gakken Bunko, 1994. Republished in
Gakken M Bunko, 2000. Republished in *Shin'en wo Aruku Mono*
[Those Who Walk in the Abyss] by Tokuma Dual Bunko, 2001. (Nov-

elization of script by same author for Japanese TV production of
Shadow over Innsmouth.)

Shin'en wo Aruku Mono [Those Who Walk in the Abyss], *Horror Wave*
01 (1998). Published in *Shin'en wo Aruku Mono* [Those Who Walk in
the Abyss] by Tokuma Dual Bunko, 2001.

Dagon, *Uchūsen* 88 (1999). Published in *Shin'en wo Aruku Mono*
[Those Who Walk in the Abyss] by Tokuma Dual Bunko, 2001.

Shiny [A Little Help from the Gods], in *Igyō Collection XII* [Freak Show
Collection XII], Inoue Masahiko, ed., Kōsaidō Bunko, 1999. Repub-
lished in *Shin'en wo Aruku Mono* [Those Who Walk in the Abyss] by
Tokuma Dual Bunko, 2001.

Kudō Mushū

Ankoku Shinwa [Dark Myths]. Arkham Advertiser No. 10, in *Teihon
Lovecraft Zenshū* [Standard Lovecraft Collection] vol. 10, Kokusho
Kankōkai, 1986.

Kurasaka Kiichirō

Kagami no Nai Kagami [Mirror without a Reflection]. *Gensōran* 10 (August 1987).

Benjo Otoko [Toilet Man]. *Gensōran* 16 (May 1985). Reprinted in *Chitei
no Ago, Tenjō no Hebi* [Jaws of the Earth, Snake of the Heavens],
Gensō Bungaku Shuppankyoku, 1987. Reprinted in *Hyaku Monogatari Ibun* [100 Alternate Ghost Stories], Shuppan Geijutsusha, 2001.

Insider. *Gensō Bungaku* 11 (June 1985). Reprinted in *Chitei no Ago,
Tenjō no Hebi* [Jaws of the Earth, Snake of the Heavens], Gensō
Bungaku Shuppankyoku, 1987. Reprinted in *Hyaku Monogatari
Ibun* [100 Alternate Ghost Stories], Shuppan Geijutsusha, 2001.

Ikai e no Shūshoku [New Job in a Different World]. *Bessatsu Gensō
Bungaku 2* (May 1987). Reprinted in *Chitei no Ago, Tenjō no Hebi*
[Jaws of the Earth, Snake of the Heavens], Gensō Bungaku Shuppankyoku, 1987. Reprinted in *Hyaku Monogatari Ibun* [100 Alternate Ghost Stories], Shuppan Geijutsusha, 2001.

Michinaru Sekkō wo Motomete [In Search of the Unknown Red Luminance]. In *Chitei no Ago, Tenjō no Hebi* [Jaws of the Earth, Snake of the Heavens], Gensō Bungaku Shuppankyoku, 1987.

Gyoei [Fish Shadow]. In *Ayakashigatari* [Eerie Tale], Shuppan Geijutsusha, 1998.

Midori no Genei [Green Shades of Illusion]. Shuppan Geijutsusha, 1999.

Kurimoto Kaoru

Shichinin no Madōshi [The Seven Sorcerors]. *SF Magazine* (October 1979). Published by Hayakawa Bunko JA, 1981. (First side novel in Guin Saga.)

Makai Suikoden [Demon Chronicles], 20 vols. *Yasei Jidai* (irregular issues, September 1981 to June 1991). Published by Kadokawa Novels, 1981 to 1991 (vols. 1 to 20). Republished by Kadokawa Bunko, 1986 to 1993 (vols. 1 to 20). Republished by Haruki Horror Bunko, 2000 to 2002 (vols. 1 to 8).

Makyō Yugekitai [Demon Borderland Raiders], 2 vols. *Yasei Jidai* (June 1984). Published by Haruki Bunko, 1998.

Nekomeishi – Shinnippon Cthulhu Kitan [Cat's Eye – A New Japanese Tale of Cthulhu]. *SF Magazine* (July 1987). Published as *Mayonaka no Kirisaki Jack* [Jack the Ripper at Midnight] by Shuppan Geijutsusha, 1995. Republished by Haruki Bunko, 1997.

Makai Suikyoden Gaiden [Demon Chronicles, side novels], 4 vols. *Yasei Jidai* (irregular issues, November 1991 to October 1992; vols. 1 to 3). Published by Kadokawa Novels, 1991 to 1995 (vols. 1 to 4). Republished by Kadokawa Bunko, 1994 to 1995 (vols. 1 to 4).

Yumema no Yottsu no Tobira [The Mouth of the Morbid Mares]. Hayakawa Bunko JA, 1998. (Fourteenth side novel in Guin Saga.)

Makino Susumu

Enka no Mokushiroku [Apocalypse Song]. In *SF Bakabon Hakusaihen Plus* [SF Fool's Book, Chinese Cabbage Edition], Misaki Keigo and

Ōhara Mariko, eds., Kōsaidō Bunko, 1999. Republished in *Rakuen no Chie – Aruiha Hysteria no Rekishi* [Knowledge of Paradise – or, a History of Hysteria]. Hayakawa SF Series J Collection, 2003.

Murakami Ryū

Kane ga Naru Shima [The Island of the Ringing Bell]. *Yasei Jidai* (1981). Republished in *Kanashiki Nettai* [Sad Tropics], Kadokawa Bunko, 1984.

Daijōbu, My Friend [All Right, My Friend], Shūeisha, 1983. Republished by Shūeisha Bunko, 1985.

Nagasawa Ichirō

Atlach-Nacha. Wani Books CaRROT Novels, 2001. (Novelization of game of same name.)

Nakajima Ramos

Uchū Keiji Vorukuban – Toraware no Joshikōsei wo Kyūshitsu Seyo [Space Detective Volkvan: Free the Imprisoned High School Girls]. France Shōin Napoleon Bunko, 1997.

Nakajima Rika

Kikansha – Brennan [The Returner: Brennan]. Kōdansha X Bunko, 1999.

Natsumi Masataka

Kaima no Monshō [Crest of the Sea Demon], 4 vols. Sonorama Bunko, 1998–2000.

Nishio Tadashi

Hakaba [Graveyard]. *Shinju* (November–December, 1947). (Experimental translation of Lovecraft's *The Statement of Randolph Carter*.)

Noa Azusa

Darumasan ga Koronda Shōkōgun [The "Red Light, Green Light" Syndrome]. In *SF Bakabon Hakusaihen Plus* [SF Fool's Book, Chinese Cabbage Edition], Misaki Keigo and Ōhara Mariko, eds., Kōsaidō Bunko, 1999.

Ōtaki Keisuke

Ankoku Kyōdan no Inbō – Kagayaku Trapezohedron [The Plot of the Black Church – The Shining Trapezohedron]. Sōgen Suiri Bunko, 1987.

Ozawa Jun

Ankoku Jashintan [Black Serpent Chronicle]. In *Bessatsu Gensō Bungaku 2*, May 1987.

Sano Shirō

Donten no Ana [The Hole in the Clouds], in *Cthulhu Kaiiroku* [Weird Records of Cthulhu], Gakken Bunko, 1994. Republished in Gakken M Bunko, 2000.

Shibata Yoshiki

Ento [City Inferno]. Tokuma Novels, 1997. Republished by Tokuma Bunko, 2000.

Kato [City Catastrophe]. Tokuma Novels, 1997. Republished by Tokuma Bunko, 2001.

Yōto – Konton Shutsugen [City Eternity – Chaos Come]. Tokuma Novels, 1993.

Chūto [City Space]. 3 vols., Tokuma Novels, 2001 to 2002.

Shinjō Setsumi

Chikadō no Akuma [Demons of the Underground]. Gakushū Kenkyūsha Fantastic Mysterykan, 2004.

Shinkuma Noboru

Alhazred no Isan [Heritage of Alhazred]. Seishinsha, 1994.

Alhazred no Gyakushū [Revenge of Alhazred]. Seishinsha, 1995.

Shunō Masayuki

Kuroi Hotoke [Black Buddha]. Kōdansha Novels, 2001. Republished Kōdansha Bunko, 2004.

Sukeyasu Shigeo

Yami Kara no Yobigoe [The Caller from the Dark]. *IP Packet no Sukima Kara*, No. 54, Interface, 2003.

The Dream Quest of Unknown Text (Journey beyond the Network 31), *Interface* (April 1999).

Chika Seikatsu [Living Underground]. (Journey beyond the Network 37), *Interface* (November 1999).

Suzukaze Ryō

Zanma Taisei Demonbane [Demonbane], 3 vols. (only first two published as of February 2004). Kadokawa Sneaker Bunko, 2003. (Novelization of game of same name by Haganeya Jin.)

Tachihara Tōya

Hazakai [The Yatoura Horror]. In *Hishin – Yami no Saishitachi* [Hidden Gods – Hierophants of Darkness], Asamatsu Ken, ed., ASCII Aspect Novels, 1999.

Takagi Akimitsu

Jakyō no Kami [Gods of an Evil Religion]. *Shōsetsu Kōen* (1956). Republished in *Genshibyō Kanja* [Patient with Atomic Sickness], Wadō Shuppansha, 1958. Republished in *Yōfu no Yado* [The Eerie Innkeeper], Rippū Shōbo, 1975. Republished in *Jaykō no Kami* [Gods of an Evil Religion], Kadokawa Bunko, 1978. Republished in *Shutsugoku* [Escape from Prison], Kōfūsha, 1983. Republished in

Shibijin Gekijo [Theater of the Dead Beauty], Shunyō Bunko, 1988. Republished in *Cthulhu Kaiiroku* [Weird Records of Cthulhu], Gakken Bunko, 1994. Republished in Gakken M Bunko, 2000.

Takemitsu Tōru

Honezuki – or, A Honey Moon [Moon-White Bones, or, a Honey Moon], privately published, 1973. Republished in *Tōi Yobigoe no Kanata e* [Beyond the Distant Call], Shinchōsha, 1992. Republished in *Takemitsu Tōru no Sekai* [The World of Takemitsu Tōru], Shūeisha, 1997. Republished in *Takemitsu Tōru Chosakushū* 3 [Works of Takemitsu Tōru 3], Shinchōsha, 2000.

Tanaka Fumio

Jashintachi no 2.26 [February 26 and the Evil Gods]. Gakken Horror Novels, 1994.

Tanaka Hirofumi

Kyofu no Choenjin [Simian Says Surrender], in *UMA Hunter Umako – Yami ni Hikaru Me* [UMA Hunter Umako – The Eyes Have Had It!]. Gakken Wolf Novels, 2003.

Yami ni Hikaru Me [The Eyes Have Had It!], in *UMA Hunter Umako – Yami ni Hikaru Me* [UMA Hunter Umako – The Eyes Have Had It!]. Gakken Wolf Novels, 2003.

Dannoura no Kai [The Horror at Dannoura]. In *Onmyōji Kurōhōgan* [Onmyōji Yoshitsune], Shūeisha Cobalt Bunko, 2003.

Tateyama Midori

Tsui no Sora [The Sky at Last], *MOVIC Game Collection* (December, 1999). (Novelization of game as same name.)

Tomonari Jun'ichi

Chi no Soko no Kōshō [Laughter in the Depths of the Earth]. *Shōsetsu Club* (August 1994). Republished in *Cthulhu Kaiiroku* [Weird Re-

cords of Cthulhu], Gakken Bunko, 1994. Republished by Gakken M
Bunko, 2000.

Yūrei Yashiki [Haunted House]. Kadokawa Horror Bunko, 1995.

Tomono Shō

Tasogare ni Chi no Hana wo [Blood Flowers at Sunset]. Kadokawa
Sneaker Bunko, 2001.

Naraku ni Tokimeku Bōkensha [Adventurer in Hell], Abyss World series
vol. 3. Kadokawa Sneaker Bunko, 1997. (Based on idea proposed by
Yasuda Hitoshi.)

Tsumiki Kyōsuke

Yuganda Sōseiki [Twisted Genesis]. Kōdansha Novels, 1998.

Umehara Katsufumi

Nijū Rasen no Akuma [Devils of the Double Helix]. *Uchūjin* 188 to 198
(1990). Republished in *Uchūjin Kessakusen II* [Best of Uchūjin II],
Shuppan Geijutsusha, 1997. (Original serialization.)

Nijū Rasen no Akuma [Devils of the Double Helix], 2 vols. Sonorama
Novels, 1993. Republished by Kadokawa Horror Bunko, 1998. (Expanded novel.)

Watanabe Masaki

Yūnagi no Machi [Becalmed City at Dusk] series, (2 vols.). Fujimi Fan-
tasia Bunko, 2002.

Yamada Masaki

Gin no Dangan [The Silver Bullet]. *Shōsetsu Gendai* (April 1977).
Published in *Shūmatsu Kyokumen* [Final Scene], Kōdansha, 1977.
Republished by Kōdansha Bunko, 1979. Republished in *Cthulhu
Kaiiroku* [Weird Records of Cthulhu], Gakken Bunko, 1994. Repub-
lished by Gakken M Bunko, 2000.

Yamamoto Hiroshi

Laplace no Ma [Laplace's Demons]. Kadokawa Bunko, 1988. (Based on
idea by Yasuda Hiroshi; novelization of game of same name.)

Scylla no Kyōfu [Scylla's Terror]. Tactics Bessatsu "Cthulhu World Tour"
(April 1990). Reprinted in *Hender's Ruin no Ryōshu* [Master of Hender's Ruin], Hobby Japan, 1991.

Yoshioka Hitoshi

Odoru Ningyo – Charlotte Holmes no Bōken [The Dancing Mermaid – The Adventure of Charlotte Holmes]. *The Sneaker* (Fall,
1994).

Yumihara Nozomu

Astral Gear 1. Enterbrain Famitsu Bunko, 2001.

Zushi Kei

Utsubo [The Moray Girl]. In *Hishin – Yami no Saishitachi* [Hidden
Gods – Hierophants of Darkness], Asamatsu Ken, ed., ASCII Aspect
Novels, 1999.

Contributors

Asamatsu Ken
Editor; Author (The Plague of St. James Infirmary)

Debuted with *Makyō no Genkei* (Echoes of Ancient Cults) in 1986. Works include horror such as *Majutsu Senshi* (Magical Warrior), *Kunyan no Joō* (Queen of K'n-yan) and *Jashin Teikoku* (Empire of the Evil Gods), as well as weird historicals like *Yōshingura* (The 47 Possessed Rōnin) and *Ikkyū Anyakō* (Ikkyū – Journey through Darkness). http://homepage3.nifty.com/uncle-dagon/

He read *The Case of Charles Dexter Ward* in eighth grade (he was in Providence at the time) and has been hooked since. His favorite work in the Mythos is *The Call of Cthulhu*, because, as he explains, "It was exactly what I'd been wanting to read."

And the future? "I've spent two-thirds of my life so far on the Cthulhu Mythos, horror and the occult. And I plan to spend the rest on the Cthulhu Mythos, horror and weird historical fiction."

Stephen A. Carter
Translator (Love for Who Speaks)

A long-time aficionado of horror fiction in all its forms, Stephen Carter hails originally from a border town in the American Southwest. After a rootless spell working at mostly legal jobs, including driver, roofer, anti-nuclear canvasser, dishwasher, and experimental test subject, he lucked into a career in technical translation in Japan, where he has lived for the past twenty years.

Chun Jin
Translator (Necrophallus)

Chun Jin is the pseudonym of a freelance translator who has been translating varied subjects for more years than he can remember. Jin works mainly from Japanese into English. Translation has so far been only a livelihood. "I was never taught to equate work with fun," he says. "Work is just that – work! You do it to earn your share of fun in life." Kurodahan Press happened for Jin by chance, as did the story he translated. "Given more choice, I might have picked a different story. Not to say that I regret having translated Necrophallus. Dark and disturbing though it is, it's a story that grabs you by the collar and won't let go until it's through with you. And Makino's brisk style of writing was a treat to translate." When he's not working, Jin enjoys windsurfing.

Nora Stevens Heath
Translator (Sacrifice)

A full-time freelance translator, Nora Stevens Heath earned her BAs in Japanese and in linguistics from the University of Michigan in Ann Arbor.

She considers herself one of the luckiest people on earth to be able to do what she loves and get paid for it. Nora works out of her home in southeast Michigan, which she shares with her husband Chris and their dog Stanzie, but most of the time she's trying to find her way back to Japan. Visit her web site at –

http://www.fumizuki.com/

Hisadome Kenji
Author (The Cthulhu Mythos in Japan)

From about 1992, he began announcing a variety of publications and materials, mostly on the Internet, covering SF, horror, fantasy, detective, manga, SFX and more. He co-authored the 2001 and 2002 'debunking' annuals from The Academy of Outrageous Books. http://www.lares.dti.ne.jp/~hisadome/

He started reading the Mythos with *The Shadow Over Innsmouth* and *The Whisperer in Darkness*, in a series of Lovecraft's best works from Tokyo Sōgensha, in August 1977. He had been caught up in Robert E. Howard's *Conan* series at the time, and picked up Lovecraft after seeing him mentioned in the back of the book.

His favorite is probably Howard's *Worms of the Earth*, even though he loves Lovecraft's work as well, explaining "No matter how many times I read it, the dreary, hopeless atmosphere never fails to grab me." As a fan, he is delighted at the opportunity to join this group of Mythos authors.

Hoshino Satoshi
Author (Cthulhu Mythos Manga List)

The author makes regular rounds of second-hand bookstores in search of all kinds of horror: fiction, non-fiction, manga and more. He has authored *Kinejun Mook–Horror Densetsu* (Kinejun Special – The Horror Tradition), and co-authored *Jitsuwa Kaidan no Tanoshimi* (The Pleasure of Real Horror Stories) with Fukayasu Tsutomu. He is currently a reviewer of fantastic literature.

The first Mythos book he read was a collection of various authors in translation, and he recalls *The Shambler from the Stars*, complete with color illustrations, and others. He was captivated, however, by the introductions by Asamatsu Ken, mixing truth and fiction in a weird and effective manner; a combination of non-fiction and horror.

"While not, strictly speaking, a Mythos story, I really like *The Case of Charles Dexter Ward*," he says. "It fits right in with my interest in the weird, and the gradual disclosure of an ancient mystery through old texts never fails to intrigue me." He hopes that more book readers will discover the joys of horror as it is portrayed in manga.

Inoue Masahiko
Author (Night Voices, Night Journeys)

Took the Lupin Award in the Lupin Short-Short Story Contest judged by Tsuzuki Michio, with *Shōbōsha ga Okurete* (The Fire Truck was Late), in 1981, followed by the Outstanding Selection Award in the Hoshi Shin'Ichi Short-Short Story Contest in 1983 with *Yokei na Mono ga*. Works include horror anthologies such as *Igyō Hakurankai,* (Freak Show Exposition), *1001 Byō no Kyōfu Eiga (*1001 Seconds of Horror Movies*)*, and *Kirei* (Beautifully Weird Ghost Story) and weird mysteries like *Takeuma-Otoko no Hanzai* (The Stiltwalker Did It). Received the Nihon SF Taisho Award (Japanese Nebula) Special Prize for his work in planning and supervising the *Igyō Collection* (Freak Show Collection) anthologies.

His exposure to the Mythos began with *The Dunwich Horror*, which was in a collection of horror stories he rented in junior high school. "I can still remember the peculiar smell of that book shop – it was just the sort of place you'd expect to find a copy of the *Necronomicon* – and for me, then, that anthology was the *Necronomicon,*" he recalls. "Just as I was getting used to Lovecraft, *Die, Monster, Die!* was on the TV, and all the other children with me, my relatives, began screaming because it was so frightening. I realized later that it was the same type of horror as I encountered in *The Dunwich Horror*. I was astonished at Brian Lumley's *The Sister City*, and my conception of the Cthulhu Mythos world expanded enormously. But I keep returning to *The Dunwich Horror*, rereading it again and again."

When asked why he writes, he explained "In Asamatsu Ken's *Jashin Teikoku* (Empire of the Evil Gods) anthology, an author mentioned that what got him involved in the Mythos was that it was simply so much fun. I still feel that's the right answer."

Kamino Okina
Author (27 May 1945)

Won an honorable mention in the 1999 ASCII Entertainment Award for *Yamiiro no Sentenshi* (War Angel). Works include *Nangoku Sentai Shureiō* (Okinawa Battalion Shureiō) and *Onihime Zanmako* (Princess Onihime: The Devil-Hunting Trail).

http://www.cosmos.ne.jp/~kim-nak/

He comments "My first Mythos book was *Yōjin Gourmet* (Weird God Gourmet) by Kikuchi Hideyuki, which I read in high school. I really got stuck on the Mythos after that, and though a lot of authors have tried, I don't think I've read any better yet. In one sense, Mythos stories are similar to historical fiction: they just don't work unless you tickle the right place in the reader's imagination. And if they don't succeed, they aren't worthy of being included in the Cthulhu Mythos."

Edward Lipsett
Translator (Foreword; Night Voices, Night Journeys; The Cthulhu Mythos in Japan)

I have been in Japan now longer than I lived in America, where I was born. When I went back to the US a few years ago, I was dismayed to discover that the nation I grew up in is no longer there – I was as foreign as any native-born Japanese. I don't feel any different on the inside, though, and that's why translation is so interesting to me: I want to find ways of expressing the way things look from the other side to people who've only experienced a single culture. I spend most of my time translating technical documentation, wishing I could speak another language or two (probably Chinese and Korean, in that order) and wondering when I'll have time to read a good book next... I can usually be reached at elipsett@intercomltd.com

Ryan Morris
Translator (Lovecraftian Landscapes;
Cthulhu Mythos Manga List)

Ryan Morris is a manga addict, mahjong enthusiast, and part-time piano player. You may hear him mention an M.A. earned from the University of Washington probing the finer points of Japan's modern economy, but don't be fooled: it has no bearing on his career built on translation of the products of Japanese pop culture. ryan@frognation.com

Makino Osamu
Author (Necrophallus)

His first published work was *Ō no Nemuru Oka* (Hill of the Sleeping King), which won the Hai! Novel Prize in 1993. His novel *Sweet Little Baby* was a runner-up for the Japan Horror Story Grand Prize. Major works include *Shikabane no Ō* (King of Corpses), *Aroma Paranoid* and *Kugutsukō* (Puppet Empress).

"I cannot remember what I read first," he admits. "Clearly the influence of some mysterious force... I do remember being astounded by Yamada Masaki's *Gin no Dangan* (The Silver Bullet), however. Sort of an SFish solution to the eeriness of the cosmos."

Murata Motoi
Author (Sacrifice)

Debuted with *Yama no Oto* (Sound of the Mountain) in *SF Magazine* in 1986, and has since authored a number of horror works like

Kyōfu no Nichijō (Daily Terror) and *Ai no Shōgeki* (The Impact of Love), as well as SF works such as *Feminism no Teikoku* (Empire of Feminism). His first exposure to the Mythos was in *The Dunwich Horror*, in about 1971 or 1972. Personally, he finds most of Lovecraft's works difficult to get into, describing them as "using too many adjectives and not enough visual imagery," and classes *The Dunwich Horror* into that group as well. His favorite is Colin Wilson's *The Philosopher's Stone*, which he praises for the grand scale of the author's imagination and the realism of the detail.

Robert M. Price
Introduction and Prefaces

Robert M. Price, a half century old, dates his addiction to H.P. Lovecraft from 1967, when he first perused the Lancer paperback editions of *The Colour out of Space* and *The Dunwich Horror*. It was many years later that he entered the field of Lovecraftian scholarship with an article, "Higher Criticism and the *Necronomicon*," in the pages of *Lovecraft Studies* and soon afterwards founded *Crypt of Cthulhu* (1982). Beginning in 1990, he edited a series of Cthulhu Mythos anthologies for Fedogan & Bremer, Chaosium, Inc., and Arkham House.

Born in Jackson, Mississippi in 1954, Bob lived most of his life in New Jersey and now resides with his wife Carol and daughters Victoria and Veronica in Selma, North Carolina in a big, purple house filled with books, comics, action figures and antique furniture. You may get to know him better at his website–

http://robertmprice.mindvendor.com/

R. Keith Roeller
Translator (The Plague of St. James Infirmary)

Keith Roeller has lived in Japan intermittently since 1987. He studied Japanese independently and at Waseda University in Tokyo, eventually earning his M.A. in Japanese Language and Literature from Indiana University in 1996. After a brief period teaching Japanese he returned to Tokyo to work in publishing, and since 2002 has been writing and translating full time. He lives in Tokyo.

Shibata Yoshiki
Author (Love for Who Speaks)

Won the Yokomizo Seishi Prize in 1995 for *RIKO: Megami no Eien* (Riko: Eternal Venus). Works cover a wide range of genres, from the Murakami Riko policewoman series and other police and P.I. novels to mysteries like *Shōjotachi ga Ita Machi* (Town Where the Girls Once Were) and the Shōtaro cat detective series, suspense books like *Miss You*, light romantic mysteries such as *Misty Rain*, and the *Ento* (City Inferno) series and others in the SF and horror fields.

http://www.shibatay.com

The Dunwich Horror was his first introduction to the Mythos, in high school, although his favorite is *The Shadow over Innsmouth*. "I love the portrayals of nature and the psychology of the traveler in the first half; beautiful, and almost illusionary. It makes the plunge into horror in the second half that much more effective, more *concentrated*," he explains. "In my story here I deliberately stressed the fantasy elements over those of horror. Sort of a literary coffee break for the reader."

Kathleen Taji
Translator (The Import of Tremors)

A passionate afficionado of gilled and all four-legged mammalian and reptilian creatures, Kathleen Taji has worked as a technical translator for many years in Japan. She currently resides in Southern California with her tropical fish and desert tortoise.

Steven P. Venti
Translator (27 May 1945)

Steven P. Venti was born in 1953 in Chelsea, Massachusetts, and grew up in the town of Braintree on Boston's south shore.

Upon graduating from the University of California at Santa Barbara with a Bachelor of Arts degree in music composition, he came to Japan in 1984 and began translating full-time in 1995 after ten years of teaching. He completed a Master of Arts in Advanced Japanese Studies through a distance learning program at the University of Sheffield in 1998 and in September 2002 founded BHK Limited, a company specializing in Japanese-to-English translation and interpreting services.

He lives in the city of Suzuka, Mie Prefecture, on Japan's Pacific coast about a hundred miles due east of Osaka, with his wife, son, and a miniature dachshund.

His published translations include Ryūnosuke Akutagawa's *Toshishun* published by Shinseken, Tokyo, (ISBN4-88012-803-1) and he can be reached at spventi@bhk-limited.com

Yamada Akihiro
Cover artist

First appeared in *Padam, Padam* (Padam, Padam) in *Aran* (Aran), 1981. Extensive work in manga including *Beast of East*, *Rōdosto Senki – Farisu no Seijo*, (Record of Lodoss War – The Lady of Pharis) and *Beniiro Majutsu Tanteidan* (Magical Detectives in Crimson). Also numerous novel illustrations, most of which can be found in *Yamada Akihiro Gashū* (Yamada Akihiro: A Collection of Paintings). His first exposure to the Mythos was probably either the *Kaiki Shōsetsu Kessakushû 3* (3rd Collection of Best Weird Novels) from Sōgen Suiri Bunko, or the November 1973 issue of *Gensō to Kaiki*, a special on Lovecraft and the Cthulhu Mythos. His favorites stories are *The Silver Key* and *The Music of Erich Zann*. "I'm an artist," he explains, "And I like stories that are simply impossible to capture in a picture."

Yamada Masaki
Author (The Import of Tremors)

Debuted on the Japanese SF scene with *Kamigari* (God Hunting) which took the Seiun Award (Japanese Hugo) in 1974. A prolific author in SF, mystery, adventure and horror genres. In the SF field, he won additional Seiun Awards for *Chikyū–Seishin Bunseki Kiroku* (Terra–Record of a Psychiatric Analysis) and *Hōseki Dorobō* (The Jewel Thief) and the Nihon SF Taisho Award (Japanese Nebula) for *Saigo no Teki* (The Final Enemy). He also received the Mystery Writers of Japan Grand Prix for *Mystery Opera*.

He comments that his first Mythos book was *The Dunwich Horror*, which he read in junior high school. While merely a digest version, it still scared him. His favorite piece, however, is *The Shadow Over Innsmouth*.

Yonezawa Yoshihiro
Author (Lovecraftian Landscapes)

Began writing criticism of manga, literature, rock music and other media from about 1977, as well as authoring original fiction. Began hosting the Comic Market in 1979. Has specialized in sub-culture criticism, especially manga, from the 1980 release of the three-part *Sengo Mangashi* (History of Post-War Manga).Works include *Bessatsu Taiyō – Rampo no Sekai* (Taiyō Special – The World of Edogawa Rampo), *America B-kyū Goodsdō* (American B-Grade Goods) and *Fujiko Fujio Ron* (Studies on Fujiko Fujio). Received the Japan Society of Publishing Studies Prize for the three-part *Bessatsu Taiyō Hakkinbon* (Taiyō Special – Censored Books).

His addiction to the Mythos began in about 5th grade, when he read *The Dunwich Horror* and *The Shadow Over Innsmouth*. In 1975 he placed a serialized Mythos novel in a fanzine, and was a finalist for the Yasei Jidai Prize for New Writer. His drive to publish fiction tapered off from that point, although he remains amazed at how his imagination was captured for over a decade by merely a few short stories. And he still hasn't entirely given up the idea of writing a Mythos novel…